ALSO BY CATHERINE COULTER

THE FBI THRILLERS

TailSpin (2008)
Double Jeopardy (2008): *The Target* and *The Edge*
Double Take (2007)
The Beginning (2005): *The Cove* and *The Maze*
Point Blank (2005)
Blowout (2004)
Blindside (2003)
Eleventh Hour (2002)
Hemlock Bay (2001)
Riptide (2000)
The Edge (1999)
The Target (1998)
The Maze (1997)
The Cove (1996)

KnockOut

KnockOut

CATHERINE COULTER

**Doubleday Large Print
Home Library Edition**

G. P. PUTNAM'S SONS

New York

This Large Print Edition, prepared especially for Double-day Large Print Home Library, contains the complete, unabridged text of the original Publisher's Edition.

PUTNAM

G. P. PUTNAM'S SONS
Publishers Since 1838
Published by the Penguin Group
Penguin Group (USA) Inc., 375 Hudson Street,
New York, New York 10014, USA • Penguin Group
(Canada), 90 Eglinton Avenue East, Suite 700, Toronto,
Ontario M4P 2Y3, Canada (a division of Pearson
Canada Inc.) • Penguin Books Ltd, 80 Strand,
London WC2R 0RL, England • Penguin Ireland,
25 St Stephen's Green, Dublin 2, Ireland (a division of
Penguin Books Ltd) • Penguin Group (Australia),
250 Camberwell Road, Camberwell, Victoria 3124,
Australia (a division of Pearson Australia Group
Pty Ltd) • Penguin Books India Pvt Ltd,
11 Community Centre, Panchsheel Park, New
Delhi–110 017, India • Penguin Group (NZ), 67 Apollo
Drive, Rosedale, North Shore 0632, New Zealand
(a division of Pearson New Zealand Ltd) • Penguin
Books (South Africa) (Pty) Ltd, 24 Sturdee Avenue,
Rosebank, Johannesburg 2196, South Africa

Penguin Books Ltd, Registered Offices: 80 Strand,
London WC2R 0RL, England

ISBN 978-1-61523-033-4

Printed in the United States of America

BOOK DESIGN BY AMANDA DEWEY

This Large Print Book carries the Seal of Approval of N.A.V.H.

To my brother-in-law Larry Horton,
who has the biggest heart I've ever seen
and kindness of spirit that's bone-deep.
You are well loved.
—Catherine

KnockOut

1

"Everyone, shut up! *All of you—get down and put your faces on the floor!*" The man punctuated his order with a half-dozen shots fired into the air from a submachine gun. Chunks of ceiling plaster fell onto the marble floor. In a few seconds, everyone lay flat, no one moving a muscle, the echoes of their shocked screams thick in the air.

Savich's first thought was *Thank God, Sean's not here with me.* He slipped his hand into his jacket pocket, pressed two keys on his cell phone, and remained as still as the twenty other people in the First Union Bank of Washington, D.C. He heard some sobs, but for the most part everyone lay on their stomachs in heart-racing, petrified silence, noses against the marble floor.

He heard Sherlock's voice. "Hello? Hello?"

The man screamed, "You worker bees behind the counter, don't even think of pressing the alarm! You—yes, you, Mr. Loan Officer—get me the bank manager, now! Now, or this asshole dies!" Savich slowly shifted his head to see Buzz Riley, the security guard, an ex-cop Savich had known for five years, with a snub-nosed .38 barrel stuck in his ear by a man maybe two inches taller than Riley was, with a lanky build and big hands that made the .38 look like a toy.

Savich knew who they were, and it wasn't good. The media had dubbed them the Gang of Four, and they had made a name for themselves as they zigzagged their way across Kentucky and Virginia during the past four weeks, and now they were making their debut bank robbery here in D.C. What was different about this group was that two of the four robbers were women. That, and the fact they were killers. When they burst into a bank, people died. To date, six people had been killed, all four bank security guards and two customers. Riley had to be scared out of his mind.

Another robber fired a spurt of bullets into the air that thudded against the high, old-fashioned ceiling, raining down more plaster, digging into the graceful 1930s molding, sending chunks of wood flying down. This time there weren't any screams, only a couple of sharp, gasping breaths, then silence. No one moved. From the corner of his eye, Savich saw they were using Colt nine-millimeter submachine guns, deadly and fast, thirty-two rounds a clip.

Another robber, this one a woman, yelled, "Where is the manager?"

Mac Jamison—proud of his thick mustache, too heavy but just about ready to join the gym, he'd told Savich—walked slowly through the doors from the back, his hands clasped behind his head. "I'm Jamison. I'm the manager."

The woman said, "Think of me as your friendly Easter Bunny here to gather up my eggs," and laughed. Like the other three, she was dressed all in black, a black ski mask covering her head and face. "I know you got your delivery from the Federal Reserve, so don't give me any butt-stupid crap about not having any money here. Now, you and I are taking a trip to the vault and loading up."

"But—"

"Move!" she screamed, and sprayed a dozen bullets from her Colt, not a foot away from Jamison's head. Savich heard a window explode. She walked right up to Jamison and poked the gun barrel in his gut. *"Now!"*

One of the other robbers followed her, fanning his Colt around, whistling, of all things, covering her back. That left the other woman and the man holding Riley around the neck. She was in his line of sight, small and in constant motion, sweeping her weapon over the employees and the bank customers. Fear poured off the rows of still bodies, lacing the air with a rancid smell. Savich lay flat on his belly at the edge of the group.

He saw her scuffed-black-booted feet coming toward him. She stopped. He felt the weight of her gaze, her sharp intake of breath. "Hey, I know who you are."

This wasn't a woman's voice; this voice was young, high with excitement, a girl's voice. She kicked him in the ribs. "Well, ain't this my lucky day. Jeff, look at what we got. He's that FBI guy. Remember, we saw him on TV a couple of weeks ago?" She kicked him again, harder. "Big bastard federal cop. You're the one who brought down those rich old dorks, right?"

Jeff, the guy holding Riley, shouted, "Pay attention, kid. You're supposed to keep your eye on all these bugs, make sure they don't try to crawl away or do anything dumb. Mind your own. He's not important."

Her voice went higher, shriller. How old was she? "Didn't you hear me? I said he's this hotshot FBI agent!"

"Yeah, so who cares? Flat on his belly now, isn't he?" And Jeff laughed. For the hell of it, he kicked a woman bank employee in the leg. She flinched but didn't make a sound.

Her voice pumped with adrenaline, she said, "Hey, jerk, you are him, aren't you?"

Savich looked up full into her masked face. She was fine-boned, thin, probably had to stretch to make five-foot-three. He stared into her wild, excited dark eyes glittering behind the black ski mask. "Yeah," he said, "I'm that jerk."

She sang out, laughing, "I got me a bona fide FBI agent, right here at my feet. What a *suuu*prize! You scared yet, big man? I'm gonna get to kill me a real-life FBI agent!"

Jeff said, "Until we've got our money, we're not popping anybody." Jeff sounded on the manic side himself, forty years old, maybe fifty, a smoker's voice, and, like the girl, he seemed to be in perpetual motion.

Savich heard Mac Jamison yell, "No!" Then there was a single gunshot, obscenely loud in the close confines of the vault. The two robbers came running out carrying dark cloth bags stuffed with money. In a voice frenzied with manic pleasure and excitement, the girl sang, "You got my birthday present?"

The woman yelled, "I sure do, sweetie! Now, let's get out of here. Okay, Jeff, take care of business!"

"I got me some business too!" the girl sang out, her voice jumping high and uncontrolled.

Jeff, the robber holding Riley, shouted out, "Bye-bye, dirtbag!"

Savich had a second, no more, and no choice.

He rolled into the young woman's legs, knocking her off balance, and kicked up hard into her stomach. She yelled in pain as she staggered backward, dropping her Colt as she waved her arms to keep her balance. As she fell, he pulled his SIG from his belt clip, rolled, and shot the man holding Riley in the middle of his forehead.

Riley ducked down fast, whirled around, shoved the man backward, grabbed his .38 right out of his hand, and opened fire at the man and woman holding the money. The woman yelled and fired back, spraying bullets everywhere, into the furniture, into the walls, shattering windows, kicking up shards of marble. People were screaming, some trying to scramble to their feet, others curled with their arms over their heads. This wasn't good; people would die.

"Everyone, stay down!" Savich yelled. He lunged behind a desk as bullets ripped through the computer monitor six inches above him, spraying chunks of glass into the air. A bullet struck the keyboard, kicked it into the air, and it shattered, raining shards of plastic.

Too close, too close. He rolled to the far side, came up onto his elbows, and fired at the robber whose weapon was swinging around toward him. He shot him in the arm. The robber yelled in pain and anger, and fired back, a hot, fast dozen rounds. When the Colt's magazine was empty, he didn't seem to realize it at first and pulled frantically on the trigger, cursing. He threw the Colt to the floor as he ran for the front door, a sack of money over his shoulder like Santa carrying a bag of presents. He pulled a pistol out of his jacket and yelled, "Let's get out of here, now!"

The woman screamed, "No! Jay, come back here! Help Lissy! She's down!" But Jay didn't stop. She began firing again, not at Savich this time but at Jay, who was running out on her. He heard screams and yells, a crazed dissonant cacophony of sounds, male and female, saw people pressing together, their arms over their heads. He prayed as he came up fast and fired. She jerked when his bullet hit her in the side. Her curses mixed with the screams, but the bullet didn't stop her. She was firing again, wildly, out of control. It would be a matter of seconds until people started dying. Savich fired again but missed her as she jerked to the side. Suddenly Riley shouted at her. When she whipped around toward him, Riley fired a single shot. Her neck exploded, and blood fountained out in a huge arching spray. She dropped her weapon and the bag of money, grabbing her neck. Savich watched the blood spurt out from between her fingers. Her Colt skidded across the floor and fetched up against the tellers' counter as she fell, gagging and keening as she choked on her own blood. The bag of money went skating the other way, hit a desk, and broke open, sending sheaves of hundred-dollar bills billowing out, fluttering down over the people on the floor. Savich saw the girl he'd kicked in the stomach elbowing her way across the floor toward the downed woman, sliding in the blood, screaming over and over, "No, no, no—this was supposed to be fun, this was our big score—"

He brought his boot down in the middle of her back, flattening her. "Stay still. It's over." She was crying, gasping with pain, trying to bring her legs up, but he held her still.

"Dillon!"

He turned toward the most beautiful voice he'd heard in his life, Sherlock's voice. His foot lightened, and the young girl reached under her black sweater and jerked out a .22. He saw the flash of movement as she yelled, "Die, you bastard!" He felt the bullet split the air not an inch from his ear. He dropped his full weight flat on her and slammed his fist against her temple.

The bank alarm went off.

Savich heard another dozen shots and his heart stopped. Then, to his blessed relief, he heard Agent Ruth Warnecki scream from the now open door of the bank, "Hold your fire! He's down, he's down!" They'd gotten the robber who'd run out of the bank.

Agent Ollie Hamish shouted over the pandemonium and the wildly screeching alarm, "Okay, folks, it's all over now. We're FBI. Is anyone hurt?"

Savich yelled, "Ollie, the manager is in the vault. They shot him. Riley, shut down that alarm!"

Sherlock fell to her knees beside him. "Are you all right?"

"Yeah, yeah, I'm okay."

"What's this?"

Savich knelt beside the girl, turned her over, and jerked off the ski mask. He looked at her young face, deathly white, mouth bloodied from biting against the pain, dark hair matted to her head. "This is one of them, Sherlock. She's only a kid." The girl moaned, her eyelashes fluttering. When her eyes opened, he stared down into her pain-glazed dark eyes. He leaned close. "What's your name?"

She spit at him.

"What's your name?" he repeated.

The kid snarled, "I'm going to kill you, shoot you in the head, watch it explode."

"Charming," Sherlock said.

"I kicked her pretty hard in the stomach. She needs an ambulance."

She was whimpering now, tears clogging in her throat, choking her, and she was saying over and over, "Mama, Mama. I want my mama."

"The manager's shot in the chest," Ollie shouted. "I've got pressure on it. An ambulance is on the way."

"Get another one," Savich shouted.

Agent Dane Carver was helping people to their feet, patting backs, and checking for injuries, his FBI voice smooth and easy.

"It's okay now. Everyone's okay—try to stay calm. Everyone head on over here and sit down. We'll get everything sorted out. That's right, breathe deeply. It's over."

Buzz Riley's voice rose over all of them, authoritative as a drill sergeant's: "Sherry, Anne, Tim, get everyone settled over in the New Accounts department. Everyone, please stay together. It's all over. Hear those sirens? More backup. Everything's under control."

Savich spoke to Special Agent Raymond Marley, four-year SAC of the Washington field office, as several agents took positions throughout the bank, calming people down. "I think it's the Gang of Four, two men, two women. This was their first foray into D.C."

Ray said, "Savich, how'd you get here so fast?"

"I was one of the customers."

"Not their lucky day to have the wolf-hound in the herd. Didn't turn out well for them, did it?"

It could have, Savich thought. *It could have turned out very differently.*

The paramedics came charging through, a dozen WPD uniforms trailing them.

In under a minute, the EMTs had Mac Jamison strapped to a gurney. Savich and Sherlock ran to catch up with them. Jamison's eyes were closed, and an oxygen mask covered his face. One of the EMTs applied pressure to his blood-soaked chest wound. "Is he going to make it?"

"He'd better," the EMT said. "I get real grouchy if anybody buys it on my watch." Seconds later they were gone.

The next set of paramedics took charge of the teenage girl whose mama lay dead not a dozen feet away, soaked in blood from her torn carotid artery. Blood was streaking in all directions across the marble floor; a dozen customers stared numbly at the snaking thick red rivers.

Bank employees were hovering around the customers, holding it together. They'd been trained for this, like flight attendants, but Savich was sure the training hadn't come close to the terrifying reality. He admired their courage. He walked over to the group. "Who's the assistant manager?"

"I am, Agent Savich," a woman said. "Is Mac going to be all right?"

"The EMT told me he was going to make it." Just a small exaggeration, but the relief flooding all the faces around him made it worthwhile. "If you guys could keep everyone calm for a while longer, I'd really appreciate it."

Four FBI agents and a couple of local cops stood staring down at the woman. It was hard to tell she was soaked in her own blood since she was dressed entirely in black. Someone had pulled off her black mask. She was about thirty-five, he thought, dark-haired and dark-eyed like her daughter. She had soft white skin and hard eyes, now empty of life.

Buzz Riley came to stand by him. "I've heard of this group, of course, got bulletins on each of their jobs. Mac and I even discussed them over lunch the other day. He said they always knew when a bank got a cash delivery from the Federal Reserve. I knew they killed all the bank security guards on their way out, but I'll tell you, Savich, I never dreamed they'd come here to Georgetown. Neither did Mac. None of us were very worried, even though Mac brought up that shoot-out of yours at the Barnes and Noble. I'll tell you, when the guy shoved that thirty-eight in my ear, I thought I was a dead man." Buzz paused a moment, swallowed hard. "Thanks, Savich. Lordy, when I tell my kids how you brought one of the robbers down and saved my life, expect a dozen excited calls."

"We're about even on that score, Buzz."

Buzz waved that away. He said, his voice still hyper, "You know, when I heard women were part of the group, I didn't know if I believed it, in my gut, you know? I mean, Bonnie Parker hit the scene long before I was even born. But this, Savich, bringing her kid with her to rob a bank. Can you figure that?"

No, Savich couldn't figure it.

"That girl—she was vicious, whacked out. I bet I'll be seeing more white hairs than I had five minutes before these bozos came charging into the bank." Buzz put his hand on Savich's arm. "You know what? When I believed in my gut I'd reached the end, I saw my grandmother, isn't that strange? I think I was a little kid and she was yelling something at me." He swallowed, shook his head.

Savich said, "It was close, but only Mac got hurt, that's what's amazing, with all those bullets flying around."

"We lucked out. We surely did." Buzz

grinned over at Sherlock, who was speaking to the assistant manager. "Your wife, right? Mac told me about her, said she was a pistol, said he was looking forward to seeing her at the gym."

After three hours of exhaustive debriefing at the Hoover Building, Savich took a call from Jumbo Hardy of *The Washington Post.* Jumbo said only one word, "Why?"

"One of the robbers had a gun in the security guard's ear. He was going to kill him for the sport of it."

Jumbo was silent for a moment. "That's Buzz Riley, right? Retired cop?"

"Yes."

A pause, then, "I spoke to him. He told me that girl was going to kill you too. Jeez, Savich, that was a hell of a risk you took."

It beat lying there watching Buzz get his brains blown out, Savich thought, and knew his own brains had been on the line too. He said what he'd said a dozen times already, the last time to Director Mueller himself: "I had no choice and no time. I had to act." Savich could hear Hardy typing on his laptop.

"Oh, yeah, I checked the hospital. The girl you kicked in the gut—of all things, you injured her duodenum, and maybe her pancreas, something the doctors only see in auto accidents. My friends at the hospital tell me she's in surgery. She'll probably make it, but she's not going to be a happy camper for a while. You know her name?"

Of course they knew all the robbers' names now. "Good try, Jumbo. You know I can't give that out yet."

"I hear the FBI agents who'd just pulled up outside the bank brought down the fourth bank robber as he was fleeing. That right?"

It was, but Savich said, "We're still sorting everything out. I'm sure you can get all the details from Mr. Maitland."

More typing on the laptop, then, "Hey, Savich, I wouldn't be surprised if a bank customer sues you for endangering his life."

He wouldn't be surprised either, Savich thought as he punched off his cell, given the deadening fear and the human need to blame someone when bad things happen. And the robbers were all dead except for the teenage girl. As he pulled on his jacket, he remembered the hundred-dollar bills scattered over the bank floor, some of them floating on the rivulets of blood from Jennifer Smiley's neck. He closed his office door, saw Sherlock, and went to her.

"Good move with your cell," she said, and hugged him. He held her carefully, a habit now, since her surgery two months before. "I've told everyone else, but not you, Dillon. We were on the road in a minute, no longer. We heard everything on the speakerphone. Riley told me the girl was going to kill you, Dillon, she was just going to shoot you and dash out of the bank, laughing." She hugged him tighter.

Agent Ruth Warnecki said, "He's alive, Sherlock, and I'd say he deserves a pizza." She paused, turned to stare hard at Savich. "Sherlock might be used to you playing fast and loose with your hide, but I'm not. I'm asking you real nice, Dillon, don't do that again, okay?"

He managed a grin. "Do you know I was at the bank to check on Sean's college fund? There was some sort of entry error that I couldn't deal with online." He shook his head, laughed at life's improbabilities.

He said, "You're right, Ruth, a pizza sounds good."

At eleven o'clock that night, Mr. Maitland called to tell him they'd found the getaway car, the image captured by ATM cameras. It was a black Dodge 2008 Grand Caravan, with swivel seats and a backseat TV. It had been stolen four days earlier from a Cranston, Virginia, dentist, and left on a side road outside Ladderville, Maryland. There was no sign of the driver but lots of fingerprints.

"I guess they should call it the Gang of Five then, since someone had to be driving that van," Savich said.

"Let's just hope this bozo's prints are in the system."

2

GEORGETOWN, WASHINGTON, D.C.
Thursday night, three days later

The first time she spoke to him was at midnight.

It's you, it's really you. I can see you. Can you hear me?

It was a child's voice, high, excited, with light bursts of breathing.

He heard her voice at the edge of sleep. At first he didn't understand, thought maybe it was Sean, but then he saw her—the shape of her small head, then a tangle of long, dark brown hair, and he thought, *Yes, it's me. Who are you?*

I can really see you, just like I could see my dad. He died, you know. Your

name's Dillon and I saw you standing in front of that bank on TV, and listened to the TV people tell what you did.

At first Savich didn't know what she was talking about. *You saw me on TV?*

Oh, yes. I told my mama you were a hero. You took care of those bank robbers, made them real sorry. She said you were crazy, said what if there'd been kids in the bank?

Raise your face so I can see you. Who are you?

She shoved back her hair and looked straight at him. *I'm Autumn.*

Autumn. Now he saw her small, triangular face, her child-white skin, beautiful eyes, a lighter blue than Sherlock's, framed with absurdly long lashes, freckles across the bridge of her nose, but there was something wrong, something—*Can you see me, Autumn?*

Oh, yes. You're all dark.

How did you get to me?

I haven't tried to call anyone since my dad died. Last night I thought real hard, and tried to picture your face, but you wouldn't come. Then tonight, I saw you in my mind standing in front of the bank, and there you were. I think you're rich, Dillon, real rich.

No, I'm not rich.

You're inside-rich and you're wide open, at least tonight you are. Mama's afraid, she's always afraid; well, I'm afraid too, since I'm the one who saw them. Mama said we have to hide real good or they'll find us. She jumps out of her skin whenever anybody comes close. I do too. They're real scary, Dillon. I told her I'd ask you what to do. Mama started to shake her head at me like she always used to do, then she didn't.

I told her I might know if they get close, and I think she believes me. I don't believe me, though. I'm just not sure about anything now. Everything's so scary after Bricker's Bowl.

Your mama's afraid of something you saw? What did you see, Autumn?

I can't, I can't—Fear knifed through her voice. He was afraid she'd hyperventilate.

Autumn, it's okay. No, don't fade out. Stay with me. Can you tell me where you are?

Mama says it's hard to hide because of the Internet, but I don't think Blessed needs the Internet. She says that's why we're in the boondocks. It's nowhere, she says, and maybe they won't find us here, maybe even Blessed won't find us here. It's real pretty, lots of trees, and the mountains are everywhere, all around you, and they go on forever, but today was real hot. She hopes Uncle Tollie can help us, but he isn't home yet, so we're waiting for him. He knows people like you, that's what Mama says.

Can you tell me who's trying to find you, Autumn? This man named Blessed? Is he from Bricker's Bowl?

Yes, his name's Blessed. It's a neat name, but he's creepy. Mama says that's because of what he's like. I think that house in Bricker's Bowl is creepier. That's where they buried—no, Mama said I can't ever ever tell because it sounds too crazy and nobody would believe us. At least we have some money. Mama found it in Daddy's safe deposit box. It's not just Blessed, Dillon, it's all of them. What do you think we should do?

First, tell me where you are. What's your last name?

Her small face blurred. *I can't—*

Yes, you can. Autumn! No, wait—

He heard a distant echo of her voice, as if she were calling him from inside a well. *I can't see you!*

It's all right. Just relax and try again.

Her voice was more distant now, only a whisper, her face a blur. *I'll try to call again so you can tell me what to do.*

But who are you? Where are you?

The little girl was gone, like someone flipped a switch. Where there had been bright color and light and a child so close he could touch her, there was now only empty blackness and his racing thoughts. Savich kept calling to her, but she was gone. It was evidently only a one-way circuit. She hadn't connected psychically with anyone except her father, now dead, so she would have to learn to control the psychic communication with him. Autumn and her mother were in big trouble, and here he was helpless, since he had no clue who she was or where she was.

Well, that wasn't exactly true. Her name was Autumn and she was in the mountains, probably in the Appalachians, he hoped close by, maybe somewhere in Virginia.

Tomorrow he'd make some calls to police chiefs and sheriffs he knew throughout the state, have them call others. She and her mom were new to town. That would help. Uncle Tollie? He'd throw his name in the computer, see what popped up. Retired? What was his real name? Surely not Tollie. He sighed, closed his eyes, and tried once again to call her.

No answer. No flicker of an image.

He lay there, arms crossed behind his head, staring up at the dark ceiling. Did Autumn's mother really accept that she had this amazing gift?

Sherlock's sleepy voice sounded against his neck. "Dillon? Why are you awake?"

He settled her face against his shoulder, kissed her nose. "Go back to sleep, sweetheart. I'll tell you in the morning."

3

TITUSVILLE, VIRGINIA
Saturday evening, two days later

Ethan Merriweather felt hopelessness sweeping over him like a tsunami. It didn't help that the sky was blacker than the bottom of a cauldron tonight—no moon, no stars, only drooping, bloated clouds pressing down on the thick-treed hills like so many black hats. His grandpa would have poked his arm and told him he was sounding like a long-haired poet again. His grandpa would have said it with a sort of Scottish lilt in his heavily accented voice, a spoken song, Ethan had always thought, one of his thick, white eyebrows arched higher than any eyebrow Ethan had ever seen. He'd practiced for hours in front of a mirror but never achieved his grandfather's lift.

He knew it was time to call it a day. Or a night.

Where are you?

Ethan's cell screamed out "Blood on Your Hands," a grinding death-metal rock ringtone that spiked his brain better than a double espresso. He picked it up and said right off, his heart speeding up a bit, "Tell me she's been found."

"Sorry, Sheriff, still no sign of her," said Ox, his senior deputy. "I called to tell you the three rangers from Thunder Ridge district are ready to call it quits for the night, said they can't do anything more now that it's dark."

"Yeah, they're right. I'll call Faydeen, have her round everybody else up, tell them to go home. We'll pick it up tomorrow morning. How you feeling, Ox?"

"I'm hunkered down beside you in a swamp of worry, Sheriff. Even my evening infusion of Turkish tar didn't hold me up long."

Ethan said, "There's lots of room in my swamp, so welcome aboard. See you in the morning."

"You going to go home too, Sheriff?"

"Yeah, to feed the critters, then I've got to see Mrs. Backman in town, let her know what we're doing. I'm nearly finished driving the perimeter of the wilderness." *Again.* "Damnation, where is she, Ox? We've covered all the roads, the rangers have checked and rechecked the trails and campsites without a sign of her, and no one's seen hide nor hair of her in or out of town. Nothing more to do until it's light again. Go home to Belle, Ox."

"Yeah, my sweetheart and I deserve big steaks, then we'll have a nice run in the woods."

Three more miles, Ethan thought as he punched off his cell, and he'd hit Rural Route 10, a winding two-lane country road that would take him to Highway 41, and back into Titusville.

Titus Hitch Wilderness. He'd grown up here, knew every inch of the four thousand and fifty-four acres. He'd climbed the highest peak, called Titus Punch, many times and fished since he was four years old alongside his grandpa in the Sweet Onion River that flowed below the Appalachian Trail. He'd eaten tuna-salad sandwiches on Sod Drummer's Ridge, a jagged, toothy line of rocks that cut the wilderness in half, and painted the endless stretches of tree-carpeted hills in every season. He'd explored the treacherous gullies, like knife gashes made by pissed-off giants, his grandpa had said, spent nights in almost all the caves. He'd even run through it in hundred-mile ultramarathons every year until a torn ACL, nearly rehabbed now, had brought him down on the last one the year before.

But none of his knowledge had helped. His birthplace, his sanctuary, had turned a deaf ear. He felt itchy and cold, and the creep of fear for the single little girl. At night the trees and hills seemed to draw in around you here, smothering all light, like the devil closing his black fist.

He hadn't found one seven-year-old little girl, missing since this morning. He didn't want to let the thought in, but he couldn't help it. She could be lying somewhere hurt, unable to call for help, or even dead. Someone could have lured her away, maybe even killed her, buried her, or left her for the animals.

He hated it.

He punched in the sheriff's office number and got Faydeen. She sounded tired, and no wonder, but he knew she'd make sure every searcher was thanked and asked to start up again in the morning. He started to call Gerald's Loft, the B-&-B where the mother and child had been staying, but disconnected. No, better to tell her everything in person. He had some questions for her.

Ethan had seen her and the little girl around Titusville for the past week—summer visitors, he'd been told when Mavis had introduced them in the checkout line in Blinker's Market a couple of days ago. She hadn't met his eyes. She'd backed her cart away. For some reason he couldn't figure, she didn't want to be anywhere near him. Because he was a man? Or because he was the sheriff? A short vacation, that's all he'd gotten out of her. He realized he didn't really know a thing about her, since he'd been so anxious to get on the road and find the child. She'd handed him a photo, not meeting his eyes. "I was taking a nap. Autumn was playing with her dolls—the three princesses, she calls them. I only slept for an hour, not more, I'm sure of that." He heard fear and soul-rotting guilt in her voice.

"When I woke up and called her, she didn't answer. She wasn't here." Her voice hitched, and she abruptly rose and began pacing the small sitting room. "She simply wasn't here in the room, she wasn't playing in the hallway. I ran downstairs to Mrs. Daily, and she hadn't seen her, but of course she's in and out all the time. She and I went out to ask everyone, but no one had seen her." She still didn't meet his eyes, and why was that? He couldn't help wondering. "When we couldn't find her, I came to you."

"You should have come to me immediately," Ethan said, angry with her because she'd wasted valuable time. She shook her head, still not looking at him. He thought about black bears and bobcats and the four-thousand-plus acres of wilderness, dense with oak, hickory, maple, and pine trees, all clustered close together. He thought about the ditches and gullies and the Sweet Onion River, deep enough to drown an adult, and he thought of one little girl, alone and lost, and turned it off. It wouldn't help. She said then, "Autumn's sick. She hasn't had her pill today. She'll be fine, but she does need the medication. Today and tomorrow." And she shut her mouth, shook her head. He wanted to ask her exactly what was wrong with her daughter, but he saw tears sheen her eyes, her hands clenching and unclenching, and didn't push it. He asked other questions, but she couldn't tell him anything useful. Or she wouldn't; he really didn't know which it was.

It was time to get serious with her.

Of course the little girl didn't have to be in the wilderness. She could be anywhere, but he didn't think so, or someone would have spotted her. They'd searched every building and house in Titusville. No sign of her. And that left the wilderness. She had to have a pill today and one tomorrow. He wished he'd asked Mrs. Backman what was wrong with her.

Had she wandered off? And that brought him back to whether someone had lured her away.

She's dead.

No, he couldn't, wouldn't, allow himself to think that yet. Not yet.

It was hot during the day, but now at nearly nine o'clock at night, when summer darkness finally hit, the temperature began its nightly drop to the forties. It was getting colder by the minute. Ethan turned on the Rubicon's heater, felt the rush of hot air on his face.

When he pulled into the driveway of his 1940s bungalow, tucked into a mess of pine trees a half-mile outside Titusville, the first things he heard were Lula's and Mackie's loud, desperate meows punctuated by Big Louie's ear-piercing bark.

He loaded up the cats' food bowls while both of them weaved frantically between his legs, talking nonstop. He fed his patient Big Louie, then took him for a quick walk. Then, just eight and a half minutes after he'd arrived, he drove into Titusville to report to Autumn's mom that they hadn't found her daughter yet. He had to get more information out of her, like what was wrong with Autumn, and where her damned husband was.

He hated it.

4

Every light at Gerald's Loft was on. It had quickly become the search center, where Ox had patiently handed out assignments, gathered reports, and called Ethan periodically.

Inside, Ethan saw Gerald Ransom and Mrs. Daily, brother and sister, refilling the giant coffee urn, laying out heaps of Oreos donated by Mavis at Blinker's Market. There were still a good two dozen people wandering around the Victorian entry hall with its dark paneled walls and florid red cabbage-rose wallpaper, and in the sitting room across from the reception area, loaded with so many knickknacks that Ethan's mom always said dancing on water might be easier than dusting that room without breaking anything.

Pete Elders of Elders Outdoor Gear spotted him, and slowly everyone turned to him, many of the faces lived-in, seamed, and weathered, all with the same expression—hope. Conversation died.

Ethan simply shook his head and saw their collective hope dissolve. He thought the air felt suddenly heavier. He searched the group but didn't see her.

"Where is Mrs. Backman?" he asked Mrs. Daily, a large-boned, buxom woman, formidable in her man's tie and black suit. She dwarfed her brother Gerald.

"I sent her upstairs, Sheriff, before she passed out on the floor. The girl's a mess. No wonder. I tried to feed her, but she threw up. She was out searching until Tommy Larkin hauled her back here."

He turned to the group. "Thank you very much for all your hard work today. Whoever can make it, we'll begin the search again tomorrow morning."

"Coffee's here and free," Mrs. Daily called out, saw her tightfisted brother start to shake his head, and stared him down.

Ethan turned to walk to the stairs, then said over his shoulder, "We'll find her."

He heard Cork Thomas, owner of the Bountiful Wine Shop, say, "To answer your question, Dolly, I haven't seen Autumn in three, four years. She was just a toddler the last time she visited Tollie, cute as a button. Tollie carted her around everywhere right on his shoulders. She's gotten big, and so bright she is. Those eyes of hers look right into your soul. She's smart. Surely she wouldn't have climbed into some stranger's car. Damnation, where the blazes is she?"

"What a shame Tollie's out of town until next Tuesday," said Tuber Willis, owner of the local nursery and a tulip fanatic.

"It wouldn't have happened if Tollie'd been here, that's for sure," Pete Elders said.

Ethan stood stock-still. He couldn't believe this. Everyone knew Mrs. Backman and her daughter except him? What was Tollie Tolbert to her? Why hadn't anyone said anything? *Well, duh, maybe for the simple reason they assumed you already knew everything they did, being you were born and raised here. They forgot you've been back for only a little more than three years.* And gone for a whole lot longer before that, back for only short visits. Fact was, though—and he frowned—Mrs. Backman had given him the distinct impression this was her first time in Titusville. Had she out-and-out lied or simply tiptoed to the line? And why?

He heard low-voiced conversations pick up as he climbed the wooden stairs with its center strip of Berber carpeting.

Her door opened before he got to it. Joanna Backman looked pale as a quarter moon that had finally cleared the mountains, her eyes bruised-looking and swollen from crying, as if she was waiting to hear the worst. Her gaze held not a flicker of hope. Her hands were fists at her sides.

"Mrs. Backman," he said, walking up to her. "We haven't found Autumn yet, but we will, you've got to believe that. Do you hear me?"

"I hear you," she said, her voice a dead monotone, and took a step back into her room. She continued to walk backward, away from him. When her knees hit the bed, she sat down, her head lowered. He walked over to her, looked down at the top of her head. Her hair was a dull, dark brown with a thick hank hanging along the side of her cheek, the rest pulled back in a straggly ponytail. She wore old jeans and a wrinkled white shirt, and her long, narrow feet were bare. She was tall and looked thin. *Well, no wonder.*

He said, "Listen to me, you've got to keep optimistic. I will find her. Now, I know you've given this a lot of thought today." He paused a moment, considered his words. "What more can you tell me that would help us find your daughter, Mrs. Backman?"

"Nothing, Sheriff, nothing. I've told you everything I know."

His cop antennae blasted red at the crackling lie, but he'd been well trained and kept his voice calm. "I see. I guess we'll just have to start at the beginning, then. Talk to me, Mrs. Backman."

Her head whipped up. "Just what do you think I haven't told you about Autumn?"

He pulled the big paisley wing chair toward the bed and sat down. He said patiently, "You told me Autumn is ill, that she had to have one pill a day for a week. That leaves today and tomorrow. What will happen if she doesn't get the full dosage?"

"The ear infection won't be completely knocked out, I suppose, but in terms of symptoms, maybe she'd have headaches again, earaches, and a high fever." She shrugged. "I really don't know. It's never been an issue before."

She looked over at him, met his eyes a moment. He saw despair and something more, something buried deep, something that scared the crap out of her.

"I'm told you're always with Autumn. Think. Did you see anyone who perhaps looked too interested in her?"

"No."

"Everyone says she's very outgoing, friendly, really cute."

"Yes, that's true," she said, and began twisting her hands together.

Ethan left his chair, came down on his knee in front of her. "Look at me."

Slowly she raised her head, and he looked into eyes bluer than the sky in the middle of summer. "I can think of one very big thing you neglected to tell me."

She became Lot's wife, didn't move a single muscle, didn't blink.

"It appears that everyone but me knows you and knows Autumn. Why did you imply to me that this was your first time visiting Titusville?"

She had the gall to shrug. He wanted to jerk her up and shake her. "I didn't tell you because it wouldn't have helped. Besides, it's none of your business."

To keep himself from grabbing her, he jumped to his feet, took a step back. "None of my business? Are you nuts? Think, woman. Someone took your child and you're telling me it's not important that people here in Titusville know her? That they could come up to her and say, 'I remember you, you're Autumn, right? Long time no see. Hey now, aren't you a big girl now?' That didn't occur to you?"

"No. That's not what happened."

He wanted to strangle her. "Why are you playing games with me? This is your daughter's life in the balance here."

She leaped to her feet, her fist headed for his jaw. He grabbed her wrist. "Not smart to hit the law, ma'am. We don't take kindly to it. I strongly suggest you tell me some of the truth now. For your daughter. I want to find her, Mrs. Backman. I want to find her alive."

She jerked away from him, crossed her arms over her chest, and rubbed her hands up and down her arms, as if she was freezing. She probably was, from the inside out.

"Talk to me, Mrs. Backman."

5

She opened her mouth, then she slowly shook her head. She still wouldn't look at him square in the face.

He realized she was afraid, not only for her child—there was something else too. Worse, the fear had frozen her. He knew from a good deal of experience that she wasn't going to tell him anything, probably couldn't get her brain together enough to figure out her options, at least not tonight.

Ethan pulled a card out of his shirt pocket, wrote his cell number on the back, and handed it to her. She didn't want to take it, but he was patient, simply stood there with the card held out. She took it. He said, "You know, as unlikely as it seems to you right now, you can trust me," and he turned and left her room without another word. As he closed the door behind him, he heard her deep, harsh breathing.

He paused a moment in the hallway, praying she'd come running out of the room to catch him, but she didn't.

He gave a little wave to the dozen people still in the reception area and nodded to Mrs. Daily, who was standing next to the now empty cookie platter.

He was home in seven minutes. When he walked through the front door, Lula and Mackie raced to him, meowing their heads off, Lula trying to climb his leg. He knelt down and let Big Louie lick him to his heart's content, then went to the kitchen and fetched treats for all of them.

"Big Louie, here's a bone for you. Think of it as your dental floss." He started tossing kibble, a game they played every night. The cats ran their paws off to grab the treats out of the air, like kibble Frisbee. He tossed the kibble farther and farther, and watched Lula rip across the wood floor, skid, and bat at the treats, then eat them off her paws.

Mackie liked to leap into the air to catch his. "Why won't the woman talk to me, guys? I'm the law. She's supposed to trust me. Well, I know why, now don't I? She's scared out of her wits. I just wish I knew what her problem was." He sighed, threw out more treats, listened to Louie gnaw and grind down on his bone. He threw the last treat to Lula, high, six feet behind where she was crouched, and she flew to grab it out of the air. "Enough, guys," he said, dusted his hands on his jeans, and stood up. "Do you know what? I'm going to find Autumn despite her."

He heard something, a slight shuffling sound that wasn't just a house noise in the night. Ethan didn't move a muscle, then slowly drew his Beretta and fanned it around him, eyes and ears on full alert.

Nothing.

He said, his voice soft and calm, "Is anyone here?"

Nothing for a moment, then a soft, "It's only me. I was watching you and the cats. They're wonderful and so fast. Can I play with them?"

He spun around to see Autumn Backman standing in the doorway, her long brown hair straggling out of a ponytail, her jeans and T-shirt rumpled. She wore orange sneakers on her small feet. In twenty years, he thought, she'd be the picture of her mom.

"Are you all right?"

She nodded.

"How long have you been here?"

She looked at him, her big blue eyes unblinking. She was afraid of him too? "If you don't talk to me, how will I find out anything?"

She stared down at her sneakers, frowned. He saw that one of the laces was coming undone. But she didn't move. She said, "You're the sheriff."

"Yes, I am, and I've been out with about fifty other people looking for you for hours and hours. I've been scared for you. Did someone try to take you and you got away?"

Slowly she shook her head. She still wouldn't look at him. Just like her mother. But at least the daughter trusted him enough to come to his house to hide out. From whom? From what?

Ethan walked slowly to the little girl, aware that Big Louie, Mackie, and Lula were hanging back, watching. They'd known she was here and yet they hadn't been hiding as they usually did from strangers, Big Louie included, all three under his bed, three twitching tails never quite all the way under. He came down on his knees in front of her, as careful as could be not to frighten her.

"Why did you come here, Autumn, really?"

"Since Uncle Tollie isn't here, I decided to come here so you can protect me."

But if someone came inside while I was out looking for you, I wouldn't be here to protect you. No, no, keep it simple. "Who would I protect you from?"

That was too much; he saw that immediately. She shrank back, wrapped her arms around herself. She looked ready to fold in on herself. Lula meowed. The little girl looked up. Mackie meowed, Big Louie barked, all three now a line behind him.

"They're nice," she said.

"They're varmints," Ethan said, but with a smile and a laugh, and was pleased to see her arms drop back to her sides. "Lula is a calico. See all the black and gold splotches on white? She's so independent,

I have to make an appointment with her before she'll give me the time of day. Now, as for Mackie, he's the big orange-and-white tabby, so big you'd think he could go bring down his own dinner, but he's also a wuss, lives to eat and sleep and have me rub his ears and tell him how handsome he is. As for Big Louie, he's a black Labrador, tough and so sweet you want to hug him all the time. He and the cats get along—what a surprise, but it's true."

She said, "Lula? Mackie?" Ethan watched them stop their slinking and bound toward her. Independent Lula, to his surprise, began to rub herself against Autumn's legs. As for Mackie, he had no shame. He stretched out his full length against her, his paws on her chest. She laughed and picked him up, then staggered before Ethan could steady her.

He said, "Why don't you call me Ethan?"

She shook her head. "Mama said I was to stay away from you. Far away."

Now that wasn't much of a surprise. "Did she tell you why?"

The little girl whispered, "She said no way would you believe us."

"But you came here anyway."

"Yes," she whispered, and he saw a small white hand stretch out toward Big Louie. "He's bigger than me."

"Yeah, he is, but you know, he wouldn't hurt you unless you tried to steal his dog bone. Then it'd be close. Would you like me to call your mother, Autumn?"

"If you do, she'll come out here and he'll come and she'll try to stop him and it could be really bad."

She was rubbing Lula's back as she arched against her hand, purring with lots of horsepower. Mackie swatted at Lula. Lula whipped around and hissed at him.

Ethan said, "Come on, you guys, don't be rude around Autumn. That's a pretty name—Autumn."

"My daddy wanted to name me that. He's dead."

"I'm sorry. Was he ill?"

She shook her head. "It was bad, real bad." Slowly she held out her hand to Mackie, who turned slinky now, twisting and turning around her, teasing her. Big Louie nudged her shoulder. Ethan said, "Listen, you guys, how can I get to know Autumn if you're all trying to take over?"

She laughed, a very small laugh but still

a laugh, and he found himself smiling in return. "Are you hungry? This trio sure was. You watched me play kibble Frisbee with them?"

She nodded. "They're good."

She fell silent, looked profoundly worried.

He wanted to ask her why she hadn't come out then, but he knew why. She'd been too scared. He said, "I can make hot chocolate. I think I've got some Fig Newtons."

She licked her lips. He had her. He held out his hand. And waited. It seemed like a year, but at last she put her hand in his. He rose. She walked beside him into the kitchen. "Why don't you sit down and play with the varmints while I work. Are you hungry?"

She nodded.

Ethan thought about her mother. *Another five minutes,* he thought, get the little girl to tell him what was going on first. And he knew to his boot heels that whatever was going on with her mother, it wasn't good. "You know, I'm hungry too. Why don't I see what's in the fridge?"

There was leftover pepperoni pizza, four

big slices. The best kid food in the land. "Look what I found."

"I was afraid to eat it," she said. "I didn't want to make you mad."

What to say to that? "I'm glad you didn't eat it cold. The cheese would stick to your teeth. Let's warm it up."

He turned the oven on high and laid the slices on a cookie tray that was so old he imagined the first cookie was baked on it during Prohibition.

He made hot chocolate from an old can of cocoa in the cupboard. As he stirred it into the milk on the stovetop, he said, "How did you get into my house?"

He didn't think she was going to answer him, then in a near whisper, she said, "Your bedroom window was up a little bit. Big Louie was barking his head off. I got stuck, and he grabbed my shirt sleeve and pulled me into your bedroom."

"You're some watchdog, aren't you, Big Louie?"

Big Louie wagged his tail. Ethan watched him nuzzle his face into the little girl's hands as she sat all straight and proper on a kitchen chair.

He poured the hot chocolate into a mug.

"Here, give this a try. It's not too hot, I stuck my finger in it."

He watched her sip, then she smiled. A beautiful smile, he thought, no fear in it, at least for the moment. "Are you a worrier, Autumn?"

She cocked her head to one side and stared at him. She nodded. "I have to."

"Why?"

She buried her face in the hot chocolate. Mackie meowed and jumped lightly onto her lap. Mackie was sixteen pounds of muscle covered with gold-and-white fur. If he sprawled out over her legs, his paws might have reached the floor on either side of her.

Back off, back off. "I need to call your mama. She's scared, Autumn. You want her to know you're okay, don't you?"

The little face sported a chocolate mustache. She looked pale and frightened. "I don't want her to die."

6

His heart skipped a beat, but he spoke easily, not a bit of uncertainty in his voice. "She won't die. That's why you came to me, you knew I'd take care of you, and I'll take care of your mom, okay? Do you believe me?"

"You don't know," she said, her fingers stroking through Mackie's thick fur. His purr went up a notch. Lula sprawled against Big Louie, who was lying on the floor on his side, tail thumping on the tile, both sets of eyes fastened on the little girl with Mackie in her lap.

"Then you'll have to tell me, won't you?"

She shook her head, rubbed Mackie harder, then buried her face in his fur.

"Okay," Ethan said. He rose and pulled the pizza out of the oven. "It's perfect. Let's eat."

After he watched her take a huge bite, Ethan said, "Do you like Titusville?"

She took another bite, chewed slowly. Mackie, now on the floor, meowed up at her.

"Take a hike, Mackie, no pizza," Ethan said. Mackie meowed several more times, his patented "I'm starving" meow, and walked to sprawl down beside Lula, who was still leaning into Big Louie.

"Mama said she brought me to Titusville once, but I don't remember it. She said I was just a little kid." She chewed. "She said she took me to three caves she'd explored, and I thought if I really tried I could remember them and find them, but I couldn't."

"So you came here instead. How did you know where I live, Autumn?"

"I heard a tourist talking to Mrs. Daily about this charming cottage he and his wife had seen. He described it real good and asked if it was for rent. Mrs. Daily told him the sheriff lived there, it had been in your family since way back before the Big War. She said your mother lived there before she went to Florida, and your older sister lived in Baltimore."

He nodded, gave her another slice of pizza, then took another big bite of his own, suddenly aware that he was as hungry as she was. Maggie, his twice-a-week housekeeper, had brought the pizza and forgotten to take it home with her when she left, thank the good Lord. Or maybe she'd left it for him. With Maggie, he never knew. "What about your folks, Autumn?"

"My mama's mother died last year because of the big C. I don't know what that is, but it's bad."

"I'm sorry." He cleared his throat. "I'm going to call your mama now. I don't think it's fair for her to keep on worrying about you, do you? And here you are, stuffing my excellent pizza down your gullet."

She gave another little laugh. He smiled as he dialed Gerald's Loft.

When he had Joanna Backman on the phone, he said only, "She's safe. She's here with me, at my house. She's eating pizza and playing with my pets."

She didn't say a single word. The cell cut off, and he could see her running out the door, maybe remembering it was cold here in Titusville at night and running back to get her jacket and her purse. She'd be here in under five minutes, he'd bet on it. He called Faydeen, asked her to start the chain of phone calls to alert everyone that the search was over, that the little girl was safe and sound. When he closed his cell, he saw Autumn was eating the last piece of pizza, stuffing it in her mouth. One hungry kid.

"I still don't know a blessed thing."

She suddenly dropped the pizza onto the paper plate and stiffened tight all over. He realized he'd spoken out loud. "What's the matter?"

"You said his name," she whispered. "How did you know his name? I only told Dillon his name."

I said his name? Whose name? Who's Dillon? He simply looked at her, his head to one side in question.

"You said his name. Why did you say his name?"

I still don't know a blessed thing. Blessed? No, he couldn't have heard her right. The man was actually named Blessed? That had to be the weirdest name he'd ever heard. He said, his voice casual, easy, "Who is Blessed?"

She was keening from deep in her throat. She shoved back her chair and slithered out of it. She would have run past him, but he managed to catch her. She fought him, tears streaming down her face, shaking, making that awful sound. Ethan didn't think, he simply brought her up onto his lap and held her tight against him. He whispered against her hair, "It's okay, sweetheart, I promise it's okay."

He heard a car drive up. He smoothed her hair back from her face. "I bet that's your mama. Come on, sweetheart, don't be scared, of anybody. I'll hurt this Blessed if he comes anywhere near you, all right?"

"You don't know, you just don't know." She was shuddering but no longer fighting him. He heard the front door open, heard Joanna Backman running, calling out, "Autumn? Autumn?"

Well, wasn't that bright of him? He hadn't even locked the front door. He said, "We're in the kitchen. Come on in, Mrs. Backman."

When she ran into the kitchen, she

pulled up sharp. "Oh my God, what happened to her? What did you do? What's wrong?"

He heard the growing hysteria in her voice and said very slowly, very calmly, "It's all right. Autumn is afraid of this man Blessed. I'm trying to convince her I can handle anyone who tries to hurt her or you."

"I don't think so," she said. She pulled her daughter out of his arms and plastered her against her chest, rocking her back and forth, kissing her hair, her small face, and kept speaking, trying not to cry with absolute relief. The animals, strangely enough, hadn't moved much, hadn't dashed for his bedroom as they usually did whenever a stranger invaded the house. All three of them sat on the kitchen floor, as if nothing at all were going on.

Ethan said finally, "Would you care for some hot chocolate, Mrs. Backman?"

"Wha-what?" She looked at him, dazed, and pulled her daughter more tightly against her.

"I gave her hot chocolate. Autumn liked it, didn't you, Autumn?"

The little girl pulled back in her mother's arms. "It's good, Mama, real good."

"I used nonfat milk. To add balance, she had pepperoni pizza."

Autumn said, "I'm sorry, Mama, but I had to keep them away from you, and I knew this was the safest place, even though you don't trust Ethan. He fed me, Mama, and his animals like me too."

"Thank you, Sheriff."

"You're welcome, Mrs. Backman."

"I suppose you should call me Joanna."

Ethan nodded. "Joanna, who is Blessed?"

She ducked her head down, her hair veiling her face. "We need to leave. I never should have come to Titusville, shouldn't have waited for Tollie to come home. I'm an idiot."

Big Louie came to his feet, barked once, and stared at Joanna. Ethan grabbed him, rubbed his rich, black coat. "That took you long enough, Big Louie. Calm down. Autumn's just saying hello to her mama, so she's currently tied up, dude. You've got to stay with me a little while."

Autumn laughed.

Ethan said easily, "You won my pets over, Autumn. Did you feed them until they were your slaves?"

"Oh, no, I know better than that."

He heard someone knock on the cottage door. Two sharp raps, a pause, then two more, harder raps. Both Joanna and Autumn turned to stone.

"It's all right. I'll be right back."

"No, no, Sheriff, don't go, please—"

"It will be all right. You two stay here." Ethan pulled his Beretta as he left the kitchen. He called out, "Who is it?"

No answer.

He opened the front door—not terribly bright, he knew—but no one was there.

He called out again, walked to the edge of the porch, and stood quietly, his eyes adjusting to the night light. He heard no other sound except the night wind whistling through the trees, the crickets, an owl, and then an answer from its mate.

He closed and locked the door, then walked back into the kitchen to see Ox, his senior deputy, a man he'd known for three years, holding Joanna back against him, his gun jabbed against her neck.

"Well, now, I surely do believe that's far enough, Sheriff." It was Ox, but Ethan had never before heard him speak in such a high, piercing voice. He felt gooseflesh rise on his arms.

7

Autumn whispered, "I'm sorry, I'm sorry."

What did a little girl have to be sorry about? Ethan stared at Ox, knowing what he was seeing, not willing to accept that this manic voice he was hearing, this mad voice, was from the Ox he knew. He stood very quietly. "What's going on, Ox? What are you doing? Put down that damned gun, you hear me? Let Mrs. Backman go and tell me what's going on. Now."

Ox turned his head to the side and spit on the tile kitchen floor. He pressed the muzzle of the gun harder into Joanna's neck. "I don't have much time, so put your gun on the floor, Sheriff, and kick it over to me. If you don't, I'll kill the bitch."

Bitch? Ethan had never heard Ox say anything like that about a woman.

"I'm not a bitch, you monster!" Joanna shoved her elbow back into his gut so fast Ethan barely registered what she'd done. Ox grunted, and she hit him again as hard as she could with that elbow. He screamed curses as she hit him a third time. He stumbled backward, yelling all the while at her, and raised his gun.

"Ox, look at me!" Ethan yelled, and brought up his Beretta. His heart dropped to his gut when Autumn kicked Ox in the shin, jumped up, and grabbed Ox's flailing gun arm.

Ethan yelled, "Autumn, let go!"

But Autumn didn't let go, she hung on for dear life. Ox jerked her right off the floor.

Joanna yelled, "Let her go!" When he twisted toward her, Joanna kicked him in the crotch.

Ethan yelled, "Drop, Autumn! Now!" and the little girl dropped and rolled away. Ox screamed, his gun flying as he sank to his knees. Joanna yelled her daughter's name even as she watched the gun skid across the tiles to bounce off a chair leg.

"Keep away from him," Ethan yelled at Joanna. He grabbed Ox around his neck, jerked his head back, and yelled into his face, "Ox!"

Ox was cursing, moaning. "I'm going to kill the bitch, kill her, kill her, kill her, and I'm gonna take the little girl and—"

"No, you're not," Ethan said, and grabbed his collar and hauled him upright.

Ox took a mad swing at him, but Ethan leaned back on his heel and kicked Ox square in the gut. Ox dropped without a sound to the kitchen floor, his arms clutching his belly. Ethan kicked him again in the chin.

Ethan stood over him, watched his eyes roll back in his head. He lay perfectly still.

No one moved. There wasn't a sound in the kitchen except for Ethan's hard breathing and Autumn's small gasps and hiccups. Joanna stared down at Ox, unmoving, watchful, her eyes narrowed, her foot up and ready to kick him again.

A minute passed—*more like a damned year,* Ethan thought—before he saw Ox open his eyes. He stared up at Ethan. Suddenly he didn't look like a madman bent on murder, he looked very scared. Ethan wanted to shout with relief because now he saw Ox behind those eyes, saw Ox's confusion. Ox—the Ox Ethan knew—was back. Had the violence, the pain, brought him back?

"Is he all right?" Joanna asked.

"Yes, he's himself again."

"It was the pain that brought him back," she said. "Pain somehow breaks the hold."

Brought him back from where? What hold? What happened to him? Had someone done this to him? This Blessed?

Ethan came down on his knees, pulled Ox up in his arms, and shook him slightly. "Ox? Come on now, wake up. You okay? You there?"

It seemed to everyone in the kitchen that another year passed before Ox said, his voice low and gravelly, like he'd been screaming too long and hard and bruised his throat, "Yeah. Ethan—what happened? My jaw and my guts feel like they've been kicked through my backbone by Old Hestus's mule. Why'd you kick me like that? And Mrs. Backman kicked me in the ba— She kicked me and I wanted to puke and die. And the kid, she attacked me. What's going on here, Ethan? Why?"

"It's over now, everything's okay." Now that was a whopper of a lie. As Ethan pulled Ox up, he looked closely into his clearing eyes and dusted him down. "You sit down, get yourself together." After he'd settled Ox into a kitchen chair, he speed-dialed Faydeen. "Get all my deputies at my house right away. This is a bona fide emergency. I don't exactly know what's happening, but there may be a very dangerous man here, so tell them all to come armed and be very careful. Hurry, Faydeen. . . . Yes, yes, I've got Mrs. Backman and Autumn with me. They're all right. Do it, Faydeen, now." He turned to Joanna, who was holding Autumn against her side. He saw that the little girl was trying very hard not to cry. He came down on his knee in front of her.

"You did really good, Autumn. You grabbed his arm, kept your mama safe. I'm very proud of you."

She snuffled once, then gave him a very small smile.

He patted her arm and rose. Joanna was as white-faced as her daughter. She looked panicked, ready to bolt. He said quietly, "Tell me what happened to Ox."

She grabbed his arm, shook him. "I'll explain later, but that's not important now. Listen to me, Sheriff, you saw what he did to your deputy. He's close by, probably right outside the window. He can make anyone do things, horrible things if he wants, crazy things."

"Who's close by?"

"A very scary man," she said, trying not to pant with fear, trying not to lose it in front of her daughter. She lowered her voice. "We've got to get out of here." Then she slapped her palm to her forehead. "No, I'm an idiot. He's out there, and I can't take the chance he'll get Autumn. How are we going to get her away from here, away from him?"

Joanna grabbed for Ethan's Beretta on the kitchen table. He closed his hand over hers. "No, stop. Dammit, you've got to tell me what's going on. What the hell happened to Ox? You say this man made him act crazy? That's true enough, but how? How did Blessed make Ox do this? How did hurting Ox break the hold? Talk to me, Joanna, stop holding back. If some crazy man is here, I need to know all about him, now."

Joanna was so scared she thought she'd vomit. She saw him, through the kitchen window, saw him—yet in her brain, she knew it was only shadows, tree branches shifting in the night winds. It didn't matter, she had to get that gun and shoot him. Or would he make her turn the gun on herself and blow her own face off?

Ethan shook her, then noticed Autumn ready to leap on him to protect her mother. He didn't yell at her, he kept his voice low and quiet. "Joanna, look at me. I'm big and I'm mean and I know what I'm doing. You are not going to take my gun. I can protect you and Autumn, but you've got to tell me what and who I'm protecting you against." He grabbed her and shook her again. Her head snapped back on her neck. "Pay attention here! Talk to me. Tell me what's going on."

"Leave my mama alone! Leave her—"

Ethan looked over at Autumn. "Listen, honey, Mama needs to talk to me so I can help you, okay? I'm not hurting her, I promise."

Joanna said, "He's not hurting me, Autumn." She drew a deep breath. *He's right, stop it, stop it.* She sucked in a shuddering breath, steadied herself. Autumn was making small mewling sounds. She had to get it together; she couldn't fly out of control. Autumn ran to her, and Joanna hugged her against her legs. "It's all right, sweetie, I promise. The sheriff will help us, you'll see. Now, stay strong for me, okay?" She looked at Ethan. "Sheriff, listen to me. Blessed is here. He is very dangerous. He's not right in the head; he has the ability to look at you and sort of hypnotize you. He can make you do anything he wants you to. You saw yourself what he just did to your deputy. You've got to believe me."

"Okay, say I believe you," Ethan said, but of course he didn't. "Who exactly is Blessed? No, forget that for the moment." He streaked his fingers through his hair, then turned to stare at Ox, who was rubbing his stomach. He still looked confused, and his face was white with pain.

Ethan, voice calm, filled with authority, said, "Don't bother making another grab for my gun. Now, I want you to take Autumn and Ox back into my bedroom. Lock the door and stick a chair under the knob. I want you to close and lock the windows, pull the drapes so no one can see in. Turn off the lights. I want all of you to sit on the floor on the opposite side of the bed. Don't move until I call you. Don't open the bedroom door except for me. Do you understand?"

"But—"

"Do it, now," Ethan said over his shoulder as he went to the back door, looked out, and slid the dead bolt home. He pulled his grandma's lacy curtains over the kitchen window and took one last look at Joanna, Autumn, and Ox, still sitting there looking dazed and lost, his jaw grinding because he still hurt. "Turn out the kitchen lights. Autumn knows where everything is. Go!"

Autumn clutched her mother's hand. "Come on, Mama, we've got to hurry."

Ethan hoped she'd obey him. He didn't have time to convince her. He turned and ran toward the front of his house.

Joanna patted Ox's arm as she bent down and picked up his gun. She saw he was still too disoriented to take care of himself. "You need to come with us, Ox. It's not safe for you to sit here right now, okay?"

Ox raised dazed eyes to her face. "I don't understand what happened. Why did you all hit me?"

"I'm sorry, but now you've got to come with us. It's dangerous. It's what the sheriff wants. I'll take care of your gun until you get yourself together again." Actually, she had no intention of ever giving up that gun. They turned off lights in their wake as they half dragged Ox to the back of the house, to Ethan's bedroom. It was dark as a pit once Ethan had turned off all the front lights. Joanna shut the bedroom door and locked it, but she knew, simply knew, that Blessed was outside the window. What was the sheriff doing? What if Blessed killed him? Or made him kill himself?

Ethan stood quietly beside the locked front door. He heard them dragging Ox down the hallway, heard the bedroom door close, heard the lock click. *Good. They were safe.*

The house was completely dark now. He wasn't worried about the animals. If they weren't under his bed, he knew Mackie, Lula, and Big Louie were hiding beneath the desk in his study, all three of them huddled together.

Who was this man they were so frightened of who'd made Ox act crazy-dangerous, like some mad killer? A powerful hypnotist? That's what Joanna believed. He had to be if he'd made Ox act against everything he was at his core.

The man's name was Blessed; the name itself sounded crazy. Was he some sort of gifted psycho who wanted Autumn? But why? And both mother and daughter knew him and were terrified of him.

He stood sideways to the front door and slowly, carefully, eased back the corner of the blind to look outside. It was perfectly black, the dark clouds hanging lower now, obscuring the quarter moon. It would begin to rain soon. He stood very still, watching for any shift in the deep shadows, listened for any sound that didn't belong to the night, but there was nothing except the shimmering of the thick-leafed oak branches in the night wind.

He heard the owl again, then the answering call of its mate.

Nothing else.

Then he heard glass shatter.

8

Ethan spun around so fast he nearly fell. The sound had come from the back of the house—from his bedroom.

He banged opened the front door and then ran full-out around his cottage. He saw a man standing on a lawn chair, leaning into his broken bedroom window, a gun in one hand.

He was tall, long-limbed, with a ski mask pulled down over his head and face. *Blessed?*

Ethan heard him say softly, his voice scary slow, mesmerizing, "I know you're in there, Joanna. I heard the sheriff tell you

what to do. You can't get away again. I
know the bedroom door's locked. I know
the sheriff heard the window crashing.
When he roars through that door, I'm
gonna blow his head off. You hear me? I'm
not kidding now. You want to see him die?
Send Autumn out. I don't want to take a
chance of shooting her. Send her out now,
Joanna."

Ethan raised his Beretta and said, "Drop
the gun now, Blessed. I won't tell you
twice."

The man jerked around, his hand coming up fast. A shot rang out from inside the
bedroom before Ethan could fire his Beretta. The man screamed as he twisted
back and fell off the lawn chair, grabbing
his arm. "You weren't supposed to have a
gun! You didn't have to die, but now you
are. I'm going to kill you for shooting me,
bitch, kill you, you hear me?" He was rolling and off the ground before both Ethan
and Joanna fired again, both bullets missing him. He whirled around, saw Ethan
bearing down on him, and fired wildly toward him. Ethan fell to his side and rolled
behind an oak tree, firing off a half-dozen
rounds. The man returned fire but only

three shots. Too bad Joanna hadn't hit his gun arm. Then he heard a repeated clicking noise. So he had a revolver, not a pistol, and he was out of bullets. Blessed made a weird high-pitched wailing sound and ran in a crouch toward the woods.

Ethan fired at him a couple more times as he leaped to his feet, and ran after him. "Don't shoot me, dammit!" he yelled at Joanna, who was climbing out of the window, Ox's gun in her hand. She ignored him, finished off the clip, but she didn't hit Blessed. He heard her say, more to herself than to anyone else, "I only got him in the arm, dammit. I missed him but good this time." She yelled after him, "Get him, Sheriff, get him!"

Ethan ran into the woods, stopped, and listened, all his training and experience coming to bear. He didn't hear anything, not even a breaking twig. The man had known enough to stop too. That meant he wasn't a fool and he knew the woods. Ethan heard Joanna yell at the top of her lungs, "Sheriff, don't get too close to him. Don't look him in the eye!"

Just what he needed. "Stay back!" he yelled, then stilled again. Ethan knew these woods as well as any Titusville native, any ranger, knew them certainly better than this maniac. He heard Blessed now, heard him running, breaking branches, stumbling, heard his hard breathing, and he smiled. He ran directly to his left, knowing where to run to keep as fast and quiet as possible. He was nearly to the road. It was then he heard the sirens blasting through the still night. Blessed had to hear them too, had to know they'd block off the road.

Ethan smiled. *Gotcha.* He broke out of the trees not six feet from the asphalt when three patrol cars raced by. He fired his Beretta into the air. All three cars screeched to a stop. Marco Hayes leaped out of the driver's seat, his gun drawn.

"Sheriff? What's going on?"

"A man alone, tall, kind of skinny, ski mask. His gun's empty, but he could have another one. He's close, in the woods. His vehicle has to be nearby. Did you see a car by the road when you went by?"

None of them had seen a car, but it was dark, and they'd been over the top with excitement, focused on getting to his house. The car could be well hidden.

Ethan put his finger to his lips and

listened. He couldn't hear Blessed moving now. Was he still again, and waiting? Had he walked here from Titusville? No, that made no sense. He had to have a car, or maybe a motorcycle.

But where had he gone?

And then Ethan knew. Adrenaline rushed through him, making him nearly airborne. He yelled to his deputies, "Everyone get to my house. He's gone back. Hurry!"

Without another word, Ethan took off running into the woods, not trying to mask his noise. When he neared the edge of the woods at the back of his property, he heard a gunshot not twenty feet from the side of his house. The man had another gun or he wouldn't have gone back. Or maybe Joanna had been the one to fire. Only a single shot, and that scared him more than a firefight.

He saw cars pile into his driveway, heard men's shouts fill the night. He didn't see Blessed.

"Joanna!"

She didn't answer. When he reached the shattered bedroom window, he realized he was afraid to look inside, afraid he'd see that Autumn was gone, her mother bleeding on the floor. And Ox?

He heard his deputy Larch yell, "Sheriff, front door!"

He ran around the side of his house to see Ox and Blessed, locked together like wrestlers, burst out of the front doorway, roll across the porch, and land hard on the flagstone steps. Both men were grunting and heaving as their fists pounded, blood from Blessed's arm spreading over both of them. Ethan saw Blessed had a gun.

"Stay back!" Ethan yelled at his deputies. "Don't shoot! You might hit Ox!" He got within six feet of where the men pummeled and battered each other when Blessed managed to jerk his arm out of Ox's hold and fired. The bullet barely missed Ox's face. It was so close it had to deafen both of them.

Ethan raised his gun. Enough was enough; he had to end it. He aimed carefully, only to have Ox suddenly roll on top of Blessed. All of them watched, guns leveled at the two men, when suddenly it seemed like Blessed was embracing Ox, but Ox wasn't fighting him now. He was holding Ox close, and the two were staring at each other, Ox's body blocking any shots. Neither man moved.

Moments passed before Ox came to his feet, Blessed coming up behind him, pressed against his back. Ox stood there, not moving, protecting him. All of them saw the gun pointing to Ox's neck.

"Stay back, all of you, stay back, or this boy here's dead!"

The Ox Ethan knew, the Ox he worked with, a man who was so tough he could beat the stuffing out of most other men without breaking a sweat, simply stood there, no expression on his face. He knew his deputies couldn't believe Ox had folded, that he'd stopped fighting. It looked like he was now willingly protecting Blessed, letting him press his gun into his neck. Ethan raised a warning hand. "Blessed, we're not moving. Look around you. You're surrounded. Let Ox go, tell him to lie down. I won't let you take him as a hostage. You hear me, Blessed?"

Blessed laughed, eerie and low. "No, Sheriff, Ox is my little buddy now, right, Ox?"

Ox didn't move, didn't speak, simply stood quiet in front of Blessed.

"Right, Ox?" Slowly Ox nodded.

Blessed yelled, "I want the kid! Bitch, I know you can hear me. You've probably got your gun aimed right at me. You send Autumn out now or this good old boy buys it. Now!"

Ethan heard her curse, knew she had no more bullets. She kept clear of the front door, but she was close. She shouted, "You're not taking Autumn, you monster! Go back to that mad old woman and tell her it's over. You're not getting Autumn!"

His deputies were staring at Joanna, whose head came around the front door, but no one moved a whisker. Ethan figured he had maybe three more rounds in his clip.

He called out, "Why does the mad old woman want Autumn?"

Blessed screamed, "She's not mad! It ain't none of your business, Sheriff. I'm gonna hurt you bad for that, Joanna. Now I'm gonna kill me this big guy."

Ethan said, "Wait, Blessed! Talk to me, maybe we can work something out. Tell me why you want the little girl. Tell me why she's so important to you."

He didn't think Blessed would answer, but he did, his voice high, nearly a wail. "I gotta have her. You hear me? That's all you gotta know."

Joanna walked slowly out of the front door.

Ethan felt his heart drop to his boots. "Joanna, get back inside!"

"No, Sheriff," she said, her voice as calm as the night. "He can take me if he'll let Ox go. You just have to take care of Autumn, give her her last two pills."

"Joanna—"

She waved him away. "Will you let him go, Blessed, and take me?"

"You thieving, conniving bitch! What would I want you for?" Blessed yelled. "We should have put your lights out as soon as Ma realized—" Blessed jerked the gun away from Ox's neck and fired at her as she jumped back into the house.

9

Blessed fired again into the open front door, and the bullet chipped off a huge hunk of the door frame. He yelled and stepped back toward the woods, pulling Ox back with him, firing at them with each step. Then his gun clicked empty, and he turned and ran. Ethan's deputies fired after him. He doubted any of their bullets hit him this time unless through blind luck. It was simply too dark, and he'd been running like a berserker, in and out of the shadows and the trees.

Ethan knew Blessed had to be running scared. He'd not only failed, he was wounded. Ethan split up his eight deputies into pairs. To the three pairs who were going after Blessed in the woods, he said, "Listen to me carefully—this is not bullshit. Do not look at this guy in the face, you hear me? He'll hypnotize you, and you'll start acting like Ox. Yeah, that's what he did to Ox, believe me. Do not look at his face!" He sent his other two deputies to their cars, watched them roar out of his driveway to cover the road. They'd try to keep Blessed pinned inside the woods until the others found him. If they didn't, Blessed would disappear into the Titus Hitch Wilderness, at least that's what Ethan would do. He had no clue whether Blessed was experienced in a wilderness. Maybe Joanna would know.

Ethan wasn't surprised when Faydeen roared up in her old Chevy Silverado. Between them, they got Ox into her truck and on his way to Dr. Spitz's house.

Ethan stayed at the house, afraid to leave for fear Blessed would come back yet again. He spoke to his deputies on his cell phone, instructing them to push into the woods if they couldn't find an escape vehicle. Push in and take care—who knew if Blessed had a third gun? At this point, nothing would surprise Ethan. He heard Joanna speaking quietly to Autumn just inside the front door.

Ethan's deputies hunted Blessed Backman for two hours. They found no car, no truck, no motorcycle. He'd either vanished in a puff of smoke or gone so deep into the wilderness it would take a week to find him. Ethan called the ranger station, told them the situation, had Joanna give them Blessed's description—mid-fifties, maybe five-foot-ten, thin, not more than one hundred fifty pounds, long, thinning gray-brown hair, brown eyes. With a look at Ethan, she'd told them his last name was Backman. Blessed Backman? They were related to this maniac? Ethan had never liked alliteration, and at this moment, he hated it. No, Joanna had no idea if he had a car, a criminal record, or any scars.

Ethan called law enforcement in the half-dozen towns surrounding Titus Hitch Wilderness. He had them check their criminal databases, but there was nothing on Blessed Backman. He couldn't think of anything else to do, except find out whatever he could from Joanna.

He called his deputies back in. None of them, they told him, had seen a thing. Because of what had happened to Ox, Ethan spoke to each of them in turn. They all seemed okay, thank God.

When Ethan walked into his living room at nearly two o'clock in the morning, it was to see Joanna stretched out on his sofa, spooning Autumn, both of them deeply asleep. Even though it was empty, Joanna still held Ox's gun, a Colt that had belonged to his grandma, an old lady known hereabouts for extinguishing a cigarette at ten feet with a shot.

Ethan stepped outside to give instructions to his two deputies, Glenda and Harm, stationed in his driveway for the rest of the night. "Listen carefully. I know you realize there's something hinky about this guy, and there is. Remember what I said—if he comes around, you don't look at him, okay? You saw what he did to Ox. Keep your eyes down if you see him, and keep shooting."

"Sounds like this guy's some major-league voodoo artist," Glenda said, and looked him square in the eye.

"I think we can start with that. I think he's also a lot more—he's out of control."

Glenda ran her tongue over her lips. She was scared, and that was good.

He had no idea what Blessed would do next. "Keep alert," he told them at least twice.

When he called Dr. Spitz, he told Ethan it appeared that Ox was going to be all right. His headache had lessened in the past hour. Dr. Spitz said he'd never seen the like, but this deal about hypnotism, he couldn't swallow that. Maybe it was drugs or some sort of psychotic episode. Even with all Ethan's assurances that it appeared to be some sort of powerful hypnotism, Dr. Spitz remained skeptical.

All Ethan was sure of was that Ox would have shot Joanna Backman without a moment's pause.

Who was Blessed Backman? Who was the mad old woman?

He stepped back inside and stared down at Joanna, a woman he hadn't known existed four days before, and her little girl. Autumn suddenly twitched in her sleep— probably a nightmare, and no wonder. Should he wake her? Before he took a step toward the sofa, Joanna began rubbing the little girl's cheek, soothing her. From what he could tell, she was still asleep. It was an instinct, he supposed, and he wondered if you just did that when you had a kid.

Autumn stopped moving. She sighed deeply, pushed back against her mother's stomach.

Joanna Backman. Who was she, really? Why did Blessed Backman want Autumn so badly?

"Meow."

Ethan looked down to see Mackie rubbing his face against his jean leg. He scooped him up and, out of long habit, smoothed his whiskers. It was then he noticed Lula tucked in tight against the little girl's stomach.

Beneath the coffee table, Big Louie snorted in his sleep, crossed his paws over his nose. He opened one eye to stare at Ethan a moment, then closed it again. He wasn't more than two feet away from the sofa.

Ethan picked up one of his grandmother's afghans off the back of his big TV chair and covered them with it. Just before the cover went down, Lula stared at Mackie, gave him the fish eye, and scooted closer to Autumn.

Ethan looked out to see Harm and

Glenda talking in the front seat of the patrol car.

He went downstairs to the basement, turned on the single hundred-watt lightbulb, and fetched a piece of plywood from behind an ancient rattan patio set dating from the fifties. He boarded up the window in his bedroom, Mackie padding at his heels, not making a sound, his ears forward. Mackie was on alert, rightfully so.

Ethan didn't think he'd sleep with all the questions ricocheting around his brain, and the gnawing concern that Blessed might still be out there, waiting, but he did, Mackie curled up against his neck, his whiskers twitching against his ear.

10

Sunday morning

Ethan smelled coffee. For a moment it surprised him because he never programmed the coffeepot before he went to bed. Was he imagining it?

He sat up in bed. No dream; it was coffee he smelled, real and rich and sinful.

Then he remembered. He leaped out of bed, dislodging Mackie, who gave a pissed-off meow, and ran toward the door. He realized he was wearing only boxer shorts, grabbed his jeans, and jerked them on. He stopped to pull on a sweatshirt and paused in the kitchen doorway. He saw Joanna standing in front of his brand-new

Kenmore stove, an egg carton, a quart of nonfat milk, onion remains, and a depleted bag of four grated cheeses he used to sprinkle on his tacos lined up on the counter next to her. He watched her whip the mixture with a fork, then pour it into a heated skillet. The sound of the sizzle, the smell of the butter, made his stomach growl. He realized he hadn't eaten since lunch the previous day—well, not counting the pizza slice with Autumn. He smelled the turkey bacon microwaving and inhaled deeply. Big Louie and Lula sat on the floor, staring fixedly at the microwave, not moving, waiting for the ping. Mackie threaded through his legs to join his sister and Big Louie in their vigil. Autumn was setting the table. She was saying, "I like these plates, Mama, they're cute."

They were a Mexican motif, bright and cheerful, presented to him by his mother three years ago when he'd moved back to Titusville. He'd packed his own very nice Italian service away, and thanked her.

"Don't forget the milk for the coffee, sweetie."

Autumn lifted the carton of nonfat milk from the counter and set it on the table.

She began folding paper napkins, placing them carefully beside each plate.

It was such a domestic scene, so very normal. It reminded him of years ago when there were three yelling, laughing children banging around the kitchen, ready to eat every scrap their mother served up. It was remarkable. He said from the doorway, "I hope you made three extra slices of turkey bacon for my anorexic pets."

Joanna dropped the wooden spatula and made a frantic grab for Ox's Colt, six inches from her hand.

He held out both palms. "It's okay. It's me, please don't shoot me in my own kitchen."

"Not a problem," Joanna said. "The clip is empty."

Autumn froze at the sound of his voice. Then she gave him a huge grin. Big Louie barked, Lula meowed, and Mackie never looked away from the microwave, which pinged a half-second later.

"Good morning, Sheriff," Joanna said. "I hope you don't mind our taking over your kitchen." She opened the microwave door, pulled out the covered plate of bacon, dabbed off the extra grease with a paper towel, and looked down at the animals. They were talking nonstop, at full volume. Ethan took down paper plates from the cabinet and crumbled a single crispy bacon slice on each plate, set them in a straight line on the floor. The barks and meows died, the silence instant.

Her fear was still palpable. How was he to get information out of a woman who was still so scared, still so on edge she'd have shot him? He said, "I'm tempted to join my varmints. Everything smells great."

"I took coffee and peanut-butter toast out to Glenda and Harm. What a name, where did it come from?"

"Her dad really liked *The Wizard of Oz*, but her mom insisted on the normal spelling."

A laugh spurted out. "No, Harm's name, not Glinda the Good Witch."

"His granny was always preaching at him to never get 'In Harm's Way,' always spoke it with capital letters. It stuck when he was about twelve. He doesn't use his real name. Thank you, Joanna, for feeding them."

She nodded and picked up the spatula, went back to the eggs while Ethan opened cans for the animals. He petted each of them. "Okay, guys, you've had your dessert, now go over and eat your main course. That's a nice name you've got, Joanna. Where'd it come from?"

She was weighing how much to tell him; he saw it clearly on her face. He'd love to get her in a poker game, she'd lose her knickers.

"Joanna was grandma's name," Autumn said, carefully placing a knife beside a plate Ethan saw was chipped. "I never met her; she died when I was little. Remember, I told you, Ethan. She died of the big C."

"I remember. I'm sorry," Ethan said to her.

Joanna shrugged. "She was actually my great-grandmother, and she was ninety-four."

Ethan watched her spill out the last capsule from a prescription bottle and hand it to Autumn.

"Down the hatch, sweetie. Last one."

"You gave her one last night?"

Joanna was nodding when Big Louie raised his head from his now empty food bowl and barked. Both Ethan and Joanna went on instant alert.

A moment later, Harm's face appeared

in the kitchen door's window. Ethan opened the door and stepped back. "What's up, Harm?"

"I left the house last night without my aloe vera, Sheriff, and my face hurts something fierce. Glenda told me Faydeen said you probably had some."

Joanna was staring openmouthed at his burned face, quite clear in the bright morning sunlight. She hadn't noticed when she'd delivered their toast and coffee. Autumn asked, "What happened to your face, Mr. Harm? What's aloe vera?"

Ethan said, "Harm was trying to get himself ready for a Myrtle Beach vacation. He wanted to look like a tanned hunk before he leaves, you know, to hit the beach looking like a local dude."

Harm grinned. "Unfortunately, I didn't listen to Mylo at Golden Tan. I insisted on going the full time three days in a row on his three-sixty tanning bed, and I didn't keep my face covered."

Ethan laughed. "Hold on, Harm. I'll get the aloe vera." He heard Joanna telling her daughter, "Aloe vera's a slimy green gunk that takes the sting out of a bad sunburn."

Autumn stared up at Harm. "I thought

you were dark like my best friend Timmy Jeffers. Now I see you're dark red. That must hurt. I'll bet your mama really yelled at you."

That was all it took for Joanna to spurt out a laugh. Big Louie jumped up on Harm's leg. Ethan just shook his head as he walked to his bathroom to fetch the aloe vera Faydeen had bought for him after the blistering hot Fourth of July parties six weeks ago when he'd roasted himself but good. He wondered again how he was going to pry any information out of her, wondered how he could make her believe he could help her. He didn't want to spook her, make her run away. He had to be patient, had to try to gain their trust. He didn't think he had a choice. There was something really bad going on here. He knew in his gut he had to know what was going on to keep them safe.

11

Mr. Maitland said, "She's gone."

Savich pulled his cell phone closer to his ear. "Who's gone?"

"Melissa—Lissy—Smiley. You remember, Savich, the sixteen-year-old-girl bank robber you put in the hospital six days ago for repairs? I just got a call from Agent Daugherty guarding her at Washington Memorial."

"What do you mean she's gone? She died?" Savich said, half an eye on Sean and his buddy Marty, who were shooting baskets at the hoop set beside his garage door. Both children were pretty good if you took into account their combined ages barely reached ten and the basket hoop was three feet lower than usual. They had a lot of misses. He'd painted the garage door three months before. Time to give it another coat.

"No, no, a guy walked up smooth as silk to our agent sitting in his chair outside Lissy Smiley's room, pulled his FBI creds out of his jacket pocket, let Daugherty see his SIG clipped to his waist in the process, and told him he was there to take a shift, give Daugherty some rest. Daugherty had no reason to question what he said, and, I will admit, it's Sunday after all, and the Red Sox and Yankees were playing. It did occur to Daugherty to check with his supervisor during the seventh-inning stretch to ask when he was expected back, since he hadn't been notified about any change, and his supervisor proceeds to tell him there was no replacement sent and he was an idiot. He topped it off by not remembering the agent's name. Long and short of it was Ms. Smiley was long gone with the guy by the time anybody got back to the hospital. The guy was the getaway driver for the Gang of Four."

"Pretty impressive. I wonder where he got the fake ID," Savich said.

"I don't know that yet, but I will know soon. I'll tell you, Daugherty will be cleaning toilets on the fifth floor of the Hoover Building until Christmas. This isn't good, Savich."

Sean shouted, "Did you see that, Papa? I made two free throws in a row!"

Marty Perry, Sean's best friend since they were both two, yelled over him, "Mr. Savich, Sean wasn't behind the free-throw line! He's cheating. You give me the ball, Sean, or I won't let you play my sax. It's my turn!"

"Well, I won't let you play my piano." Sean ran away with the ball, Marty ran after him, and the two of them went at it. At least they rolled around in the thick summer grass rather than on the concrete driveway. The basketball—kid-sized and bright orange—went rolling out onto the street, hit a fire hydrant, and came to a bouncing stop against the curb.

Astro, Sean's Scottie, and Marty's big golden retriever, Burma, were dancing around them, barking as loud as they could, tails wagging furiously.

Savich said into his cell, "Excuse me, sir, but I've got to separate two warring basketball factions and rescue the ball. I'll call you back with Sherlock in a couple of minutes."

"I had four warring factions in my house, in any sport you can name. Call me back when you can," Maitland said, laughed, and hung up. He had four grown sons, all bruisers.

Since it was safer to let both children pummel him rather than each other, Savich soon had both kids climbing on top of him, trying to hold his arms down on the grass. Marty's mom, Lucy, trotted up, stared down at Savich, and grinned. "Ah, I think they might have you pinned, Dillon. Tell you what, let me take these ferocious wrestlers off your hands. Come on, Marty, let go of Dillon's arm," she said to her daughter as she peeled her off Savich. "As for you, Burma, stop licking faces. Come on, boy. That's it. You too, Astro." She said to Savich, "I can see I owe you or Sherlock a favor here for physical distress. Okay, Marty, Sean, how about both of you come with me. The magic genie sent some fresh lemonade and chocolate-chip cookies, extra walnuts."

Sean and Marty instantly forgot their wrestling match with Savich and their own disagreement, and jumped to their feet, yelling together in victory. Savich hoped she'd made a couple dozen cookies, since both kids had hollow legs.

"I'm the champ!" Sean yelled. "Extra walnuts?"

"Yep, I asked the genie especially for extra walnuts, just for you, Sean."

Marty was torn. "I don't know, Mom. Mr. Savich was saying he'd play with us, you know, show us some moves."

Burma, tongue lolling, barked, Astro joined in, and the two children laughed.

"You'll need your strength," Savich said. "Cookies first."

Lucy said, "You might have to fight those mighty dogs for the cookies. You'd best hurry now, guys, chocolate chips don't last forever, you know."

The little boy and little girl went whooping across the front yard and next door to the Perry house, the dogs racing beside them. Lucy gave Savich a hand up, patted his shoulder, and took off after them. She called over her shoulder, "I'll bring Sean and Astro home in an hour or so."

He was dusting himself off when Sherlock appeared in the open doorway, wearing white shorts and a flowy pink top. She was lightly tanned, her hair pulled up in a curl-packed ponytail, the sandals on her feet showing off toenails painted a soft pink. She looked about sixteen. Savich felt the familiar kick in his blood when she waved and smiled at him. *Ah,* he thought, *a hot afternoon, a fan stirring up the air over the bed, the blinds pulled, and blessed quiet—surely some things were meant to be.* On the other hand, maybe not. There was Mr. Maitland to call back. He sighed and thought maybe they'd have some time this evening. Around eight o'clock might be lovely, not dark yet in the deep summer— he'd check her scar as the air cooled down around them, and who knew? Maybe Sean would miraculously be eager to climb into his own bed.

Fat chance.

"I'd sure like some lemonade too," Savich called out.

Sherlock laughed. "Then you've got to help me denude the Meyer lemon tree."

He looked at her closely. "You're not doing that, are you? Remember, your spleen became history only two months ago. Rest, Sherlock, you've got to rest."

"Yeah, yeah, I was growing mold. It's good to be back to work, back to doing important things, like making lemonade." She touched her fingers to his cheek. "I'm okay. I won't overdo, I promise."

"You already did. You came roaring down to the Georgetown bank. Ruth told me you were outside running after that fourth robber, that Dane had to grab you."

"Nah, it wasn't any big deal—oh, all right, that was a little much, but I'm better every day, Dillon. Don't worry."

Still, he worried, and she knew he worried, and they'd both be worried for another month or so, until she was one hundred percent again.

12

After Savich drank down half a glass of tart lemonade, something Sherlock made very well, he said, "Mr. Maitland called. Lissy, our sixteen-year-old-girl bank robber, is no longer under guard at the hospital."

"What?"

He nodded. "Yep, she's in the wind, probably with the help of the missing getaway driver." He told her what Mr. Maitland had said.

Her first comment was, "Daugherty isn't stupid, Dillon, he'd spot fake creds in a nanosecond. And if they weren't fake—now that worries me."

"You're right," he said. He dialed up Mr. Maitland, punched on the speaker. "Sorry it took so long. Both Sherlock and I are here now."

Maitland said immediately, "Bless Daugherty's little pointed head, he finally remembered the last name of the agent on the FBI ID the guy flashed at him—Coggins. Turns out he's Peter Coggins, an agent in the Richmond field office. Agents got over to his house fast, found his sister untying him and pulling duct tape off his mouth. She says she was pretty surprised to see him tied up on the kitchen floor. She'd brought him over a strawberry pie."

"That sure sounds good," Savich said.

"Yeah, it does. At least the guy didn't kill him. Now, here's how it went down, according to Coggins. He was mowing his backyard when this young guy trots up and asks for directions to Interstate Ninety-five into Washington. When Coggins turned to point, the guy bashed him over the head, stole his ID and his SIG. The Richmond SAC had just gotten our alert about Lissy Smiley escaping and called me pronto."

Sherlock said. "Is Agent Coggins okay?"

"Yeah, the doc said he's got himself

only a minor concussion, which, naturally, doesn't make his head feel any better. He should be back in the saddle in a couple of days."

Savich said, "As you know, you asked us not to work this case, sir. This guy, do you have any ideas about him?"

"Oh, yeah, we know who he is—her cousin. Actually, we already knew about him. Agents were trying to locate him in connection with the case, as soon as we got positive ID on Lissy and the others. Oh yes, you guys won't believe this. As you know, a major rule for bank robbers is never carry ID. Well, this crew did, all nice and neat in their pockets. Pretty unprofessional of them and good for us. Now, the cousin wasn't at his address in Winnett, North Carolina, and nobody had seen him for a good six weeks. He told a neighbor he was going backpacking in Europe for a couple of months. Both Daugherty and Coggins identified him from his driver's license photo, so we already have it plastered everywhere."

"Does he own a car?"

"No, a motorcycle."

Sherlock asked, "What's the guy's name, sir?"

"Victor Nesser. His mother was Jennifer Smiley's half sister, Marie. She married a Jordanian, Hasam Nesser, Victor's dad, and the two of them moved back to Jordan four years ago. Victor was nearly seventeen at the time and didn't want to go—we don't know why—so he went to live with his mom's half sister, Jennifer Smiley. At the time, Lissy Smiley was twelve years old."

"Bad choice," Sherlock said. "So Jennifer seduced him over to the dark side?"

"Maybe, or he went willingly enough," Maitland said. "But don't forget, when all the bank robberies began, Victor wasn't a seventeen-year-old kid anymore, he was an adult, twenty-one years old."

Savich said, "I wonder what his relationship is with Lissy Smiley. That was quite a risk he took to get her away. Something's there, something deep."

"Don't know, but we need to find out. Jennifer Smiley hails from Fort Pessel, Virginia, a small town down near the North Carolina border that dates back to the Civil War. We already had agents search the Smiley house for the stolen money and interview everyone of interest, but they haven't found out anything real helpful yet about her or Victor Nesser. Lots of rumors about the family, but, bottom line, they kept themselves real private, never socialized, seldom did business locally, except grocery shopping, that's about it. Oh, yeah, and they liked the local KFC.

"They paid their bills, never pissed anyone off, so no one thought about them much. They were just sort of there.

"Agents did track down a couple of Lissy Smiley and Victor Nesser's teachers. Only two teachers and a coach were in town. A lot of the teachers seemed to have escaped town for the summer. What a deal they've got."

Sherlock said, "Yeah, but in some places I bet they wish they had Kevlar vests."

Maitland said, "Forget I said that."

"Tell us about the other two robbers, sir," Sherlock said.

13

"Like I told you, the boobs carried their ID." They heard rustling in the background. "Here we go. Jeff Wicky and Jay Fisher, they were imports from out West—Oregon, to be specific—longtime hoods for hire. The Salem field office sent agents to their former addresses, but there wasn't anything to find except new tenants who hated the thin walls.

"Wicky and Fisher got out of jail about the same time—six months ago—rented apartments in the same building in Salem for four months, then disappeared. They told the bartender at their favorite dive they were driving cross-country. To see all the beautiful scenery? The bartender didn't think so, since they were badasses, but he wasn't about to ask. We don't know yet how they hooked up with Jennifer Smiley."

"I'll wager Sean's downsized orange basketball it's more than just hooking up," Savich said. "A family tie, some sort of connection, got to be."

"Or maybe a friend in common in prison," Sherlock said.

"We're looking. No word yet. Thing is, guys, we never even considered the possibility of Lissy Smiley's escaping. Damn, makes us look like idiots. Now it's a whole new ball game."

Savich said, "We know Lissy Smiley is a killer, but what about Victor? Any arrests, fights—anything to indicate how he'd behave at crunch time?"

Maitland said, "Best guess from behavioral sciences—he isn't a psycho. He didn't kill Coggins or Daugherty, though he could have. And don't forget, he was always the driver, never a real player in the actual bank robberies. To verify, we double-checked all the banks' security videos. Never a sign of him."

Sherlock said, "Victor Nesser's twenty-one, barely old enough to grow face hair. How could Daugherty possibly think he was an FBI agent?"

"Yeah, yeah, I know, but Daugherty says he looked at the creds and never questioned his age."

Savich asked, "How old is agent Peter Coggins?"

There was a moment of agonized silence. "He's thirty-one."

"Ah," Savich said.

"I know, it's obvious Daugherty didn't pay attention. He says the guy pulled his ID away real fast, that he wasn't really thinking about anyone gutsy enough to walk right up and flash another agent's ID."

Sherlock said, "Excuse me, sir, but that's bull."

Maitland laughed. "Yeah, it sure enough is. One of my boys calls it *caca de toro,* and busts a gut laughing at his own law school wit. I bet the guys won't let Daugherty forget this until next summer, if then."

A moment of silence, then Savich asked, "Why exactly are you calling us, sir?"

"Because Lissy Smiley kept telling Daugherty she was going to kill you for murdering her mama. I want you to keep your eyes open."

Sherlock said, "But Dillon didn't kill her mother, it was Buzz Riley."

"I know. Lissy Smiley didn't mention him, but I called Mr. Riley, told him to take a vacation until we catch her and Victor. I helped him clear three weeks off. No one wanted another employee shot. I suggested Buzz pay a nice little visit to Aruba. I even got him on an evening flight."

Savich grinned as Sherlock rolled her eyes. He said, "It's a beautiful Sunday afternoon, sir, and I appreciate the call. I mean, the warning is thoughtful, but now tell us what you really have in mind."

Silence on Maitland's end.

At Sherlock's nod, Savich gave it up. "I know you've got a team already in place, sir, but with Lissy Smiley on the loose and threatening me, I'd like to be front and center on finding her and Victor Nesser."

Savich would hand it to his boss, he put on a good show. Finally Maitland said, "Well, if you really insist, Savich. I'm gonna have to pull some strings. Last thing I want is any turf problems, any duplication of effort, or stumbling over each other. I'll send links to everything we have to MAX."

Savich appreciated that Maitland tried not to sound too pleased with himself about getting what he wanted.

Savich said, "I think Sherlock and I need to go down to Fort Pessel tomorrow, check it out, then maybe on to Winnett, North Carolina, find out what we can about Victor Nesser. I'd like to get a personal feel for where they lived and the people who know them."

"If that's what you want, Savich," Maitland said, and Savich knew he was grinning like the cat in the canary cage. When Savich hung up the phone, he told Sherlock, "I'll say one thing for Victor. Taking out an FBI agent, stealing his ID, taking himself to Memorial to free Lissy—that took guts and steadiness. He's got to feel really attached to Lissy to take a chance like that. He moved to Winnett, North Carolina, when he was eighteen, evidently right after he graduated. The question is why? What happened?"

Sherlock said, "Lissy was only thirteen when he left."

He nodded and said, "Did he leave because of Lissy, or maybe a falling-out with his aunt, Jennifer Smiley?"

Sherlock raised her face to his, touched her fingertips to his cheek. "We need to see if he's got a passport, maybe dual passports, one Jordanian."

"Yeah, we'll do that first thing."

She said, "I wonder why he didn't want to return to Jordan with his mother and father. Ah, well, we'll find out everything about him in due course. We don't know what he's been doing since he graduated high school, how he's earned a living. We'll go first thing to Fort Pessel and Winnett, find out about these two."

"I'm sure some of that legwork will be in the info Mr. Maitland sends us."

"Yeah, yeah, you know it's not the same thing." She added as she looked at the kitchen clock, "I figure we've got another thirty minutes before Sean comes home from the Perrys' on a sugar high. I want you to tell me everything about Lissy Smiley and how things went down. Paint me a picture, Dillon. I want to hear it out of your mouth again. I know you've thought about it, relived it. Now that Lissy is free, I need to know what you think. Talk to me."

And he did. She didn't add that the thought of a crazy teenager out to kill Dillon scared her to her toes.

". . . Riley saved my bacon, shot Jennifer Smiley through the neck. I will never forget thinking of a blood fountain."

He'd been so close to death again, she thought, *too close. A fountain of blood.* She got herself together. "We've got to find out what sort of relationship Lissy Smiley had with Victor. It could be the key to what makes them tick."

Savich agreed, only he really didn't care at this particular moment in time. He grabbed Sherlock and kissed her. "I'll get to work with MAX on this tonight. Ah, how much time do you think we have before Lucy brings Sean home?"

"At least fourteen minutes," Sherlock said, and ran up the stairs.

The only thing missing from this perfect picture, Savich thought as he followed her, was that they didn't have a ceiling fan in their bedroom. He hoped he'd have time to install one next weekend. He thought about Autumn. He prayed she'd call him again tonight. It had been too long. He'd gotten a couple of phone calls from several small-town sheriffs, but as yet, nothing on Autumn. His Autumn. He was getting really worried about her.

14

TITUSVILLE, VIRGINIA
Sunday

The Washington Post lay neat and un-opened on the living room coffee table, delivered as always on Sunday morning from the 24/7 Quick Shop by little Buddy Grubbs, Amy Grubbs's youngest. Ethan had gotten into the habit of reading the *Post* when he'd lived in Washington during his three-year stint in the DEA. The idea of putting his bare feet up on his coffee table and reading it on this fine Sunday morning, a cup of coffee in his hand, seemed a world away.

Ethan sat down on the comfortable worn sofa that had cushioned many of his family's butts over the years, carefully moved the newspaper to the side of the coffee table, and set his cup down on the glass top. He waved a hand. "It's just as well Autumn's playing in the bedroom with the cats. I need to talk to you, Joanna. Sit down a moment. You probably heard me on my cell phone. All my deputies are out looking for Blessed Backman, with as much neighboring law enforcement help as they can spare. Unfortunately, he doesn't appear to have a driver's license or a Social Security number. And that means, officially, he doesn't exist."

"Surely he must drive. How else did he get here?"

"Yes, it only makes sense that he drove up here. It could have been a car, truck, motorcycle, whatever."

"I know Blessed is still out there, probably real close. He hasn't got Autumn yet, and believe me, he wants Autumn very badly. I need to get her away from here. I've been thinking Colorado might be a nice home for us."

Her heels looked dug in like a mule's, and so he said easily, "And what do you intend to do, Joanna? In Colorado?"

"I'm not completely down-and-out like you seem to think, Sheriff. I was an office manager in a big medical facility in Boston. I have a business degree." She sighed. "Who am I trying to kid? Actually, I was okay at it, but I hated it, being cooped up all day, every single day, living for the weekend. I did it only to help support Autumn. I do speak Russian fluently."

"Yeah, so who wants to learn Russian in Colorado?"

She plowed right over him. "What I'm really good at and enjoy is teaching skiing and snowboarding in the winter and taking people hiking in the mountains in the summer, rock climbing, white-water rafting, camping, that sort of thing."

"Autumn told me your husband passed away."

"Yes, recently."

"I'm sorry."

"Look, Ethan, I might not have much money right now, but I do have enough to get Autumn and me set up in Colorado until I get a job. I'm thinking Leadville."

"Leadville is quite a place," he said. "I was there with my brother and sister once, cross-country skiing and some downhill, of course. I remember a couple of days the city was actually in the clouds."

"Yes, well, it's two miles high, after all."

"And all those old Victorians, it made me want to pull on some chaps and climb aboard a horse. So is that why you've been coming to Titusville for so long—your parents were outdoors fans? Did you spend a lot of time in Titus Hitch Wilderness?"

"A fair amount through the years, Sheriff. Why are you smiling? Don't you believe me?"

"Sure, I believe you. Actually, I'm glad to hear you weren't all that happy being a city wuss, all decked out in suits and panty hose and killer high heels. I can clearly see your little nose pressed against the office glass, desperate to get outside."

"City wuss? I've got some city girlfriends who would deck you for saying that. Some women I know who work in Boston could chop up a mugger and fry him for breakfast."

"Urban survival skills, that's different. I'm more interested in a woman who can set up a camp, cook on a Coleman stove and boil up coffee, kill a snake and bake the sucker if she had to, know when a bear is looking at her like breakfast. See? Different kinds of skills. Don't get up, Joanna, just relax. I'm not going to bite, all right?"

She knew he was trying to get her to relax, smile even, so he could herd her in the direction he wanted. He was very good. But she didn't want to be herded, she couldn't afford to be.

He sat back in his chair, laced his fingers over his belly. He said, "Tell me about your folks, Joanna. Did they teach you about the outdoors? Teach you how to ski?"

Why not? It wouldn't matter. "My folks were both ski instructors at Whistler Mountain, north of Vancouver. I was raised in British Columbia. As soon as I could walk, they put me on skis. We camped, hiked, swam, rock-climbed, whatever else was available, in the summers, and skied in the winters."

"It sounds like a wonderful childhood."

"It was the best." She took another sip of her coffee.

"Are your parents still in Canada?"

She shook her head, her lips pursed.

He sat forward and asked quietly, "What happened, Joanna?"

She didn't look at him. He watched her

long fingers pleat the afghan beside her. Finally, she said, "My mom passed away when I was fifteen. Then my father was killed trying to save some idiot hotdog French skiers from an avalanche. I swore on that day I never wanted to see another snow-covered mountain."

"Once again, I'm sorry. That's tough."

She gave a half laugh. "I was in my freshman year at CSU in Fort Collins. I transferred the next year to Boston University. And became a business major. Then I met my husband in my junior year. Sheriff, it's time for me and Autumn to hit the road."

"When did you begin skiing again?"

"After I'd worked in an office for a week, it was time to head up to Loon Mountain Resort on White Mountain in New Hampshire. I skied for a week straight."

He wanted to ask her if her husband had gone skiing with her, but he let it go.

He noticed that her mug of coffee said: GOOSE ME OR GIVE ME COFFEE. He pointed to it. "The mug was my grandpa's, it's forty years old if it's a day, holds a good twenty-four ounces. If you chug that all down, Joanna, you're going to be flying high.

Why don't you tell me why you ran here to Titusville? Other than its being the butt end of nowhere. An incredibly beautiful butt end, but still—"

"Tollie lives here. We've known him since he was good friends with my dad's older brother. My folks were close to him, and I was too. Tollie knows lots of people—he used to be in law enforcement—and I knew he'd help us."

Ethan said, "Yes, Autumn mentioned Tollie. You're right about his knowing people, he's former FBI. So you didn't know about his yearly trek out to the Everglades? You came here without talking to him?"

"We couldn't reach him by phone, so we just drove here. We've been waiting for him. It doesn't matter now, it's too late. They've found us."

"Who is 'they'? The Backmans?"

She nodded. "There's a nest of them, Sheriff. I thank you for all you've done, I really do, but Autumn and I are going to be leaving now. I will keep in touch."

"How many times did you rehearse that little departure speech?"

"Three, four times, in front of the mirror.

That doesn't change the facts. Autumn's in danger here. I want to take her away from the danger, it's that simple."

"Blessed would have murdered you, probably me as well."

"Yes, I suppose so, through Ox."

"I'll bet Ox feels really lousy that it was his finger on the trigger."

"Look, I'm really sorry about what happened to Ox." She set the mug on the coffee table beside his and rose, smoothing down her creased jeans with her palms. He slowly rose to stand in front of her. He was big and barefoot, he hadn't shaved, and his Beretta was clipped to his jeans. He imagined he looked like a thug who needed a shower. He hoped she might be intimidated, but he gave it up when she merely raised an eyebrow at him and looked amused. He said, "I don't think it'd be too bright to ignore this. You know, running from trouble might save you for the short term, but trouble always catches up. Always."

She stared down at his grandpa's mug.

"Look, Joanna, I get that you're afraid for your daughter."

"Yes, and myself."

"Tell me about Blessed and the 'mad

old woman.' Tell me all about the Back-mans. Blessed referred to his ma?"

She sighed. "I could tell you, and maybe you could even talk the local police chief into going to see them, but trust me on this—nothing would be done, and that's because everyone's afraid of them, even that good-old-boy sheriff, Burris Cole."

"Where is this? Where do they live?"

Since she ignored the question, he continued, "I can see being scared spitless of them, after seeing what Blessed can do to another human being. What makes you think when we find Blessed our charges won't stick? After all, he'll be here, not with his own local sheriff."

"Maybe because the judge would look at Blessed and dismiss the case, or the prosecutor would look at him and never bring a case, or, better yet, the cops sent to arrest him would look at him and they'd let him go, maybe even give him a lift to wherever he wanted to go—better yet, even forget why they were there in the first place. This is not what could be possible. This is exactly what would happen. Believe me, Sheriff."

He said, "I gotta admit, you've hit a solid

point there. We'll get to that in a moment. I don't want you to think I'm just this boon-docks sheriff who doesn't know his butt from his boots. I was this big law enforce-ment honcho back in Washington, a DEA agent."

That drew her up short. "DEA?"

"You know, the Drug Enforcement Ad-ministration. Maybe I wasn't a real big hon-cho, but I think I did some good."

"Then how did you get to be a sheriff in the boondocks?"

He gave her a big grin. "Like you, I couldn't stand being trapped inside a build-ing, wearing a suit and wing tips. Don't get me wrong, if they'd let me out in the field, I'd have been happy as a clam, but they wanted me in a Washington tactical desk job."

She picked up his grandfather's mug. "I need a refill."

"No, you don't. Step away from the mug, Joanna."

She laughed, couldn't help it.

"So tell me about Blessed. All he has to do to hypnotize someone is to look them straight in the eye, that's it? Can he do it to anyone?"

How had he gotten her off on this track, and talking? This was bad. She wasn't amused at his macho show now, probably because he wasn't playing at it any longer, that hard look on his face all too real. Because she'd known such fear in the last two weeks, felt so *paralyzed*, it almost hurt to say it, but she did.

"I don't know. I guess so. I only saw him do it to one other person besides Ox. It was instant, what he did."

Ethan said slowly, "I've always heard you can't hypnotize another person into acting contrary to their wishes. But here's the thing, Joanna. Last night, it seemed to me that Ox would have killed you, killed me, killed anyone who happened to get in his way of nabbing Autumn. You don't know Ox, but I do, and that guy last night wasn't the man I know. He didn't even sound like himself, exactly—manic, excited, quite mad, really. It was more than hypnosis, I'm thinking. It's scary, Joanna, what he did to Ox."

"Sheriff, I appreciate your wanting to protect us, but Blessed is out there, mending his arm, making his plans. Autumn and I must leave. We've got to stop at the

B-and-B and pack our things. I do thank you for what you've done for us, Sheriff."

"You're welcome, but I've just begun to fight. Now, I'll take you to the B-and-B. While you're getting your stuff together, I'll make some calls. We're staying together, Joanna, get used to it."

15

NORTHEAST WASHINGTON, D.C.
Sunday, late afternoon

Buzz Riley looked one last time at the bed he and his wife, Eloise, had shared for more than thirty-six years. He'd never been gone from home for long since she died of ovarian cancer the year before. He missed her every single day, a steady ache. Was the ache less than it had been six months ago? He didn't know. His three kids worried about him, and hovered. At first it was good, but soon it was driving him nuts. He figured out they'd made a schedule to see him, especially on the weekends, and that drove him nuts too. He tried to tell them he needed time alone, to reflect, to remember, to enjoy fishing in his new fifteen-foot Blue Fin Dory, but they wouldn't pay any attention. One of his kids and some of his grandkids were always with him, the kids pressed against his back at the center console.

He fastened his ancient army duffel bag, checked to see that all the kitchen appliances were turned off, something Eloise had trained him to do, locked the front door, and carefully set the house alarm. He walked to his 2007 blue Chrysler Sebring, the first convertible he'd ever owned. They'd bought it from their mail carrier—only nine thousand miles on it—a year before Eloise died. She loved to ride around with him with the top down, laughing like a teenager sometimes, until one day she stuck her head out the side and an insect hit her front teeth. Buzz grinned at the memory of her shriek. He could still see her scrubbing her fingers manically over her teeth, trying to find a Kleenex.

He tossed his duffel into the passenger seat and slid across the soft black leather, closed the door. He patted the dashboard, still looking good as new, since he kept his baby cleaned and polished inside and out. He loved this car, only wondered in that moment if the damned thing had taken some of Eloise's place in his affections.

"Nah," he said aloud, and turned the key in the ignition.

Nothing happened. The engine didn't even turn over.

He centered the steering wheel and turned the key again.

There was a small grinding noise that didn't sound good, but then the engine roared to life, hummed smooth, and happy. He gave it some gas, listened to the sweet music. "Ah, there you go, beautiful."

Buzz backed out of his driveway slowly because the neighborhood was always hopping, kids playing in the street, riding bikes. Didn't matter if it was nearly seven o'clock in the evening, if it was still light there was action.

He waved to a couple of teenage boys who looked like they were going to smoke dope the minute he was out of sight, and they waved back. He was a retired cop, seven years now, but still a cop, and they knew it. His fingers itched sometimes to grab the little yahoos by the scruffs of their necks and shake some sense into their buzzed teenage heads.

He took a last look at his house, wondered how long it would be until he was home again. He knew he had no choice but to leave, with those crazy loons from the bank out for his hide—that young girl, Lissy, especially. Mr. Maitland had told him Lissy was probably sprung by the guy driving the getaway car, and confided that Dillon Savich would be taking over the case. Buzz liked him. Mr. Maitland treated Buzz like he was still a cop, even thanked him for saving Savich's life.

Buzz had been to the Caribbean only once, with Eloise, on a cruise they'd hated, what with all his fellow cruisers running like pigs to the trough, and the threat of a hurricane, which, thankfully, hadn't materialized.

He figured if he got bored on Aruba, he could always island-hop—after all, he was on leave with pay. Island-hopping, that might be good, but not if it meant being stuck on a rocking boat for seven days. At least he'd get a break from his kids cluttering around him all the time, trying to feed him, siccing his grandkids on him. It had been a zoo with them since he'd nearly bought the big one in the bank robbery. Buzz hadn't called any of them to tell them he was leaving. Nope, he'd sent a blanket e-mail, and hadn't answered any phone calls. He'd send everybody postcards.

The Sebring wasn't running right. He had noticed some sputtering earlier, and now it was skipping, running rough. Whatever it was, it was getting worse. Maybe he shouldn't drive the car to the airport. He had time to leave it at Jimmy's—yeah, that's what he'd do. He pulled out his cell phone and called Jimmy at home, told him he was going to leave it, and called a taxi.

Buzz switched lanes and drove over to Pepper Street, down a couple of blocks, and pulled into his friend Jimmy Turly's auto shop, Honest Abe's Repairs. Buzz once asked him if there really was an Abe, but Jimmy said his mom told him it had a good sound to it, trustworthy and all.

Buzz left his convertible at the tail of a row of other broken-down cars, left the keys on top of the front driver's-side tire, and climbed into the taxi that had pulled up sooner than he expected. They made it to Reagan Airport in under an hour. His plane wasn't late—a miracle—and he checked his bag and made it through security without having to strip to his shorts or empty his carry-on. He boarded his 737 to Aruba, a flat island, he'd heard, with lots of casinos and white beaches. He didn't like to gamble, but he did like to lie in the sun. No one could ever tell he had a tan, he was already so dark, but he liked the idea of just lying in the sand and listening to the waves break. He could still feel the mad rush of adrenaline and the pounding fear when that maniac stuck his .38 into his ear, and the leap of joy and excitement when he could finally fight back. And he'd made it, with Dillon Savich's help, even managed to shoot that woman who was leading the gang. In thirty years as a cop he'd never come that close to dying, and had never had to kill someone. *The Washington Post* had called him a hero, run his picture with Savich standing next to him, looking like one mean dude, despite his grin. At least he was alive, and although Eloise was gone, it felt wonderful.

He smiled. What an experience. It had changed something in him, he thought, made him feel more involved again in what people were doing around him, what they thought, how they felt. He liked it. He realized it felt vaguely familiar.

Buzz sat in a window seat, glad the seat next to him was still unoccupied, and looked out into the dying day when he noticed a closed utility door next to their gate slowly open. A young man, dressed in jeans and a gray T-shirt, stuck out his head. To Buzz's experienced eye, he looked furtive, like he was somewhere he shouldn't be, wanting to do something he shouldn't be doing. What was this all about? The young man looked straight up at the plane, and Buzz would swear the young guy looked straight at him, although Buzz doubted that was possible. He saw something change in the boy's expression. He turned to speak to someone still inside, and suddenly Buzz clearly saw Lissy Smiley come out from behind him. He'd seen her up close the day of the robbery when Savich had pulled her ski mask off, stared at her for some time. No doubt in his mind it was her, even though he couldn't see her crazy dark eyes from here.

He knew why the two of them were here. They'd come to kill him. But they were too late.

He wanted to wave his fist at them, yell and laugh at them that he was safe. Then

Buzz wondered how they followed him here, remembered the trouble with his car. Had they rigged it to break down on the side of the road? Or to blow up? Had that taxi arriving early saved his life? He quickly turned his cell back on and dialed Dillon Savich, but there was no answer. He left a message.

Buzz watched the two young people fade back into the terminal, watched the utility door automatically close. He continued to ignore the flight attendant and dialed Mr. Maitland. He didn't want to take a chance of Honest Abe's blowing up, Jimmy along with it.

16

TITUSVILLE, VIRGINIA
Sunday evening

Joanna and Autumn wore clean jeans and T-shirts, and probably clean socks on their feet. Ethan thanked the Lord he had convinced them to unpack, to stay with him at least while his deputies were out searching for Blessed. But he hated waiting. He hated not knowing what he was up against.

After a dinner of macaroni and cheese with a side of peas and a salad Joanna made without anyone asking for one, he set Autumn in front of the TV in his bedroom and took Joanna to the living room. "Sit down."

She said, "Why don't you throw that

sweatshirt away? It's got a hole under the right arm and it's all frayed around the neck. I know, I know, you're a guy and you've worn that sweatshirt since you were sixteen."

"Seventeen, actually."

"And why don't you have shoes and socks on? You'll get splinters."

Ethan put his feet up on the coffee table, arched an eyebrow at her.

She said, "I finally tossed a Fort Lauderdale T-shirt last year a boy bought me when I was eighteen."

"There you go. Tell you what, I'll be strong and toss my sweatshirt if you tell me everything you know about these people."

"That's a beautiful piano. Do you play?"

Anything to divert him. He nodded. "Thank you. It was my grandmother's piano. I'll play some jazz for you later if you like. You know, Joanna, I've been patient with you, but now it's time. I'm worried about my deputies as much as I'm worried about you and Autumn. What if they get close to Blessed? What will he do to them? Tell them to run off a cliff? You have to tell me what you know about him. I think you owe it to us, don't you?"

She chewed on her lip, studied the inch of cold coffee at the bottom of the mug, then said, "I don't want anyone to be hurt, I really don't."

He nodded. "Go on, then. Talk to me. Please."

She put her feet up on the coffee table next to his, frowned at those two pairs of feet, put hers back on the floor, and said finally, "We were in the cemetery at my husband's funeral, just a week ago. Blessed caught a young man hiding behind a gravestone. He had a camera and was taking pictures, like a Jimmy Olsen cub reporter. Blessed went into a rage, screamed at the kid, 'Well, if it isn't little snotty-nosed Nat Hodges,' and jerked him to his feet, looked into his eyes—the young man never said a word. Blessed told him to drop his camera and stomp on it. Nat Hodges did it, no hesitation at all. At first I thought he was just scared to death, but then he simply stood there, all still and quiet. Blessed laughed at him and started making him do things, like elbow-crawl on his chest, rip off his shirt, rub dirt in his hair, humiliating things. The boy didn't seem to be there anymore. He was completely in

Blessed's control, just like Ox was last night.

"Then Grace said, 'Stop it, Blessed, we've got guests and we're burying Martin,' and Blessed huffed out in a pissed voice, 'Can't have the little scheiss taking pictures.' Then he shook the kid until his head snapped back. I remember I took a step toward them, but Grace said in my ear not to worry, that Blessed was just bringing the boy back, something I really didn't understand. But the boy seemed to wake up.

"Then Blessed grabbed the kid by the collar and told him he was going to run back to his boss at the newspaper and tell him he quit. And he said, 'If I catch you around here again, I'm going to put you in one of those graves, you hear?'

"I remember the young guy was moaning, said his head hurt. I watched him run, just like Blessed told him to, trying to hold his head at the same time. I watched Blessed take the smashed camera and throw it into the open grave. He said, 'Now Martin can take pictures of all the saints.' He turned to his mother, Shepherd, and she nodded, didn't say a word, simply nodded, and it was over.

"I was so shocked, so terrified, I stood there like a stone, my hand over Autumn's eyes. She was plastered to my side. I could hear her breathing." Joanna stopped a moment, looked over his left shoulder toward the grand piano.

"Since it happened, I'd been thinking about it, though, what we saw, and it seemed that being shaken or hit, or jarred, is what brought the boy back to himself. That's what I was trying to do last night with Ox. I have no idea what Ox would have done, though, if you hadn't hit him so hard. No, I do know. He would have killed us to get Autumn."

He nodded. "It was like he was hard-wired to do whatever he had to do to get his hands on her. Dr. Spitz still won't accept that Ox was under the control of someone else. He checked him for drugs and alcohol, and he wants Ox to have an MRI and an EEG, to see if his behavior was the result of a seizure or a brain tumor.

"You spoke about a cemetery, and you mentioned your husband, and you were there for his funeral. Tell me about the rest of the family, and why you were there with them."

"I hadn't met any of them before last

week." She didn't say anything else, just began to worry her thumbnail.

Ethan said, "Blessed—his name makes me think of some sort of weird-ass preacher for one of those off-the-wall religions that doesn't have much to do with God."

"All their names are like that. For example, Grace."

"Grace? Yes, you mentioned his whispering to you. Blessed and Grace? What, they're brothers?"

"Yes, Martin's brothers."

"Okay, what can you tell me about Grace?"

"Grace is thin as a rail, holds himself real quiet. But you're always aware of him when he's around. He's creepy."

She started to say something again, and he sat forward, touched her wrist. "What? Say what you have to say."

"I could be wrong, really wrong."

"What, Joanna?"

"I only heard Grace speak a very little bit. His voice was soft, sort of hollow, almost dead." She shuddered. "That sounds ridiculous. I can't really explain it, but—"

"But what?"

"Ox, last night, when he spoke—"

He waited.

"Ox sort of sounded like Grace. Not all soft and quiet like Grace, but the cadence of his voice.

"It sounds crazy, I know. It's not that it was Grace's voice, but it was the way he spaced out his words, like I said, the cadence—it was so familiar."

17

Later, he thought, he'd visit that snake pit later. Ethan knew there was even more; he knew it. He had to keep her talking. Maybe all of it would come out at last.

"Are you ready to tell me where this happened? Where they live?"

"In a strange little town called Bricker's Bowl. It's near the Alabama border."

"Bricker's Bowl? I've never heard of it."

"It really is more a bowl than a valley, curves up on both sides with houses marching right up the hills. I guess, from the air, what with the houses on the surrounding hills, it does indeed look like a bowl. Their family's been there for generations, his mother told me."

"Tell me about Ma."

"She's rich. She, Blessed, and Grace live in a huge Victorian mansion, filled with expensive antiques, mostly nineteenth-century English, and lots of manicured grounds. They have a six-car garage, although I never saw the cars inside, so I can't tell you what they are. They've got their own private cemetery.

"She's very proud of their wealth. She loves to show you every antique in the place—and there are a lot of them, since there are maybe fifteen rooms. She told me this is all due to her husband's talent."

"Was the husband around?"

She shook her head. "He's dead. When she first told me about him, I thought she was batty, but now I'm not so sure. She confided in me that Theodore had the most useful talent in the family. That's what she called it—a useful talent."

Ethan found himself sitting forward. "What could Theodore do?"

"She said he had this beautiful gift,

discovered quite by accident when he was in Las Vegas once and played the slot machines. He won."

"Yeah. So what?"

"Evidently he won a great deal. Actually, she told me he never lost."

"*What?* You're telling me Theodore Backman was some sort of diviner?"

She had to grin, but it fell off her face fast enough. Ethan was staring at her, an eyebrow arched.

"As Shepherd explained it, where the reels stop is supposed to be random, but somehow Theodore could make the reels stop where he wished. She said he talked to the slots."

"Oh, come on, Joanna. You mean he had this force field that reacted to the reels themselves? Or he had this internal magnet that brought the reels to a stop? What?"

"Look, I thought it was nuts too, even though Mrs. Backman told me he'd made them all rich."

"It sounds like one of the crazy stories they'd tell us in the DEA as a cover for illegal income," Ethan said. "It never flew in court. How'd he die?"

"Mrs. Backman told me he walked out of a casino in Reno and a mugger killed him. He hit the mugger with his cane, but the mugger hit him on the head with a hammer and left him to die, which he did."

"A cane? How old was Theodore when the mugger got him?"

"Mid-seventies."

"How old is Blessed? Grace?"

"Blessed is in his fifties. Grace is a bit younger, late forties, maybe."

"So you're telling me Blessed and Grace and their mother—what's her name?"

"Shepherd."

"Like the guy on FOX News?"

"More like the guy who herds the sheep. She told me, all preening, that her husband gave her that name, the mother of his small flock. I wondered what her birth name was, but I was too freaked out to ask."

"Okay, so these folk say they're rich because of a man who could line up three cherries. Now the million-dollar question. How did you hook up with these people? If they're your husband's family, why did you only just meet them?"

When she remained silent, he said, "You might want to consider me the prince of bad, Joanna. I can handle just about anything."

That made her laugh, then draw a deep breath. "All right. Martin, my husband, was the third and youngest brother. Autumn and I met them for the first time at his funeral."

"But he couldn't have been as old as Blessed or Grace, was he?"

"No, he was thirty-six when he died, much younger than both his brothers. Shepherd was in her forties when she birthed him."

"Your husband died—a natural death?"

Her mouth seamed tight, but the words were pushing to get out. Why didn't she want to tell him? Was she still grieving too much?

He pulled on a thread hanging down from the left sleeve of his sweatshirt. "An accident of some kind?"

She shook her head, looking hard at him pulling that thread, and the words came out in a burst, but lifeless and without fury or pain. "He died in prison," she said, her eyes still on that gray thread.

He nearly fell off the sofa with surprise. He stared at her, unable not to. "Why was your husband in prison?"

She shook her head. All right, so she wasn't ready to face that yet with him. He shifted gears. "So you found his family's phone number—where?"

"The warden sent all Martin's stuff to me. There was pitifully little, to be honest. There was this lone phone number in a small black notebook—no name, only an out-of-state phone number—and so I called it to see who it was he knew in Georgia. It was his family.

"I spoke to his mother and told her Martin was dead. She wept, Ethan. Then she begged me to have him buried with his family, not in cold Boston where he hadn't known anyone except me and his daughter. Did we feel he had any deep roots there? 'No, not really,' I told her. 'Then please,' she begged me, 'please bring him home.'

"She begged me, Ethan, and she was crying again, so I said yes because she was right. I didn't have family in Boston—no family anywhere, for that matter. And so after a memorial in Boston with all our friends, Autumn and I drove Martin's urn from Boston to Georgia so his mother could bury it in the family cemetery."

He waited for her to continue, but she didn't. She sat there as if frozen, as if her words were stuck in her throat.

He said quietly, "Your husband never told you about his family. You never asked?"

"Yes, of course I was curious, but Martin refused to talk about them. *They are not the sort of people you want to know, Jo. Neither do I. I ask you to accept that.* I remember he once said unwittingly that he'd managed to escape them, that they didn't know where he was. I didn't know what he'd meant about escaping them, and he never told me. I suppose I thought it was a runaway-kid sort of thing."

"He didn't change his name? He kept Martin Backman?"

"Yes."

"I wonder why he didn't change his name. With the Internet, you could probably find a missing pet. Didn't he care if they found him? Bigger question—why didn't they find him? They found you and Autumn, didn't they? Real fast."

She nodded. "They did find us fast, but I don't understand how they did it."

"You must have talked to them some

about your own family. Did you mention Titusville?"

"I'm sure I didn't, not directly. When I first met him, married him, I simply let it all go as not being important to me, important to us. I loved him, found him fascinating and funny. But now—it's obvious I didn't know him, didn't know a big part of him at all. Who was the man I married? Believe me, I would really like to know."

She lowered her face into her hands.

"I'm sorry, Joanna."

She jerked up and Ethan saw sudden anger and pain radiating off her, like waves of heat laced with poison.

18

He rose. "I'm going to lock us in for the night, Joanna, then we can go on."

She followed him out to the foyer, watched him lock and dead-bolt the front door, and turn on the alarm.

They checked Autumn. She was curled up asleep on his bed, Mackie in her arms. Ethan covered her with an afghan.

He got them two mugs of tea and motioned her back to the living room.

"You started to tell me about his mother when you first arrived in Bricker's Bowl."

She nodded. "His mother was alone when we drove up. At first I thought she was his grandmother, but she wasn't. Like I told you, Martin was born long after Grace.

"She was very nice, showed me the Backman cemetery, but I knew she was upset that I'd cremated Martin and brought him in an urn, not in a casket as she obviously expected. There were a lot of graves in the cemetery, maybe upwards of forty, maybe more. Must be an old family, I thought, looking out over it. I remember all the graves were set in overlapping triangles, so there were no rows or paths. I asked her about all these triangles, and she said her husband's grandparents designed it that way when they'd moved to this spot from the other end of the bowl, and had all the caskets moved here. Then she said the weirdest thing: 'They knew to keep the old ones with them, because the old ones know how to draw the power from the earth.' I was so surprised—so creeped out, really—that I didn't pursue what that meant.

"There were all these oak trees, nearly growing together, some branches pushing down on others, vying for space, and they seemed to huddle over the graves as if trying to protect them, or hide them.

"But then, the next morning, I thought I'd overreacted because it was peaceful and warm, a sun bright overhead—serene, even. It felt right that Martin would end up being buried with his family. His grave was already dug. It hadn't been there when we'd arrived the day before, so I guessed Blessed and Grace dug it out after Autumn and I went to bed. She told me the space was meant for her, but she could always move, now, couldn't she? I remember watching her wrap the urn in a lace tablecloth she said her mother had made herself. I watched Blessed climb down a small ladder and lay the urn on a wooden platform at the bottom of the grave. It looked so small in that deep hole. Then she handed Blessed a wood-framed mesh sort of thing that looked like a chicken coop and he set it over the wrapped urn. Grace climbed down and smoothed another white tablecloth over that. Both Blessed and Grace were wearing shiny black suits, and they took turns filling in the grave. It was just the five of us, no one else, not even a minister. Blessed read from an ancient Bible—ashes to ashes, dust to dust—read on and on for quite a while, in a low drone. When

I realized no one was going to say a prayer, I did. Then we all stood staring down at Martin's grave, the raw dirt piled high, all loamy and black. Autumn was clutching my hand, but she wasn't crying. Her hand was terribly cold. She was so still, never made a sound.

"I wanted to leave immediately after we'd buried his urn, but his mother begged me to stay, just one day, she said, only one single day so she could spend some time with her granddaughter. She reached out to touch Autumn. Autumn didn't move, didn't seem to even breathe when her grandmother stroked her hair."

"And did you stay for one more day?"

She shook her head. "We couldn't stay, not after what Autumn saw—"

She looked terrified. He waited a beat, then asked, "What did Autumn see, Joanna?"

"She said she saw them burying dead people in her daddy's grave."

She'd said it, insane words, unbelievable and terrifying.

Ethan's expression didn't change, but she saw clearly he wasn't going to accept that.

She saw them burying bodies? In her daddy's grave?

Ethan knew there were all kinds of monsters out there, but this was a story from a little girl. He said, "Who did she see burying dead people? Blessed? Grace? Shepherd? All of them? Come on, spit it out."

"It was that night—"

Autumn appeared in the living room door. "What's wrong, Mama?"

Joanna looked pale and exhausted, but she looked up and smiled. It was well done, Ethan thought, but Autumn wasn't buying it. She came running to her mother, grabbed her arm. "Mama, you were telling Ethan about Daddy's funeral, weren't you? You look all white and stiff, like you did that day."

There'd been too many lies, to her daughter, to herself, to others. And so she told her daughter the truth. She nodded. "I was telling Ethan about your daddy's family, sweetheart, about how they behaved, what they were like." Autumn tightened all over. Joanna said, "Did you get some rest, sweetie?"

Autumn nodded. "I woke up from my nap,

Mama. Big Louie was licking my toes and Mackie hissed at him."

Ethan asked, "Big Louie only licks big toes. Did you keep them from fighting?"

"I guess because my feet are a little smaller than yours, Ethan, he got them all. Mackie only swatted his nose once."

"And what did you do?"

"I hugged him, kissed his nose, and then he nearly licked my face off." She pressed closer to her mother and whispered in a small voice, "You told Ethan what I saw them doing?"

Joanna nodded.

Autumn looked at Ethan. He saw such fear on that little face, it was like a punch in the gut. Joanna held her hand tight and said, "Why don't you tell him about it yourself, Autumn?"

She licked her lips. "It's too scary, Mama."

Ethan said, "You tell me and then it won't be so scary anymore. I promise."

She thought about it, then slowly nodded. "I was supposed to be asleep beside Mama, but I couldn't stop thinking about them, how scary they were, how I knew they didn't like Mama, even though they pretended they did. And they looked at me funny, you know, trying to pretend they weren't looking, but they were.

"Mama started moaning in her sleep, so I got up. I put on my clothes without waking her and climbed out the window." She swallowed. "I walked to the cemetery, and that's when I saw them, and they were digging up my daddy's grave and there were these bodies on the ground beside them." She was shaking, both her voice and her small body, and she pressed even harder against her mother's side, as if she wanted to become part of her.

Joanna gathered her close, kissed the top of her head, whispered, "It's okay, sweetie, I swear it's okay. Ethan is—" Joanna cleared her throat. "Ethan is going to help us."

He swallowed hard at that vote of confidence. He looked at the mother and daughter and marveled at what life had dished onto his plate in a single day. He said, "Autumn, I told your mama I'm the prince of bad and that means I can help you with just about anything. Now, kiddo, tell me who you saw out there."

"Blessed and Grace were digging, and Shepherd was standing beside the dead people." Her voice caught, and she looked terrified.

"Okay, Autumn, that's enough for now. I want you to take some deep breaths and shake your arms around; it'll loosen you up. That's it—good. Now, let your mama talk for a while. Joanna, let's back up. After the funeral, what did you and Autumn do?"

Joanna said, "I made some excuse, and I drove us to Bricker's Bowl, only about a half-mile away. Like Autumn, I wanted to get away from all of them. I was tempted to keep driving west, let me tell you. I wish I hadn't gone back there now, wish I hadn't taken Martin's urn to be buried in a chicken coop."

He wondered what would have happened if she'd kept driving west. Would they still have found her just like they found her here? "Okay, after you drove into Bricker's Bowl, what did you do?"

"Just walked around. Everyone knew who we were—how, I have no clue, but I knew they were talking about us, wondering about us, I guess, wondering, maybe, if we were weird. I'll tell you, I don't blame them a bit.

"We stopped at the small grocery store because it was hot and Autumn wanted an ice cream. There was a woman in there who looked at us like we were members of the devil's fold. I'll never forget how she stared at Autumn and said, 'She looks just like him,' and she crossed herself. I was appalled and grabbed Autumn's hand to get her out of there but the woman said then, 'I was very glad Martin escaped. I'm very sorry he's dead. Everyone liked Martin, but no one knew when he was going to be buried. Preacher Michael even called Mrs. Backman, but she didn't tell him a thing.' And then she shut up and shook her head."

"The lady asked me what kind of ice cream I liked best," Autumn said. "I told her I really liked butter pecan, and she said that was good because she'd just made some."

Lula strolled into the living room, tail high. She meowed when she saw Ethan, padded quickly to him, and jumped up on his lap. She began kneading his leg.

Autumn leaned over to pat her and

Lula stretched under her hand and kept kneading.

Of course Mackie wasn't to be left out. He was soon seated on Ethan's other leg, his claws sharper than Lula's, who'd had a manicure only two days before when Maggie had come to clean up the cottage and managed to catch her. Mackie had escaped clean.

Autumn yawned and leaned back against her mother's chest, all boneless, like the cats when they were with him in bed at night. "Mama," she whispered, "I think we can trust Ethan. We started to tell him about those poor dead people. I think we should tell Ethan more of it, Mama."

19

Joanna was pale and quiet. He gave her a moment to think about what Autumn had said, and slowly stood up. "I think both of you could use a soda. How about it?"

Joanna looked at him, drew in a deep breath, and slowly nodded. "Yes, a drink would be nice. Autumn, stay here, sweetie, sit on my lap."

When Ethan came back to the living room, he popped open the cans and passed them on. He kept his voice easy and slow as he said to Autumn, "You were telling me about seeing them burying people. Did you see how these people died?"

Those stark, unbelievable words hung in the air. Autumn stiffened up, pressed her back against her mother's chest. Ethan sat forward, reached out his hand, and lightly touched her shoulder. "You know me now, Autumn. Your mom knows me too, in fact, she even knows I play the piano. I'll play for you later, but first, it's time we cleaned up this mess, and that means you've got to tell me what you saw. All right? Can you do that?"

Autumn gave him a long look, then said, her voice clear and steady, "The people were already dead, Ethan. They were lying next to each other. Blessed and Grace were digging Daddy's grave even deeper so those dead people would fit in it."

"You're sure they were people, Autumn?"

Even as she nodded, Ethan saw her small face cloud over. He knew what she was thinking: *He doesn't believe me; he thinks I'm a stupid little kid.* She couldn't have been clearer if she'd spoken out loud.

"Could you tell how many dead people there were?" Now wasn't that real smart, asking a seven-year-old how many bodies were piled around.

Autumn sat forward, her small hands making fists on the table, her eyes on his face. "I was so scared, Ethan, I just couldn't think. I ran to Mama."

Joanna said clearly, "Yes, she came to tell me what she'd seen, Sheriff."

"Did you go and look?"

"At that point I didn't think it was necessary."

At that point? What did that mean?

He said, "If my kid came to tell me she saw dead bodies, I think I'd be up like a shot to see what was going on. Oh, I see, you thought Autumn was making it up."

"No, Mama didn't believe that," Autumn said. "She just didn't think I saw what I thought I did."

Joanna Backman's face was so leached of color he thought she'd faint. He waited for her to say something, but it was Autumn who spoke. "I wanted Mama to come with me so I could show her what they were doing, but she wouldn't. She pulled me against her and rubbed my head and told me it would be all right, and we were leaving first thing in the morning, and I wasn't to worry about it. I'd forget about it—that's what she thought. But I knew it wouldn't go away.

How could it? I saw them digging up Daddy's grave, and I saw them burying dead people in it."

Joanna took her daughter's hand. "She's right. I believed Autumn was seeing something in her head, but I didn't believe the Backmans were actually in the cemetery at that moment burying people. Autumn had just lost her father; she was grieving for him terribly. Perhaps she'd misinterpreted whatever she'd seen."

The thick silence in Ethan's living room was broken only by Lula and Mackie's purring.

He said slowly, "You believed Autumn was seeing horrible things in her head because of what you'd both seen earlier that day in the cemetery? You thought she was dreaming it?"

Joanna saw incredulity on his face, heard the disbelief in his voice. She said, "That's what I hoped at the time. I mean, who wants to believe something that horrible was actually happening right below the bedroom window?"

Ethan said, "You went to the cemetery, didn't you, Joanna?"

"Yes, I planned to, alone, so I could come

back and reassure Autumn. I was walking toward the center staircase when I heard the three of them come through the front door. They were talking. I couldn't make out what they were saying, so I tiptoed down to the bend in the stairs. I heard Mrs. Backman then, her voice was really clear, so I stopped right where I was and listened. I couldn't have misunderstood her. She sang out, sounding happy as a lark, 'Well, boys, I'm thirstier than a desert in hell. We got it done, all solemn and proper, and it's over. Nobody could complain we didn't do it right. That big pile of dirt will settle down soon enough. Now, I need a nice whiskey sour. Grace, you know exactly how to make it. Blessed, you want a Diet Coke?'

"Blessed said he did, with a slice of lemon. Grace didn't say anything. I would swear they should have heard my heart pounding. They'd just buried people and she wanted a whiskey sour? I wanted to run, but I knew I had to wait and listen, but for the longest time I didn't hear them say anything more. I stayed bent down, in the shadows of the bend of the stairs. I thought they'd gone when Shepherd said, 'We'll take care of Joanna in the morning. Make it look like an accident, Blessed; we don't want Autumn to distrust us. Everyone will be so pleased she's here at last, where she belongs. She's strong. I know it now, stronger than Martin.'

"I heard Blessed grunt and say he'd stymie me easier than Nat Hodges. That was the word he used, 'stymie.' Then Grace said something, but I couldn't make out the words.

"I felt frozen, so terrified I couldn't think, couldn't move, could scarcely draw a breath. Finally they moved away, probably to the kitchen, so Blessed could make this horrible old woman a whiskey sour.

"Later, probably after three o'clock in the morning, Autumn showed me the tree branch outside the window and we climbed down."

Ethan said, "Did you go to the cemetery before you went to get your car? To know for sure?"

Autumn turned in to her mother and wrapped her arms around her back. "It's all right, sweetie."

Autumn nodded and turned back. "Mama wanted to see it with her own eyes. But she said she believed me now after what she heard Mrs. Backman say. She knew I didn't see it in my head."

Joanna hugged her daughter tightly to her. She kissed her hair. "Know this, Autumn, from now on I will always believe exactly what you tell me." She gave her daughter a lopsided grin and another hug. "However, whether or not I want to believe you is a very different matter." She looked up at Ethan. "It was too dangerous to stay. We had to get out of there."

Ethan studied the little girl's face. "Tell me, Autumn, what were you doing in the cemetery so late, and alone. When you saw them burying the people?"

She wouldn't meet his eyes. She glanced at her mother, then quickly away. Finally she said, "I wanted to say good-bye to Daddy."

Joanna looked like she'd collapse in on herself.

Ethan said matter-of-factly, "Okay, thanks for telling me. So, Joanna, you got out of there fast?"

He'd thrown her a rope and she grabbed it. "You bet. Thankfully my car was on a bit of an incline in front of the huge garage, and I put it in neutral, pushed, then jumped in as it gained speed and steered it back down that long driveway. I didn't have to start the engine until we were nearly at the road that runs past the driveway."

Autumn said, "I was looking back, and I didn't see any lights go on. I told Mama we'd be okay."

"I drove until morning. Believe me, I never stopped, even for an instant."

Autumn said, "I tried to call Daddy, and that was stupid because there couldn't be an answer now since he's dead. But before he died, I spoke to him when he was in prison. Do you know, Ethan, Daddy would talk to me about everything, but he wouldn't ever talk about his mother or his brothers. I guess I know why now. They're creepy. I'm glad he ran away."

Ethan asked without thinking, "Your dad had telephone minutes?"

Autumn cocked her head at him. "I don't know."

"Yes, he did," Joanna said. "That's enough for tonight, Sheriff."

"One last thing you might help explain, Joanna. Blessed must know we're aware of who he is now, where his family lives, yet he still tried to take Autumn. What did he intend to do with her? Where did he think he could take her? And why? And what did Shepherd mean by saying Autumn was stronger than Martin?"

"You'll have to ask Blessed that, Sheriff. He didn't exactly share it with us."

20

GEORGETOWN, WASHINGTON, D.C.
Sunday evening

"That was a good call on Buzz," Savich said to Jimmy Maitland, who'd stopped by after dinner. "He's safe now, no way the two of them can get to him in Aruba. That would mean passports, and Lissy Smiley doesn't have one."

"Victor Nesser does, but the alert's out on him. I would strongly doubt they have the sophistication to obtain good forgeries," Maitland said. He accepted a cup of coffee from Sherlock, cocked his head at her. She said, "Yeah, yeah, the coffee god over there made it, not me."

Maitland toasted her with his cup. "You're

looking pretty good, Sherlock. Like I told my wife, in the long scheme of things, I'd rather lose a spleen than some other parts I can think of."

Sherlock wanted to whine about how her body still wanted to sleep when she wanted to keep working—even piddling everyday stuff—how a nice sweaty work-out was still at least a week away, but she smiled. "I'm feeling it less and less every passing day." She handed Dillon a cup of hot tea.

He said, reading her quite clearly, "An-other couple of weeks and you'll be throw-ing me all over the mat at the gym. Be patient."

Maitland looked at the two of them, saw the shadow of fear still in Savich's eyes from the thought of the bullet she'd taken. Then Savich lightly touched his fingertips to her cheek. "I take that back. If you were being patient about this brief vacation, I'd wonder where my Sherlock was."

Maitland said, "Sit down, Sherlock; let's talk about what happened at the airport." He took a sip of coffee, sighed, and smiled. "Okay, after Buzz called me, we got over there fast, but Victor and Lissy were gone.

"We looked at the security videotapes, saw Victor helping Lissy across the terminal, straight to the Caribbean Air counter, then flat-out running with her toward the line at security. But they missed Buzz; he was already through and on his way to the gate.

"Next we saw them ducking through an employees-only door that led down to the tarmac. This part borders on the hard to believe—Buzz was not only sitting in a window seat, his seat was on the terminal side. To top it off, he just happened to be looking out the window to see Victor sticking his head out the door, Lissy behind him. Then he calls me, tells me what a lamebrain he is because he didn't suspect a thing when he dropped off his car at his mechanic's, didn't think about anything hinky until he saw Lissy and Victor eyeing him from that employees' doorway.

"We sent the bomb squad over to the car, but it wasn't rigged. They only found water mixed in with the gasoline in the gas tank. Buzz was lucky he got as far as he did."

Maitland paused a moment, took a drink of his coffee. "I guess because of how close this was, I decided to make doubly certain Buzz will be safe. He'll stay only one night in Aruba, then one of our agents is escorting him to Barbados on a private plane so there'll be no earthly way for Victor and Lissy to trace him. I may be going overboard on this, but I like the guy."

Maitland grinned. "Buzz said he was going to visit the horse-racing tracks in Barbados first thing—he was feeling real lucky."

Savich said, "Okay, so that means Victor and Lissy got to his neighborhood just a few hours after she escaped. They found Buzz still home, spiked his gas, and followed him to the car shop, then on to the airport. What undoubtedly saved him was that Lissy's injuries slowed them way down. Pretty smart, though, not taking Buzz on at home where he was armed. They knew he wouldn't be carrying a gun on his way to the airport."

Sherlock nodded. "I'm wondering, though, what would they have done even if they'd caught up with Buzz? Would they have shot him right there in the terminal?"

"I believe she'd sure give it a try," Savich said. "During the bank robbery, Lissy Smiley was out of control, whether from drugs or a misfiring brain, I don't know."

Sherlock said, "The word *nuts* comes to mind."

Maitland set down his coffee cup, picked up the plate with the small slice of apple pie in the center, the only slice left after Sean had demolished it. "But why sneak out to the tarmac? Were they thinking they could shoot him as he boarded? Blow out the landing gear? What?"

Savich said, "I can see Lissy pushing it to the end, without hesitation. Each moment for itself, no thought or reflection of what might happen, that's Lissy."

Sherlock said, "All spur-of-the-moment, just reaction when they saw Buzz hop into that taxi."

Maitland said, "So now they look like losers again. And that leaves you, Savich. I really don't want them to blow up your new Porsche."

Sherlock said, "Our insurance carrier would kick and moan, that's for sure."

Maitland saw she was both mad and worried, and that was good. She said, "I wonder why Lissy went after Buzz first when you were the one she threatened?"

Savich shrugged, sipped his tea. "I'm thinking I'm the frosting on her cake."

"She and Victor will figure out we live in Georgetown," Sherlock said. "After all, you were in one of the local banks."

"I expect they'll find out our address. Remember, they found out about Buzz's flight to the Caribbean, so one of them's pretty clever. We'll know which one soon enough. Sherlock and I are going down to Fort Pessel, see what we can find out.

"One other thing, sir, can you get round-the-clock surveillance on both the Smiley house in Fort Pessel, Virginia, and Victor Nesser's apartment in Winnett, North Carolina?"

Maitland got to his feet. "All right, for three, four days. You think we can get them in that time?"

"From your mouth to God's ear," Sherlock said.

Savich said, "I've got this gut feeling they'll go back to one or both places before they come after me, hunker down, and try to come up with a plan. Too, Lissy Smiley can't be feeling great. How she managed to run at all at the airport is astounding. She must be feeling the results of that now. She'll have to rest, maybe several days."

"I can't see them taking the chance of going home though," Maitland said.

"They're kids," Sherlock said, "and it's home. At least Lissy's a kid."

Savich said, "I have a feeling Lissy wants to take me down herself, and she's got to be one hundred percent to do that, and she knows it. She's got to lie low for a while."

Sherlock said, "I keep wondering why Victor left the Smileys three years ago. What do you think happened for him to make that abrupt break? And why did he get back together with them?"

Maitland said, "Sex, drugs, or rock and roll; gotta be one of those."

21

NEAR PAMPLIN, VIRGINIA
Sunday evening, dusk

"I feel like crap."

"I know, Lissy, I know," Victor Nesser said, and pulled over on the shoulder. "It's time. Here, take your pain pill." He unscrewed the water bottle and handed it to her. "Fifteen minutes and you'll be snoozing." He came around to the passenger side and tried to get the front seat of the old Chevy Impala to recline more, but it wouldn't. They should have lifted themselves a newer car where the seats went down flat like a bed. "But you're better today than you were yesterday. That run through the airport didn't help things."

"Yeah, yeah, I'll live." She smacked her fist against the warped glove compartment and cursed, sucked in a couple of deep breaths, and tried not to move.

He slid his palm over her breasts, patted her cheek. "Rest now." And he got them on their way again.

Lissy's eyes were closed, her hands were on her belly, lightly massaging her fresh scar because it hurt. Another ten minutes, she just had to hang on another—it had to be only nine minutes now—and that sweet numbing haze would float over her brain. She said, "We should have taken him out at the mechanic's place, a nice, big, stupid target—"

"Not possible. Remember? The taxi pulled right up. Instant witness."

"I could have popped him too."

"We didn't have any time. And there were probably more witnesses than we can count."

She said, "Who cares who saw us? They're never going to catch us, never."

He laughed. "No, I'm careful. I'm the brains, Lissy, since your ma died, remember? And you're an invalid with a big mouth. Be quiet and go to sleep. Let me do the worrying. Get yourself well; you're not fun like this."

She smacked her fist against her palm and winced. "I couldn't stand seeing that old dude wearing his ridiculous Bermuda shorts, whistling, happy as a clam on his way to the Caribbean. If we'd only caught him at the curb at the airport, I could have snuck right up behind him, popped him fast and clean."

No way would that have happened, Victor thought, *she was still too weak.* But they'd both been caught up in it, both so revved up that all they wanted to do was find that plane and—well, the guy had seen them, and wasn't that a kick in the butt? He'd looked more startled than scared, but Victor knew he wouldn't forget. It was a start. Let them think they'd won. It was just a matter of time. "We'll get him when he comes back from his hideaway. Do what I told you, Lissy, close your eyes and get some sleep."

She closed her eyes and said, "I want to fly down to the Caribbean and find him, shoot his ass down there. My mom knew people who could make really good fake papers, driver's license, passports, the works. We have the money at home to get the best."

"No," Victor said, shaking his head for emphasis. "That's way too risky. Stop thinking about it. We'll get the old man when he gets back, when you're well again."

She continued to rub her stomach, eyes still closed, but her voice was vicious. "He killed my mother, Victor. You didn't see it. The bastard shot her in the neck and all her blood just burst out of her." She smacked her fist on the glove compartment, moaned at the shock to her belly.

Victor leaned over, lightly slapped her face, then caressed her cheek. "Shut yourself down, you hear me? Take some slow, deep breaths."

She settled into the seat, breathed deeply like he said. She felt the throbbing pain ease back. She knew it was still there, but it felt duller now. "We've got to get some more pain meds though. I've only got one more."

"That's 'cause you took so many you nearly croaked yourself. Don't worry, we'll get you some more."

"It was sure nice of that nurse to leave her pill cart in the hall," she said. "Dammit,

Victor, we should have blown that old dude to hell and gone." She turned her face to look at him. "But you insisted you could make his car break down. Talk about crappy information, and look what happened. Big fat zero."

Victor shrugged, speeded up a bit. "It looked good on that website, but I'm no car expert."

"That's for sure."

He raised his hand, then lowered it. "Shut your trap. I'm the one who found his damned house. Don't you rag on me, Lissy, you know I don't like it. I remember my dad always telling my mother to stop her nagging. I don't remember that she did all that much, but he thought so."

"That's why you hit me sometimes, isn't it?"

He looked at her. "Don't you accuse me of being like my dad. He was dead-on mean. He'd clip me whenever it suited him. I told you how he smacked Mom more. I didn't like him much. When I hit you, you deserve it, that's all. When he and Mom went back to his beloved Jordan, I saw my chance to get away from him."

She said, her voice dreamy, since she

was beginning to fade out, "And you came to me, Victor. You thought I was a little girl, but I wasn't."

Victor remembered that long-ago night waking up with Lissy licking his belly. "Yeah, I came to you. Your mom is nothing like mine. Mine's all soft and boring. You mom, well, she'd shoot the nuts off a squirrel if she felt like it."

Lissy giggled. "She had to be tough, since it was just her. I thought Mama was going to shoot you when she found a pair of your shorts under my bed."

Victor remembered that day, remembered how he'd protected Lissy, taking all responsibility—after all, he was five years older, which made Lissy only a kid—but her mom knew her daughter, and that was why, he was convinced, she didn't shoot him and bury him in the deep woods behind the house. She just ordered him out, which was bad enough.

The three years he worked for that bush-league home-security company in Winnett had been boredom punctuated with bursts of huge happiness when Lissy e-mailed him. He said, his voice hoarse with the memory of her absence, "I didn't see you for too long, Lissy. I nearly went crazy without you. Then your mom called me up to ask me if I'd like to rob banks."

"Yeah, I talked her into it. I told her you could drive the car. She said that was fine since you were a pussy."

"I'm not a pussy, dammit!"

"All right, all right," she said, her voice soft, dreamy. "Do you remember how we'd get under a sheet and play, my flashlight on?"

The memory made him jerk the steering wheel. He thought about those horrible hours when he didn't know if she was alive, deadening hours when he'd lurked on the surgical floor, listening to the FBI agents speaking to the nurses and doctors about her. He went to the men's room and vomited when he heard she was going to be all right. He said, "No pussy could have gotten you out of that damned hospital. Don't you remember that big FBI agent sitting outside your door? Well, I fooled him good, didn't I?"

"You saved me," she said, her eyes closed, her hands over her belly, gently kneading. "I love you, Victor."

He felt a fist squeeze his heart. "Yeah,"

he said, "that's good, real good. Why don't we just leave now? Why do we have to hang around? I'm thinking I'd like to visit Hollywood, maybe see Angelina, learn how to surf, make love on the beach."

Her eyes popped open. "Victor, I've gotta kill that old man, blow his brains from here to Oregon. He murdered Mama. I can't let that go. And that FBI agent, Dillon Savich." She started rubbing her belly harder now, her hand jerking. "What he did to me, what he did, I can't let him get away with that, I can't."

"All right, we'll kill those two, then get out of here. Give your mouth a rest. I'll wake you up when we get to Fort Pessel. Go to sleep."

Four minutes later Victor heard a siren. He looked in the rearview mirror and saw a police car, lights flashing, closing fast. He felt a punch of panic, then rage. Why was this jerk on him? He hadn't done anything wrong. No way did they know this was a stolen car. Too soon for that.

He took a deep breath and slowly pulled the Impala over to the side of the road. It simply wasn't possible somebody had already discovered the old woman's body and reported her frigging car stolen. His hands felt cold and clammy. He hated it. He rubbed his hands on his jeans, breathed deeply, calmed his pulsing heart.

Sheriff's Deputy Davie Franks shined a flashlight into the young man's face as Victor lowered the window. "Nice wheels you got," he said. "I had me an old Impala like this when I was about your age. You got a driver's license to show me?"

"What's the problem, officer?"

"You've got a busted taillight."

That old bitch had a busted taillight and she didn't fix it? Stupid old cow. Victor swallowed his bile. "Thank you, Officer. I'll get it fixed in Fort Pessel."

Davie Franks shined his flashlight over on the girl, whose head was back against the lowered seat, her eyes closed. He said, "She sick?"

Victor said, "A case of the summer flu. She's been puking, but she'll be okay now."

"May I see your driver's license?"

Deputy Franks watched the young man hesitate, then reach for his wallet. He glanced again over at the young girl. Her eyes were open now and she was staring at him, her eyes sort of glazed. Was she really sick or high on drugs?

As he took the driver's license, he asked, "Where are you kids going?"

"I'm not a kid. I'm twenty-one," said Victor. "My cousin and I were visiting relatives in Richmond and we're going home now. Like I said, she's got a touch of the flu."

"Where's home?"

"Fort Pessel. Look, Officer, I'll get the taillight fixed as soon as I get home."

Davie shined his flashlight on the license, read the name, checked the photo, then said aloud, "Victor Alessio Nesser. You from the Middle East?"

Now the jerkface thinks I'm a terrorist? He said, all stiff, desperate to get this guy out of his face, "I am an American. It is my father who is from the Middle East—Jordan, to be exact."

"You don't look Jordanian—I guess your mom was the blond, passed it on to you. Good thing for you. Always lots of trouble over there—" Davie glanced once again at the girl, then back down at the driver's license photo; his eyes snapped alert with recognition and he jumped back, his hand going for his gun. "Get out of the car—"

But Davie didn't have time to get his gun clear of its holster or to finish his sentence. Lissy brought her hand up smooth and fast and shot him between the eyes. He was grabbing for the door, but he was dead before his fingers touched the handle.

"Hey, what's going on? Davie!"

"Well, look at this—another one," Lissy said.

Victor opened the driver's-side door, leaned down low, and waited for the female deputy to get close. She was talking into a cell phone, her voice urgent and her gun out. She saw his gun and yelled, "Stop!"

Victor shot her in the chest.

She dropped her gun and grabbed her chest, blood oozing out between her fingers, looked down at her partner staring back at her, a hole in his forehead, and said, "Why'd you shoot us?"

"You got in my face," Victor said, and watched her collapse to the ground, maybe two feet from her partner.

"Check her, Victor. Make sure she's dead."

Victor got out of the car, looked down into the glazed eyes of the young freckle-faced woman who lay at his feet, her chest covered with her blood, blood snaking out of her mouth. Her cell phone was on the ground beside her, and he heard a man's voice yelling, "What's happening? Talk to me, Gail!"

Victor kicked the cell phone across the road.

"Is she dead?"

Deputy Gail Lynd tried to look for her gun but couldn't move. She stared at the man—a boy, really—who'd shot her. She watched him turn and yell to someone in the car, "Shut your yap, Lissy. She's not quite dead yet, but she will be soon."

He looked back down at her, met her eyes, dumb with pain. She saw the buzz of excitement in him and doubted there was mercy there.

Lissy called out, "Pay attention, Victor. My mama said you gotta shoot 'em be-tween the eyes, put their lights out right away. That way there's no one hanging around, surviving, telling stories about you before they take their boat ride to hell. So stop your hee-hawing and put out her damned lights!"

"Yeah, yeah, all right." Victor leaned down close and winked at the deputy as she whispered, "No, please, don't kill—"

He fired. A chunk of concrete flew into the air not six inches from her face. She stared up at him.

He winked at her again.

Gail heard a mad cheer come from the car, then a yell: "Put a notch in that boy's belt!"

22

Victor pulled the Impala into the Amesey gas station on High Street, just inside the Fort Pessel city limits, one he'd never used before because his aunt Jennifer hated Loony Old Amesey, as she called him. *Some city,* he thought, nothing but a dippy loser town that had nothing going for it except a long-ago dumb little Civil War battle that had passed over the grounds of city hall, an ugly gray stone heap built back in the thirties. He'd hated the place for the year and a half he'd had to plunk his butt down with his crazy Aunt Jennifer. He hated breathing the air that always smelled like old cigarette smoke. But it was better than traveling to Jordan with his parents, meeting his father's family, who were probably just as crazy-mean as he was, maybe getting shot for just existing. You couldn't even drink or smoke pot there, and they'd chop your hands or your nose off for selling drugs, or even your head.

There was an old geezer chewing on a stick of straw, sitting on a tilted-back chair against the side of the grungy little market, which was flashing a green neon sign that had only the letter R left glowing. It was Loony Old Amesey.

"Hey," Victor called as he got out of the car. "I need a new taillight. Can you help me?"

"Nope," the old coot called back, not even bothering to move. "We're closed. Come back tomorrow. That's Monday, ain't it? Monday's always a busy day, but my boys could maybe find time for you."

Victor cursed, got back into the car, slammed his fist on the steering wheel. Lissy said, "I'm thinking maybe that female cop could have written down our license plate. I mean, she was sitting in the cop car with nothing else to do, right? And you said she was talking on her cell—no telling how close the cops are to us, Victor."

He took a deep breath, nodded. He hated it when she told him what to do. It made him feel small and helpless. He looked over to see her eyes unfocused and knew she was in pain again. He hated that a lot more. He only nodded to her.

Thirty minutes later they were driving a little blue Corolla, the old Impala now tucked away behind a bowling alley next to an overflowing Dumpster that stank in the hot night air.

It was dark already; the few businesses in downtown Fort Pessel that opened on Sunday were shut down tight now. Victor pulled into the alley behind Kougar's Pharmacy on Elm Street. He took her bottle of pills and quietly got out of the Corolla. "You stay still," he whispered to Lissy. "Don't come in after me, you hear me?"

He jimmied the back door, eased it open. The alarm didn't go off, just as Victor knew it wouldn't. Old Mrs. Kougar hadn't ever had the alarm fixed after it burned out in the big storm of 2006, and everybody knew it.

Victor held his .22 in one hand, the

bottle of pills in the other. All he had was a big flashlight, and he hated to use it, too much of a risk. He went behind the pharmacy counter, switched the flashlight on just long enough to find the narcotic pain meds, then off again. Thank God everything was labeled or he'd never find the right pills for her. He didn't spot the same pills that were in Lissy's bottle, but he did find Vicodin, and that was just fine. He filled up her bottle, and his pockets, put the nearly empty pharmacy bottle carefully back on the shelf. No one would know until morning that anyone had been here.

His heart nearly stopped when a light flashed toward him and a croaky old woman's voice yelled, "Hey! Who are you? What do you want?"

Victor shot toward her voice without aiming. He heard her yell and run into something, heard boxes go flying. He fired again. It was either turn on the lights and nail the old biddy or get out of there. Somebody would have heard the shots, called 911. Old Lady Kougar would call the cops for sure, but she hadn't seen him, at least he didn't think she had. He was too afraid to think, so afraid he wanted to puke. He ran flat-out through the back door. He jumped into the car, cranked it hard, and rolled out of the alley.

Sweating, breathing hard, he threw the bottle of pills to Lissy, forced himself to take some deep breaths, and slowed down. He drove them out of town, telling her what happened in fits and starts until he calmed down again.

"You didn't kill her?"

The disappointment in her voice steadied him. He even grinned a bit. "I don't think so. It was dark as a pit in there. I didn't hear her hit the floor or anything like a moan."

"I never liked Old Lady Kougar. Always sticking her snout in everybody's business." She sat back, closed her eyes again, and said, "I'll never forget the look she gave me when I bought condoms. Well, at least you shot at her. The bitch deserved it."

Fifteen minutes later, the rush of adrenaline had eased off, and his blood slowed. Victor had already looped back toward town, and soon turned, slowly and carefully, onto Denver Lane. The Smiley house was on the end of the cul-de-sac, surrounded on three sides by thick oaks and maple woods that stretched behind the house a good quarter mile before a two-lane hardtop cut through them. They passed the closest neighbor a hundred feet down the street, Ms. Ellie at number 452. Not a single light was on in her house, since she always went to bed at seven-thirty. She'd cackle that she needed her beauty sleep, say that every single time she saw him. He and Lissy would slow down and stare at her shaky old hands when she waved to them, laughing about how they should send her to her reward. Lissy was serious, thought it would be fun to dump the old cow in the freezer in the garage, just another steak.

Suddenly, Lissy grabbed Victor's hand. "Stop!"

He braked smoothly and pulled over to the side of the street. "Why? What's wrong? The Vicodin hasn't kicked in? You still feel bad?"

"No, no. You said the cops might be watching our house, waiting for us to come home. You're too close."

He wanted to tell her not to be stupid, he knew exactly what he was doing. He wished she'd learn to trust him. He shrugged. "Look, we talked about this, Lissy. You said they'd never find the bank money Aunt Jennifer stashed in the house, and you know where it is, right? I wasn't just going to drive up. I was going to go around the back."

Lissy felt mildly nauseated from the Mc-Donald's hamburger and fries she'd eaten an hour before. She shouldn't have eaten them, but they tasted wonderful. But the spike of energy was long gone. She felt weak and shaky. And that made her angry again, angry at that big FBI guy who'd kicked her and that ridiculous old security guard who was probably sipping a rum punch somewhere in the Caribbean by now. She wanted to sleep, but first things first, that's what her mother always said, her mother who'd bled to death on the beautiful marble bank floor, hundred-dollar bills fluttering down beside her.

She got a look at Victor in the interior car light. He looked tired too, burned out to his toes, on edge. Well, after they got the money, they'd rest, take it easy for a couple of days, and she'd get well.

Victor pulled the Corolla off the road behind the house and into the trees. He helped Lissy through the woods to the far side of the house. It was nice and dark, clouds covering most of the stars, no moon to speak of, and it was still really warm. They slipped quietly from behind one oak tree to the next, studied the few cars parked on Denver Lane. Most looked familiar, and those that weren't were empty—no federal agents with infrared glasses looking out, no movement of any kind.

"What do you think?" Victor whispered against her temple.

"Mama always said the cops were stupid, didn't know their butts from their earlobes."

"Yeah, but she's dead, now, isn't she, so maybe she wasn't right all the time."

"Mama was never wrong. Those guys just got lucky," Lissy said. "I don't see anything, do you?"

"No, nothing."

"Maybe they've already been here, searched for the money, and left. You think it's okay?"

He started to say yes when Lissy saw a tiny arc of light come from her bedroom, then disappear. She grabbed his arm to pull him back and it hurt so bad she sank down against a tree. She was gasping a little. "You see that? Someone's in my bedroom with one of those little flashlights." She cursed. "I knew they wouldn't just leave, I knew it. Victor, let's sit down and let me rest a minute."

Victor saw she was in pain and said, "All right, Lissy, rest. When you're ready, we'll get out of here. We can hide someplace close by and come back for the money in a couple of days."

Lissy jerked awake when a blade of sun slashed through the oak branches and splashed across her face. She blinked, tried to remember where she was.

"Good morning," said Special Agent Cawley James, standing above her, his gun aimed at her heart. He was wearing black slacks, a white shirt, and loafers, as if he'd just been to church. Lissy jerked up her gun, but he kicked it out of her hand. "No, you're not going to shoot me, little girl." He took a step back and said, "Hey, Victor, time to rise and shine and let me escort you to jail." Then he spoke into his radio. "Hey, Ben, Tommy, I've got them, a hundred yards southwest of the house. Get over here!"

Victor moaned where he lay and twitched. But didn't move. He turned his body slightly away.

"Come on, let's go," Cawley said, and nudged him with his toe. He raised his head, shouted, "Tommy, Ben, get yourselves over here."

Victor moaned again, turned fast, brought up his .22, and shot Cawley in his right arm. Cawley's gun went flying. He yelled out and kicked at Victor, but Victor was already rolling, twisting around to shoot again. "Stay out of the way, Lissy! Do you see his gun?"

Cawley ducked behind a tree and kept yelling for Tommy and Ben.

"Victor, we've got to get out of here!" Lissy was scrambling around, looking at the ground. "He kicked my gun away, I can't find it. I don't see his either, it's still too dark. We've got to go."

Victor cursed, fired the rest of his clip toward where the cop was hiding, then jerked Lissy into the woods. They ran, branches cutting their arms and faces, not stopping until they drew up, panting, to jump into the Corolla he'd left sheltered beneath the full-leafed branches of an oak tree just off the two-lane road.

They heard male voices yelling, heard them crashing through the trees. The Corolla screeched off in two seconds, Lissy leaning out the open window, dry-heaving, Victor's empty .22 loose in her hand.

Victor looked in the rearview mirror, saw the men burst out of the trees, guns in their hands, one of them on a cell phone. They were a long way from their cars.

But they didn't have much time. Lissy spotted an old black Trailblazer in the driveway of a house at the end of Miller Avenue, eight twisting blocks from Denver Lane. It took Victor three seconds to hot-wire it. Lissy stayed in the Corolla, Victor on her bumper in the Trailblazer, to the woods outside of Fort Pessel, then he drove it into the trees.

"We're going to Winnett," Victor said. "Maybe they don't know about me yet, and I know that place, know where we can hang low. If they do know about me, it won't matter. We'll trade out this piece of junk in another fifty miles. We'll stay there until it's safe to come back here and get the money."

"Okay, let's do it," Lissy said, her face tight with pain. He handed her a couple of pain pills, watched her pop them right down with half a bottle of water.

"I just wish we could have taken a couple of those jerks down."

Victor said, "Who knows? Maybe you'll have your chance. I'm going to see to it things turn out different in Winnett. You rest, Lissy; that was a crazy run through the woods. Hey, we're okay, and that's all that matters."

23

RANDALL COUNTY HOSPITAL
FORT PESSEL, VIRGINIA
Monday morning

Special Agent Cawley James's arm hurt bad. On the bright side, the bullet hadn't hit an artery and he hadn't bled to death. He stared at the morphine drip machine they'd hooked up just a minute ago, willing it to kick in. His arm was cleaned, stitched, and bandaged, and the anesthetic had worn off. Now his arm was screaming at him.

"It's only been one single lonely minute since the nurse started the drip," said Galen Markey, SAC of the Richmond field office. "She said it was faster than a shot. Stop whining, you're going to live. You should be thankful, the doc said you won't end up with any movement or rotation problems. No thanks to your pitiful brain."

"Yeah, yeah, kick me while I'm down," Cawley said between gritted teeth. "Listen, Galen, I've a bottle of twelve-year-old scotch for you if nobody calls my mom. She'll fly here on her private jet, her doctor in tow, and demand you let her take me to her villa in Cancún. I can see you're pissed, ready to tell me I'm a screwup. All right, so I should have waited for Ben and Tommy, but I stumbled over them, and she was just a teenager, after all." He sighed. "Then she woke up and tried to shoot me. What was I supposed to do? I told you, she wasn't the problem. I mean, she could have been if she'd been faster."

"If she'd been faster, you'd be stone-cold dead."

"Maybe. Look on the bright side. It was that damned guy, he faked me out. I'll admit it. Why didn't I just shoot him? But I thought the scrawny little dude was asleep. He was fast, Galen. Holy mother, my arm feels like it's burning off."

The ER nurse called out in a chipper voice as she hurried by his cubicle, "Another minute, tops. Suck it up, Agent."

Sure enough, only a few more seconds passed before he felt the monster fangs pulling out of his arm.

Galen said, "I should cut off the morphine, you being such a Señor Nacho hot dog. Either or both of those lunatic kids could have killed you, Cawley. What didn't you understand about 'armed and dangerous'? And don't forget crazy."

Cawley said, "Don't you mean Señor *Macho* hot dog?"

Galen stared him down.

"Okay, yeah, so you're right, pull the morphine. I should suffer. Too late. Ah, I'm basking right now in the total absence of pain."

Galen said, "I doubt it'll blunt the pain you're going to feel when our brothers from Washington show up. Ah, speaking of brothers, here he is right now. And we've got one sister."

Galen stood up as Savich and Sherlock came into the room. "You might have lucked out, Cawley," he said over his shoulder. "Look who it is."

Cawley brightened when he saw Sherlock. He didn't know the woman, had never seen her before, but she was something.

His brain swam happily in the morphine, and he hummed looking at her.

Savich said, "No, he hasn't lucked out. Hello, Galen." He turned to Cawley. "Are you the brain-dead yahoo who let them get away?"

Cawley moaned.

Galen said, "Yep, in all his wounded glory."

Sherlock only nodded to Galen Markey, walked up to Cawley, and got right in his face. "You jackass! I'm the one you should be afraid of, the one who's going to kick your butt into your backbone when you're back on your feet, not Dillon. Do you hear me? I am royally pissed. You could be stretched out on the autopsy table, like that"—she snapped her fingers—"with all of us standing over you, shaking our heads. How could you let this happen? Uncontrolled testosterone? Because you didn't wait for backup, those two young psychopaths are in the wind again and you've got a bum arm." And she jabbed him hard in his good arm.

Her punch didn't hurt him because morphine was still the main ingredient in his bloodstream. He looked up at her, gave her a dopey grin. "I don't know who you are, but I love your hair and all those soft, wild curls around your face. Would you go to dinner with me when I'm able to cut my meat again?"

"Go out with a birdbrain like you?" She nodded toward Savich. "Don't you know who he is?"

"Well, yeah, that's Agent Dillon Savich. I aced one of his computer refresher courses at Quantico last year. He likes me, he thinks I'm smart."

Savich said, "I have revised my opinion of you, Agent James. I'm beginning to see you in a new light, one that doesn't have that many watts."

Sherlock said, "No, I won't go out to dinner with you. I happen to be married to that guy, who, at this moment, would probably enjoy throwing you out the window. What floor are we on?"

Cawley said, "The ground floor."

Sherlock knuckle-tapped him on the head. "Your lucky day, bozo. You will now begin at the beginning and tell us everything. Please, feel free not to spare yourself. Trust me, self-mortification is the way to go here."

Cawley cleared his throat, one eye on Savich. It was difficult for him to reconcile that he was in deep trouble, since he felt so very nice. He cleared his throat again. "The sun was just coming up. Tommy was checking the other side of the house, Ben was inside making coffee, and I was making rounds through the woods and all around the cul-de-sac.

"I couldn't believe it when I practically walked over the two of them leaning against a big oak tree, snoozing away. They looked so innocent, so young—well, until she opened her eyes and my nerve endings started screaming. She brought up a gun real fast, a big old whopper Bren Ten, probably a ten-millimeter auto. I kicked the gun out of her hand."

Sherlock said to him, "Good thing you did. If she'd shot you in the arm with that sucker, you'd probably have bled to death, or at least lost your arm and have to learn to tie your shoes with your teeth. Lucky for you Victor shot you with a twenty-two."

Galen said, "I wonder where Lissy Smiley got hold of a Bren Ten?"

Sherlock said, "Maybe a granddad in

World War Two? You may continue now, Cawley."

Cawley shuddered. "The other one, the young blond guy—Victor Nesser—he didn't move, like he was asleep. I wasn't about to shoot him in mid-snore but then the little creep came up with that gun so fast I—"

"Mortification of the self, Agent James," Sherlock repeated. "It's best in this situation, trust me."

When he finished, Savich had to admit he hadn't spared himself—very difficult, since all of them knew he felt very fine, what with the morphine on board. When he finished, Savich said, "Okay, they dumped the Corolla and stole an ancient black Trailblazer. I'm betting they dumped it once they got maybe fifty miles from Fort Pessel."

Galen said, "I've got state and local law enforcement out looking for them. They didn't get much of a head start, but if Savich is right and the Trailblazer's hidden somewhere and they're driving something else now, it won't be easy to spot them until we get a stolen-car call."

Savich asked, "What were they wearing, Agent James?"

"The girl was wearing a loose white man's shirt, skinny-legged blue jeans, and black sneakers. The boy, he was in a pale blue T-shirt with a John Deere tractor on the front, baggy blue jeans, and white sneakers. He had a nondescript ball cap pulled low, no writing on it."

"Can you describe him?"

"He looked real young, and he was very fair-haired, light-complexioned, not even any a.m. whiskers on his face. Both of them were slim. *Lithe* is a better word for her, *scrawny* for him. He looked pretty tall, but she looked like a child." He paused. "Until she opened her eyes and looked at me. There's something really wrong going on behind her eyes."

Sherlock said, "Did you get any impression she was hurting?"

Cawley shook his head. "I saw Nesser jerk her up and pull her after him into the woods. Then I was putting pressure on my arm and trying to get to my SIG, hoping I wasn't going to die. Ben and Tommy came up and we took off after them."

A few minutes later, just as Cawley James was about to fall into a morphine stupor, Savich gave him his cell phone number.

"Call if you think of anything else." He paused in the doorway, turned. "You didn't deserve to be shot, Cawley; you did okay in that impossible situation." He shook Galen Markey's hand. "If you really want to punish him, call his mother."

Cawley moaned.

Sherlock laughed.

Galen Markey caught up with them just as they were leaving the hospital. "Hold up a second. We've got a report of two sheriff's deputies shot last night near Pamplin, about sixty miles up the road from Fort Pessel. One of them is dead. The other deputy was sending in the license number while her partner made contact. When he was shot, she went to help and was shot herself, in the chest. They've taken her to surgery twice; don't know if she'll make it."

24

Savich got a call from Galen as he stepped into Carly Schuster's house, telling him a hiker had found the Trailblazer in the woods just over the North Carolina border, and a dark blue 2001 Chevy Malibu was reported stolen from a small tobacco farm a half-mile away.

He pocketed his cell, turned, and smiled at her as Sherlock said, "We appreciate your taking the time to speak with us, Mrs. Schuster. The principal told us you have no official affiliation with the high school, but you've tutored a number of students in computer science through the years, one of them Victor Nesser. Could you please tell us about him?"

She waved them both to the sofa as she said, "Goodness, yes, I taught Victor everything I knew. He was self-taught to that point and really quite talented. I'll tell you, he was beyond me in a few months. He's a natural, the first one I've seen. He didn't do that well in his school courses, a teacher friend of mine told me, and he never took any computer classes. He didn't tell me why. But he was hungry for learning it, you know?"

Savich smiled. "Yes, I know what you mean."

"Ah, do I have a kindred spirit in my living room?"

Savich only smiled. "Can you tell us what you remember about the Smileys?"

Her lips unseamed and her very white buck teeth appeared again. Carly Schuster nodded. "Ah, yes, the Smileys. I didn't know Jennifer Smiley very well, saw her in town from time to time, nodded to her, you know, said hi and how are you, but nothing more than that. I'll tell you though, the word is Mrs. Smiley's a piece of work. She managed the Lone Star Bar out on Route

Thirty-three, just south of town. Lots of stories about how the place got drunk and rowdy on the weekends, and she with it. She lived off and on with the owner, a biker with tattoos. I wondered how she could let Lissy live in the same house with that man. Then he was killed driving that motorcycle of his, ran headlong into a bridge abutment.

"Everyone thought Jennifer Smiley would inherit the place, but he left it in his will to a cousin from up north somewhere. She was very angry about it, I heard. Then one day, maybe three months ago, she and Lissy were simply gone. Yes, it was right after school was over, I remember, though I don't see how it mattered, since Lissy hardly went. Then *poof*—they were gone, their house locked up. Their neighbor, Ms. Ellie, thought they'd gone on a long vacation. It had been just the two of them, you know, since Victor left right after he graduated high school three years ago."

Suddenly her lips seamed shut over her buck teeth and she was shaking her head. "Oh, goodness, since you're FBI agents, that must mean Victor has done something illegal. And the Smileys? Will you tell me?"

Savich said, "We're looking for both Lissy Smiley and Victor Nesser. They're wanted in connection to a series of bank robberies."

Sherlock said, "Did you hear about the bank robberies in Kentucky and Virginia by a group called the Gang of Four? Most of them were killed up in Washington, D.C."

Carly Schuster shook her head. "Sorry, I refuse to watch the news, it's too depressing."

Savich wanted to see those buck teeth again; they made her smile quite charming.

Carly said slowly, "So you're saying Jennifer Smiley was also involved in this Gang of Four?"

Sherlock nodded. "From what we know now, she was the leader."

"Oh, dear. And Lissy? And Victor?"

Savich said, "Yes. Two other men as well. Jennifer Smiley was shot dead in the middle of a bank robbery in Washington. Lissy and Victor escaped. We're trying to locate them."

"But this is a small town, nothing bad ever happens here; well, not like this. I haven't heard anybody say anything. My husband won't believe it. He liked Victor, said he was okay for a scruffy geek. I liked him too."

She pursed her lips, did some thinking, and said, "I just can't get over Victor. Lissy, now she's a different story. I hate to say this about a sixteen-year-old girl, but I'm not at all surprised she's involved. Lissy is . . . Well, I'm not sure quite how to say this . . . but she's off, but it's more than that. She's strange in the head, and the way she some-times looks at people, it's frightening. The thing I finally realized was that she's a cha-meleon, no other way to say it. She can charm you if she wants or look like she's bored to tears."

"How do you know all this about her, Ms. Schuster?" Sherlock asked.

"She dated my son for four months," Carly said simply. "I saw her up close and personal. Of course Jason talked about her. I know she was having sex with him, and I'll tell you, that scared me."

Savich and Sherlock waited.

Carly drew in a deep breath. "He broke up with her last spring. Though he wouldn't admit it, I think he was a little frightened of her. After the breakup, she threatened to kill him. That might sound like a melodramatic teenager, but I was afraid for him. She accused him of sleeping with another girl, though he hadn't. A few days later, the girl, Lindy, was struck by a car while she was riding her bicycle, broke her leg. We never found out who hit her. Lissy didn't ever hurt Jason, but someone slashed the tires on his old Honda."

"Is Jason around, Carly?" Sherlock asked.

"No, I'm sorry. He's in Spain with his father, my ex. He won't be back until September. You know, I think Jason breathed a big sigh of relief when Lissy and her mother left town."

25

They'd just climbed into the Porsche when Céline Dion's beautiful voice sang out the theme from *Titanic* on Savich's cell phone.

"Savich." He listened, then said, "I'm betting on a twenty-two and a Bren Ten, ten-millimeter auto ammo. Yeah, verify when you know." He slipped his cell back into the pocket of his leather jacket. He met Sherlock's eyes.

"You wanna know something fantastic? The deputy is alive, out of surgery, and we can head up to Overlook Hospital in Pamplin, try to speak to her. The hospital is filled with her family and cops. The sheriff said we're to go directly to the ICU on the third floor. He'll meet us there."

"It had to be Victor and Lissy, on their way down here. I wonder why she's alive?"

"I don't know, but I'm sure hoping she can tell us."

Sherlock said, "The license number was off an old Impala, right?"

He nodded again.

Sherlock closed her eyes, remembering clearly getting shot herself, wondering if she would die. "What's the deputy's name?"

"Gail Lynd. She's been in law enforcement for six years. She's married, two small kids. As for the deputy they killed, he also had a family."

"We've got to get them fast, Dillon, before they kill anyone else."

"My gut keeps telling me Victor will head for home, for Winnett, North Carolina, though I know that doesn't make sense. We were right about Fort Pessel, but they're not stupid. Everyone and his mother are looking for them. But they've got to go under for a while before they try for me.

Maybe Victor knows a place to hide in or near Winnett. I want to get home, though, after we speak to Gail at the hospital."

When Savich pulled into the parking lot in front of the hospital, Galen called again, told him about the break-in at Kougar's Pharmacy in Fort Pessel, and the couple dozen stolen Vicodin. "Maybe that's why she fell asleep."

Sherlock and Savich walked the long third-floor corridor. The walls were a light green, meant to be restful, she supposed, but it didn't work for her. She felt itchy, jumpy. They passed some uniformed officers and what must have been family in the waiting room but didn't slow or look in.

The sheriff wasn't waiting for them.

Nurse Dolores Stark eyed them and their creds over her bifocals. "The sheriff had to leave on an emergency."

Sherlock said, "Talk to us about Deputy Lynd."

Dolores, an ICU nurse for twenty-three years, tough as her mother-in-law, said with a big smile, "She got through surgery, both of them. Dr. Lazarus worked on her for four hours, and then had to go back in for bleeding. They lost her twice but got

her back. She's going to make it, barring
anything else coming down the road we're
not expecting. I'm not sure she can speak
right now, they just extubated her a couple
of hours ago. Ah, Dr. Lazarus, these are
Special Agents Savich and Sherlock, here
to see Deputy Lynd."

Dr. Lazarus didn't look happy. But neither did he look like he'd spent the night inside someone's chest. He wasn't rumpled,
didn't have any bags beneath his eyes, like
he wanted to fall over and sleep for a year.
Instead, he looked like he'd just waltzed in
from the golf course but had shot too many
bogies. "You can't," he said. "She's not up
for it yet. Maybe tomorrow. Call me."

Sherlock gave him a lovely smile, walked
up into his face. "Would you like to accompany us, Dr. Lazarus? We're hopeful she's
with it enough to give us information about
who shot her. What room, Nurse Stark?"

"Room Three forty-three," said Dolores.

Savich and Sherlock walked quickly
down the hall, Dr. Lazarus on their heels.
"Wait! You can't do this. I can't allow—"

Savich waved Sherlock on and turned to
say easily, "You can monitor, Dr. Lazarus,
all right?"

When they walked in, it was to see Sherlock bent over Gail Lynd, her fingertips lightly stroking her forearm. "Gail, can you hear me?"

No response.

"You see, she's not—"

"Gail? Can you hear me? I'm Special Agent Sherlock, FBI, and I really want to find the yahoo who shot you and throw him in the Mariana Trench. That deep enough for you?"

Gail Lynd moaned.

"That's it," Sherlock said, and continued to lightly rub her fingertips over Gail's forearm. "You don't have to open your eyes, but I would like to see you, if you can manage it, and you to see me."

Deputy Gail Lynd managed to open her eyes. She looked up into blue eyes the color of the August sky. "The Mariana Trench should be fine," she whispered.

"It's good to meet you, Deputy Lynd. We both have blue eyes. Call me Sherlock. Do you think you can tell me what happened last night?"

"Last night? It was just a moment ago, no, it was—" Gail felt something wonderfully cold and wet rubbing lightly against her mouth, and she licked it. Sherlock turned to Dr. Lazarus, who looked like he wanted to leap on her to protect his patient. That made her smile a bit. "Water?" she asked him. "A little bit?"

At his unsmiling nod, Sherlock held Deputy Lynd's head up a bit and put a straw between her lips. "Just a little bit, we don't want you to get sick to your stomach."

"Thanks," said Gail Lynd, her voice a croak. She blinked, surprised she could actually speak.

"Are you in pain?"

Gail thought about that a moment, then shook her head. "No, fact is, I feel dead from the neck down."

"Probably a good thing," Sherlock said. "Now, Gail, I don't want you to overdo. If you get tired or there's pain, tell me and we'll stop."

She started slowly, but ended in a rush. ". . . and I heard the shot, saw Davie go down, and I went running toward the Impala, yelling at Davie, and then this young guy leans out of the driver's side and he shoots me." She looked at Sherlock, her eyes pooling with tears. "No one ever shot me before. I know what it's supposed to be like, you know, we discuss it, but it wasn't like I thought—it slammed into me like a sledgehammer, knocked me backward. I saw him coming down over me. I heard the girl yelling at him to shoot me between the eyes because if I didn't die right away, I could live long enough to tell someone. Her mother told her that." She broke off, held very still for a couple of moments, raised her eyes to Sherlock's face. "Her mother," she whispered. "This is what her mother told her to do."

"Thankfully for the world, her mother is dead," Sherlock said matter-of-factly. "Did she say anything that might help us find them?"

"She was crazy, Agent Sherlock. I don't know about him, but that girl was crazy. I couldn't do anything except lie there, helpless. It was . . . horrible. To wait, knowing you're going to die. Just waiting, and you hurt so bad you can't really accept it, not really, and you wait."

Sherlock gently wiped the tears that were seeping out of the corners of Deputy Lynd's eyes. "You want to rest now?"

"No, no, let me finish it. I want you to catch these two. The thing is, when the young guy—she called him Victor—when he came back down over me, I knew he was going to shoot me right between the eyes, I knew it, and I was helpless. Helpless."

No one said a word. Dr. Lazarus stared at the young woman whose life he'd managed to save. Sure, he'd been inside her chest, taking out the bullet and repairing her lung, he'd watched her heart stop twice, but now he was inside her head, living her memories with her of being shot with that bullet, of what it was like to almost die, and know it. He didn't think he'd ever forget this moment as long as he lived. He took a step back from the big FBI guy in front of him. He rubbed his hand over his chest. It hurt to listen to her, hurt—

"It was so weird; he winked at me, twice, and he fired, only the bullet hit the pavement maybe six inches from my head. I heard her yell, 'Notch that boy's belt!'— something like that. I heard Randall—he's the dispatcher—yelling on my cell, and I knew in that moment that maybe I had a chance." She raised her eyes to Dr. Lazarus. "You saved my life?"

He nodded, wordless.

"Thank you, Doctor. Agent Sherlock, will you please get these two killer kids?"

"Yes, we'll get them."

"The girl, Lissy, she shot Davie?"

Sherlock nodded.

"She would have shot me between the eyes too."

Again, Sherlock nodded.

"I wonder why he didn't?"

Because Victor knew Lissy couldn't see what he was doing. Sherlock closed her hand around Gail's, squeezed just a bit. "That is an excellent question. Maybe there's something in him that can still be redeemed."

Sherlock leaned close. "I know it was horrible. You will always remember this as being horrible, but you know what? The shock of it, the pain, the hopelessness of what you felt, it will fade when you begin to laugh again, when you smile at yourself in the mirror, when you hug your kids. I was shot not long ago, and you know what? It is beginning to fade.

Never forget, Gail, you survived. I'll be checking on you. You get well, no setbacks, okay?"

Gail Lynd managed a smile as she closed her eyes.

26

TITUSVILLE, VIRGINIA
Monday morning

Ethan walked into his kitchen to see Autumn throwing kibble to Lula, Mackie, and Big Louie. She was laughing. When she saw him, she gave him a huge smile. "Ethan, when Big Louie slides, you can hear his fingernails scraping the floor."

He leaned down and hugged the little girl. She was wearing a pink T-shirt with tulips on it. "You sleep okay, kiddo?"

She hugged him back before she nodded. "Mama didn't. She had a nightmare and started moaning. I had to wake her up."

"No wonder. So much has happened.

I'm glad you didn't have a nightmare too. Would you like a bowl of Rice Krispies and some toast?"

She nodded and threw another piece of kibble to Lula, who went flying out of the kitchen after it.

"It was the last one," she said, and rubbed her hands on her white shorts. "I hope you catch Blessed today, Ethan."

From the mouths of children. "I do too. Everyone's trying, Autumn. Sit down now." He poured cereal in a bowl and handed her the milk. As she poured it, she said, "I'm going to try to call Dillon again tonight."

She took a big bite and chewed while he pushed the bread down in the toaster, then stared at her. "Dillon? Who's he?"

She grew very still. She looked scared.

He came over to her, knelt down beside her chair. "What's wrong, sweetheart?"

"I'm not supposed to say anything."

"Anything about what? About Dillon?"

"Even my mama doesn't know about me calling Dillon. I didn't want to tell her. I knew it would upset her, and she's so scared right now, so worried about me. But I know she was going to tell Uncle Tollie."

Tell him what?

The toast popped up. He frowned as he buttered and added strawberry jam to each slice, one for him and one for Autumn. "Here you go. My mom made this jam; it's pretty good."

She gave him a guilty look and ducked her head. She didn't eat, only sat there. Big Louie trotted over and laid his head on her leg. She began petting him.

Ethan waited.

He said, "Did you use your mom's cell phone to call Dillon?"

Autumn cocked her head to one side. "No, I don't know his number."

What was going on here? "Then how did you call Dillon?" She kept her head down, petting Big Louie faster.

"Autumn, sweetheart, you've got to know you can tell me anything. If you've got something to say that will help me help you, you should tell me."

She looked up at him then, and sighed. "Uncle Tollie would help us, but he's not here. You're here, Ethan."

Ethan nodded and waited.

She looked him straight in the eye and said, "I called Dillon last Thursday night, real late. I think he was asleep. I haven't been able to speak to him since then. He hasn't been there."

"How did you do that?"

She closed her eyes a moment, then whispered, "Mama will be mad at me."

He waited, impatient now, wondering what she was doing.

"I called him because I saw him on TV, standing in front of a bank. He stopped a bunch of bank robbers. He was a hero. I knew he could help us, so I waited until it was real late and then I thought hard about him, made him clear in my mind, and he was there and he could hear me and see me too, just like Daddy when he was in prison. He wasn't scared or anything. I told him Mama and I were in big trouble. I'm going to try to call him again tonight, when it's real late again."

What was he to say to that? *Some imagination you've got there, kiddo, but could you eat your cereal and throw kibble to the varmints and get back to the real world?*

He said instead, "What did Dillon say to you when you told him you and your mama were in trouble?"

"Well, I had some problems because I hadn't spoken to anyone like that since

Daddy died. He knows my name but not my last name, and he doesn't know where we are. I've got to call him and tell him so he can come and help you find Blessed."

Joanna walked into the kitchen, carrying Lula in her arms. The small smile fell off her face when she looked at her daughter. She grew very still. Lula meowed, and Joanna set her on the floor. "What, Autumn? What did you say to Ethan?"

Autumn didn't say a word. She took a big bite of her toast and kept her head down.

Ethan said, "She told me she spoke to someone called Dillon last Thursday night, like she used to speak to her daddy, and she's going to try to call Dillon again tonight to come help us. Has she told you stories like this before, Joanna?"

Autumn whispered, "Dillon's a hero. Remember, Mama? He shot those bank robbers in Washington. I called him, just like I called Daddy, and he talked to me."

"Oh, Autumn, baby, you didn't. I told you—" She broke off and gave a sideways look at Ethan. "Well, never mind, we can talk about this later, Sheriff. I'm hungry. How about I make some pancakes?"

"No," Ethan said, walking to her. "I don't

want pancakes. I want to know what's going on with Autumn. Did you believe her story about speaking to her father in her head when he was in prison hundreds of miles away, and speaking to this Dillon last Thursday night? Is that why you doubted her story about the cemetery, because she's told you stories like this before?"

Joanna wrapped her arms around herself and began pacing the small kitchen.

"Joanna?"

Autumn said, "Mama, I told Ethan we were going to tell Uncle Tollie, and he's not here. We need to tell Ethan, explain it to him."

Ethan said, a hint of sarcasm breaking through, "I'd sure appreciate anything you deign to tell me about all this, Joanna."

That got her. She drew up and stared him straight in the eye. "Very well, Sheriff, I will. Autumn has a special gift, one I didn't believe at first either until I met the Backmans in Bricker's Bowl and saw what Blessed could do. She inherited it from her father, and I think that's why they want to get her back, because she has the same gift her father had."

"You mean that Autumn has the ability to do the things Blessed can do?"

"No, she can't hypnotize people. But I believe Autumn can speak telepathically to some people. Not all that many people, but naturally with her father, and it seems this Dillon as well. Autumn, you really called this man who killed the bank robbers?"

Autumn nodded and took a small bite of her toast.

Joanna said, "He was crazy, what he did. What if there had been children in that bank?"

"He's a hero," Autumn said again, her chin going up. "He was real nice to me, Mama. I mean, he was surprised when I called him, but he didn't freak or anything like that. We talked. But I've tried to get him a bunch more times, but he wasn't there. I'm sorry I didn't tell you, but you're so worried about me, I didn't want to scare you more. And you told me not to talk to anyone except Uncle Tollie."

Ethan looked from one to the other. He wasn't angry for the simple reason that he'd had to accept Blessed as a reality. He didn't want to believe any of this, but there was Blessed, always Blessed, and

Autumn was Blessed's niece. "Can you speak to your mother telepathically, Autumn?"

Autumn shook her head. "I wish I could, but Mama can't hear me. I don't try to talk to people anymore. If they hear me, they think they're crazy. Well, there was the boy at the gas station, and he liked talking to me in his brain, once he got used to it. He called me dude. He'd say, 'Hello, dude.' He was always wanting to borrow money from me. He thought I was a teenager, like him."

"Try to talk to me, Autumn."

She did try, and so did he. He concentrated on her, concentrated on relaxing, on opening up, but nothing happened. He had to admit he was relieved.

Joanna said, "I overheard Shepherd say she knew Autumn had her father's gift. The only thing is, I don't really know how she knew it." Joanna broke off and looked at her daughter. "Oh, no, you didn't say something to them, did you, baby?"

"She sneaked it out of me, Mama. She was handing me a glass of really bad lemonade and she asked me—like she wasn't really paying attention or she didn't care—if I spoke to my daddy very often and I nodded before I thought about it. She smiled at me and said when my daddy was young, he could always call her from wherever he happened to be. She'd always been sorry she couldn't talk back to him when he called her, but she couldn't, but she bet I could, couldn't I? I nodded. I told her I could talk to Daddy anytime because it never cost any money.

"She said she just knew my daddy hadn't called her in more years than even she could count, and wasn't that sad? I didn't think it was sad because she's so scary, but I didn't say so. She said she'd tried and tried to call him, but it never worked. She asked if I would try to talk to her in her head, but I knew that wasn't good. I ran away. I'm sorry, Mama."

Joanna hugged her tightly. "It's all right," she said, though she knew it wasn't okay at all. "I can see how it happened, sweetie."

She looked at Ethan. "Martin never hinted that he had a gift. It was probably all tied up in his mind with his family, and he wanted no part of it. It was only after he went to prison that he called to Autumn telepathically, maybe because he missed her so much. She was only four years old, but he got right through. Apparently they could see each other while they spoke, so he did see his daughter growing up. Martin didn't want Autumn to tell me about it until she was older because he knew I'd be upset, most likely not believe her, think she was sick. Then he died unexpectedly and Autumn told me.

"I knew Autumn was grieving him terribly, and I thought she was imagining it, that it was her way of not letting him go. But after visiting the Backmans, I believe her. I've talked to her about it for a very long time this past week, and she's told me things her daddy said that she couldn't have known about without his telling her.

"I wasn't ready to tell you or anyone, Sheriff, because I haven't figured out yet how I can protect this child, not only from Blessed but from anyone else who would take advantage of her. But I will do anything to keep her out of the Backmans' hands. Anything."

For the first time in his professional life, Ethan felt uncertain to the soles of his size-twelves. Joanna obviously believed it all, but she couldn't prove it to him, or to anyone else. He was an earthling, and he felt like someone had thrown him into an alternate universe. Something within him fought against believing it, demanded more proof. But there was Blessed.

Always Blessed.

27

GEORGETOWN, WASHINGTON, D.C.
Monday evening

They arrived home about nine o'clock, the Porsche's gas tank nearly kissing empty. They were greeted by a hysterical Astro, who'd been chasing kernels of popcorn Sean was throwing to him. Gabriella was on the living room floor, laughing as Astro jumped over her, back and forth, chasing more popcorn. They joined in the game but not for long. Both of them were exhausted.

Autumn called him at midnight.

Dillon? Are you there?

Autumn? That's you, isn't it? Where have you been? Are you all right? I tried to call you but you didn't answer.

He turned on the bedside lamp. He was clearer to her now. She saw he had black whiskers. She could see his dark eyes. He looked wonderful.

She was so happy he was there she nearly burst with it. *Hello, Dillon. I'm okay but just barely. I'm sorry you didn't get me. I'm kind of new at this, just you and Daddy, really. Ethan told me how you were off chasing bank robbers.*

Yes, I've been real busy here. I'm sorry. Tell me your last name, Autumn, and where you are. Who is Ethan?

I'm Autumn Backman, and my mom and I are in Titusville, Virginia, with Sheriff Ethan. He's real nice and wants to help us.

Can you turn on a light, Autumn? I can't see you as clearly as I'd like.

No, my mama's asleep next to me. I don't want to wake her up.

A beat of silence, but she saw a brief smile on his mouth. *Tell me what's been happening.*

She told him about Sheriff Ethan Merriweather and his three pets, particularly all about Lula, who always caught the most kibble. She told him how maybe the sheriff really believed now that she was talking to Dillon, but . . . *He doesn't want to believe me because it's weird and I'm a little kid. People don't want to believe you when you're only seven.*

She told him how Blessed put the whammy on Ox, but Ethan had helped snap him out of it with a hard kick to his chin, how they'd been looking for Blessed, but he was hiding real good.

I need you, Dillon, my mama needs you. You've got to catch those bank robbers so you can come here and help us. Things are bad. Blessed is here. Blessed is scarier than the Phantom of the Opera.

Then she floored him. She told him about the dead people in Bricker's Bowl, told him about Shepherd and Grace. She didn't wink out once, her voice and face steady. *Mama and I got away and drove to Titusville, but Uncle Tollie wasn't here. He knows a lot of people, Dillon, but he's old, maybe too old for you to know him.*

What's his full name, Autumn?
Tollie Tolbert.

She saw him scratch his chest. Then he smiled at her, sort of embarrassed because he'd forgotten she could see him. *I know about Tollie Tolbert. He was an FBI agent, just like me. Everyone called him T Squared, you know, because both of his names begin with a T. So he lives in Titusville, Virginia, and you and your mama know him. I'm relieved, Autumn, because Tollie's tough, doesn't take grief from anybody. He knew my dad, worked with him occasionally in New York. My dad always said Tollie could make a witness talk faster than opening a can of tuna fish. He had this evil-eye thing going. Where is he, Autumn?*

In a place called the Everglades. That's in Florida. He hasn't come back yet. We've been waiting for him.

Okay. Ah, maybe I'd better give you my cell phone number. Can you memorize it so you won't have to turn on a light and wake up your mama?

He repeated his cell number three times, listened to her repeat it after him each time. *Good. Now, Ethan was right. I'm up to my neck here in a pile of bad guys. I'll call him in the morning, maybe get to Titusville in the next couple of days. How's that?*

I wish you were here right now. I don't know if Ethan's a hero like you are.

I'll bet you Ethan is a real big hero. He's watching over you and your mom now, isn't he?

Savich clearly heard a woman's voice say, "Autumn, sweetie?"

And Autumn said, "Mama, I'm talking to Dillon like I told you."

He heard nothing else. Autumn said, *Mama doesn't want to believe I'm really talking to you, Dillon, but she says hello.*

Hello to your mom too.

Will you get Blessed?

I'll do my best.

Thank you, Dillon, and she was gone.

28

"That was Autumn?"

"Yes." Savich looked up into Sherlock's face, then turned off the bedside lamp. Her face was shadowed, since there wasn't much of a moon to light their bedroom. He touched her hair and smiled. "She and her mom are in Titusville, Virginia, with Sheriff Ethan. She didn't tell me his last name. They're in trouble, according to Autumn. At least they're staying at the sheriff's house, deputies everywhere." And he told her everything Autumn had told him.

"You never mentioned this Tollie Tolbert—what a name. He really knew your dad?"

Savich nodded. "He's been retired quite a while now. Last time I saw him was at my dad's funeral. I'd feel a whole lot better if he were there, but Autumn said he was visiting the Everglades. The sheriff sounds like he's doing all the right things—of course, this is all from a seven-year-old's perspective.

"I'm thinking given this special ability she has, Autumn has had to be growing up a lot faster than normal. She was pretty cogent, Sherlock, she spoke really well, but you know what, when I looked at that beautiful little face of hers, I wanted to drop everything and pluck her out of harm's way fast. She's in fear of some very strange relatives."

"As strange as Blessed?"

"Yep. There's Shepherd Backman, Blessed's mom, and Grace, his brother."

Sherlock tilted her head at him.

"What is it?"

She said, "I thought Blessed's name sounded familiar, but I let it go. But those three names." She ducked her head down to tuck against his neck. "I've seen those names. Where was it?" She reared up and smacked herself on the head. "Okay, I re-member now. I was doing online research for that cult case we've got going out in Idaho, reading about religious cults, what they do, how they operate, how they indoctrinate their members."

Savich eased his hand beneath her short pajama top and began rubbing her back. "What'd you find?"

"There were hundreds of blogs written by the cults themselves—recruiting, I suppose—and there were newsletters, some out every month, subscription only. I found one that had to do with the supernatural power of the mind, and it talked about three people who had names like that—Shepherd, Blessed, and Grace, I think. First names only."

He gave her a huge kiss. "You're incredible," he said, rolled her off him, and got out of bed. She grinned as he grabbed a pair of sweats and pulled them on.

"Tell me the name of the blog."

"Something about sunset, sundown— something like that. It's in my files. Wait, I remember—it's 'Children of Twilight.'"

He shook his head at that. "I've got to take a look at this. Thanks, sweetheart. Go to sleep."

29

TITUSVILLE, VIRGINIA
Tuesday morning

Ethan woke up at six o'clock in the morning. He knew better than to get up or the animals would begin pretending they were starving with barks and loud meows punctuated by cat storms, Big Louie in pursuit, all through the house. He didn't want Autumn or Joanna to wake up that early.

So he lay there, listening to Lula snore lightly, watching Big Louie twitch in his sleep. As for Mackie, he cocked an eye open at Ethan, stretched, and went back to sleep. Ethan lay there, wide awake as soon as he thought about Blessed.

Blessed was still here, had to be, lurking

somewhere, probably in the wilderness, waiting, biding his time to get Autumn. He wondered if somehow Blessed had gotten himself into Autumn's head without her knowing it, and that was how he'd found her. Joanna had mentioned this, but this was the first time Ethan had let it into his brain as a real possibility. He shook his head. He was beginning to think as if he actually believed everything Joanna had said. Well, maybe he did. There was one thing he was doing, though, that wasn't good—he was building Blessed Backman up to be an omniscient monster.

Where are you, Blessed?

He nearly leaped off the bed when his cell phone rang. "Merriweather here. What's up?"

"Ethan, this is Chip Iverson, Titus Hitch ranger district."

Ethan had known Chip for two years. The man sounded like he'd had his brains shot out of his head. No, he sounded like he was in shock. Ethan slowed his voice. "Chip, talk to me. Tell me what's going on."

Ethan heard the rock-solid Chip draw in breaths, knew he was trying to get himself together, and Ethan felt his own heart kick up, felt the jump in adrenaline.

"Sheriff—Ethan, we've got a bad thing here." Chip's breathing broke off and Ethan heard him gagging, then vomiting.

Ethan waited. He heard Chip gasping for breath, heard a man say something behind him, heard him chug down some water, spit it out. Finally Chip came back on the line. "Ethan, it's a dead man, he's been savaged by a bear, but it's not right, just not right. Please come fast."

Ethan drove his Rubicon as far as he could into the wilderness on the fire road, Big Louie in the passenger seat, his head out the window. Then he and Big Louie ran the quarter mile to the southern fork of the Sweet Onion River.

It had taken fifteen minutes, and every one of those minutes, Ethan was thinking, *A man savaged by a bear?* How was that possible? There was plenty of game, no reason for a bear to seek human prey. It didn't make sense. It happened rarely, but sometimes some brain-dead idiot would bait a black bear, just to see what happened.

"I don't think so, Big Louie," Ethan said, petting his head as they neared the sound of muted voices. "I don't believe in coincidences, way too convenient. It's Blessed, Big Louie, I know it."

Everyone in uniform within fifty miles was looking for Blessed Backman. Ethan had spoken personally to as many of them as he could and had given out the facts he had, that Blessed had tried to kidnap a young girl and had shot at several police officers. He also told them Backman was a powerful hypnotist, so you couldn't look him in his face, told them the safest course was to shoot him on sight. If some of them doubted that, they didn't say so. He knew they would use deadly force, and whatever the legal rules, he knew it was righteous. It was the only way to bring the man down.

Big Louie began to whine, low in his throat. He pressed against Ethan's leg. The four people, rangers all, stood in the water reeds that grew wild beside the Sweet Onion River, two of them actually in the water up to their ankles.

Big Louie whimpered.

Chip Iverson called out, misery in his

voice and in his eyes, "Over here, Sheriff. We haven't touched anything."

The four rangers moved aside for him. Ethan looked down at the devastated remains of a man who'd probably been alive and laughing twelve hours before. His body was sprawled beneath a huge willow tree. He indeed looked like he'd been savaged by a bear.

Big Louie backed away, then stopped, threw back his head, and yowled. One of the rangers went onto her knees and hugged him to her, and spoke to him, tried to calm him.

Ethan swallowed the bile that rose in his throat, accepted the handkerchief a ranger handed him, and tied it around his face against the overpowering stench. He went down on his haunches and forced himself to study the man's face, what was left of it.

Chip was right. This man had been torn apart. One of his eyes was gone—ripped out by teeth or claws—and his other eye stared up at Ethan, sightless, filled with black blood. His throat was torn open, his chest flattened, his entrails ripped out. His clothes were shredded.

"This isn't right," he said aloud, twisting back to look up at the four faces. "You can see for yourself—tracks, claw marks, a bear for certain, but here's the thing. A bear ripped him apart, but why would he do that without devouring him? There are no major parts of him missing."

Four voices, hollow, terrified, sickened, agreed this wasn't right. A moment later Ethan saw the tangled threads of a skinny rope beneath one of the man's mangled wrists. A rope? No animal he knew of could tie a man's wrist, except the two-legged variety. *Blessed,* he thought again. *Of course it was Blessed.*

Ethan looked at the man's feet and nearly dry-heaved. The man's feet and lower legs were mangled nearly beyond recognition. The rest of him was bad, nearly unendurable, but not like his feet and lower legs. Thing was, they weren't feet any longer, but gore and bone, the ankles nearly gnawed through as—what? As the bear pulled and jerked his body down. Ethan heard Big Louie still whimpering, heard a soothing voice. He continued to breathe lightly into the handkerchief. He said aloud, "Look at his feet. Why would a bear do that?"

The four voices were silent.

Chip said, "We found pieces of his boots. They were ripped off his feet and chewed to bits, covered with blood."

Ethan nodded, then leaned down to gently remove the threads of the rope beneath the man's wrist.

"What's that?" Chip asked, staring down at that frayed rope, wet and black with blood.

Ethan showed him. He rose to look up into the thick branches of the willow tree. It didn't take him long to find the branch someone had tied the man up to. The branch was hanging low, nearly broken off, because the body that had hung from it had been pulled and jerked down. He could picture it happening. Someone tying his wrists together, throwing the rope over a low branch, and hauling the body up, but not too high up, no, only high enough so a bear would have to stretch himself to grab at his feet and ankles, to pull him down.

This was what the killer wanted to happen, what Blessed intended to happen.

Chip said, "The bear must have jerked and pulled until the rope tying his wrists gave way. See, the bear pulled him nearly to the water's edge, about ten feet from the tree."

"A bear doesn't feed like this," said Primo, a ranger from Montana who'd been at Titus Hitch six months. "Animals eat what they kill. If the bear wasn't ready to eat him, he wouldn't have mauled him like that. He'd have just come back later. The sheriff's right, this doesn't make sense."

Chip was shaking his head. He said, "What doesn't make sense is why anyone would do this to another human being. I mean, what's the point? Only a monster—"

Chip broke off as he studied Ethan's face. "You think Blessed Backman did this, don't you? He went to all this trouble to kill this man and set him up for the bear to obliterate him?"

Ethan stood up. He still held the rope. "Oh, yes, Blessed did this." He looked at each of the rangers. "Have any of you ever seen an animal wreak this kind of damage on a human being"—he forced out the words—"without some sort of encouragement?"

Paulie Burdett had been in the Park Service for twenty-four years, and was usually unflappable. But not now. Now he was mad.

"In the Serengeti I remember a guide was savaged like this, but he'd been reduced to bones. I've never seen animals who went to the party but didn't eat the cake."

No one laughed.

"Thanks for that image, Paulie," Chip said.

Ethan checked the man's pockets. No ID.

Ranger Junie Morgan said, "We'll have to check the camps, see if he was out hiking, whatever. So far we haven't had a report of anyone missing. Listen, Sheriff, if you don't need all of us, I'd sure like to get started tracking that bear."

"He had to be dead, didn't he?" Chip asked all of them and no one. "I mean, no one would haul a guy up and tie him to a branch, then eviscerate him so the animals would come and finish the job . . . No, I can't believe that."

Ethan said, "There's so much devastation, I can't even guess the cause of death. The ME will have to tell us that."

Ethan got the man covered, called his deputies to the crime scene, called the county ME. Then he pulled out his cell and called the Hoover Building in Washington,

D.C. He was surprised when he was put right through to Special Agent Dillon Savich. He'd expected—what? To be told to leave another voice mail, since the big man was too busy?

A man's deep voice said, "Savich."

"Dillon Savich?"

"Yes."

"I'm Sheriff Ethan Merriweather from Titusville, Virginia, and I've got myself a huge problem here."

"Hello, Sheriff. I gather you've already spoken to Autumn this morning?"

30

Ethan stared at his cell phone, felt his flesh ripple. "Ah, no, I got called out early. I haven't seen her yet this morning. I was out of the house before she and her mom were even awake. I, ah, gather you've met her?"

"Let's just say we spoke. She told me what's going on out there. She even told me about Big Louie, Mackie, and Lula. What's happened, Sheriff?"

No, he couldn't accept this, he couldn't, but Autumn's ability was staring him right in the face. "Well, what's going on right this minute is that I'm looking at the mangled

body of an unidentified man in his six-
ties, in torn hiking clothes, lying beside the
Sweet Onion River in the Titus Hitch Wilderness, about fifteen minutes from my
house. The body's an ungodly mess. For
whatever reason, a bear savaged it. If Autumn told you anything about Blessed, you
know why I think he was responsible for
this."

Savich hummed a moment, then, "Do
you have a good forensic team available
to you, Sheriff? An experienced ME?"

"We've never had the need before for
a hotshot medical examiner. I called the
county ME, and he's okay, as far as I know.
I guess the best ME would be in Richmond."

"I'll make some calls, get some people
up there. Don't let your deputies trample on
the crime scene, Sheriff, otherwise these
folk from Richmond will kick your butt.
They're very serious about what they do."

"You got it," said Ethan.

"Is there something else you'd like to tell
me?"

"Yes. Blessed is still free. Since Saturday night we've been scouring the area for
him, and believe me, everyone understands

how dangerous he is. I know he's here, hiding in one of the hundreds of caves that pock these mountains. And I know he won't leave without Autumn, and that's why I'm keeping the search parties in close to the house. But to find him out here in the Titus Hitch Wilderness—the chances aren't that good."

"If he wants Autumn, he'll come out. As I said, Autumn told me everything she knew about Blessed. The only thing is, she's seven years old, so a linear presentation isn't her forte. I've still got lots of questions.

"I'm hoping Autumn's mother, Joanna Backman, has more to say. If she's having trouble facing it, I can't say I blame her."

Ethan said, "Actually, I'm the one who can't bring myself to accept it. Joanna's been a trooper. She's told me a great deal already I can fill you in on. And there's Autumn, her actually calling you telepathically—well, I have lots of questions for you as well."

"I'll be there sometime today," Savich said. "Sheriff, you're completely sure that Blessed Backman did this?"

"Yes."

"Then don't you find it strange he'd select this particular time to commit this gruesome murder, a murder, I might add, that isn't all that close to Autumn?"

Ethan exhaled a curse. "Damn me for an idiot. Blessed knew I'd be called right away, knew I'd be tied up with this mess. He wanted me out of the house. He had to be watching the house, waiting for me to leave. There are only two deputies there guarding her."

Ethan punched off his cell as he ran through the forest and back to his Rubicon, Big Louie barking and racing beside him. They jumped in and Ethan floored it, barreling down the rocky dirt fire road.

He didn't know Joanna's cell number, so he called the landline at his house. There was no answer.

He called again a minute later. Still no answer.

Curse him for a moron. Blessed had delivered up a horror to him, and he'd been sucked right in. He'd gotten him away from Autumn.

He called Larch's cell. Three rings. Ethan was ready to panic when Larch came on, his good-old-boy voice deep and rich.

"Larch, it's me. What's happening there?"

"Nothing at all, Ethan. Everything's quiet."

Ethan thought he'd pass out with relief. "Larch?"

"Yo."

Typical Larch, the fewer words spoken, the better. Nothing hinky sounded in that "yo," nothing of Blessed. "Put Glenda on."

"Can't, Ethan. Glenda's turn to check the house and grounds. Then I think she was going to the little girls' room."

"She's inside the house? How long?"

"Well, now that you mention it, she's been gone a good ten minutes. She's probably talking to Joanna and Autumn. You want I should get her?"

"Put a call out and get people into the woods around the house. I'll be there in a minute." Ethan turned into his driveway at that moment, spewing dust. Larch jumped out of his cruiser when he saw him.

"What's up, Ethan?"

Ethan's cell phone rang. He ignored it. "If you see Blessed, Larch—don't forget—do not look at his face or what happened to Ox will happen to you. Get out your gun and stay behind me."

The front door was unlocked. Ethan quietly eased through, his Beretta at the ready, Big Louie behind him.

He heard Larch whisper, "You think Blessed got to Glenda?"

They heard a woman's low, gravelly voice, Glenda's voice. Ethan put his hand up, waved Larch back, and moved quietly toward the kitchen.

Glenda yelled, "Stop trying to creep up on me, Sheriff. I know you're out there; you made more noise than a herd of elephants."

Joanna called out, "Ethan, stay back. She's got a gun."

"Yeah, right, lady, and if you try anything, I'll blow your head off. I don't need you."

Joanna said, "You're going to shoot me anyway, aren't you?"

"Well, now, let me just say I'm doing things like I'm supposed to. You're not enough to stop me anyway. Sheriff, you stay out of here, you hear me?"

"Yeah, I hear you." Ethan heard the low murmur of their voices, but he couldn't make out the words. Then he heard Autumn's voice, clear and loud. "I don't want to go back with you—I won't go back! And don't touch my mama—"

He heard Glenda scream, "You shut up, you hear me? Shut up!"

Joanna yelled, "Big Louie!"

Big Louie bounded past Ethan, barking wildly, lost traction, and careened into the kitchen doorway, and bounded straight toward her, his nails a mad tattoo on the kitchen tiles. He heard Glenda yell, heard a gunshot, obscenely loud in the small kitchen. Ethan raced into the kitchen after him.

He saw Joanna hit Glenda in the jaw with a hard right jab. Glenda's head snapped back with the force of the blow. Big Louie was barking his head off, his jaws locked around Glenda's leg. She rolled her head, trying to get clear again. Autumn grabbed a pot and swung it hard at Glenda's back, and got her good.

It was all Joanna needed. She hit her again, hard, in the temple. He watched Glenda's eyes roll back in her head, watched her hit the center island and slide to the kitchen floor. He eased his Beretta back onto his belt. "Big Louie, that's enough, lad. You did good."

He picked up Glenda's gun and stared at Joanna standing over his only female deputy, rubbing her knuckles.

She looked up, and he couldn't believe it. She was grinning like a loon. "I hope that was hard enough to snap her out of it. Thanks, Big Louie, you're a prince." She went down on her knees and hugged the big Lab against her. He licked her face, then turned his head to take a couple of licks at Autumn's face.

He hadn't been needed, but his dog had been a nice addition.

He said, "Usually Big Louie hides under my bed at the first hint of trouble. But he didn't this time." Ethan scratched Big Louie's head.

Glenda moaned. Ethan went down on his knees beside her, checked her pupils. Her eyes opened. "Ethan? What happened? Oh, goodness, my head hurts."

"It'll be okay now, Glenda, just hang in there. Larch, get Glenda to Dr. Spitz's house as soon as the others arrive. Don't leave her, okay?"

"Jeff's gonna freak," Larch said.

"Yeah, he will, but she'll be okay."

"She's going to have a big shiner. Jeff's

not going to like that. They've only been married six months."

"I'll talk to him. Go, Larch. Glenda, you take nice light breaths and stay awake, okay?"

Glenda nodded and moaned.

Joanna said, "Glenda, I'm sorry I hit you so hard, but I had to. I had to break you free of Blessed."

"I don't know," Glenda whispered, her hands pressed against her head. "I can't remember." Larch nodded as he pulled Glenda up against his shoulder and walked her out of the kitchen.

Ethan hugged Autumn against him. "Did you see Blessed? Do you know where he is?"

Joanna said, "No, Sheriff. But when Glenda came into the kitchen through the back door, I knew Blessed had gotten to her—her walk was different, and she had this look, scared me to death. That sounds stupid but—"

"No, it doesn't. Autumn, if your mom leaves anything out, you just pipe up, okay?"

Autumn pressed even closer, nodded against his waist.

Joanna said, "She had her gun already against her side, but the thing is, like Ox, she didn't want to hurt Autumn, and that meant I could act."

Ethan said with a calm he wasn't close to feeling, "She could have shot you between the eyes in an instant."

"But she didn't," Joanna said, giving a sideways look at Autumn.

Autumn pulled away a bit. She smiled up at him. "Mama slammed her twice, Ethan, right in the head. Did you see her? She was awesome." She sent her mother a beaming smile.

Ethan heard his deputies outside, and relaxed. He picked her up and hugged her until she squeaked. "I'm proud of both of you."

Joanna scooped her daughter out of Ethan's arms and kissed her face a good half-dozen times, until the little girl was giggling. "We're a good team, sweetie. You got her in the back with that pot—what a swing. I think I see a Yankee in the making."

Autumn patted her mother's cheek. She looked over at Ethan. "I'm glad you came back, though, Ethan. I was a little worried."

Joanna said, "Why did you leave, Ethan?

It was really early when I heard you drive off."

He looked at Autumn, shoved the horrific words back in his mouth, and shrugged. "I had something pretty urgent to take care of."

He saw her stiffen. She guessed, he thought, that Blessed had done something to get him away from the house, something awful. She swallowed. She didn't want to know, at least not yet.

Thirty minutes later, Faydeen called to tell him they'd identified the victim. "His name is Harold Spalding, sixty-six, a retired bush pilot from Sitka, Alaska. A neighbor of his at the campsite said his daughter and her family were coming in today and they planned to spend a week exploring Titus Hitch. He was going to teach his grandkids about survival skills in the wilderness."

Only now he wouldn't. Blessed had seen to that.

Ethan knew he'd have to meet with Harold Spalding's daughter and family. He'd tell her that her father had been murdered, but no more. But what could he tell her about the motive? He felt battered, and his rage at Blessed was beyond anything he'd ever known, though he'd been powerfully angry when he'd been at the DEA at what he'd seen the drug lords do. He walked back into the kitchen and poured himself a cup of coffee from the pot Joanna had brewed. It was strong and rich. It cleared his head but didn't lessen the anger in his gut.

31

Tuesday afternoon

A black FBI helicopter set down on the country road in front of Sheriff Ethan Merriweather's house, whipping up the hot afternoon air and bringing everyone outside. Autumn yelled, "Oh, my. Look, Ethan, Mama, it's the President! He just landed on the road!"

"Shows you how important we are," Ethan said, and grinned. "I didn't even have to call him. Service right to our front door." He watched a big man wearing a white shirt with sleeves rolled up to his elbows, black slacks, and boots climb down. He turned to help down a woman, tall and slender, dressed as he was, all the way to the black low-heeled boots. She had incredible hair, a beautiful red, vivid as an Irish sunset. The man waved to the helicopter pilot and the bird lifted off.

The two of them were carrying leather jackets over their arms, and the man held a black computer case.

So this was Dillon Savich. Ethan had forgotten how sharp a fed could look. He had dressed like that himself three years ago, before he'd realized they'd cast him in a role he didn't want to play in the long run and had come back home to the mountains and to flannel shirts, boots, and jeans. He wondered if his deputies would have thought he'd looked as cool as these two back in the day. It seemed like a hundred years ago.

He felt Autumn's small hand slip into his. He grinned down at her. "Sorry, babe, I don't think it's the President. But maybe it's somebody you know."

She became very still, shaded her eyes. She shouted, "Dillon!" and broke away from Ethan and her mother and dashed across the front yard, Big Louie barking at her heels, toward that fed who looked hard as nails, his black hair whipped up by the helicopter blades.

Savich recognized the little girl instantly and pulled up. "I believe it's my midnight visitor," he said to Sherlock, then caught the little girl when she opened her arms and leaped at him. "Hi, Autumn," he said. He kissed her cheek and held her close, breathing in her kid smell, different from Sean, not better or sweeter, just different. *A little-girl smell,* he thought, *and wouldn't that be nice?* "I like finally seeing you in the real world, in real time."

"Real time," she repeated. "I like that too." She reared back in his arms and lightly touched her fingertips to his cheek. "You're awful handsome, Dillon."

"Well, my wife thinks so," Savich said.

"You're almost as handsome as Ethan."

"*Hmmm.* Say hello to my wife Sherlock. Sherlock, this is Autumn, who just kicked my ego in the chops."

Sherlock lightly touched the little girl's hand, smiled at her. "Do you know we have a little boy? His name is Sean."

Autumn slowly shook her head. "Dillon didn't tell me. Is he as big as me?"

"Not quite," Sherlock said. "And he's got

a terrier named Astro. Astro's all white, a live wire, and he fits right in Sean's arms."

Savich said, "Is that your mama standing over there, Autumn?"

The little girl nodded happily and called out, "Mama! This is Dillon. And Sherlock. They've got a little boy named Sean. And Astro. It sounds like Big Louie is lots more dog than Astro."

"Nice job of ice-breaking," Savich whispered to Sherlock. "Let's meet everyone, Autumn. Would you introduce us?"

An hour later, Ethan was cooking ribs and chicken and vegetables and foil-wrapped potatoes on his backyard grill, his eyes searching the woods for any sign of movement, any sign of Blessed. Savich turned twelve pieces of corn on the cob on the grill with a long-handled fork, whistling, asking more questions as they occurred to him, getting a feel for the place, and this bizarre situation, and drinking the best iced tea he'd had in a very long time.

He said, "Did you tell Joanna any details about what happened to the hiker?"

"Not all of it. I couldn't. She took it pretty hard."

"This Bricker's Bowl, where the Backmans live—since you know Blessed's identity, did you call the local sheriff?"

Ethan turned a chicken breast, slathered on more barbecue sauce as he said, "Yeah, I called Sheriff Cole, for all the good it did me. He asked me straight off if I could identify Blessed Backman as the man responsible for all the trouble, and of course I couldn't. I never saw him without his mask. I asked him to e-mail me a photo of Blessed and Cole said yeah, yeah, sure, he'd do that. When I told him about what Autumn saw, he sort of chuckled and said it was a private cemetery, no law against shuffling bodies around, now, was there? Of course, in this case, it sounded like the little girl dreamed it all. Sure, he'd go talk to Miz Shepherd, blah, blah. I wished I could have reached his throat through the phone."

Savich said thoughtfully, "I'm thinking Sherlock and I should pay a visit to Bricker's Bowl. I followed up on some Web research Sherlock told me about. I found a mention of what may be the Backmans in a blog by a group that calls themselves Children of Twilight. They traced the IP address of the server to northern Georgia, near Bricker's Bowl. The blog claimed to be written by a Caldicot Whistler, who wrote with the snake-oil charm of a charismatic cult leader. It mentioned only their first names—Blessed, Grace, and Shepherd, as disciples who had developed the powers of mind under Whistler's guidance. A cult requires money. I want to find out where the money's coming from."

Ethan knew where all the money came from, supposedly, but he simply couldn't bring himself to tell Savich that Theodore Backman was a slot-machine whisperer.

Finally, Ethan couldn't stand it. As he brushed barbecue sauce on the ribs and flipped the onions, he said, "Did Autumn really suddenly appear in your head one night and talk to you?"

Savich nodded as he carefully turned over the tinfoiled potatoes buried in the coals. He looked at Ethan. "It surprised me but good. At the time I was racing Lance in the Alps, both exciting and scary, since my bike was maybe three inches from a cliff, when there she was, right in front of me. I tell you, at first I thought I'd crashed my bike right over that cliff. I remember it was midnight on the dot."

"She . . . just appeared? Like that?" He snapped his fingers. "In your head?"

Savich smiled at him. "Yes. Her voice was clear as a bell, but I couldn't see her clearly. I asked her to bring her head up so I could see her face. She's a precious little girl, all that dark brown hair, her blue eyes and the line of freckles across her nose; she's the image of her mother. She'll be as beautiful as her mother someday. It's quite a gift she's got."

"But that means you've got it too," Ethan said, and he felt weirded out all the way to his boots saying such a thing. "Has this happened to you before?"

"Yes, several times. Once we were chasing a killer as dangerous as Blessed, called Tammy Tuttle. She was a horror, and if Blessed is anything like her, we'll have to focus on him like a target on a shooting range. Look, I know getting your mind around what Autumn can do is tough. But it isn't as important now—getting Blessed is."

"Fair enough," Ethan said.

Savich nodded as he turned the zucchini and squash slices and the mound of onion rings on the tinfoil, all coated lightly with olive oil. The smells were incredible, and he breathed in deeply. "I love summer," he said. "Even when it's so hot in Washington you feel like you're frying, there's something in the air, something sweet and alive.

"You've got a nice setup here. You use the grill a lot?"

"At least twice a week in the summer. Friends I haven't seen all winter show up."

"Well, I suppose smells this good travel fast."

Ethan fidgeted with the bottle of barbecue sauce. "But you were surprised when she suddenly popped up, right?"

"Sure. Look, Sheriff—"

"Call me Ethan."

Savich grinned, which didn't make him look like any less of an ass-kicker. "Ethan. The last sheriff who asked me to call him by his first name was Dougie."

"Did you ask him why his parents hated him?"

Savich laughed. "He was sporting bib overalls at the time, his gun belted on top."

Throughout the afternoon Ethan's deputies were in and out, drinking a couple of gallons of iced tea Sherlock and Joanna made, with Autumn's help, all of them eager to meet the two feds and trying not to act impressed or intimidated. When Glenda came into the kitchen with Larch just before dinner, Joanna walked right up to her, studied her face, and said, "I'm sorry I hit you, but I had to."

Glenda nodded. "I know. You had to get him out of me, so you're forgiven. Thank you."

Ethan introduced Savich and Sherlock. Savich said as he shook Glenda's hand, "You knew someone was there, in your head?"

Glenda frowned. Her head still ached, although the pain pills Dr. Spitz had given her had reduced it to a dull throb. She knew what she'd said had sounded like she'd been taken over by an alien. The pain in her head spiked, and she closed her eyes.

"Here," Joanna said, "drink some iced tea and relax. Stop thinking about it."

Glenda drank, took a few slow, light breaths.

Ethan said, "That's right, try to throttle down, Glen. Take it easy, don't think so hard about it. Look, when Blessed put the whammy on Ox, he still hasn't remembered."

Thankfully the pain eased off again.

"I can't believe Jeff let you come over."

"He didn't want to, but I told him it was my job and I didn't want to get fired." She gave Ethan a big grin and looked over at a big rope bone in the corner of the living room, chewed to grimy bits by Big Louie. "You're right, I don't remember, but the thing is, Ethan, I do know I wasn't there inside my head until Joanna hit me in the jaw. Her first punch didn't knock me out, but I remember the lightning slap of pain, and shaking my head, and for a moment I felt something inside my head slip, like a slippery hand losing its grip on a door-knob, off balance and trying hard to regain control."

She clammed up and looked terrified. "I can't believe I said that. I'm crazy, aren't I?"

"If you're crazy," Ethan said matter-of-factly, "then we all are."

His words did the trick. Glenda's eyes cleared. "It's true. He was there, inside me, but I didn't know it, not until she hit me. Thank God you hit me again, Joanna. That second whack must have knocked him right out of me. I don't remember anything until I woke staring up at Ethan's face."

Larch said, "You scared the crap out of me, Glen. Would you look at that mouse. What did Jeff say?"

"He thought it was cute once I convinced him I wasn't going to croak."

32

Ethan said to Sherlock and Savich, "Jeff Bauer, Glenda's husband, is a ranger with the Glenwood District, a real hardnose— I've seen him stare down a bear that was stealing food. He and Glen have only been married—what? Six months? He's one of the many out looking for Blessed. I'm surprised he isn't here hovering."

Glenda smiled. "I told him I was okay, but you know Jeff. Don't be surprised, Ethan, if he comes charging in here any time now. He did freak when I called him, since he knew about what happened to Ox. He came running over to Dr. Spitz's."

Savich said, "Glenda, at any point, did you hear Blessed speaking in your head, telling you what to do?"

She shook her head. "It was like I was gone, or buried so deep I might as well have been gone. I was only there after Joanna hit me that first time. And there was Big Louie biting my leg, and then Autumn was hitting me in the back with a pan." Glenda patted Autumn's cheek. "You and your mom mounted a full-blown attack on him. Really, thank you. You too, Big Louie." She leaned down and scratched behind Big Louie's ears.

Sherlock felt her own shoulders tighten at the overflowing tension she heard in Glenda's voice, even as she'd tried to joke about what had happened to her. She asked Ethan, "Where did Big Louie get his name?"

Ethan laughed. "My grandfather's old hound dog was called Big Louie. I remember my folks called him Saint Louie, since my grandfather was such a piece of work and they figured the hound had to be a real saint to put up with him. But the truth is, the two were closer than ham and rye.

"Big Louie was ancient when he died,

and he died a couple hours after my grand-father passed. My dad had them buried together. Believe me, no one told the authorities about that. Big Louie was my constant companion when I was a little kid. I guess I didn't want to let him go. Big Louie doesn't mind being Louie the Second, do you, boy?"

Big Louie woofed and butted Ethan's hand with his nose.

Glenda's husband, Jeff, came striding into the room at that moment looking like a wild man until he heard his wife laugh. He sucked down a deep breath, looked at his wife, winced at the black eye. "Oh, babe, I told you not to mix it up with Cloris over at Ty Harper's bar."

Glenda laughed. The headache was nearly gone. "I could take bigmouthed Cloris, trust me."

Some of the tension leaked out of the room. *Thank God,* Sherlock thought.

Twelve people ate outside on a long picnic table covered with two red-and-white checkered tablecloths and what seemed like enough food to feed them twice over.

Sherlock saw one barbecued rib left on the huge platter, a couple of pieces of zuc-

chini, and that was it. She was so full that
the single lonely rib dripping with barbecue
sauce didn't even tempt her. They drank
coffee and tea and soft drinks under the
slowly darkening sky. The air was cooling,
and Joanna put her own sweater around
her daughter's shoulders. It was turning into
a fine evening, what with the beautiful
mountains hunkered around them, chang-
ing colors every minute in the fading light.

Jeff took Glenda's hand and rose from
the large picnic table. "I need to get my
princess to bed, maybe put another ice
pack on her eye."

Slowly, everyone got themselves together, and the mood changed. For a while
there, it was sharing a meal with friends,
the conversation light, but now, as night
was closing in, Blessed loomed large
again.

Two deputies would remain, keeping
watch.

Savich and Sherlock remained seated.
Joanna knew there would be more discus-
sion. She thanked each of the deputies,
watched her daughter solemnly shake their
hands. When only the five of them remained, Autumn leaned up and whispered

to her mother, "I have to go to the bath-room."

"I'll take you," Ethan said immediately, and started to get up.

"No, no, I'll go with her," Joanna said. "We'll be right back."

They walked into the cottage through the kitchen, Autumn's hand in her mother's. Big Louie, so full he could barely move, followed them, tail at half-mast.

Joanna was opening the door to the half bath off the kitchen when she heard Lula hiss. She had been sleeping on the rocking chair in the guest bedroom. Joanna didn't hesitate. She shoved Autumn inside the bathroom and whispered, "Stay put, Autumn. Don't you move, you hear me?" She quietly closed the door. She nearly yelled Ethan's name at the top of her lungs, then stopped. If Blessed was here, it meant she could kill him, then it would be over. She'd had to give Ox back his Beretta. She raced to the gun cabinet she'd seen tucked away just inside Ethan's bedroom and pulled out a small Smith & Wesson, checked the clip. It was full.

She heard a man curse softly. He was in the guest bedroom. She crouched down and listened. Joanna knew to her soul it was Blessed this time, not some poor soul he'd hypnotized and sent after them. She wanted to end it right this minute, end it once and for all. Joanna ran down the hallway. She heard Lula hiss again, then saw her come flying out of the guest bedroom, tail bushed out, growling deep in her throat, more indignant than afraid.

Joanna was terrified, but it didn't matter. She crouched and ran toward the bedroom. She knew he was in there, waiting for what? Autumn to come strolling in? Or her? *Don't look at him. Just shoot him.* She went in low, like she'd seen on TV, saw him standing beside the bed, Autumn's blue pajamas in his hands. He'd pulled them out from under her pillow.

Joanna knew he was looking at her; she felt the weight of his will pulling at her to look back at him, to look at his eyes, but she kept her head down, stared hard at his hands holding Autumn's pajamas. They were rough hands with thick purple veins standing out on the back.

Shoot him! Now!

"Hello, Joanna."

She aimed her gun straight at where

she knew he stood. She stood too close to miss. All she had to do was pull the trigger and he'd be dead, but her finger wouldn't move.

His voice was soft and deep, mesmerizing, almost singsong. "You were a surprise, Joanna, you and Martin's daughter. Did you know he changed his name when he was twelve, said he couldn't stand his real name? Do you want to know what his real name was? His name was Harmony. Mother loved his name, but he hated it, said it sounded like he was a New Age dip, and he wouldn't back down.

"Mother thought you were a good mother, Joanna, but I didn't. I saw through you to the selfish twisting rot in you right away."

His words nearly made her jerk her head up. Nearly. Why wouldn't her finger pull the damned trigger? "Turn around, Blessed. I won't look at your face, you hear me? Turn around! Now, or I'll shoot you!"

"No, you won't, Joanna; you really don't want to." His voice continued, soft and soothing, deeper now. In her mind she felt his voice turn to thick liquid that was flowing warm into her blood, then racing through her veins to her heart. As if from a great distance, she saw him raise Autumn's pajamas in his hands and rub them against his cheek, and her heart pounded, filled to overflowing with revulsion, and something else. He said, his voice making her blood boil inside, "You can't, and you know it."

Joanna couldn't help herself; she jerked her head up, met his eyes for only a fraction of time, and fired.

33

The explosion was huge in the small room. It deafened her instantly, and the recoil made her stumble back a step to keep her balance. The room was spinning around her, and she felt nausea roil up into her throat. She wanted to fall down, but she didn't, she just stood there, weaving like a drunk, the gun now hanging loosely at her side.

The world stopped, simply came to a halt and left her standing alone with nothing on her mind, her only focus Blessed, standing directly in front of her, closer now, his eyes, hazy and deep, like fingers, lightly feathering her face, and his mind flowed in her blood, smooth and sweet. No, that couldn't be. Why was she thinking like that? Why wasn't he dead? She'd shot him straight-on. But he was standing in front of her, studying her face as if she were an insect he'd never seen before. She stared back at him, felt his mind probing at her, and she hated him, hated him so much she was choking on it. Why couldn't she move?

Autumn, she thought, but the image of her daughter floated away.

In a very deep part of her, Joanna knew she'd failed. But she couldn't fail, she had to destroy this evil. She tried to focus the gun on him again but couldn't find the will or the strength to even lift it. She heard him laugh, heard him say, in that same soft velvety, singsong voice, "You were mine the second you walked into the room, Joanna, and you'll do what I want you to. You're not going to use that gun, except maybe in your mind, or on yourself. I want you to lie down on the bed and fold your hands over your chest, look like you're dead rot, lying in a casket. That's a nice start."

"Mama!"

Autumn ran into the bedroom, her eyes on her mother, not on Blessed, who was smiling at her. "Mama! Are you all right? Mama, what's wrong?" Autumn ran up to her mother and hit her hard on the arm. Joanna didn't move; she was looking at the bed. She took a step toward the bed but Autumn shoved her back.

"Come here now, Autumn. Come to your uncle Blessed."

Autumn looked him dead in the eye and said, "No. You're a bad man. Go away. Leave us alone."

"Don't be afraid of power, Autumn. You and I will go away together to where you'll be surrounded by people who will value you, who will help mold you into what you're meant to become. Your mother doesn't understand, she never will. She's common, unimportant, merely shackles to be cut away to free you." He extended his hand to her, the thick veins bulging madly, purple and ugly.

Autumn yelled as she hit her mother again, "You're horrible! Let my mother go! Mama, come back." She kept hitting her mother, on her arm, on her shoulder, jerking on her hand.

Blessed looked bewildered. "You're an amazing girl, Autumn—you can look at me and still you can resist me." He slowly shook his head at the child who was staring right into his eyes. He then spoke in his natural voice, higher and sharper, with a kind of a country whine, "You're really looking at me, aren't you? Well, it makes sense, since you're Martin's daughter. I couldn't stymie Martin either. See, you don't know what you can do because your mother can't teach you anything; she can't even accept you for what you are, what you will become.

"Come here now, Autumn. You and I have a long road to travel. I imagine that idiot sheriff will be coming along real soon now. We have to go."

Autumn didn't move.

"You will come with me or I will have your mother hurt herself. Look, she wants to, all I have to do is tell her to pull the trigger."

"No!" Autumn looked at her mother, who was still standing motionless, looking at the bed, the gun held out in front of her now, straight at Blessed. She looked vacant, like she wasn't there. Autumn shook her mother's arm hard. "You took my mama!"

"Yes, I did, but she'll be all right if you come with me. If you don't, I will make her kill herself."

Autumn closed her eyes.

"Open your eyes. Stop that foolishness. What are you doing? What—?"

Dillon had taken a sip of tea as he listened to Ethan describe Blessed's attack on Saturday night when Autumn screamed at him, *Dillon! Help, he's in the bedroom and he's hurting Mama. Dillon!*

The tea spewed out of Savich's mouth. He had his SIG in his hand and was running toward the house in under three seconds, yelling over his shoulder, "Ethan, get your deputies outside Joanna's bedroom window; you cover the front of the house. Blessed is here!"

He slammed through the kitchen door, Sherlock six feet behind him, heart pounding, her SIG in her hand. She was running into the back hallway when she heard a man's voice yell, "You keep away or I'll kill Joanna, you hear me?"

Autumn screamed at him, "Dillon, don't look at him!"

"You look at me right now, fella, or she's dead, you hear me?"

Savich raised his face to stare at Blessed Backman. He didn't know what he'd expected Blessed to look like, but this pallid, middle-aged man with his stooped narrow shoulders, his baggy pants belted too high over a golf shirt, his light brown hair thinning—this man wasn't it. He didn't look like a bogeyman in a horrific nightmare. Except for his eyes. There was something moving behind his eyes, something corrupt, something hot and twisted. This man looked like he saw things others didn't. He looked like he saw the flames burning in hell and warmed his hands over them. They were Tammy Tuttle's eyes.

He watched Blessed's face take on an immense focus, felt his ungodly need to get inside his head, to control him, destroy him. And he felt the instant Blessed realized he couldn't get in.

Savich smiled. "I guess not, Blessed."

Blessed's eyes flared wild and panicked, and he howled, "No! Who are you? There can't be two of you!"

Savich said, never taking his eyes off Blessed's face, "Autumn, look at this man who let his gift be corrupted. Let Joanna go now, Blessed. Release your hold on her."

Blessed swung those mad burning eyes toward Joanna. "Oh, no, the bitch will do as I say."

Joanna brought the gun up slowly, very slowly, and she aimed it at her head.

Savich shot him.

The force of the bullet knocked Blessed against the wall, sending a picture thudding to the floor beside him. As he slid down the wall, he stared hard at Savich. He looked momentarily bewildered before he slammed his palm against his shoulder, and his mouth opened and closed as he watched the blood ooze bright red between his fingers.

Tammy Tuttle's face was bright in Savich's mind. This man was as mad and dangerous as she had been, and he knew he should kill him because he would never stop, never. But he slowly lowered his SIG.

Sherlock ran to Joanna, took the gun, stuck it in her belt, and shook her by the shoulders. Autumn kept hitting her mother's arm. Sherlock yelled right in her face, "Wake up, Joanna!"

Tears streamed down Autumn's face as her fists flailed at her mother and she cried over and over, "Mama, come back, come back!"

Sherlock continued to shake her until Joanna blinked, her eyes finally focusing on Sherlock's face. She looked dazed, but she was herself again. "What happened? Autumn? Where are you?"

Autumn clasped her mother around her waist, squeezed hard, and whispered, "Dillon shot Blessed. It's going to be all right now. Sherlock, you're sure Mama's okay?"

"Yes, I'm sure," Sherlock said, and hugged the two of them against her. She saw Dillon jerk the case off a pillow, watched him drop to his haunches and apply pressure on the wound.

Blessed was moaning in short gasps, deep in his throat, obviously hurting, and that was fine by Savich. His eyes popped open, and he stared up at Savich.

"How did you do that?"

"Sounds like a question for your guru, Blessed. Press your palm hard over this pillowcase, and the chances are good the bleeding will slow. Don't press hard enough and you might bleed to death right here in the sheriff's guest bedroom. I doubt anyone would feel sorry about it."

Joanna walked to stand over him, but she didn't look at his face. She looked at the blood smearing his hand and kicked him hard in the side.

He moaned, tried to spit at her but couldn't. "I stymied you. I should have had you put that gun in your mouth right away and—"

"When you stymied me? That's what you call it? I felt you, you bastard, trying to make me crazy, trying to make me see and feel horrible things. I should have walked in here shooting. I should have emptied my gun into you." She kicked him again, in the ribs, and he gave a long, lovely cry of pain. "You got anything else to say, you monster?"

He looked at her hard, but she still didn't raise her eyes to his face. "Look at me, woman!"

"Forget it, Blessed, or I'll shoot you again," Savich said. "You should step back, Joanna." He looked up to see Ethan standing in the bedroom doorway, his two deputies behind him. "Ethan, could you call 911? We're going to have to do this carefully, blindfold him so he doesn't attack anybody else. I'll ride in the ambulance with him."

Joanna said, "Stymie. That's what this pathetic worm calls what he does to people's heads."

"Stymie," Ethan repeated, as if tasting the bizarre word. He went down on his knees beside Blessed, pulled a handkerchief out of his pocket, and tied it around Blessed's head, covering his eyes. "Try to take off the blindfold, Blessed, and I'll kick you from here to the Sweet Onion River." Only then did he dial 911. Faydeen answered on the first ring, as Ethan knew she would. Whenever she was on call for 911, she walked around with her cell phone clipped to her bra.

"Sorry to interrupt your lovely Tuesday evening, Faydeen, but we need an ambulance out at my place. We got Blessed Backman here, and he's got a fresh bullet wound in his shoulder."

"Good going, Ethan. Hey, why didn't you kill the miserable bug?"

34

When Ethan closed his cell he said to Savich, "Faydeen wants to know why you didn't kill the miserable bug."

Savich said, "I seriously considered it for a second, but I had to let it go. Sorry."

Ethan shook his head. "We can't kill him now, dammit. I mean, I'd like to, but I can't, you know? Now we even have to keep him safe. All right, we'll deal with it."

"He couldn't stymie Dillon," Autumn said. "Dillon's like me. We're—what's the word, Mama?"

Joanna patted her. "You and Dillon are

gifted, thank heaven. You're both special in a very good way."

Autumn appeared pleased with that. Gifted. Savich realized it was a good word, the right word, and Joanna had taken a giant step in understanding her daughter's gift to think of it in that way.

Savich rose and looked down at Blessed. He felt Sherlock's hand on his arm and placed his hand over hers, squeezed. "We got him, sweetheart. It's over."

Joanna looked at him now. "He looks so ordinary. That makes him even scarier."

That was the truth, Savich thought. They listened to Blessed moan and curse, and, strangely, ask for his mother. Sherlock pulled him away, said quietly, "You remembered, didn't you, Dillon? You remembered when you got close enough to Tammy Tuttle you saw her clearly. She couldn't fool you like the others. She couldn't—what does Blessed call it?—she couldn't stymie you."

He nodded. "Yes, I remember. I guess it makes sense."

"No," Sherlock said, shaking her head, "it doesn't make sense. None of this makes any sense." She drew in a deep breath. "You lucked out."

Savich shrugged. "Fact is, there wasn't a choice. He was going to make Joanna kill herself. I had to stop him."

Joanna said, "That much power in this paltry little man, it scares me to death. Thank you, Dillon, for my life."

Savich smiled at her.

Ethan said, "Joanna, you don't look woozy or disoriented. Actually, you look okay. How do you feel? Headache?"

"No, no, I'm fine, don't worry, Ethan." She sounded surprised, and vastly relieved. "Maybe he didn't have enough time with me."

"Possibly so," Savich said thoughtfully. "Okay, later, when we get this squared away, I want you to tell me exactly what you felt the moment you looked at his face, his eyes."

She nodded. "I can do it now—fact is, I don't even remember looking at him, not at first, but it didn't seem to matter. Do you know, I was certain I'd shot him, that I'd fired my gun, dead-on. For whatever reason, he wanted me to believe I'd pulled the trigger. But I hadn't." She looked down at Blessed again, at his blindfolded eyes, and kicked him one more time, on his leg. He jerked and gasped out, "You damned bitch, I'm going to have you roast yourself, have you hop right into a bed of coals, get you ready for hell."

Joanna said, "Yeah, right, you pathetic monster. You'll be the one heading to hell, leading that family of yours."

Blessed gasped out, pain and anger in his voice, "Martin was my family. Is he in hell?"

"No, because he saw your evil and he escaped from it, from you and Grace and your mother."

"I'll bet you killed him, murdered him."

"No, I loved him, but since you're crazy, I'm sure you'll believe what you want."

"You burned his mind! You burned him up, made him nothing, like you. You're weak and stupid, Joanna, and that's what you made him. You'll pay for that."

Autumn yelled at him, "Mama didn't burn up my daddy's mind; his mind was wonderful. Don't you call my mama weak and stupid!" She kicked him with the toe of her sneaker.

Joanna pulled her back, gave her a quick hug. "Good shot."

They listened to him curse her, one good meaty curse, then another, then his head lolled to the side.

Savich watched him for a moment and said, "I'll wager that if we took the blindfold off him you could look right at him and he wouldn't be able to do anything. He's too weak now to focus, to affect your mind. On the other hand, I could be dead wrong."

Savich said to Blessed, "You're awake, I saw you twitch. You'd best pay attention, Blessed. You're bleeding again because you're not pressing hard enough. Get yourself together if you want to live."

Blessed licked his tongue over his lips, managed only one faint curse, and moved his hand back to his shoulder.

Joanna said to Savich, "You should have killed him, Dillon. What will happen now?"

She might be right, he thought. Faydeen was right to worry, because there was no way Blessed Backman would crawl through the courts blindfolded the entire time—he could hear the defense attorney screaming at the judge how they were torturing the poor man, denying him his basic human right to face his accusers. Well, it was too late now. Ethan was right, they'd have to deal with it.

The bedroom was soon full to over-flowing with deputies, everyone talking, everyone avoiding looking at Blessed's face, even though he was blindfolded and seemed to be helpless, like a snake with no fangs.

Sirens blasted through the night, grow-ing closer. Savich said, "I'm going with him. I'll be sure all the EMTs know to keep his blindfold on, and why. I'm going to scare them."

35

It was close to midnight before Sherlock and Savich were tucked in bed at Gerald's Loft, snuggled close because the temperature had plummeted the instant the sun had fallen behind the mountains. Despite the late hour they'd turned up, Mrs. Daily, bouncing with excitement, wanted to feed them.

Sherlock reared back and punched him in the arm.

"What? Hey, what's that for?"

"I don't care what you say—you took a big chance, looking that madman in the face."

Savich pulled her down on his chest. "You know I had no choice."

"Yeah, that gets you off the hook, but I know you, Dillon, you were testing it out."

She knew him well, he thought. He said mildly, stroking his hand through her hair, "It really wasn't all that big a risk, Sherlock."

"Yeah, right. You jerk." She punched him again, but she didn't have any leverage because he was holding her against him.

He laughed, grabbed her hands, and kissed her. "That roasted corn on the cob was delicious, particularly the couple of ears snuggled down in the coals for a long time. The kernels just fell off into my mouth—no gnawing at all."

She said against his mouth, "Yeah, make me laugh, try to distract me. That only works with Sean, and then it only works sometimes." She bit his neck, then kissed him. "Now that Blessed is safely put to bed at the hospital, so to speak, what's next, Dillon?"

"I want to check in on Blessed tomorrow, see when he might be stable enough for transport to Quantico. I want him where we're really in control. Then I figure we'll go down to Bricker's Bowl, Georgia, meet Sheriff Cole, Mrs. Backman, and brother Grace. Children of Twilight. I wonder, are the Backmans running this cult with Whistler? Or are they subordinate? And where does the money come from, and flow to?"

Sherlock said, "I hope those bodies they buried weren't cult members they'd finished bleeding dry of what they owned, or who wanted out." She sighed, drummed her fingertips on his chest. "Dillon, there's so much going on. We've got to attend to Lissy and Victor."

"I think we've got some time, two, maybe three days while Lissy's still mending from surgery, before they show up again. I've been working with MAX, checking out any possible real estate they could have access to outside of Winnett, North Carolina. The cops are looking for them there, along with the FBI and the state police. Not much else to do until they come out of hiding."

"Happy thought. You know she'll come dancing to Georgetown to kill you." She tapped him lightly on the nose. "You know what I'm thinking?"

That was not a business tone of voice. Savich stared up at her and waited.

"I'm picturing fractal art in my head—all wild colors and chaos and unpredictability, so I'm thinking a smart woman should take her opportunity while all the bedlam's still outside the door."

"Yeah? What opportunity?"

She leaned down and kissed him.

36

ROCKINGHAM COUNTY HOSPITAL
NEAR TITUSVILLE, VIRGINIA
Wednesday morning

"Sheriff Merriweather, I simply don't understand any of this. You say this man—who, by the way, is not only older than I am but is also too weak to even open his eyes—is so dangerous he has to be blindfolded at all times or he will somehow hypnotize me?"

"If he wants to, yes. You and anyone else who looks at him." *And,* Ethan thought, *I've told you this three times now, you idiot.*

"And I'm telling you it's simply not possible for a person to somehow take over another person's mind. And keeping his hands strapped down to his sides so he can't pull off the blindfold—come on, Sheriff Merriweather, don't you think this is a little over the top?"

Well, yeah, the blindfold and the tied wrists did look like they were over the top, or maybe they looked just plain crazy, but he had to try to make this man understand, or what chance did they have of keeping Blessed in the hospital, much less ever getting him to trial? "Dr. Truitt, listen to me. You need to trust me. We must take every precaution with this guy. I can tell you I've already seen him hypnotize three different people—he took them over completely."

A gray eyebrow went up a good two inches, and Ethan's frustration burst into the stratosphere. If he couldn't convince this doctor, how could he convince anyone of the monstrous danger that was Blessed Backman? "I know you think I'm exaggerating, I wouldn't believe me either, but the fact is, I've seen what he does with my own eyes. You've spoken to Dr. Spitz, heard the stories my deputies told him. This man was this close to making Mrs. Backman kill herself."

"Isn't Dr. Spitz a country doctor, a general practitioner?" Ethan heard the smooth touch of condescension in Dr. Truitt's voice.

"And you think he's been duped, right?"

"No, no, surely not, but all this nonsense about instant hypnosis, people killing themselves through suggestion—"

Ethan could see the future stretching out in front of him, constantly explaining and justifying himself, trying to make people believe what Blessed Backman was fully capable of and fully prepared to do to anyone who got in his way or could be of use to him. He said, "I'm going to keep him blindfolded, because the minute the pain meds kick in, the minute he's able to concentrate and focus, he'll be at it again, and trust me, you don't want to be on the receiving end. So you fully understand, he brutally murdered a hiker yesterday in Titus Hitch, left him for animals to savage."

Dr. Truitt looked shocked. Ethan watched his tongue whip over his bottom lip. "Do you have proof this man was responsible?"

"Yes," Ethan said, lying cleanly.

Dr. Truitt looked at him for a long moment, then simply shook his head and looked away.

Ethan hardened his voice. "He does

look helpless, doesn't he? No threat at all. All right, Doctor, consider this an order— keep this man blindfolded at all times; keep his hands tied down at all times. I'll have deputies here around the clock to make sure that happens. All he needs is a single second to pull off the blindfold, and it'll be over." Ethan raised his finger, cocked it like a gun, pointed it at the doctor, and pulled the trigger. "He might kill you if he's able, or make you murder someone else, a colleague or a nurse."

Blessed moaned.

Dr. Truitt jumped, cursed himself for being so suggestible. Since he knew Ethan was watching him, he calmly took his patient's pulse, raised the blindfold even though Ethan was standing right beside him, and checked his pupils. "He's still out of it. If there is anything to this hypnosis business, he can't do much if he's still unconscious. The surgery went well, and his wounds, both of them, should heal. With rest, he should be okay."

"There'll be a team of FBI physicians coming tomorrow, medical and psychiatric," Ethan said. "If he's well enough, they'll begin testing him."

"What sorts of tests?"

"I assume they'll evaluate him, physically and mentally, to see if there's a consensus on when he's ready for transfer. I expect you and all hospital staff to cooperate fully with them." He took Dr. Truitt's arm, shook it lightly. "Listen to me, this man is more dangerous than you can imagine. I know now he looks about as dangerous as a toothless old dog, but he's not, Doctor, he's the most dangerous human being I've ever met in my life."

Ethan could see Dr. Truitt still wavered. He knew if Joanna were here, she'd bitch-slap him. It made him smile. Dr. Truitt said, "As long as your FBI personnel are cleared by the chief of staff, I'll cooperate with anything I think ethical. As long as this man is my patient, his welfare is my primary concern."

Even though Ethan wanted to punch him out, this little speech was a start. He nodded. "Give me a call if there's any change at all in his condition. My deputy Ox Cobin is going to stay in this room with him. And by the way, Ox is one of his victims. You want firsthand information, you ask Ox.

"Ah, good timing, Ox. Come on in.

Blessed is still out of it, but he moaned a couple minutes ago. You know what to do."

Ox nodded as he brought in a huge easy chair with an adjustable footrest. "Nurse Lowery loaned me the big man's chair. He's on vacation in Croatia."

Ethan smiled. "You're feeling fine, right?"

"Yep, but I'll tell you, Ethan, I'm hardly even going to look at that little man, even all tied down, even with a blindfold over those mad eyes of his."

Dr. Truitt harrumphed, turned on his heel, and left the hospital room.

Ox watched his progress out of the room. He said thoughtfully, "That's going to be everyone's reaction—doctors, lawyers, judges, laypeople—you know that, Ethan."

"Yeah, I know, even though I told him about Blessed murdering our visitor from Alaska. And no, I didn't try to tell him Blessed somehow whipped up a bear to savage his corpse. We've got Blessed on a dozen felony charges, even if the FBI forensic team doesn't find anything definitive to tie Blessed to Mr. Spalding's murder.

"You know, Ox, I hate to say this, but truthfully, I don't think we even have a chance to get Blessed to the lawyer stage. I have this gut feeling it's not going to be long before he walks out of this fine hospital, a load of stymied folk in his wake."

"Let me kill him, Ethan, here and now, a pillow over his face; it'll be over in no time." Ox sounded dead serious.

Ethan shook his head. "I wish we could, Ox, believe me. It's a nice fantasy, but it's no way for law officers to talk. The FBI people will be arriving soon, and they're going to take him out of here, to Quantico."

"He might be gone as soon as he's out of pain," Ox said. "Do you know Belle wouldn't come near me when I got home from seeing Dr. Spitz on Saturday night after Blessed stymied me? She sniffed and growled, danced around me like she was afraid of me, but at the same time she wanted to attack me. Scared me to my boots. Took me a good hour to talk her down."

"Now that's interesting. I've got to remember to mention that to the FBI docs when they show up tomorrow." Ethan paused, looked down at the thin, middle-aged man who didn't look like he could even raise a single finger. "Keep your eyes on him, Ox."

"You know I will, Ethan." Ox settled himself into the easy chair, pressed the button to bring up the footrest, and grinned at his boss. "Now, I could get used to this. Why would the bigwig hospital guy go all the way to Croatia when he could stretch out in this Cadillac of a chair all day, drink a Bud?"

37

Dr. Hicks, a top FBI forensic psychiatrist, was also an extremely competent hypnotist in his own right, and a huge Beatles fan. He didn't wait for the rest of the FBI team, he arrived by himself that afternoon, his eyes bright with excitement, like a kid on Christmas morning, Ox thought. Dr. Hicks introduced himself and shook hands with Ox. Ox waved over at Blessed. "There he is, sir."

Dr. Hicks turned immediately to look down at the motionless middle-aged man. He shook his head. "So this is Blessed Backman. An interesting name, don't you think? He looks harmless enough. Talk to me," he said, turning his formidable attention on Ox. "Tell me what this man did to you."

Ox told him. ". . . I wasn't there, you know, inside my own brain, at least not until the pain got me back into myself." Ox jabbed his fingers through his flattop. "Sounds stupid and weird. You believe me?"

Dr. Hicks was frowning down at Blessed again. "Of course I believe you."

He pinched the back of Blessed's hand. Blessed didn't react. Dr. Hicks lifted the blindfold, then his eyelids, stared at him a good minute, then said, "*Hmmm.* How long has he been like this?"

Savich said from the doorway, "I told Sherlock you'd be here, no way would you wait for the team. You didn't even check in at the B-and-B or stop at the men's room or eat a bagel, did you?"

Dr. Hicks gave Savich a really big smile. "I didn't even eat an apple. I couldn't wait to see this guy. Drs. Chambers and Bailey will be here tomorrow. I'll tell you, the report you gave them had them flying at me with questions and speculation, not to mention a cargo bay full of disbelief. I left them with their heads together, plotting out what kinds of tests, what kind of restraints, to arrange for him at Quantico. We can get an MRI here to see if there's a brain tumor. We can see if he can bend spoons, that sort of thing, later. I hope he comes out of it soon. I really want to talk to him."

Savich nodded. "Come outside with me for a moment, Dr. Hicks."

Once in the hallway, Savich looked at Sherlock, who nodded and said without preamble, "We appreciate your enthusiasm, Dr. Hicks; that's one of the reasons we called you. But we've got a major security problem here until we get Blessed to Quantico. We need to keep him in this room while he's here."

Dr. Hicks said thoughtfully, "I can't begin to imagine such power, to actually make someone willing to kill themselves. And you, Savich, you are immune to him. Life never ceases to amaze, does it?"

"You're right about that," Savich said. "I'm also going to set up a video camera in the room so we can monitor Blessed remotely. I sure hope it doesn't happen, but it's possible, given Dr. Truitt's skeptical response to Blessed's hypnotic ability, that we just might get a live demonstration if the hospital staff doesn't believe us. If this does happen, I just hope no one gets hurt."

"Let's have Dr. Truitt attend him," Ethan said. "See what he does."

Savich said to Ethan, "That would be justice. Ethan, you okay with this? If Blessed does try anything, there'll be living proof on film. A defense lawyer could claim it was all staged, but we'll worry about that when we need to."

Dr. Hicks held up his hands, palms out. "Hey, wait, I want to speak to him first, listen to his voice, have him talk to me. I want to look into those eyes of his. Why can't I do it? If he does anything to me, Ox here can smack me."

Savich said, "Tell you what, sir. If he wakes up while you're here, you can have a go at him. But his blindfold stays on. No more victims for him on my watch."

Ethan said, "When you get that camera set up, Savich, I'll see that Ox drags his chair out here into the hall."

38

"Is anyone there? How can I know if anyone's there if I can't see?"

"Yes, I'm here, Mr. Backman. I'm sorry about the blindfold. I'm your nurse, Cindy Maybeck. Do you need anything, sir?"

His voice sounded weak, querulous. "I need you to take off this ridiculous blindfold."

"I'm sorry, sir, but I was told to leave it in place, for my own protection, not that I believe it, but I have to follow orders. Let me take your pulse, listen to your heart."

Blessed felt her lift his wrist, place two fingers against the pulse. "It's that hick sheriff; he's torturing me because we had a disagreement. Here I'm old enough to be his daddy and he's afraid of me. Isn't that a kick? Listen, how would you like to lie in darkness, Nurse, with your hands strapped down? I can't even scratch my nose. It's inhumane, don't you think?"

"I don't know, Mr. Backman. I was told—"

"I hurt; I hurt real bad."

"Now, sir, you had a shot of morphine not an hour ago. Why don't you try to sleep? Sleep will make you heal faster. You want me to scratch you anywhere?"

Blessed hissed out a moan but didn't say anything more.

Cindy took his pulse. Nice and slow and regular. Then she put a cuff on his good arm and a stethoscope below it. He had good pressure, a little on the high side but nothing to merit alarm. She straightened, looked down at him. She said softly, "Don't cry, Mr. Backman, you're getting the blindfold wet."

He sobbed.

"You're going to make yourself all itchy if you don't stop crying, Mr. Backman."

"Just wipe my eyes for me, Nurse. Please.

What can I do? My hands are tied down, I'm helpless."

She held herself silent for a few seconds. She'd heard Dr. Truitt say all of these precautions were ridiculous; he was an old man, for God's sake. But then the sheriff and the FBI agent had told everyone not to remove his blindfold and why. He could hypnotize someone instantly? She'd never heard of such a thing. She agreed with Dr. Truitt. This poor old man, shot twice, helpless as a foal—she said, "I really shouldn't, I'd be disobeying orders. Oh, all right, but only for a moment. It'll be our secret, all right? You promise you won't tell anyone?"

His voice was liquid with tears. "I swear I won't say anything, Nurse."

Cindy eased the blindfold over the top of his head. She wiped away his tears. Real tears, she saw, and she knew Dr. Truitt was right. This poor man couldn't do anything to anybody. She studied his pale face for a moment. No, surely he couldn't—Blessed Backman opened his eyes and looked up at her.

"Thank you," he whispered. "You're quite pretty, all that blond hair. Is it real?"

"Yes," Cindy said, "from my grand-mother."

"You're a pretty, helpful girl. Unfasten the straps on my wrists." He smiled up at her.

Cindy didn't hesitate. She unfastened the straps and straightened to stand next to the bed, unmoving.

Blessed slowly eased onto his side, pressed his palm to his bandaged shoulder, and sat up. He winced, cursed softly.

Cindy said, "Can I help you?"

He looked up at her and smiled again. "No, thank you, Nurse. That is much better. Now, I want you to bring my clothes."

Cindy walked over to the patient's closet that held his shirt, trousers, and shoes. She pulled them off the hangers. "I don't see any underwear or socks," she said.

"It's all right. Bring them to me now."

Cindy turned back with the clothes over her arm.

"I want you to go outside and talk to that guard, distract him; you're pretty enough to turn the head of a dead man. Flirt with him, keep him busy until I call you. Then you can bring him in with you, all right?"

"All right."

In the hospital room next door, Savich, Ethan, and Dr. Hicks were watching them. Savich said, "Well, that didn't take long. Do you think Dr. Truitt will believe us now?"

"You said Dr. Truitt is a skeptic, Savich. He could say this was all a performance."

"Good, you sound just like a defense attorney," Savich said. "We'll play it out some more, until and unless he acts against the nurse, then we move fast." But he didn't want to. Savich watched Cindy Maybeck walk out of the room, knew she wasn't really there in her own head. Still, letting this go on was a risk, but he prayed it was a manageable risk. He forced himself to set aside all his doubts and fears. He drew in a deep breath. They watched a middle-aged man, thin and scrawny, his shoulder and arm hugely bandaged, slowly swing his legs over the side of the bed.

"I can't believe he can move around as well as he can," Dr. Hicks said. "Maybe along with his abilities, he's also able to influence his own body somewhat." He shrugged. "Who knows?"

They watched Blessed Backman slowly stand up and strip off the puke-green hospital gown, wincing and weaving a bit. They watched him awkwardly pull on his pants, then stare at the shirt. There was no way he could get himself into it, not with his shoulder bandaged so thickly, not with the pain the movement would cause him.

Blessed called, "Nurse, come here, please."

Cindy opened the door and came in. She never looked away from his face. He said, "I need you to help me into this shirt."

She did. He swore the whole time. They could see the pallor, the beads of sweat on his forehead. "He's in pain," Dr. Hicks said, "but he's still functioning. Amazing."

Blessed asked Cindy, "Where are my shoes?"

"I left them in the closet."

"Get them for me."

She did. She went down on her knees and helped him into his shoes.

"All right. I want you to ask the deputy to come in here, tell him you're concerned that I might be getting free and you want him to check on me."

Cindy nodded and turned to leave the room.

"That's it," Ethan said, and he and Savich were out of the room in a second flat. "You will stay outside," Savich told him. "No arguments." Savich walked past Nurse Maybeck into the hospital room to see Blessed reaching for his watch on the side table.

It was all on film.

"You!"

"Yeah, it's me, your worst nightmare, Blessed. Go ahead, give me your best look, come on, give it a try. Sorry, not going to happen. Party's over. That was some performance you gave us." He nodded up at the camera, Blessed's eyes following his. Savich didn't think he could hypnotize people on the other side of the camera, but he wasn't about to take any chances. He blocked his view. He looked over at the nurse, who was looking blankly at nothing at all, simply standing outside the doorway. Savich said to Blessed, "Get your clothes back off and I'll help you with the gown." Savich stripped him down because Blessed was cursing him, trying desperately to stop him and not succeeding. Blessed yelled to Nurse Maybeck, "Help me, Nurse. Help me!"

"What is that agent doing to him? Let me go!"

But Ox grabbed the nurse by her arms

and lifted her bodily onto his shoulders to get her away from the room.

Savich got Blessed back into the hospital gown and flat on his back. Blessed stared up at him, panting with pain, his eyes burning wild and hot in his white face. "I'm going to kill you. I'm going to skin you and make a lamp out of your hide. I'm going to bury you so deep no one will ever—"

"Yeah, yeah." Savich forced the straps around his wrists, clipped them to the bed railings, and slipped the blindfold back over his eyes.

"It's okay, Ethan, you can come in now."

"This is amazing," said Dr. Hicks, who stood in the doorway beside Ethan. He stared from Savich to Blessed, who was still panting from the pain. "That was the most incredible psychic phenomenon I've ever seen."

Dr. Truitt appeared next to him in the doorway. "They paged me. What's happening here?"

A half-dozen hospital personnel were soon clustered around Dr. Truitt, looking from Savich to Blessed Backman, who lay on his back, moaning, blindfolded, his wrists strapped down.

Ox stood beside the bed, staring down at Blessed Backman like he could kill him and enjoy it. Savich turned to the hospital staff. "It's over now. We do have a little something to show you, Dr. Truitt, you and the staff. It's a video in the next room. You're in living color, Blessed. Maybe this will help keep you in solitary confinement for the rest of your miserable days."

Ethan said, "I don't suppose there's a prayer of keeping all this away from the media?"

"We can try," Dr. Hicks said. "Some of these people won't want to confess to another soul that they saw a man take over another person's mind so easily. Some simply won't believe it. But the media will sensationalize any hint of psychic powers. Even if no one believes it, they'll come like locusts."

But Savich knew it would get out, knew Blessed's family would find out fast that they had him. What would they do?

Cindy Maybeck stood beside Ox, rubbing her arm where he'd hit her. She'd recognized him when he'd first arrived with Sheriff Merriweather. He'd given her a parking ticket last year. She looked up at him. "Why did you hit me?"

"Because that nice old codger took away your brain for a while. You'll be okay now. Do you have a headache?"

She shook her head, frowned. Ox knew she didn't understand, but maybe she would when he explained it to her over dinner at Marlin's Mexican if she said yes. He'd also teach her how to parallel park.

39

BRICKER'S BOWL, GEORGIA
Wednesday afternoon

"Joanna described Bricker's Bowl well," Sherlock said, staring around her. "It's like the whole town's at the bottom of a gigantic soup bowl. Very cool. It makes me want some chicken noodle. How many people live in this valley?"

"Around five hundred souls," Savich said.

"It looks like nobody's come or gone in a lot of years. It should be in black-and-white, like that old movie *Pleasantville*. Look, Dillon, there's a cell tower, power lines, all the modern conveniences. Somehow they look out of place. I'm thinking the

Backmans would have to be careful about what they do around here, you know, not soil their own backyard."

"Joanna did say she saw Blessed stymie the young guy taking pictures the day they buried Martin Backman's urn in their cemetery."

Sherlock said, "And his brother Grace stopped him."

Savich picked it up. "Blessed did tell the young man he wouldn't remember anything. Neither did Ox or Glenda or that nurse at the hospital. Blessed would have to be very careful, though, or sooner or later he'd face a mob."

Sherlock nodded. "And we're talking years upon years living here, Dillon. Look there, cows grazing, goats munching away. Makes me feel better. But what I don't understand is why Blessed doesn't simply walk into a bank and stymie a teller and walk out with a gazillion bucks. No one would remember he was even there."

"Maybe he's tried it. They could have a lot of cash stuffed in those graves. We're going to find out, I promise you that." Savich turned the rented Camry into the first filling station, Miley's. A young boy with buzz-cut wheat-colored hair was putting air in a couple of tires on an ancient Honda. A heavyset woman was seated inside the Quik Mart, the cash register in front of her, staring at them through the glass.

Sherlock said, "That woman's looking at us like we're trouble. Fact is, though, if I lived anywhere near the Backmans, I wouldn't just be paranoid, I'd move. We don't need gas, Dillon. Why'd you stop?"

He said, "That woman sitting at the register was looking at us even before we pulled in. I want to sit here awhile before I get out of the car and fill the tank. We're two strangers, doing nothing, and she looks like she's on red alert. This might end up being interesting."

"I hope we luck out and find Caldicot Whistler here. He's probably the key to this Children of Twilight cult, maybe to all of it."

"I finished putting together what MAX could find about him this morning," Savich said. "He's thirty-seven years old, a graduate of Harvard Law who worked for four years in a private law firm in Manhattan, then took off without a forwarding address after he was turned down for a partnership. No wife, no kids. Actually he has no living relatives that MAX could locate.

"We have a four-year gap until we pick him up again here in Georgia, leading this Children of Twilight cult. Surprisingly, it's the only mention MAX could find about him.

"Ah, look. Our subject behind the glass is giving us the evil eye, probably wondering if we're criminals or we're using Bricker's Bowl as a hideaway to cheat on our spouses. And that boy's putting too much air in that tire. If he's not careful, it's going to explode."

Sherlock said, "I ran searches on Children of Twilight myself."

He waited. "But?"

"Well, I did find a reference to a possible origin of the phrase, but, Dillon, it's really out there—"

"And your point would be?" Savich held up his hand. The woman on the other side of the glass was reaching for the phone at her right elbow. He said, "Tell me the origin when we're done here. It's time for me to pump gas."

Savich leisurely stepped from the car and eased the nozzle into the gas tank.

The woman at the register dropped the phone into its receiver and turned back to watch him. He could tell from twenty feet away that her face was loaded down with makeup, from bloodred lipstick to bright blue eyelids. He gave her a little wave.

He replaced the gas nozzle and walked inside to pay the woman. He saw lines of suspicion form on her face. Her blue-shadowed green eyes were lined with black.

He smiled at her. She didn't smile back.

"Hello," he said, his voice smooth, confident. "Nice dress."

She looked surprised and uncertain, the compliment unexpected, and she leaned toward him but only for a moment. Then she pulled back, crossed her heavy arms over her chest. She eased one leg over the other, letting her flowy blue print dress ease up to her knees.

"That'll be only fourteen dollars and sixty-three cents," she said, extending her hand. "Why'd you stop here when you didn't need any gas to speak of?"

Savich glanced at her name tag as he peeled the bills out of his wallet. "You're Doreen, right?"

"That's me," she said, and took his money. "You got three pennies?"

She had a deep Georgia drawl, every word syrupy-slow and with vowels. Savich shook his head no, watched her make change.

She gave him back a lot of nickels and pennies—payback, he supposed—then asked, her voice careful, "You and the missus take a wrong turn?"

"Oh, no," Savich said. "We're here to see the Backmans."

He saw the whip of fear in her eyes before she smoothed it away. "Nice family," Doreen said, looking down at an old *People* magazine with Drew Barrymore's expressive face on the cover. He saw Doreen didn't believe him. She said, "Outsiders usually pay with credit cards, not cash, particularly if they don't have anything to hide."

Savich said easily, "But then again I didn't get much gas, did I? I like to keep rental cars nice and full. Do you also know Caldicot Whistler, Doreen? Good-looking guy about your age?"

Savich loved this woman. She was wide open, every thought clear on her face. He saw the flash of recognition, then fear or suspicion, or alarm, he wasn't sure which.

"Nope, never heard of this Whistler. Dumb name."

"I don't know. I think Blessed is a pretty dumb name too, don't you?"

"No."

"Can you give me a recommendation for a place to stay?"

"The Backmans won't put you up? They got more bedrooms in that big house than that Hearst Castle place in California. How long you going to be here?"

"We haven't decided that yet. I guess we'll have to see how long our business dealings with Blessed take."

She let her breath whoosh out. "You're not—I mean, you really know Blessed?"

"Yes. Very well, as a matter of fact."

"I don't know how that can be, since Blessed doesn't leave Bricker's Bowl very often and I've sure never seen you before. Fact is, though, Blessed's not here—in town, I mean. Haven't seen him in more than a week. Heard he borrowed an old SUV from Mr. Claus and headed out. So you're out of luck."

"Then we'll deal with Grace and Shepherd."

"Haven't seen Grace either. As for Shepherd, who knows? She hardly ever leaves that mansion of hers, much less Bricker's Bowl. I heard she buried one of her sons—the Lost One—just two weeks ago. Martin was his name. We started out in the first grade together and went all the way through. He was smart."

"Why do you call Martin the Lost One?"

She shrugged her big shoulders. "After he left, Mrs. Backman started calling him that. The Lost One. And she'd cry. No one ever heard from him again, not until his widow brought him back in a miserable urn to plant in the ground since she'd had him cremated up north somewhere. People think that's not right around here, you know? I heard the urn was made of one of those new specially treated woods, last as long as metal. Can you imagine? I also imagine Shepherd wasn't happy about that, Blessed and Grace either."

"Hey, Martin's widow brought him back to his hometown and family. That was surely a nice thing for her to do, don't you think, Doreen?"

"She was gone fast enough. Della Hoop down at the dry cleaner's said she heard the widow was this city girl, all proud and proper, and Martin's little girl was cute as a button. That's what Mavis at the Food Star told her. Said the little girl liked butter-pecan ice cream. But she didn't look a thing like her daddy. Martin was dark, had a five-o'clock stubble by the time he was sixteen. Shepherd didn't like that either, I heard, the little girl looking the image of her mother."

Savich nodded. "Blessed told me how he caught that young guy from the newspaper who was at the funeral spying on them, how he told him to go quit his job."

Doreen's eyes flashed again—was it fear? Or was it par for the course when you lived in Blessed's universe? "The little snoop, serves him right, but old man Maynard wouldn't let him quit even though he lost his prized camera."

"Yeah, Blessed said he smashed the camera."

Doreen's mouth opened and Savich leaned forward a bit. Suddenly she looked out the window. Savich turned to see a big muscle truck, a Chevy Cheyenne, so spit-shined you could see your reflection in its black surface. He saw a gun rack but no one riding shotgun.

Doreen said, "That there's Sheriff Cole. Burris probably saw you, wants to check you out. He's real careful with our town. I told you, Blessed and Grace aren't here. Why don't you just leave now? I mean, you got a real full tank now, don't you? Trust me, you don't want to tangle with Sheriff Cole."

"Tangle with the sheriff? Last thing on my mind. I'm pleased you called him for me, Doreen."

40

"Sheriff Cole doesn't like strangers. He's always driving through town, watching for them, so you'd best hie yourself out of Bricker's Bowl, back up to the highway, before he hauls you in and puts the hurt on you. I didn't call anybody."

"The hurt on me? Does he make a habit of beating up strangers who come to Bricker's Bowl?"

"Don't make him think you deserve it."

"Wouldn't dream of it," Savich agreed, and gave Doreen a small salute and a smile that startled her. He walked out the door to stand in the bright sun a moment and stretch. He watched Sheriff Cole climb out of his truck, check himself in the high shine. So this was the man who'd kissed off Ethan. He watched him hoist up his tan polyester pants and settle the wide leather belt and big holster around his middle, run his fingers over the butt of his Smith & Wesson Model 29, Dirty Harry's classic .44 Magnum. What was this small-town sheriff doing with such a powerful gun? Stupid question. Like his truck, the .44 Magnum helped make him the Big Man, someone with power, someone to fear. He actually was big and muscular, in his late thirties, big hands, big booted feet. He rolled his powerful shoulders and, of all things, cracked his knuckles. Savich sincerely doubted the two of them would ever be friends. This was no Dougie Hollyfield or Ethan Merriweather. This man looked volatile, and that made him very dangerous. If Joanna was right, he was in the Backmans' pocket.

What Sheriff Cole really looked like, Savich thought, was a natural-born bully.

He came to within four feet of Savich before he stopped, took a wide-legged stance, his fingers still on his gun butt. He stared at Savich, measuring him, assessing him, as if wondering, maybe, how long it would take him to beat Savich unconscious. Savich would bet this guy would go about any beating he did with great joy and viciousness. Savich saw he was wearing two-inch boots and wondered why. The guy was already a good six-foot-three or thereabouts. More intimidation, more huge attitude. No help from this quarter, not after what Ethan had told him. The guy probably feared only three people in this town—all of them named Backman.

Sheriff Cole had a heavy twang. His voice boomed out deep and hard, filled with threat and violence. "Good afternoon. You want to tell me who you are and what you're doing here?"

Savich saw Sherlock climb slowly out of the Camry. She stood at her ease about eight feet behind the sheriff, her arms loose at her sides, her jacket shoved back so her fingers weren't more than two inches from her SIG.

"Or what?" Savich asked easily, a black eyebrow arching.

"Or, you disrespectful piece of shit, I'll

whip your ass and kick you out of my town."

"All that?" Savich smiled as he pulled out his creds and held them out. "If you will look at my credentials, Sheriff, you'll see I'm Special Agent Dillon Savich. Behind you is Special Agent Sherlock, FBI. You know, Sheriff, I really dislike foul language. You might want to remember that. I didn't catch your name."

Sheriff Cole looked around at Sherlock, narrowed his eyes, then turned back. He spit. No spray, just a wad of spit that hit maybe eight inches from Savich's right foot. "I'm Sheriff Burris Cole. What are two FBI agents doing in this little town?"

"Like I told Doreen, we're here to see Blessed Backman."

That rocked him, but to his credit, he recovered quickly. "Well, Blessed's not here, now, is he? I'll bet you Doreen already told you that. So I guess there's no other reason for you to stay."

"You've got a nice town here, Sheriff. I think Agent Sherlock and I will hang around awhile, see the sights, visit with Shepherd and Grace. Who knows? Maybe Blessed will show up. And, ah, Sheriff, could you tell us where we can find Caldicot Whistler?"

Savich thought the man would come at him on the spot, but whatever good sense he had stopped him at the last minute. He let out a frustrated breath, keeping the violence pulsing beneath the surface, and hooked his thumbs into his wide leather belt.

All in all, Savich was disappointed.

He looked into Cole's nearly colorless eyes. The sheriff's fingers dug into his belt so hard they turned white. So he did have some control. A pity.

"We don't have any Caldicot Whistler in our town."

"If not here then close by. Surely you know about his . . . organization, Children of Twilight? As a fellow law enforcement officer, I'd sure appreciate some cooperation with this, Sheriff."

The sheriff spit again, this time about six inches from Savich's left foot.

Savich shook his head, sighed. "No cooperation then. Agent Sherlock, call Director Mueller, tell him we're going to need a cadre of agents in Bricker's Bowl as soon as possible. We got us a cult leader to track down."

"On it, Chief."

Savich heard her speaking on her cell not two seconds later.

"Now wait a minute, there's no reason to flood my town with a bunch of federal guys poking into everybody's business. All right, all right, I'll help you."

"Agent Sherlock, tell the director we might get some local cooperation after all. Now, Sheriff Cole, where is Caldicot Whistler? Where are these Children of Twilight?"

"I told you, Mr. Whistler doesn't live in Bricker's Bowl, but he does visit on occasion. I don't know about any cult. 'Children of Twilight'? That sounds crazy. Whistler's a nice man, Agent Savich, wouldn't hurt a soul. I believe he sells cars over in Haverhill. Why do you want to see him?"

"I want to talk to him about his cult you've never heard about," Savich said.

"I tell you I don't know about any Children of Twilight cult. Don't you government types have anything better to do than harass car salesmen? Yeah, that's what he does—sells those fancy German cars.

Caldicot Whistler has nothing to do with a cult. Who claimed he did?"

Savich leaned forward a bit, his voice confiding. "Actually, Sheriff, the FBI knows just about everything we need to. I'm surprised that you, a law enforcement officer, haven't bothered finding out about them, or think the FBI wouldn't. On the other hand, you've been stuck in this valley a long time—don't bother with TV or newspapers, right? Now, what's Caldicot Whistler's address?"

"We got TV, newspapers, computers, even *People* magazine." Sheriff Cole wanted to kill this asshole or at least hurt him bad, and it showed. He also wanted to scratch at the itchy rash around his middle because the heavy leather belt dug into his flesh. That didn't help. As for the girl with all her red hair and white skin, her long fingers flirting with that SIG, he'd like to introduce her to other sorts of things he liked—a little bowling, a little love, a little pain.

He wondered if she knew what to do with that powerful weapon so close to her fingers. His two deputies were more than likely already over at Kandra's Kafe chowing down on "All the Tortilla Chips You

Can Eat," today's special. When Doreen had called him, he'd almost not come by, thinking about all those chips and the big bean burrito waiting for him. He could always count on Kandra to come through with the food when his wife was in one of her moods.

Stupid lost tourist who needed some hassling, that's what he'd thought. And now this. Now he had two FBI agents on his hands, this big guy whose nose needed to be broken, and the woman, probably the guy's girlfriend. He could just pull them behind the gas station, but it was too big a risk. The woman had already called the damned director.

How could the FBI possibly know about Blessed and Whistler? He remembered that sheriff calling him about Blessed from somewhere in the mountains back in Virginia. He must have called the FBI. *Damnation.*

The fed had asked him a question—oh, yeah, about Whistler. He said, the hot rage burning the air between them, "You'll have to ask Blessed for Whistler's address. I don't know it. I never knew it, you got me?"

"Not yet, but I'm beginning to think I

probably will," Savich said easily, and walked straight at the sheriff, making him hop to the side. Sherlock saw the flash of rage in the sheriff's eyes when he realized he'd been outsmarted, and tried not to smile. They watched the sheriff walk inside the Quik Mart and lean close in to speak to Doreen. They waited. After only about a minute he came out, put sunglasses on his nose, climbed into his truck, and peeled out. She arched an eyebrow.

Savich said, "Thanks for calling Director Mueller for me."

"You're more than welcome. He was right there, as if he'd been waiting for me to call him."

"I must say, you sure got a hold of him fast. I'm impressed."

"And so you should be. We're off to see Grace and Shepherd?"

"Doreen said Grace wasn't here either," Savich said. "She could have been blowing me off—we'll find out when we get to the Backmans'."

Savich stared after the black truck. "Do you know, I don't think Sheriff Cole and I are going to be best friends."

Sherlock said, "He's afraid of the Backmans, and he hates you all the way to his steel-tipped boots. He really wants to kick your butt, Dillon, big-time."

Savich quirked an eyebrow at her. "Do you think that might be fun?"

"Yeah, for you."

Savich drove down Main Street, only two blocks long, past its short row of businesses, from the Intimate Apparel boutique to Higgins Bar on the corner, with its neon flashing Dos Equis signs, to Polly's Dry Cleaners right next door. He stopped when he saw a little boy on his bike and asked him where the Backmans lived.

The boy, who was missing two front teeth, gave him a big grin and leaned close. "My ma doesn't like me to go anywhere near where the spooks live," he said, and pointed east.

"Why do you call them spooks?"

The boy said, "Everybody knows they're spooks, but my ma says I'm not supposed to talk about them. She won't admit it, but I think she's scared of them."

"Why do you think that's true?"

The boy frowned over Savich's left shoulder. "Whenever she and my dad are talking about them, they whisper."

"Got you. Do you ever see the Backmans in town? Blessed, Grace, Mrs. Backman?"

"Miz Backman sometimes talks to Dolly down at Fresh Fish Filet—that's our restaurant, you know. Ma doesn't like to eat there, says the fish is off sometimes, whatever that means."

A gold mine of information. Savich said, "What do your parents do here?"

"My dad—he's Reverend Halpert; he's the preacher at the First Pilgrims Baptist Church. He's always saying we're lucky to have more members than Father Michael at Our Lady of Sorrows. Father Michael tells my dad he's a heretic and laughs. Dad tells him he might be a heretic, but we have better potluck suppers. Catholics can't make good potato salad, he tells Father Michael, and then he laughs too."

"Do the Backmans go to your church?"

"No, they're Catholics, but they donate money to us anyways. Lots, I heard my dad say."

"What's your name?"

"Taylor."

"Well, Taylor, I'm Dillon Savich. You've been a big help. Go buy yourself an ice cream. I saw Elmo's Thirty Flavors. Are they good?"

"Oh, wow, thanks, mister. The triple-fudge chocolate's the best." The dollar bill disappeared in Taylor's pocket and he'd pedaled halfway to the ice-cream shop by the time Savich slid back into the Camry. Taylor yelled over his shoulder, "Elmo's really got thirty-three flavors, I counted them! Thanks again, mister!"

"Spooks, *hmmm*," Sherlock said as Savich pulled away from the curb. "Cute kid. So Mama's afraid of the Backmans?"

"So it appears," Savich said, and gave a nod toward a couple of old geezers who appeared to be playing checkers in front of The Genesis Spirit, the lettering stenciled in gold against black glass.

"Wonder what that's all about?" Sherlock said.

"There's a little sign beneath. Looks like it's a tarot card and palm-reading place. I wonder how a town this size can support them?"

"We'll ask Mrs. B.," Sherlock said, and gave a little wave to the two checkers players, who seemed more interested in them than in their game.

41

The driveway to the Backmans' house was long and graveled, curving first around two enormous oak trees, then threading between wildly blooming red rhododendron bushes. Oaks and maples lined the sides, full branches forming a lush canopy overhead. It was a royal approach to the palace.

The house was set in the best spot in the valley, at the eastern end of the bowl. It glistened beneath the hot sun like a wedding cake, lavishly decorated with blue and green accent colors. The house was surrounded by thick stands of oak trees. The front yard was beautifully manicured, with undulating green lawns and small yews lining flower beds filled with azaleas, petunias, and fuchsia. Rosebushes and jasmine trekked up the sides of the house on trellises. It was extravagant and romantic and utterly unexpected in a valley like Bricker's Bowl.

Savich's first thought was, *Where is the cemetery?*

"Wowza," Sherlock said, and whistled. "Would you look at that place, Dillon. I didn't get the impression of anything this grand from Joanna. She said it was a mansion and left it at that. Would you look at the accent colors—those dark blues and greens are gorgeous. I don't think I've seen more colors on the Painted Ladies in San Francisco."

The place gave Savich a headache. It was too big, too in-your-face, just too much, period, except for all the flowers. He particularly liked the iceberg roses with white blossoms so thick they looked to weigh down the bushes.

He parked the Camry in the driveway leading to the six-car garage, behind a new dark blue Cadillac that matched the blue on the house trim. Were there more cars inside? And if there were, then why had Blessed borrowed an SUV to drive to Titusville?

Sherlock said, "The Caddy looks like Mrs. Backman's wheels, I'd say, so hopefully she's home. Any idea where the cemetery is?"

He gave her a quick smile. "Probably in the back. We'll get to it."

"You know, Dillon, this place is incredible, the flowers look like they're on steroids, the grounds are lush and neat as a pin—it creeps me out."

They walked up the ten deep-set wooden steps onto a wide veranda with an inviting porch swing, white rattan table, and four matching rattan chairs, the cushions the same blue and green of the house trim. It was blessedly cool on the porch, a breeze coming from the west.

Beautiful Italian ceramic pots filled with overflowing azaleas and petunias and other flowers Savich couldn't identify hung from lacy black wrought-iron hangers, each set precisely two feet apart.

"The flowers," Sherlock said. "I wonder what Mrs. Backman uses to get them so glorious? Maybe some sort of spell or incantation?"

He laughed. "Our garden is just as spectacular."

"I wish," Sherlock said, and breathed in. "Even though I can smell the roses and jasmine giving off that lovely perfume, it still creeps me out. I don't know why."

"You know too much about the residents."

The door opened before they could knock. The proverbial little old lady in a flowered cotton housedress stepped out in beaded mules, her sturdy legs bare. She looked like a benign grandmother, fluffy white hair done up in an old-style knot on the top of her head, pearl studs in her drooping earlobes, a huge diamond on her ring finger. There was nothing frail about her. They knew she was seventy-eight years old because Joanna had told them. Otherwise they could have only guessed because officially, Shepherd Backman didn't exist. She didn't have a birth certificate, a Social Security number, a driver's license, or a recorded marriage license. Her husband had filed taxes in his name alone. Blessed filed now, showing a yearly income of about forty-five thousand dollars from driving a delivery truck, this verified by a manager of a local mailing distribution company who had been paid off at least that much. Or maybe Blessed simply stymied him every year at tax time.

Mrs. Backman said nothing, merely stared at them, not moving, her pale brown eyes darting from one to the other. They came to rest on Savich. "Who are you, young man, and what do you want?" Her voice didn't sound like it belonged to an old lady. It was deep, on the gruff side, as if she'd smoked for many years, and had authority, the voice of a person who always drove the bus she rode in. Savich wagered that Blessed, who was utterly terrifying, bowed to her orders without hesitation.

Savich smiled at the old woman and held out his creds. "I'm Agent Dillon Savich, FBI, and this is Agent Lacey Sherlock."

She studied his creds, gave them back, then held out a surprisingly youthful hand to Sherlock, who placed her own creds in her wide palm. Her fingernails were dirty. From gardening? Or maybe from digging up graves?

She studied Sherlock's ID for a very long time. Finally she handed the shield back. "Now I know who you are. What do you want?"

"We would like to speak to you and your son, Grace, since Blessed isn't here."

"Neither is Grace."

At her words, Savich went on full alert. He smiled at her. "Where is Grace?"

"I imagine he's with his brother, since they left together. They're rarely apart, those two."

"Do you know where they went, Mrs. Backman?"

"My boys are all grown up, Agent Savich. They come and go as they please. I'm only their mother. I'm always the last to know."

Yeah, right, Sherlock thought.

"Excuse me a moment, please," Savich said, nodded to Sherlock, and walked to the end of the veranda. He called Ethan's cell. Ethan answered on the second ring. Savich said, "Grace is in Titusville. Evidently both he and Blessed went to fetch Autumn. I don't know what to expect from him, Ethan, but he's close by, and maybe as dangerous as his brother. Maybe they work together or Blessed uses Grace in some way to help him focus. Remember you told me when Ox was stymied, he sounded like himself, only not quite? Was it Blessed's voice?"

"He didn't sound all that different, but what he said and how he said it, that wasn't Ox. You're thinking it might have been Grace's voice?"

"That sounds so bizarre it gives me a headache even to think about it. More likely Blessed does it all by himself, but the fact is, we don't know for sure. But Grace is there, so take care."

When Savich walked back he heard Sherlock say, "You have a lovely home, Mrs. Backman. The blue and green accent colors are perfect, and show an amazing attention to detail. They draw you right in. And the flowers—I like to garden myself."

"Thank you," said Shepherd Backman. She didn't bend at the praise of her home or gardens, nor did she budge from where she stood, blocking the front-door entrance. Well, maybe she'd slathered it on a bit too thick, Sherlock thought. She wanted to tell the old crone that even though it looked well-kept, the place still creeped her out, just to see what she'd say.

Savich picked it up. "We wondered where all the money came from to build and maintain this lovely property. Your husband's dead, isn't that right?"

"Yes, a mugger got to him outside Harrah's in Reno on November seventeenth, 1999, killed him dead."

"Your husband gambled?"

"Well, yes, he spent a good deal of time in the casinos. He was a man of many talents, Agent Savich. I have little knowledge of his financial dealings, but he always provided well for us. I built this house from the legacy he left."

Not quite the story you told Joanna, Savich thought.

Shepherd said, "The damned mugger took all Theodore's money too after he whacked him on the head, money Theo would have wired to me the next morning, nine o'clock on the dot. The local police were useless. If our own Sheriff Cole had been in charge, they would have found the murdering little pissant and hung him."

Now this was quite an outpouring.

Sherlock said, "That's a long time to go

without an influx of cash, Mrs. Backman. Has Blessed been providing for you since then, stymieing your local bank manager, for example, to replenish your checking accounts and your investment portfolio, or the car dealer to get you that new Cadillac? Incidentally, the Caddy sure matches the blue accent well."

Shepherd showed no reaction; she remained poised, well in control. Maybe she'd paled a little bit? No, unfortunately Savich didn't think so. She was a tough old duck.

Shepherd said matter-of-factly, "Blessed doesn't stymie for money in Bricker's Bowl. That wouldn't be right. We would not take from our neighbors. Those huge Mob-run casinos are a different matter entirely."

Sherlock said, "I would very much like to see the inside of your lovely home, Mrs. Backman."

"Most people would."

"May we come in?"

They could see that Shepherd Backman desperately wanted to show off her masterpiece, garner more envy and praise. But should she keep out the FBI agents or appear to cooperate? She was obviously torn about that. They could see her wheels spinning—let the enemy in or not?

"Very well, but I won't show you all the house, it's too big. You may see the living room. Then you will leave."

42

Savich and Sherlock followed her inside to an immense oak parquet entrance hall. There were fresh flowers in a huge pink vase on an antique table, an ornate Victorian mirror hanging over it, both looking as if they were straight out of Buckingham Palace. An antique umbrella stand, a grouping of several paintings—and then the Victoriana stopped. They stared at four paintings that were raw and elemental, painfully modern. Their constant subject was storm clouds, churning water, and black rocks. In each, there appeared to be a person drowning, pale arms flailing, mouth open in a scream. A terrifying glimpse into the artist's soul?

"Incredible paintings; who's the artist?" Savich asked.

"They are incredible, aren't they? My son Grace painted them. I believe they are museum-quality."

"Is this a common theme for Grace?"

"I suppose you're wondering if Grace nearly drowned in a storm? It's called artistic rendering, it's a statement of the powers and forces beyond a mortal's control." She smirked at both of them, there was no missing it. She turned on her heel and they followed her into the first room on the right, dominated by a Carrera marble fireplace with an imposing portrait of an elderly gentleman above it. The look in his pale eyes was happily mad. It had to be Theodore Backman, her dead husband.

Mrs. Backman walked spry and straight, the cotton housedress falling straight to her calves, her mules sliding over the beautiful polished oak floor. She pointed to an authentic Victorian settee.

They sat, watched her ease into a high-backed chair opposite them. She looked complacently around the large room. "It took five years to build this house and decorate it the way I wanted it. It is now perfect. But my sons, Blessed and Grace, have no interest in anything other than the pork chops on their plates and their nightly dessert of strawberry cheesecake, made for them by Marge at Phelps's Bakery every day." She waved her hand around her. "This lovely house, all the flowers, the antiques, it's all wasted on them. It is not right nor fair. I have asked them what they plan for it when I'm dead."

"And what did they say?"

"They looked furtively at each other and made up the story that they will marry as soon as they bury me so their wives can keep up my shrine. That's what they call this beautiful house—my shrine. This is a work of art, I told them, not a ridiculous shrine, and they just looked at each other and shrugged. There is nothing to be done."

Savich said, "Is that why you want your granddaughter to come live with you, Mrs. Backman? You want Autumn to grow up here and take over your place when you die? Keep up your beautiful gardens, buy more antiques?"

"That would be nice, if that is what she wished," Mrs. Backman said comfortably, not at all surprised they knew about Autumn. "However, there is no need for more antiques. She is only a little girl, and she wasn't here long enough for me to determine if she is worthy of such a gift. She carries half her mother's common blood, after all."

Whoa. Sherlock said, "Why do you believe your son's wife is common, ma'am?"

"I had only to speak to her to know what she was."

Savich said, "You must have been greatly saddened to hear of your youngest son's death. A shock."

Sherlock saw her fist tighten in the folds of her housedress. She shook her head as she said, "Poor Martin. He was confused, as are many young men. He would have come home, but that woman, she lured him away and convinced him to keep away from us. I didn't even know where he lived until she called me, but by then it was too late. He was already dead. Do you know she didn't preserve his body to be buried here beside his father?" Her voice was high now, and angry. "She had the gall to bring him home in a cheap urn. I wanted to see my boy, touch him one last time, but he was nothing but ashes."

Sherlock said, "I understand his wife had to make an effort to notify you at all, Mrs. Backman. Actually, she didn't even know you existed; she didn't know anything about you. Her husband never spoke of you or his brothers, you see. He was the one who cut all ties to you, not his wife. I understand you called him the Lost One?"

"He was lost, but he would have come home to me. Now it doesn't matter. His death was all her fault. She seduced my boy and kept him away from his family. She wouldn't even tell me how or where he died. But how do you know about Martin? Has that woman been telling you tales?"

Savich said, "But your granddaughter, Mrs. Backman, you found Autumn to your liking?"

"I told you, that woman took her away too quickly for me to judge."

"We know about Autumn's gift, and you do too, don't you, Mrs. Backman? Didn't she tell you she spoke often to her father when they were apart? Isn't that why you sent Blessed and Grace to Titusville, to fetch Autumn back to you?"

"That, young man, is quite absurd."

Savich said, "Did you tell Blessed and Grace to murder Joanna while they were at it?"

Her eyes revealed arrogance nearly off the scale. The old woman believed herself invulnerable, believed no one could touch her. She was dangerous, Savich thought, despite her age, a woman who could kill without a moment's hesitation and feel not a moment's remorse. Like Blessed. What about Grace?

If Autumn was right about the bodies Mrs. Backman and her boys had buried, then this little old lady had already killed many times. He said again, "Did you tell Blessed to kill Joanna when he got ahold of Autumn?"

"You have no idea what you're talking about, Agent Savich. For you to accuse Blessed of all this, it only shows what a small, common mind you have. You will leave now. I have cooperated with you; I have told you Blessed and Grace aren't here. I don't know when they'll be back."

"Then let me tell you about Blessed," Sherlock said, sitting forward on the settee a bit. "He is currently in a hospital, a blindfold over his eyes. His wrists are strapped to the bed railing so he can't remove the blindfold and stymie anyone."

She didn't look at all surprised. "Why is my boy in the hospital?"

Savich said, "I shot him. He had surgery last night. But Grace called you, didn't he? He told you how Blessed broke into Sheriff Merriweather's house to kidnap Autumn. Maybe Grace is afraid of what you'll do to him because Blessed was caught? Maybe Grace is afraid you'll blame him? Did you give him further instructions, Mrs. Backman? Would you like to tell us what you told him to do?"

"You're telling me you shot Blessed? You are despicable! You tried to kill my boy!" Her voice rose an octave, and rage pumped red into her parchment cheeks. Her eyes darkened to almost black.

"You will be punished for that," she said. "I will see to it that you are punished."

Sherlock said pleasantly, "If that happens, I will kill you myself so you won't know the pleasure of it. Now let's get to it." She pulled a warrant out of her jacket pocket. "This is a warrant, Mrs. Backman, to search your family cemetery for the bodies Autumn saw you and your sons burying."

The old woman wanted to blight them, they saw it in her eyes, and they saw it in her white-knuckled fists. She said finally, "That is nonsense, and you know it. You actually believe a little girl's nightmare because her mother wants you to? What, are you sleeping with her, Agent Savich?"

"Take the warrant, Mrs. Backman," Savich said. Still, she didn't reach for the warrant in Savich's outstretched hand, merely looked at them both without emotion. "I will call Sheriff Cole if you do not leave immediately and take that ridiculous warrant with you."

"But the sheriff already called you, didn't he, ma'am? About fifteen minutes ago? Telling you we were looking for you?"

"I'm going to call Sheriff Cole," she repeated. "He'll deal with you two."

Savich looked down at his watch, then up again when he heard a car outside.

"If that isn't the sheriff, then it's our forensic team here to go over your family cemetery." He stood and put the warrant in her lap. "Feel free to read it. Feel free to call Sheriff Cole again, tell him he's too slow."

"I'm calling my lawyer too."

"You might as well call Caldicot Whistler."

It was a hit, they could see it. She sucked in a breath, but she held herself together and remained quiet.

Sherlock smiled at Mrs. Backman. "I believe it's our forensic team."

43

The search was a bust.

An hour later, forensic expert and team leader Dirk Platt walked to where Savich and Sherlock stood watching the operation at Martin Backman's grave site. He was shaking his head even as he said, "Sorry, guys, but there are no bodies here."

"She moved them," Sherlock said. "Blessed notified her and she moved them. Or she suspected either Autumn or Joanna saw what they did and that's why they ran." Sherlock looked out over the cemetery. The forty graves positioned in odd triangles. The last graves were not two feet from a thick stand of oak trees that reached up the sides of the bowl to spear green and fat into the sky. The trees surrounding the cemetery laced their branches together, creating moving shadows in the breeze.

Dirk asked them, "Do you want us to dig up any of the other graves?"

"No," Savich said. "Not yet."

Dirk nodded and waved to the huge hole in the ground. "She moved something out of here. All we've got is a big hole recently filled in with dirt."

"Any blood? Any clothes?"

"No, nothing, but don't give up yet. If there were bodies thrown in that hole, we might still find something. Damnedest thing. To look around, this seems a peaceful-hidden-valley sort of place, an old-fashioned little American town where you expect to find some rustic charm, not missing bodies.

"Lori is taking soil samples, looking for traces of blood and human remains, which I don't think she'll find. She'll also be checking to see if the soil comes from here or somewhere else. If the soil is clean, you can bet it was brought in."

"When they moved the bodies," Sherlock said, "I doubt they took them far. Who'd want to take the chance, too great a risk of discovery. On the other hand, this valley is pretty large."

"Not much risk if the grave robbers are the sheriff and his deputies," Savich said. "They could have wrapped the bodies in a tarp and hauled them anywhere in the valley in the flat bed of the sheriff's truck."

"There's no sign of any recent digging anywhere else in the cemetery, so we're going to start checking the flower beds and anywhere else there's disturbed ground with GPR, ground penetration radar. I've called for a couple of cadaver dogs to complement the GPR, but if we don't find the bodies pretty close by, the cost builds up real fast."

Savich said, "I know. Do what you can, Dirk." He turned to Sherlock. "Well, things don't always go like you want them to."

44

ROCKINGHAM COUNTY HOSPITAL
NEAR TITUSVILLE, VIRGINIA
Late Wednesday afternoon

The nurse, skinny as a windowpane, with salt-and-pepper hair and a no-nonsense stride, was pushing against Blessed's hospital room door before Ox could roar to his feet and shout at her, "Hold on there. I haven't seen you before." He grabbed her skinny arm. "Who are you? What do you want?"

She stared up at him with a face scrubbed clean of makeup. He swore for an instant that he saw a five-o'clock shadow on her jaw—no, couldn't be. He shook his head as she said patiently, "I'm Nurse Eleanor Lapley. I work here. I just came on duty. Who are you?"

"I'm with the sheriff's department, here to guard the maniac strapped down to the bed inside. Do you know about him?"

"Of course. First thing when I came in, they showed me that film about him. Kind of hard to believe. Seems to me it might have been faked, don't you think?"

"Nothing was faked."

"If not, then he's quite something, isn't he?" There was admiration in her deep voice. *Not good.*

Ox said, "I'll go in with you. What do you need to do?"

"Check his vitals, see that he's not in pain, the usual."

Ox nodded and pushed the door open.

It was the last thing he remembered.

When Ox woke up he was lying on his back, strapped down to Blessed Backman's hospital bed, his eyes covered, his wrists strapped to the bed railings. He opened his mouth and yelled.

An orderly burst through the door, stood stock-still, and stared down at him.

"Whoever you are, get this blindfold off me and the straps."

"I can't, sir. I saw that film; I saw what

you do to a person. I'm not even coming close."

Ox managed to still his panic. He forced calm and reason into his voice. "Listen to me. Blessed Backman is in his mid-fifties, a skinny little guy. I'm not. Somehow he got me. That nurse—"

"What nurse?"

"Nurse Eleanor Lapley, she said her name was."

"Okay, there isn't a nurse Eleanor Lapley, not unless she started thirty minutes ago and nobody told me."

"For God's sake, look at me. Do I look like Blessed Backman?"

"Well, no, sir, but—"

"Get me loose, now! Blessed Backman's escaped. We've got to get him back."

"But—"

"You idiot! I'm thirty-three years old and I weigh two hundred pounds! Look at me!"

The orderly freed him.

Ox looked up at Savich's video camera. Where was Dr. Hicks? He pushed past the orderly and looked into the next room. Dr. Hicks was unconscious but alive, the video equipment mangled.

He knew the only official security in the

small hospital was at the front entrance, so he didn't bother alerting hospital staff. He got hold of Ethan three seconds later.

". . . This nurse, Ethan, I swear to you she had a five-o'clock shadow. I know Agent Savich told you Grace was probably here. I know it sounds weird, but do you think Nurse Lapley was somehow Grace?"

Ethan thought his brains were going to scramble. "I suppose it had to be Grace. He got in through hospital security disguised as a nurse, only I guess he couldn't quite make it realistic enough . . . A bad disguise? I sure hope so, because if it wasn't a disguise . . . no I don't want to think about that. Another couple of minutes and you would have suspected, but Grace was fast, got into the room and pulled off Blessed's blindfold, and that's why you don't remember what happened. . . . Get all our people out to my place. That's where Joanna and Autumn are. He'll head there, you know it. I'm on my way right now." A moment later, Ethan was back on his cell phone, and Joanna's phone was ringing.

"Hello?"

"Joanna, this is Ethan. Blessed's escaped, with the help of his brother Grace.

Get Autumn out of there right now. Drive back toward town. I'll meet you halfway."

She didn't say a word, punched off.

Five minutes later when he saw her rental car barreling toward him he honked and pulled his Rubicon over on the shoulder.

Joanna's first words were "I should have killed him. Dammit, I should have killed him."

Autumn was white-faced and silent, plastered to her mother's side. "Get in." He threw the passenger door open and Joanna lifted Autumn inside, jumped in beside her. "I don't have a gun. We just ran."

"I do; don't worry." That was about the stupidest thing he'd ever said. "There's a rifle in the box under the front seat. I'll take that; you can have my Beretta."

He patted Autumn's shoulder. "It'll be all right, kiddo."

If Autumn didn't believe him, he didn't blame her. He pulled his Beretta off his waist clip, handed it butt-first to Joanna.

"Where are we going?"

He saw an ancient Ford Escort in his rearview mirror, closing fast. He didn't have to see for sure who was in the car. It was Blessed and Grace. Had to be.

"Hang on," he said, and pressed down hard on the accelerator.

The Rubicon pulled away smoothly on the windy two-lane highway, and soon they were far enough ahead so Blessed couldn't see them around the turns. Ethan pulled off fast onto a potholed fire road that led straight into Titus Hitch Wilderness, not the front entrance with the ranger kiosk but a narrow dirty path barely wide enough for the Rubicon. It came to an abrupt stop at the Sweet Onion River. If they were lucky, it would take Blessed and Grace a good long time to find out where they'd gone. But they would find them, Ethan knew it.

"Let's go."

Joanna said, "You know where we are; that's good. Where to?"

"We're going to head on foot into the Titus Hitch Wilderness. We can't go back where we came from, and going forward is better than staying here. I know these woods well, know a good spot to stop."

"Ethan, what are we going to do in the wilderness?" Autumn asked him.

He looked at the mother, then at the daughter, and said, "We're going hiking."

He pulled his bolt-action Remington 700

out of his gun box. It was a gift from his father when he was twelve years old—to make a hunter out of him, his father had said. Ethan had learned to shoot the bolt action, loved the rifle as a matter of fact, but he hadn't stayed with hunting. He preferred to paint animals and take their pictures rather than shoot them.

He grabbed two boxes of boattail bullets. He had only forty rounds. He had to be careful. He said, more to himself than to Joanna, "The clip is already loaded—ten rounds, so that gives us fifty rounds." He looked up at her. "This baby is slow, but it's really accurate at distance. Here's two magazines, Joanna, fifteen rounds each, for the Beretta."

He thought about setting up a blind, shooting Blessed from a good hundred yards away, far enough away to be safe. But what about Grace? Was he good at disguises, or was he something else entirely? Ethan was very afraid he knew the answer to that.

He walked to the back of his truck, opened a metal storage trunk, and hoisted on a heavy backpack. He passed a smaller one to Joanna. "Okay, guys, let's get out of here."

Ethan led them along the edge of the Sweet Onion River, through lush water reeds, to a narrow slice of water only ten feet wide, with black stepping stones that he himself had laid fifteen years before, for a dry crossing. "Okay, Joanna, you go first, then Autumn. I'll come across last."

"Why don't we pick up the black rocks so they won't know where we've crossed?"

He said simply, "I want them to know."

Joanna looked at his rifle, then back up at his face.

When they reached the other side of the river, Ethan pulled out his cell and dialed Savich. "We won't have service for much longer."

Two rings, then, "Savich."

"Ethan here. Grace sprang Blessed. If you want the full story, call Ox. Joanna, Autumn, and I are heading into Titus Hitch Wilderness, a place I know better than you know Washington."

"We just left the Backmans' place. No bodies to be found, so they moved them. Do you want us back there?"

"You can't get to us out here any more easily than they can," Ethan said. "It has to end, Savich. I hope to end it here."

"He can't stymie me, Ethan."

"There's no time."

"Can you get a distance shot?"

Ethan grinned into his cell. "Exactly what I'm hoping for. We're going to keep moving and then camp for the night. If we don't run across them, I'm planning to lead Joanna and Autumn out across the north boundary in the morning."

"Have you called your deputies in after you?"

"No. I thought about that, but I want the only one trailing us to be Blessed. I don't want to take the chance he'd stymie my deputies. Call Ox and let him know, will you? We've got to move."

There was a pause, then, "Good luck, Ethan."

Ethan pocketed his cell phone, then turned to Joanna and Autumn. "Either of you need to rest, you just holler, okay? We're going to be going through some pretty rough terrain. I'm the only one without good footwear." He kicked a stone with the toe of his low-heeled boots. "Your sneakers will be fine. Stay close. We've got a ways to go before we get to Locksley Manor."

One of Joanna's eyebrows went up. "Robin Hood's house?"

"You'll see," Ethan said, and took the lead.

He pictured Mr. Spalding hanging in that tree, the bear ripping him down. He had no intention of ending up like him. He prayed they wouldn't run into hikers. He prayed harder that any hikers didn't get close to Blessed and Grace.

They walked a few hundred yards on narrow trails until Ethan hooked off-trail to the right, and they walked, always upward, through thick brush dotted with brilliant daisies and jasmine.

45

BRICKER'S BOWL, GEORGIA
Late Wednesday afternoon

"We need to go back to Titusville, Dillon. We can't leave Ethan on his own, even if he asked us to."

"We'll be on a flight this evening, Sherlock," Savich said, and turned the Camry onto the main road, heading east from Bricker's Bowl. "Right now I've got a surprise for you."

"Anything to make this headache go away."

"How about MAX found the address of the Children of Twilight?"

"He's been working on that for days. You're not kidding me?"

He shook his head. "Nope, got it."

"Oh, yeah, that'll do it." She snapped her fingers. "Headache's gone in four-point-five seconds. How did MAX find out where they're located?"

"Whistler's mother."

She punched him in the arm.

He grinned. "MAX couldn't find any property in Caldicot Whistler's name, so we dug into Caldicot Whistler's anteced-ents, his father, then his mother. Father's dead, so is the mother, but I had him do a property search within a hundred-mile ra-dius of Bricker's Bowl, flag anything that might be suspect. He finally found a good-sized property hidden within two holding companies, the first under the proprietary name of the second. That second compa-ny's name was listed as C. W. Huntingdon, Limited. The initials C.W.—as in Caldicot Whistler—triggered MAX's algorithm, and he went for it. Underneath all the layers, MAX discovered the property actually be-longed to Mrs. Agatha Whistler as sole trustee. She inherited it from her husband when he died some fifteen years ago. Al-though the trust isn't in the public record, it must have been passed to Caldicot when she died only last year at the age of eighty-five years. Caldicot is her only surviving child, now age fifty-two. Her other child was much older and is also dead.

"So Caldicot made a good stab at hiding the property, but MAX dug him out anyway."

The pride in his voice made Sherlock smile. "What sort of property is it?"

"An old flue-cured tobacco farm."

"What on earth is that?"

"Flue-curing is still used commonly on tobacco farms in Georgia, supposedly produces the best tobacco. Evidently they string the tobacco leaves onto sticks that they then hang from tier-poles in the curing barns. Then brick furnaces heat flues that 'cook' the green tobacco leaves.

"According to the deed, the farm was active until the nineteen thirties. There are two curing barns still standing after more than a hundred years, and a huge stone mansion, built in the early part of the twentieth century that now probably houses the cult. I can't imagine what other use Whistler would have for it. It's located about two miles outside of a small town called Peas

Ridge, ten miles from Haverhill, where Caldicot Whistler supposedly sells cars."

"May I ask when you worked with MAX on this?"

He shrugged. "I woke up early this morning, couldn't go back to sleep. You looked so happy in whatever dream you were having, I didn't have the heart to wake you. I already called Ethan about it."

Sherlock nodded. "He needs all the info he can get. Good job." She frowned at him. "You could at least act like you're a bit tired."

"Hot tea's my secret, you know that."

"All right, macho man, the Children of Twilight. I haven't told you where I think that name comes from."

"Yeah, you were going to tell me about that earlier."

"I found a couple hundred references to the name, but the one that caught my eye was a Children of Twilight group back in the fifteenth century in Spain, which was at the height of the Inquisition. They were called *Los Niños en el Atardecer* in Spanish. They'd been around for maybe a hundred years before that, living in isolation, causing no trouble.

"Torquemada himself went after the cult. You're going to like this—the Children of Twilight were all supposedly endowed with psychic powers."

Savich said slowly, "They wouldn't have called it that back then. How were they described?"

"Torquemada called them *Adoradores del Diablo*—devil worshippers—who communicated not only with each other but with the devil himself to further the devil's evil schemes."

"Not a good ending for them, I'll bet."

"No, not a good ending. Those Torquemada caught were burned at the stake. *Auto-da-fé*—an 'act of faith.' Isn't that lovely? Some escaped, but the group was never heard from again."

Savich said, "So if this present-day cult has taken up their name, that leads to an interesting conclusion, doesn't it?"

"The same direction Whistler's blog took us—a cult that glorifies psychics—and might risk a great deal for a child like Autumn. Of course, it could all be coincidence."

"Or maybe not."

A bullet whistled past Sherlock's head and spiderwebbed the windshield.

46

Savich shouted, "Hold on."

He got control of the car again, glanced into the rearview mirror at a small black Ford Focus not twenty feet back and saw the black barrel of a gun and the hand holding it coming out the passenger-side window. So there were two of them. He wasn't in his Porsche, he was in a Camry with regular gas in its tank, but it was a game little car. He sawed the Camry back and forth across the lanes, grateful there were no other cars in sight.

Sherlock slithered low across the seat as she pulled her SIG from her belt clip, then twisted around to look at the car behind them. Savich said, "Gun out the passenger-side window. They haven't fired again because they can't get a fix on us."

"Got it." She rolled down the window, leaned out, and yelled, "Now, Dillon!" She fired off three shots as he steadied the car, then he jerked the Camry hard to the left, through the other lane, nearly into the ditch, before he jerked it back. He heard the ping of bullets hitting the pavement and the car.

"I missed him. Hold steady again, Dillon!"

She emptied her clip this time. He wasn't surprised when the Ford began careening all over the road, out of control and gaining speed on the decline behind them. The driver had to be hit. He saw the shooter trying to shove the driver aside so he could get control. It was going to be close, because lumbering toward them, not fifty feet ahead, was an old silver pickup truck loaded with hay bales higher than its cab. Savich laid his palm on the horn, blasting loud into the hot late afternoon. Thank God the driver of the ancient pickup wasn't a slouch. He careened into the right lane and pulled over onto the shoulder, chewing tobacco furiously at them while they whizzed past.

A caravan of trucks and a Goldwing with a man and woman on board came around a wide bend in the road, going at a good clip. He looked at the Ford behind him, thick black smoke billowing from beneath the hood, and watched the shooter jerk the Ford hard to the right and peel off onto an unpaved country road he hadn't even noticed. He knew then they had to be locals, but he'd known that already.

Savich slowed and Sherlock fired another full clip after them, but they disappeared into a cloud of whirling dirt from the road. He had to wait for the spurt of traffic to pass, then he turned the Camry in a tight U and came in behind an old SUV, the last of the traffic he'd just let pass. All the vehicles had slowed and were rubbernecking, trying to see that smoking car. He laid his palm on the horn and got the finger in return. Finally he reached the country road and turned a sharp left onto the dirt road.

Sherlock was still hanging out the window, her hair whipping around her head.

She jerked back inside. "There, Dillon, behind that stand of trees on your left. They didn't get far."

He saw the black smoke before he saw the car. He braked fast and hard, closer than he wanted. Sherlock was out the door while the tires were still trying to grip the dirt.

"Careful," he shouted, pulled his SIG, and went out the driver's side, bent low, his eyes on the car.

The Ford exploded. No time, no time. The burst of heat singed their hair, seared the air itself, and the blast concussion hurled them backward. Savich grabbed her as they went down, protecting her as best he could, and rolled with her beneath the back of the Camry as burning pieces of the Ford rained down around them.

Sherlock, coughing and trying to suck in air at the same time, finally managed to whisper against his shoulder, "I really didn't mean to, but guess I got the gas tank. You think those guys are still inside?"

"Yeah, probably," he said. "Don't move." There were still hot flames and foul-smelling smoke gushing upward like black geysers, pieces of the car still hissing and exploding off the frame in the heat, setting nearby bushes on fire. Then there was silence, absolute silence.

Savich slowly eased from beneath the car, came up on his elbow over her, and studied her black face and the cut along her hairline, snaking a line of blood down her cheek. He touched the cut, saw it was superficial, and drew a deep breath.

"I'm okay, Dillon. How about you?" She was grinning at him, teeth whiter than his shirt had been before the explosion.

"I'm fine, but you're hurt."

"Just a little cut. My hair will soak it up. You're okay?"

He consulted his body parts, nodded. "Do I look as bad as you do?"

"Yeah, but you know, kind of black-ops sexy."

He pulled a handkerchief from his pocket and dabbed at the cut. It was indeed as shallow as he'd thought, nothing much really, thank you, God. He realized he'd been shaking. It had been too close, simply too close, and here she was cracking a joke. He grabbed her and pulled her hard against him on the ground, pressing her into his shoulder.

"I'm all right. Come on, Dillon, I don't want to, but we have to check to see if those guys are still in the car."

He wanted to hold her for at least another hour and breathe fresh air, tons of it, but fresh air would be in short supply here for a while, and the shooters could have gotten out of the car. He gave her a final squeeze, then they slowly got to their feet.

"Careful," he said. SIGs drawn, they made their way to the smoking ruin of the car.

Sherlock stepped around a burning running shoe with a foot in it and swallowed bile, swallowed again when she felt the heave coming. There was a smell of burned flesh mixed with the foul smell of burning plastic and gasoline. When she got ahold of herself, she said, "I guess they didn't get out."

Through the smoke they saw blackened remains huddled together in what was left of the front seat. Two men.

Savich pulled out his cell and called the Atlanta field office. "Beau? Savich. Sherlock and I have got ourselves a pretty gnarly situation here."

And he told the SAC, Beau Chumley, what had happened.

He said to Sherlock, "Guess we're not going to get to have dinner with the Children of Twilight."

They waited in their car, cleaned up as best as they could with water from Sherlock's fizzy water bottle. Savich tried Ethan several times but no go—no cell service that far out in the wilderness. He knew this, yet he tried once again. Then he looked at his wife and said slowly, "I'm dumb as dirt. I forgot about Autumn. Let's see if I can reach her." He closed his eyes and pictured her face in his mind.

Dillon? It's you, really you?

Hi, Autumn. What's happening?

We're resting for a minute, Dillon, so I can talk. What happened to your face?

Sherlock and I had a spot of trouble here in Georgia, but we're okay. I need you to speak to Ethan for me, okay?

That beautiful child with her hair in a ratty ponytail, and her mother's freckles marching across her small nose, giggled.

I'm going to be a TV.

Yep, with picture and sound. Okay, ask Ethan to tell me where you are.

Savich watched Autumn turn away from him. Oddly, he couldn't see anything else, only her profile, nor could he hear her speaking to Ethan. So did that mean Autumn couldn't see Sherlock? Autumn turned back to him. *Ethan says he's taking me and mom to Locksley Manor. He said it's a cave and he knows it real well. We're going to hide there.*

Savich knew exactly what that meant. Ethan would leave Joanna and Autumn in the cave and go after Blessed and Grace. Since that was what Savich would do as well, he couldn't say much of anything except, of course, warning him about not looking at Blessed, but Ethan knew that. Ethan also knew what he was doing. He knew the wilderness, and he knew what was at stake. He settled for asking Autumn to tell Ethan to be careful.

She nodded, turned away again.

A minute later she was back. *Mama is staring at me because she knows we're talking to each other and she doesn't want to believe it, but, well, she has to. Ethan told me to tell you he's got a plan, but he won't tell me what it is. I'm scared, Dillon. What's going to happen?*

What to say? Then he knew.

Sherlock and I are going to try to get

Blessed and Grace to leave the wilderness and come back fast to Georgia. Tell Ethan we're going to see Mrs. Backman again. Tell him we're going to cut off the head of the snake. You be brave, Autumn. I'm here when you need to speak to me.

She smiled at him, a smile filled with such hope and confidence—in him.

When SAC Beau Chumley arrived by helicopter an hour later at twilight, the local sheriff and his three deputies were already there, along with the white van of the county forensic team. The first words out of Savich's mouth were "Can you take over for us here, Beau? We've got to get back to Bricker's Bowl to arrest Mrs. Shepherd Backman." He looked toward the forensic team, who looked both grim and resigned, and was thankful he didn't have their job.

47

TITUS HITCH WILDERNESS
TITUSVILLE, VIRGINIA

Ethan cleared away enough brush so he could slip through onto a narrow stone ledge beneath an overhang and into the cave he'd named Locksley Manor when he'd been seven years old, reading Robin Hood and exploring with his grandfather. The cave was well hidden since he'd planted bushes all across the front of it, hoping to prevent hikers from finding it, which had worked, and keeping animals out, which hadn't. A bear hibernated in this cave most every winter, but it was August now and quite empty, thank God. It smelled like bear, not a bad smell, just thick, kind of oily. The chamber was small, unremarkable, really, giving no hint to the several magnificent chambers to be found deeper in the mountain, each of them with ceilings so high you couldn't see the top.

He made his way out through the bushes and brought in Autumn and Joanna. Then he pulled the bushes back into place, covering all signs of a cave entrance.

He pulled off his backpack as he watched Joanna and Autumn's faces in the pale light of their sanctuary. He said, "It looks pretty humdrum out here, but as it burrows farther back into the mountain, it becomes quite spectacular. I'll bring you guys back here to explore it. Let me show you the goodies I brought." He pointed to his bulging backpack that he'd slung onto the cave floor. "You never know when a tourist is going to get into trouble, and so all of us officers around here are prepared. My backpack is basically a survival kit— water, a half-dozen PowerBars, first-aid stuff, three of those high-tech sleeping bags that weigh a few ounces and keep you warm at twenty below. Not our problem, but it will get cold tonight, cold enough to appreciate them." He reached in the pack and pulled out a plastic bag. "And the most important, coffee and a couple of mugs."

"But we don't have—"

"Oh ye of little faith," Ethan said as he pulled out another small package and opened it. He took what looked like a metal disk, unfolded it into a cylinder, shoved another piece of metal into a bracket at the side, and within a few seconds he was waving a small pot in front of him.

Without thought, Joanna threw her arms around him. "That is miraculous, simply—"

She broke off, quickly stepped back, only to hear Autumn say, "I don't drink coffee but I think you're miraculous too, Ethan."

They all laughed. It felt good to smile, to feel a little wash of relief pour through you. It put the fear aside, if only for a moment or two.

Ethan looked at the stack of logs he'd left here last year. Above the logs were twenty-five deep scratch marks in the stone, marking each year since he'd found the cave.

He decided against lighting a fire, not

wanting Blessed and Grace to smell the smoke. He made do with a small Coleman burner just large enough to hold his pot.

Joanna boiled water, Autumn spread out the high-tech space sleeping bags, and Ethan checked all their weapons.

Ethan looked at the three sleeping bags in a neat line and said, "Here, Autumn, I've got your dinner. Eat slowly, you only get two bars, okay?"

It was quiet, and soon it was nearly dark in the deep wilderness. The trees were so thick that night fell quickly. Autumn fell asleep inside one of the sleeping bags, her hands cupped beneath her cheek.

When Ethan seated himself beside Joanna, his legs stretched out in front of him alongside hers, his back against the cave wall, he said, "Joanna, have you thought about how Blessed and Grace found you and Autumn here in Titusville?"

She shook her head, then sighed, leaned back against the cave wall. "Well, of course I have. I really don't know, Ethan, but I know without a doubt they'll find us. You know it too."

He nodded. "When Autumn was talking to Savich earlier, Savich told her to tell me he was going to see Mrs. Backman again, to cut off the snake's head."

"A good name for the old witch."

"Is he thinking it's Mrs. Backman who's the tracker, not Blessed and Grace, that she somehow directs them? Do you think that's possible?"

"I've thought about it, but when it comes down to that it's so outside anything that makes sense to me, to any of us, it makes my head ache."

"What we already know about them is remarkable enough. Truth be told, I don't know why they haven't tried to take over the world. What Blessed alone can do— why isn't he president? Or dictator of a small country?"

"I'm thinking he's got to have limits. Maybe he can stymie only a couple of people at a time. Maybe the hypnosis fades after a day, two days, whatever. Maybe there are a whole lot of people he can't stymie—both Dillon and Autumn can resist him, after all."

Ethan said, "Limits—that sounds reasonable, if anything can be considered reasonable about what Blessed does."

"And Grace. We don't even know what

he can do. It's interesting the Backmans never moved out of Bricker's Bowl to look for a larger canvas. Mr. Backman left but always came back, again and again. It's like they're somehow tied to Bricker's Bowl, they're afraid to leave, or can't leave."

Ethan poured them each another half-cup of coffee. "That's the end of it. Do you like it?"

"It's the best coffee I've had today."

He chuckled and raised his cup to hers in a toast. He paused a moment, then said, "I meant to tell you, Joanna, I really like your freckles."

Her hands immediately went to her cheeks. "Freckles, the bane of my existence. You said you like them?"

"Yeah, I do."

"They breed in the sun."

Her dark brown hair was pulled to the back of her head and held in a big clip. Hanks of thick hair fell around her face. He would have told her he liked her mouth too, and how her smile filled the very air with pleasure, but it really wasn't the time. He prayed there would be a time. He couldn't remember a more dangerous situation, and he knew he couldn't fail. It wasn't an option. Ethan watched her pull out the clip, smooth her fingers through her tangled hair, gather it all up again, and hook the clip back in. He said, "Autumn is the picture of you."

"What? Oh, no, she's beautiful. I've always thought she looked more like my mother."

"Nope, she's a copy of you. There's nothing of her father in her?"

"She'll look at you sometimes with her head tilted to one side, like she knows what you're going to say and is waiting for you to get on with it. That's her father. And when she's mad, her cheeks turn redder than a sunset. That's her father too."

"Ready to tell me about Martin Backman?"

She swallowed, shook her head.

Ethan waited, saying nothing more, and sipped his coffee, so thick with grounds now it was probably growing hair on his tongue.

"He was a mean drunk, that's what he told me when we dated, and that was why he didn't drink. He said something snapped inside him when he drank, and he lost it. He hadn't had a drink in seven years. I admired him because he'd recognized the problem and dealt with it.

"I was visiting some friends in Boston when I met him. I fell in love, married him right after I graduated from Bryn Mawr, and moved to the big bad city of Boston. Became a Patriots fan, and the Red Sox— you can't help but love them. Then Autumn came into our lives."

"What did your husband do?"

"Martin was in advertising."

"TV commercials?"

"Yes—television, primarily. People, humor, screwy situations, mostly. He was very good at it, very intuitive. He had a knack for knowing what would and what wouldn't appeal to people, and he was usually right. Not long after we married, he was made the head of the agency branch in Boston—he was only twenty-eight."

"Do you think his gift somehow played into this? Gave him an edge?"

"You're probably right. Sometimes it was scary how right-on he was. Autumn was four years old when his company wanted to bring him to New York—a big promotion, more money than you can imagine."

"What happened?"

"He went out with people from the firm in New York to celebrate and, without thinking, he drank a toast. He didn't stop, couldn't stop, I guess. He hit a man in a brawl with a chair, and the man died. He plea-bargained down to manslaughter and went off to jail to serve a minimum of nine years." She shrugged, staring down into her empty cup. "He was murdered in prison, stabbed by an inmate in the shower who turned out to be related to the man Martin killed in that bar.

"You want to know what was strange, Ethan? Autumn knew her father was dead before I told her. Not dead, necessarily, but that he wasn't there anymore. And she knew he would never be there again. She told me they spoke every single day, only I refused to accept it as being real even though I knew in my gut that it was, even then. I couldn't figure out why Martin had never told me about this gift of his, never told me about his family, refused to even speak of them. Now, of course, I understand.

"He didn't want me to know about any of it, even this so-called gift that terrifies."

Ethan took her fisted hand, smoothed out her fingers. "Autumn isn't her father. She's herself, and what she can do is a miracle."

She gave a hard laugh. "Yes, a real miracle."

He pulled her against him and pressed her against his chest. "Thank you for telling me. I'm very sorry. How long ago did he go to prison?"

"Nearly three years ago, up in Ossining. He refused to let either Autumn or me come to see him. He wrote to me every single week, although, of course, he must already have known everything that was going on, since he spoke to Autumn every day.

"By the time he died, I couldn't even remember his smile, and I felt guilty because maybe I didn't want to remember." She sighed. "It was all so pointless."

He smoothed his thumb over her eyebrow, traced his fingertips over the line of freckles. "I've been meaning to tell you, you look familiar to me."

She closed her eyes. "I did a TV commercial for a new kind of potato chip. It was a way to make some extra money."

"Was that you in the wheat field, chewing on this square, lacy chip?"

She grinned. "The director wanted the light just right so it would show up my freckles; he said they made me look like the girl next door. Do you know, those chips are quite good."

"I remember I bought a bag because of you."

He shouldn't have said that, he should get down to business, but not just yet. He leaned down, kissed her mouth. She tasted of oat and apricot PowerBar. "I'm very sorry for all that's happened to you, Joanna, both you and Autumn, but we'll get through this. I'm heading out now to find a good spot to watch for Blessed. It's the perfect night for it, hardly any moon but enough light for me to see. You watch over Autumn, all right?" He kissed her again and rose.

Joanna slowly got to her feet and faced him. He supposed he expected her to blast his plans but all she said, her voice quiet and calm, was "Yes, it's time. I'm going with you. I don't want to leave Autumn, but she'll be safe enough here. I'm hoping she'll stay asleep. She's a really good sleeper." She pulled her gun out of the back of her jeans.

"Mama? What's going on? Is Blessed here?"

48

BRICKER'S BOWL, GEORGIA

The car lights made the trees lining the Backman driveway shadowy; a light breeze made the leaves flutter.

The air was heavy, and star jasmine sent out its seductive scent.

Only forty minutes had passed since they'd left the burning car with its two dead killers inside. Savich and Sherlock, with two agents from the Atlanta field office behind them, saw the huge house, lights dotting the downstairs and the front veranda. Savich pulled the Camry to a stop, the two agents in the Toyota pulling up beside him. The four of them walked lock-

step up to the Backman porch. Standing
there were Sheriff Cole, and Mrs. Backman at his elbow, both now lit by several
lights suspended off the overhang. Tonight, Shepherd looked like a tough old
boot. Tonight, she looked like a very old
witch with her white hair loose around her
heavy face.

As for Sheriff Cole, he was still in uniform, looking determined. His hand rested
on his gun. Was the man insane? There
were four federal agents standing in front
of him. He felt Sherlock move closer. He
heard the two agents breathing fast.

Sheriff Cole slowly lowered his hand
from his gun, held it loosely at his side, and
gave them all a full-bodied sneer. "Well,
now, Miz Backman, isn't this ever a treat? I
thought we'd got rid of these outsiders."

Savich said, "Nope, the outsiders are
back. Best keep your hand away from that
weapon of yours, Sheriff."

"Nosy bad pennies," said Shepherd
Backman. "You can't get rid of them."

Sherlock said easily, looking from one
to the other, "Mrs. Backman, your mistake
was to try to get rid of us. The two men you
sent to kill us are dead. We're here to arrest

you for conspiracy to murder two federal agents."

To Savich's surprise, there wasn't a hint of awareness on Sheriff Cole's heavy face, there was only astonishment. The old lady sprang back. "Shoot them in the face, Burris! Kill them!"

"*What?* I can't shoot them, ma'am, I can't. We need to calm down here, think this over—"

"Do it!"

Savich saw the sheriff turn to look at the old woman, whose face was filled with malice and rage. She looked straight at the sheriff, and he at her.

Sherlock said, "Look at me instead of the sheriff. Mrs. Backman, don't tell him that again, or I will shoot you both dead. Then I will burn this damned house down. Do you understand me?"

Agent Todd stepped forward, his SIG in his hand.

"We've got it," Savich said over his shoulder. "Things are under control. Now, Mrs. Backman, I guess you didn't realize there are four of us, all FBI agents. You're coming with us to Atlanta. Trying to kill a federal agent is, naturally enough, a federal offense. The FBI doesn't like having its agents shot at."

Sheriff Cole stepped in front of her, blocking her from their view. "You can't do that, Agent. Miz Backman is a citizen of Bricker's Bowl, our leading citizen. Her roots are here. You can't take her. Whoever it is that shot at you, you don't have any proof."

Sherlock stepped into his face, raised her SIG up to his nose, and said very quietly, "Listen, Burris, if you don't want to share a cell with this malevolent old witch, I suggest you drop that gun to the ground. Now."

He wanted to drop-kick her off the veranda, belt the damned girl agent in the chops. But he knew dead serious when he saw it, and he believed her. He pulled the gun from its holster and dropped it. It thumped on the wooden veranda, bounced once, and came to a rest six inches from his foot.

"Now you will move yourself back six steps. I'll count them for you. Go!"

Sheriff Cole stepped back until Sherlock told him to stop, with his back pressed against the front door.

Agent Todd stepped onto the porch and

picked up the sheriff's gun, Dirty Harry's Magnum, one he'd like to own himself. He raised an eyebrow at Savich, who said, "If the sheriff behaves himself from now on, I'm willing to let him slide. I just want Mrs. Backman." He asked her, "Do you wish to make a call, ma'am?"

"Yes, to my lawyer."

Once again, he said, "Caldicot Whistler?"

She gave him a malignant look and shuffled away in her mules. The sheriff jumped to the side so she could open the door. She flung it open so hard it hit against the inside wall. Savich wouldn't have guessed she had that much strength. Savich watched her walk to where a phone sat on a lovely Victorian marquetry table. He watched her pick up the phone and dial.

None of the agents could hear what she said; none of them stepped inside the house. When she came back, Sherlock said, "Did you call your lawyer?"

"No," she said. "I called someone of far more help than that pitiful excuse."

Savich didn't care at the moment whether she'd phoned someone or used telepathy, so long as what she'd done would get

Blessed and Grace away from Titusville, away from Ethan, Joanna, and Autumn.

"Nice touch," he said to her, "using the phone like that."

She turned on him, head thrown back, and snarled at him through her teeth, "I'm going to boil you alive, you miserable shit."

Sherlock walked right up to her, got in her face. "Really, ma'am, that isn't at all polite. Now you're going to get cuffed." She unhooked the handcuffs from her belt and slapped the old lady's hands together.

Shepherd Backman lifted her face to the heavens and shrieked. That mad, guttural howl raised gooseflesh on their necks. Agent Ruley and Agent Todd stood still, watching the old woman, their SIGs drawn. Neither man could think of a thing to say.

49

TITUS HITCH WILDERNESS
TITUSVILLE, VIRGINIA

Autumn sat straight up. "Mama? You can tell me, is Blessed here?"

Joanna palmed her gun into Ethan's hand and moved quickly to kneel down beside her daughter. She touched her hair. "Blessed isn't here; everything's okay, sweetheart. You're safe."

Autumn looked from one to the other of them, her eyes too adult, too filled with an understanding she shouldn't have. "You're going with Ethan to go after them, aren't you, Mama?"

Joanna looked into her daughter's beautiful blue eyes. *Her* eyes? Ethan thought so. She stroked out some of the tangles in her hair. She needed a brush. "Ethan wants to go alone, but you and I both know that's too dangerous. One look and he'd be under. I want to be at his back, to keep him safe."

"Your mother is staying here with you, Autumn."

Autumn looked up at Ethan, again with too much awareness in her eyes. She said slowly, "Mama's right, Ethan. I'll be okay here. You take Mama and sneak up on them. I won't be afraid, I promise."

"It would be too dangerous for her," he said. "Joanna, you have to stay here and protect Autumn."

Autumn gave him a look that clearly said, *What a stupid thing to come out of your mouth, and here you are, an adult.*

Ethan said, "I don't like it."

"You can't keep me from following you, so we might as well go together," Joanna said, voice honey-smooth because she knew she'd won. How could she possibly consider taking a risk of dying as winning? He watched her hug Autumn hard against her, heard her say against her hair, "You stay here and wait for us, all right? We'll be back. I promise you."

"Be careful," Autumn said, and looked toward where her sneakers were lined up next to her silver sleeping bag.

Once outside the cave, Ethan and Joanna made sure the bushes covered the entrance without any trace they'd been there. Ethan said, "Even if Blessed accidentally comes along, even if he tracks her near here, he won't know where she is, precisely, because he can't see the cave entrance in the dark."

Joanna prayed that was true. She knew he'd said that to convince both of them. She said, "It's too dark for you to track them. How are we going to find them?"

He said, "Tell me how experienced you are in the woods, Joanna. At night."

"At night it's pretty much been limited to leaving my tent to go to the bathroom. But I'm very good. I don't clomp around and trip over plants and bushes. I'm a shadow, a ghost."

He grinned.

"Seriously, I can keep up with you, Ethan. Where are we headed?"

"I told you I know this wilderness. I know they're after her, but even if they can somehow track her to this area, I don't think they'll even try to come for her tonight. It's too dark, they don't know the terrain, and any light they used would give them away. If all that's true, and they're not all that far away, I have a good idea where they would have stopped for the night." Without another word, Ethan started toward a cliff they'd skirted to reach the cave entrance.

"Be careful, Joanna. Now that it's dark, it's far more dangerous going down than coming up. From now on, don't talk." He picked up a dry branch as they made their way down the narrow winding path. When Ethan came upon a loose mess of rocks, he poked the branch at it, alerting Joanna. Neither of them stumbled. Ethan had excellent night vision, and Joanna kept close, copying his steps.

At the bottom of the cliff was a narrow creek that flowed into the Sweet Onion River, nearly dry now in the deep of summer. He decided they'd cross it right there, to get out of the clearing and away from the faint reflection of the water.

They made their way easily over smooth

stones in the creek bed, stones laid down by someone who'd traveled the wilderness before Ethan was born. The creek wasn't more than three feet wide at this point. When they reached the other side, Ethan turned and held out his hand to help her up a steep incline on the opposite side. She smiled at him and shook her head. He whispered, "It's a little rough here, be careful."

Joanna slipped once after all. His hand was there to grip her wrist and pull her up. He nodded to her when they reached the top.

He took them through a patch of underbrush so thick she didn't see how they'd get through, but Ethan managed to push forward steadily, not making much noise at all. He stopped and pulled her very close, whispered against her ear, "The land flattens out up ahead and opens up for a while. We'll walk where the trees are thick, so watch for branches."

Ethan knew the terrain so well he recognized individual trees as they moved in the intense darkness. It brightened only a bit when at last the trees thinned out and the few stars overhead came into sight. He leaned close again. "There aren't any trails within a quarter mile of us, then there's a nine-mile stretch of the Appalachian Trail through the wilderness. It's well marked. I'll wager Blessed and Grace are close to it. If they were following Autumn, this is the only way they'd come. I suppose they could have tried to get through that thick undergrowth, but not for long. They'll stay in the open, maybe at or near one of the campsites up ahead. You see movement, a shadow, tell me. I'm counting on them using a nice big flashlight sooner or later, long enough to give them away."

Ethan took them around the edge of several deserted clearings. They reached a mess of outcropping rocks blocking their way. Ethan said nothing, merely took her hand and somehow led her through them. If he told her he could see in the dark, Joanna would have believed him. She stayed very close, nearly matching his footsteps. He stopped suddenly and she bumped into his back. He nodded, pointed ahead.

She leaned around him to see—what? She kept looking. There, she saw it, a light, only a flash of light, but it was there, off to their right, maybe forty feet away, not more. Then the light winked out.

Gotcha, Ethan thought, and put his finger against his lips.

He led her in a wide circle. Ethan stopped every few steps to listen. Joanna couldn't hear or see anything. She said nothing. She felt her heart pounding, her breath catch in her throat. Truth be told, she'd rather have to fight a couple of black bears than Blessed and Grace. She knew they were close; she could feel them. She also knew what they could do to both her and Ethan with a single look. The flash of light they'd seen, it had to mean they weren't asleep. Did they sense Ethan was close? Did they sense her? Were they waiting? Was the flash of light bait?

Ethan whispered, "Stay here. Don't move. Don't even breathe."

She watched him slither between two scraggly pine trees, then he was swallowed up by the darkness. The night seemed to have turned blacker than the bottom of a witch's kettle.

She waited until she couldn't stand it. She took one step, felt his hand on her back, and nearly screamed. He said against her temple, "They're asleep, Joanna. We've got a chance now."

"But what about the flash of light?"

"One of them probably got up to relieve himself. We'll wait another ten, fifteen minutes, just to make sure."

He sank down to lean against an oak tree, Joanna next to him, and they waited. After a minute, she began to hear the night sounds return, a cricket, an owl hooting, small creatures moving in the underbrush.

They waited. Joanna was stiff with cold, but she didn't say anything. When she believed her teeth would begin chattering, Ethan rose, pulled her up beside him. They both stretched to get their muscles working again.

She followed him, her hand on his back, trying to move as quietly as he did through the underbrush, under the tree branches, trying not to trip on the rocks and the rotted vegetation. She could see only his outline in front of her. She heard a sound beside her foot and stopped suddenly. Ethan stopped too. It was a small animal, a possum or a weasel. Ethan smelled a whiff of smoke, the light taint of a burned-out campfire in the night air.

Close, they were very close. When they reached the edge of a small open space, not more than six feet across, Ethan saw the small fire they'd built was nearly out. There was no movement that he could see. On either side lay a sleeping bag. Everything was quiet, a postcard kind of night.

Another owl hooted. An answering hoot came quickly, then another.

The air was soft against their faces, soft and cold. Joanna shivered. She pressed against Ethan's back. He whispered, "They must have stolen the sleeping bags, if it's them. We'll have to shine a light. I'll take the sleeping bag closest to the fire, all right? You take the other. Remember, don't hesitate. If ever our lives will be on the line, it's now." He stared down at her for a long moment. He knew she couldn't see him clearly, but he could see her. He touched his palm to her cheek. She looked scared, and determined. It would be enough. "Let's do this and get back to Autumn."

She nodded, her throat suddenly dry as desert sand. She'd never really understood wanting to kill another person, but she understood now. She felt a wild need to kill Blessed, watch the life flow out of his mad eyes. Then at last Autumn would be safe. And Ethan, a man she'd known only for a week or so. That was amazing.

She stared at the unmoving sleeping bag not ten feet away from her. She thought she saw the shape of a head, but she couldn't make out who it was. It didn't matter.

They approached silently, their weapons raised, Ethan breaking away from her toward the closer sleeping bag.

Ethan felt something flutter behind him and froze. He knew without looking. He whipped the Remington up and whirled around, his eyes down, and fired.

He heard a little girl's scream of pain. He jerked his head up and looked at Autumn, standing not six feet from him at the edge of the trees, and she was bleeding, a gaping tear in her small chest, a river of blood flowing from her small body.

Joanna screamed her daughter's name but swung her gun around and fired down at the sleeping bag, again and again until the clip was empty. There was no sound, no movement. *Autumn—oh, God, no, no.*

"Ethan. Mama. Why did you shoot me?"

She was dead. Joanna had seen the huge bloody hole through her chest.

She was hearing her dead child's voice.

50

"Ethan, Mama, that's not me. I'm over here."

Ethan watched as the little girl he'd shot fell slowly to the ground onto her back, watched that little girl change—a second, that's all it took—like a shift in the air had lifted a veil, and Grace became himself. Ethan shook his head, not wanting to believe what his eyes had witnessed. It was madness, but it was nonetheless true. His life had flown out of control since these two had come into it. Grace lay on the ground, his hands pressing frantically down on his gut, blood and fluid seeping through his fingers, and he was hissing with pain.

Ethan yelled to Joanna, "Where is Blessed?"

"I shot him in his sleeping bag," Joanna said as she ran toward Autumn. "Finally he's dead, thank God, he's dead. I emptied my clip into him."

"No, you didn't, Joanna."

She whirled around, stared him right in the face.

"No!" Autumn screamed, and launched herself at Blessed. He turned to grab her small arm. He looked at Ethan as he jerked up the Remington. "You don't want to do that, Sheriff."

Ethan froze.

"Autumn, my little niece, my little sweetheart, it's all right now—no, it's not, I can't lie to you. He shot Grace, that sheriff shot your uncle, Autumn. Look at him, it's bad."

Blessed dragged Autumn to where his brother lay curled up on his side, his palms flat against his belly, his blood now gushing through his fingers, whimpering with pain. Gut shot, the sheriff had gut-shot Grace. Blessed knew if he didn't get him to the hospital fast, Grace would die. His guts would twist up, and they'd turn green and black, and Grace would rot. He would die screaming. Martin was dead, and now Grace. He'd always protected both of them, always paid back, with bloody interest, anyone who bullied them because they were different, because they were special. But the bullies beat his brothers up only once, because Blessed nearly killed them. And now Grace was shot, shot bad, in his belly. Blessed had failed him. He wanted to howl, to shriek, but not pray, never pray, because Mama had told him prayers from him could bring up the devil and then things would really get bad.

He stood there staring down at his brother, his brain squirreling about madly. He knew little Autumn was terrified, he couldn't blame her for that, but Grace was lying on the cold ground, weeping and screaming. What was he to *do*?

Grace's eyes fastened on his brother, tears running in dirty rivulets down his thin cheeks. "Blessed," Grace whispered. "Listen to me, Blessed. Kill me, kill me. There's no choice. Oh, Jesus, I can't stand it."

"Oh, no, no, you can't ask me to do that, Grace. No!"

"Do it, Blessed. I can feel the bullet in me, feel it burrowed deep. I know there's no way to get me out of here. I shouldn't have tried to fool the sheriff like that. He was afraid it was you, so he shot me before he looked at me, my fault.

"I love you, Blessed. Tell Mama I'll look down on her. Tell her I'll prepare a welcome for her and a special place for her. I know I'm dying, Blessed. Do it now, please, just do it now." Grace drew up his knees, still clutching himself, and turned his face away. His sobs were all they could hear in the silent forest night.

Blessed said to Ethan, "Give him a kill shot."

Ethan turned to Grace, brought up his Remington, and fired. The bullet struck Grace between his eyes. His body lurched up, then collapsed again. He died with his eyes open, his face riddled with pain, his hands still clutching his belly.

"Stand back, Sheriff."

Ethan took a single step back. Blessed pulled Autumn with him as he dropped to his knees beside his dead brother. He touched Grace's face, closed his staring eyes. "I'm sorry, Grace. This is gonna kill Mama, and she's gonna blame me even though it was what you wanted. I couldn't take you to a doctor, and you knew it." He leaned down and kissed his brother's tear-streaked face. Blessed straightened, swiped the back of his hand over his mouth, then turned to Ethan. "You killed my brother."

Autumn hit him with her fists, yelled in his face, "Don't you dare hurt Ethan or Mama! You monster, don't you dare!"

Blessed controlled his killing rage. He stared down in shock at the little girl, his own flesh and blood. "I'm not a monster. That's not a nice thing to say to your uncle."

"I hate you. I wish you weren't my uncle. I wish you were in hell. That's where you should be."

"I am your uncle and I love you." Autumn was hiccupping, tears streaming down her face. He thought for a moment and said slowly, "If you promise to come with me willingly, I won't kill them even though the sheriff did murder my brother. If you promise to let me and Mama teach you how to use your gift, I won't. Do you promise?"

Autumn looked at Grace and thought, *You're dead, you're dead, you're dead.* But

Blessed wasn't dead. He wasn't like her, that was a lie, he was a monster, and monsters could look like anybody they wanted to when they snuck into your dreams or crashed into your face. Autumn knew death was the end of things, like her father had gone away forever, and now Grace wasn't here anymore either, and that meant sometimes death was good. But Blessed—what should she do?

She looked at Ethan, then at her mother, both of their faces blank, as if they weren't there.

She heard his rough old voice saying again, "I promise I won't kill them, Autumn, I won't, if you do what I want."

Blessed's words fluttered over her. Autumn wanted to run to her mother, to shake her until she was back into herself again, and she jerked her arm to try to get away from him, but Blessed tightened his hold. She wanted her mother, she wanted her laughing and holding her, telling her everything would be all right. She nodded up at the old man whose eyes were hard and soft at the same time.

"Say it. Say, 'I promise, Uncle Blessed.'"

It was hard to get the words out, but she

did, finally. "I-I promise." She tried to say his name, but she simply couldn't. She hated his name, it scared her. Autumn lowered her head and cried. Through her hiccups, she whispered, "I want my mama back."

"You will have her, but just not yet," Blessed said. "Sheriff, you will dig a grave for my brother."

Ethan said, "I don't have a shovel."

Autumn's head snapped up. Ethan sounded like himself, it was his voice, but in a way it wasn't. His voice sounded dead, uncaring, flat as the strawberry pancakes she'd tried to make for her mother on her birthday.

Blessed said, "Then you will dig with sticks and your bare hands. Woman, you will help him. Both of you."

He loosened his hold on Autumn's arm. She ran to her mother, but Joanna ignored her, dropped to her knees beside Ethan, and began to dig, pulling up clumps of dirt and grass, tossing them as far as she could.

"Mama." Autumn pulled on her sleeve, but Joanna paid her no attention. Autumn grabbed Ethan's jacket, but, like her mother, it was as if he wasn't even there. "Come back, come back," she whispered, and couldn't even whisper anymore because her throat was clogged with tears. She drew back her fist and hit Ethan as hard as she could. He didn't flinch, he didn't react at all, he continued digging up dirt, big handfuls of it, throwing it over his shoulder. It was horrible what she was seeing, but Autumn couldn't do anything to stop it. She listened to the thuds of earth strike the ground. She didn't look at Grace; she couldn't. She fell to her knees and began to dig up clots of earth.

"Stop that! Come here, Autumn," Blessed said, and pulled her away.

"I'll help them. Let me help them. Let me dig too."

"No."

Blessed pulled Autumn down to the ground beside him and held her there. She sat beside the monster for what seemed like hours, watching her mother and Ethan dig a grave for Grace, and finally, so exhausted her brain finally closed down, she fell asleep.

When the grave was deep enough, Blessed wrapped Grace in a sleeping bag and told the sheriff to lay him at the bottom of the four-foot hole. He did.

"Now come out."

Ethan climbed out of the hole and stood silently beside Grace's grave.

Autumn slept, her face against her cupped hands. Blessed had taken off his jacket, covered her with it.

He said, "Now, both of you, fill the grave."

Throwing handfuls of dirt over Grace's body didn't take as long as digging his grave. When it was done to Blessed's satisfaction, he told them to stand respectfully on each side of Grace's grave. "Sheriff, you and the—" He took a quick look at Autumn, saw that she was sleeping soundly, and said, "You and the bitch will pray for my brother."

Ethan said, *"The Lord is my shepherd, I shall not want . . ."* After a moment, Joanna joined him.

Blessed thought of his mother, at the awful soul-tearing grief she'd feel, and felt his throat clog. He prayed she'd understand. She had to. He'd had no choice. He listened to the smooth, even cadence, a monotone really, no feeling to the words at all. At least they knew all the words. It was good.

Blessed slapped his hands against his arms. He was getting cold without his jacket, but that was all right, Autumn needed warmth more than he did. She was only a little girl, after all, so small and fragile, and she was his niece. She was important. He wished she understood. But it was too soon and the child was too young, too dependent on her mother, the bitch who controlled her. She would come to understand, to know he'd done the right thing. Blessed tucked his jacket more closely around her. He didn't want her to get sick. Autumn still slept—a blessing, Blessed thought, and smiled at the irony of it—a blessing, and that's what he was, that's what both his mother and his father had told him. His smile fell away. How was he to tell Mama the story hadn't ended right, that another one of her sons was dead, dead because of the sheriff?

My fault, Grace had said. No, it wasn't Grace's fault, Blessed would never accept that. Grace had a gift, he was good, his soul was in heaven with Martin. Was Martin in heaven? He hoped so, but he'd been away from his family for so many years, nearly half his life, and Mama had finally said, *Let him go, let him go, he'll come back, on his own.* But Martin had been corrupted, all her fault, and then the bitch had brought him home in an urn.

And now Grace was dead too, and he'd rot inside that sleeping bag covered with a mound of heavy black dirt because he'd been doing what he had to do. It hadn't turned out right. It had all gone wrong and Grace was dead. He'd lie out here forever.

It wasn't right.

Blessed felt his rage build until he shook from the inside out. It was so strong, his need to kill both of them, to wipe them away as if they'd never existed. It would be hard with Autumn, though, if he broke his word to her. He didn't know what she'd do, and Mama said he had to get her back. She had to have Martin's daughter. He looked at them. They were filthy, covered with Grace's grave dirt. He supposed he couldn't leave the wilderness with them looking like this.

"Take us to the nearest stream, Sheriff."

Blessed picked Autumn up in his arms and followed Ethan and Joanna. Thankfully, she still slept because those two had exhausted the poor child, dragging her through the wilderness, probably not giving her enough to eat or drink in their rush to get her away from him and Grace. The sheriff seemed to know where he was going, even in the dark. Blessed was impressed.

51

ATLANTA, GEORGIA
Thursday morning

An orange glow lit up the gray dawn sky. Even this early there was lots of traffic on the road, mainly trucks and vans. They checked into a small Hilton because they were both exhausted, but sleep didn't come. Sherlock finally sat up. Hazy morning light now filled the room. She saw Dillon was awake, staring up at the ceiling.

"We've got Shepherd out of circulation," she said with satisfaction. "She's behind bars, scaring her fellow inmates with her chants."

Savich turned his head to look at her.

He smiled. "When she screamed at one guard, I thought he was going to faint."

"See? We did good. You told Ethan we were going to cut off the snake's head and we did." She kissed his ear, then looked toward the windows at the bright morning sky. "Well, I don't think sleep is going to happen." She called Ox's cell and, glory be, got through to him. She turned on the speaker and Ox told them they were getting ready to go in since it was light enough now. But Ox sounded really worried.

"I'll call you guys as soon as we find them, or I know more."

She told him about Shepherd in jail in Atlanta, then, "Ox, we think Blessed and Grace are headed back home, to Bricker's Bowl. Please keep in touch."

When she punched off her cell, Savich said, "I've tried to call Autumn, but there's no answer." He sighed. He was scared for them, really didn't see a good outcome here if Ox and all the rest of the deputies hadn't heard from them. Then again, there wasn't much reception in the wilderness.

Sherlock was right. They'd had one victory. He thought of everyone's shock when they first saw the little old lady in cuffs, being hauled into booking. The chanting and screaming took care of the shock. Shepherd was tucked away tight. That left Grace and Blessed. He felt panic nibbling away and wanted to smack it out of his head. Well, he'd gotten what he'd wanted. He'd bet his gym membership Shepherd had somehow contacted Blessed and Grace.

He had four FBI agents at Bricker's Bowl, staking out the house, waiting for them to come back. But what if they didn't come back? Maybe Joanna and Ethan were both dead. No, Savich couldn't accept that, he simply couldn't. He had to stop this, he was driving himself crazy.

He said, "I wish Autumn would pick up my call." He gathered Sherlock against him and they fell into an exhausted sleep.

It was near eleven o'clock in the morning when Savich's cell phone sang out Rihanna's "Umbrella."

It was Ollie Hamish. Just as Sherlock had done with Ox, Savich turned on the speaker.

"Savich, everything's okay, let me say that first off. Lissy Smiley and Victor Nesser somehow found your home address. As you know, we've been keeping your house under watch. Dane Carver and Jack Crowne spotted them trying to sneak around to the back just after dawn this morning. They spotted each other, actually. They'd managed to get back to their car and floor it out of there before Dane and Jack could bring them down. Lissy was hanging out the passenger-side window, shooting at them for all she was worth. Victor knocked down a couple of mailboxes and mangled a kid's bike on the way. Thank God none of your neighbors were up and about yet.

"Jack told me it was a wild honker chase, with a half-dozen local cop cars joining in. They left an injured pedestrian and a small Volkswagen flipped over on its side near the Potomac, and got across the bridge before we could close it. Then they drove right into the gates of the Arlington National Cemetery."

Savich was gripping his cell. It was hard to be silent and wait and listen. He wanted to shake the words faster out of Ollie's throat. Finally, he couldn't stand it. He said, his voice flat, "They didn't get them. Lissy and Victor got away."

"So far," Ollie said. "They blew out a rear tire driving over the grass and bushes, knocked over some of the grave markers, and skidded into a tree. Dane said the car was totaled, both front and back windshields shattered from gunfire. But Lissy and Victor were out and away before they reached the car."

Savich said, "That means they'll have to get a car, and they'll carjack one if they have to, doesn't matter how many people are around."

"Yeah, we've got local police patrolling the streets within a mile of Arlington National Cemetery, setting up a perimeter, checking all the houses. You know, Savich, Lissy can't be back to one hundred percent yet, so she's got to slow them up. We may get them yet."

But Savich wasn't at all sure about that. It was a whole lot easier being a killer than a cop—cops had to follow rules. Lissy and Victor could have grabbed a car and been on the road again in five minutes, if they were willing to create havoc—and they were indeed willing, Savich knew. They didn't care what they left in their wake. Lissy would kill everyone in the car if it would give them a few minutes before the bodies were discovered.

Dane, Jack, and Ollie knew it too.

Savich said, "I'm an idiot. I should have had Sean and Gabriella moved out right away, but I didn't think there was a chance Lissy and Victor would be back so quickly. Sherlock and I were going to Titus Hitch or maybe back to Bricker's Bowl, we weren't sure yet exactly where, but not now, not with those two running around in Washington. We're coming home, Ollie, as soon as we can."

Ollie knew he'd do the same thing; he'd run all the way back if he had to, to ensure his child was all right. He said, "I understand. Listen, our agents will continue the watch on your house in Georgetown. Go to the airport. I'll call you as soon as I have a couple of reservations for the first flight to Washington. Listen, guys, Sean's okay."

When he flipped off his cell, Savich felt Sherlock's warm breath on his neck. "That was too close, Dillon, way too close. They're not going to give up. Lissy won't stop until she's in handcuffs or she's dead."

"I agree. Revenge is what's driving her, nothing but rage and revenge. If Lissy's driving the horses, and I think she is, we can expect more crazy behavior and not much planning. What they did early this morning—trying to break into our house in Georgetown, the sheer craziness of it— scares me to death."

"We've got to try to find them before they try another attack. And the fact is, we don't know where Ethan and Joanna and Autumn are right now. But maybe we can get Victor and Lissy."

"It could be," Savich said slowly, "that Victor's really scared, that he wants to find a rock and crawl under it. But not Lissy, never Lissy. Still, even though we know she's the alpha dog, I'm betting they're going to go back to Winnett." He shook his head, shrugged. "But what do I know?"

"You know it in your gut, don't you?"

He nodded, and she kissed him and tossed him his pants. "Let's get dressed and get to the airport. We'll have a better idea of what's going on after we get home."

Savich thought about Autumn. He tried contacting her once again before they boarded the plane, but she didn't answer.

52

GEORGETOWN, WASHINGTON, D.C.
Thursday

Savich held Sean close, smoothed his fingertip over his boy's left eyebrow. He felt such blessed relief that he was all right. Sherlock was tickling his ribs. Sean was laughing and yelling at Astro to save him. Astro was jumping on them, yipping his head off, his tail whipping back and forth so fast it was a blur.

Savich smiled over at his mother, who stood close, watching and smiling too, a plate of chocolate-chip cookies in her hand. Behind her stood Congressman Felix Monroe from Missouri, a widower of ten years, and he too was smiling as he watched.

Savich didn't know the congressman well, since he'd just begun seeing his mom. Savich felt funny about it but knew he shouldn't. He looked over at his mother, saw the worry in her eyes that she managed to hide from Sean.

Dillon? Are you there? Where are you, Dillon?

Savich said, "Sherlock, take this monkey, stuff a cookie in his mouth. I've got to take a call."

"Autumn?"

He nodded.

"Thank God. Go, Dillon. Hey, sweetie, let's go scarf down some of your grandmother's cookies, okay? I can see Felix is drooling for some, too."

"Astro loves cookies," Sean told Felix. Sean considered Felix cool since he'd showed him how his iPhone worked.

"Your mom's right. I do too," Felix said. "Your grandmother makes the best I've ever eaten."

"But you can't give Astro any chocolate, Sean, it'll make him sick."

And naturally, the first question out of Sean's mouth was "Why?"

Savich walked swiftly from the living room,

down the hallway toward the kitchen, and into the half bath on the main level of his mother's house. He closed the door, then closed his eyes for the simple reason that it immediately cut all distractions. *Autumn? Are you all right? Your mom? Ethan?*

He saw her then, clear as day, her back pressed against a wall, her legs drawn up to her chest, her hair in a tangled ponytail, tear streaks dried on her pale cheeks. She didn't look hurt, but she did look wrung out.

Tell me what happened.

Blessed guessed I called you before, Dillon, back at Ethan's house. He told me he'd kill Mom and Ethan if I called you again, so I couldn't take a chance until now. We're in a motel somewhere. I'm in the bathroom. I heard him tell Ethan and Mama that we were going back where I belonged. I don't belong at that bad place with my grandmother, do I, Dillon?

No, of course not. I won't allow that, Autumn. Neither will Ethan and your mama. Tell me how you managed to call me now.

Blessed wanted to go to sleep, so he tied Mama and Ethan to chairs. I think he was afraid if he left them and went to sleep he couldn't control them anymore. He locked me in the bathroom, told me he'd know if I called you, but I don't believe him. He doesn't know, does he, Dillon?

No, he doesn't know. It's all right. Thank God Ethan and Joanna were alive. *Good, Blessed's asleep. Is Grace there?*

No, Dillon. Grace is dead. Ethan shot him with his rifle.

One down. *Do you know where this motel is? Did you see the name of the motel?*

She thought and thought. He saw tears come to her eyes.

Too much, too fast. She was just a little kid, a couple years older than Sean, and here he was questioning her like he would an adult. But again, he saw she was looking thoughtful, focused. He felt a strong pull of affection for her, and admiration. She was smart, she had grit. Even this young, she hadn't frozen.

Did you drive a long time, Autumn?

I don't know, Dillon. I slept because I

was so tired. I think Blessed did all the driving. I don't know why he didn't have Ethan or Mama drive. Maybe you can't drive when you're stymied.

That's possible. Tell me about the highway you were driving on. Was it big? Lots of lanes going both directions?

Yes, it's real big, with a million cars. Blessed pulled off an exit and bought us some Wendy's hamburgers, then he looked at a motel across the road, but he shook his head and drove onto this old road. He pulled up to this motel.

Did you see the name of a town?

I don't think so.

Did you see the name of the motel?

She frowned and her fingers began to fret. *I can't remember it, just some old sign—it's orange and some letters are missing.*

If only he could help her remember. *Autumn? I want you to close your eyes and listen to my voice, okay? Don't worry about Ethan or your mama, don't worry about anything, just try to relax and listen to me. Will you try?*

She nodded, then cocked her head to one side and obediently closed her eyes.

Good girl. Now, get comfortable, that's it, lean back against the wall, put your hands on the floor, and pretend you're floating in a swimming pool.

Bless her, she did exactly what he said. He saw her small hands, palms up, on the cracked linoleum floor beside her. He watched her fingers uncurl.

Autumn?

Yes, Dillon.

That's really good. Now, you were eating your hamburger. In the car?

Yes. Blessed went in and brought back bags of food. I was sitting in the front seat beside Blessed. Mama and Ethan were in the backseat. They were just sitting there, like they were dead, but they're not—

He saw her breathing hitch, saw her stiffen up. *It's okay, sweetheart, it's okay, I promise. Your mama and Ethan will get through this. That's it, just don't worry about anything right now, listen to my voice. That's right, that's good. You were eating, all right? Did you have mustard on your hamburger?*

No, Dillon, I like catsup, lots of cat-sup. I squeezed a whole bunch from

those little plastic packets, more than Mama usually lets me have. I know it's bad, but—

A little more catsup is all right, your mama wouldn't mind. Was your hamburger good?

It was real good. Blessed was eating a hamburger too, and a bag of french fries, but he didn't put catsup on them. All Mama and Ethan did was stare straight ahead and eat. I wanted to talk to Ethan and Mama, but when I turned around they didn't even look at me.

I know, sweetheart, I know. Now, Autumn, Blessed started up the car again, right? And he drove away from the highway.

She nodded, never moving. *Yes. He drove us down this little road, but just a little ways. Then he smiled, and he pulled into this bumpy parking lot and stopped the car by the office. He has a horrible smile, Dillon.*

I know. I've seen it. What kind of car are you in, Autumn? He held his breath, this was right out of the blue, he couldn't really expect her to know, to even under—

It's a white van. He had Ethan steal it out of somebody's driveway not long after we left Titus Hitch.

Okay, you were sitting in the front seat in front of the motel. Did you see a sign?

Yes.

Describe it to me.

It's kinda old, a real ugly orange color, and the sign isn't hanging exactly straight.

Now, the name, look at the name. Can you read it?

It's two words, but I've never seen them before. I can't read them.

Picture it in your mind and show it to me.

Where had that come from? And then he saw that orange sign, couldn't believe it, but there it was, bright and clear right before his eyes. She was right, there were some letters missing.

LIZ RD'S HIDEA AY.

He's coming, Dillon, he's coming! He's going to know and he'll kill Mama—

No, he won't. Look up now, Autumn. That's right. Everything is fine. Go wash your hands in the sink. Keep washing until he comes in and sees you. You went to the bathroom, okay? You're fine, sweetheart. Go.

53

Fifteen minutes later when Savich and Sherlock walked to his Porsche, he heard his boy singing at the top of his lungs in an off-key duet with his grandmother. It was recognizable—Bobby Darrin's "Beyond the Sea," the closing song to one of Sean's favorite movies, *Finding Nemo*. Even though he was hyped, nearly running, Savich turned back and smiled when he heard Felix's baritone join in.

His Porsche roared to life. He was backing into the street when Céline sang out "Nature Boy."

He said into his cell, "Savich here."

"Ollie here, Savich. Lizard's Hideaway is in Tennessee, thirty miles from Chattanooga, right off Highway Seventy-five. What do you want to do?"

Good question. "It's too dangerous to send a fleet of local cops to the motel; they might end up shooting each other or Autumn. I think Blessed is driving home to Bricker's Bowl." Savich knew he was the best person to bring Blessed down.

He said, "Ollie, how about you get some agents from the Chattanooga field office, have them follow Blessed but emphasize they're not to be seen, and they're not to try to take him down. Okay?"

"You got it. Now about the car they're in—"

"A white van; I don't know the license plate number."

Ollie was silent. "Okay, we'll get the highway patrol involved. When we identify the van, we'll have agents follow them."

"Good. Call me as soon as they're spotted. I want to know where they are all the time, okay?"

"Not a problem." Savich heard Ollie draw in a deep breath. He knew it was about Lissy and Victor, and he knew he wasn't going to like what Ollie said.

"I've got an update on Victor and Lissy. Dane called to tell me a resident living three blocks from Arlington National Cemetery phoned 911 about a hysterical neighbor boy who'd run over to her house shouting that his parents were bleeding all over the kitchen floor.

"The dad will survive, but the mother is iffy, headed for surgery. Of course their car was gone, a red 2007 Chevy Cobalt. The little boy said the car is real pretty and shiny. His mother calls it Honeypot." Ollie's voice broke. "This shouldn't have happened, dammit. We're going to get them, Savich."

"Thank you, Ollie. At least we have the description and the license plate. Keep in touch." And Savich punched off his cell and told Sherlock what had happened.

"Honeypot," she said, shaking her head. "Thank God that little boy isn't going to be an orphan. Thank God Lissy didn't try to murder him too. But his mother Dillon, I can't stand it."

Savich thought it made more sense the child had been upstairs and Lissy simply hadn't known he was there. He didn't credit her with a crumb of conscience. He found himself praying for the mother to survive.

He said, "Lissy and Victor aren't going to give up, Sherlock." His fist hit the steering wheel. "It's my fault, that family is all my fault, no one else's." And he knew in that moment he had to make one of the most difficult decisions he'd ever have to make, but not right now. Now there was nothing to do but wait.

Four hours later, Céline sang out "Nature Boy" again.

Savich and Sherlock were in the CAU on the fifth floor at the Hoover Building. When Savich punched off, he said to Sherlock, "That was Agent Cully Gwyn. Lissy was spotted at a Kmart north of Winnett, North Carolina. He and Agent Bernie Benton are covering Victor's apartment building in Winnett. He wants to know what I want him to do."

"You know what to do," Sherlock said.

And Savich made his decision.

54

When Ethan woke up, for one terrifying moment he didn't know who he was. He only knew he wasn't where he had been, and he was now someplace different, someplace he didn't recognize.

Memory flooded back. He was Ethan Merriweather, and he'd been—away. He felt a spurt of fear, then forced himself to think, to remember. He had a rip-roaring headache, and it pounded so hard it was difficult to focus, but he did, and he remembered. He saw himself at the campsite in Titus Hitch Wilderness, remembered whirling about, bringing his Remington up fast to shoot Blessed but not fast enough. Blessed had gotten to him. How much time had passed? What had Blessed made him do? Something inside him didn't want to know.

He saw sunlight coming around the edges of the draperies. That meant it was daylight, but how late? He knew he'd slept and awakened back into himself. So what did that mean? Blessed couldn't hold him beyond a certain number of hours? Sleeping broke the hypnosis, or whatever it was? *Joanna and Autumn.* They had to be all right if he was; surely he wouldn't have hurt Joanna, but he could have. Blessed could have told him to do anything and he'd have done it as fast as he could and to the best of his ability. Even murder. It was in that moment he realized he was tied to a chair, his hands behind his back, nearly numb. He tested the knots. They were solid. He gritted his teeth against the pain in his head and studied the room.

Cheap dresser, ugly brown draperies, threadbare and dirty, covering a set of skinny windows. The brown-painted door looked like a kid could shove it open. It smelled like air freshener. *A motel.* He was in a cheap motel. *Where?*

He heard slow, even breathing behind him. At first he didn't understand—it was Joanna and she was probably tied to the chair behind him, still sleeping or unconscious.

"Joanna?"

No answer. He worked his hands more but the knots held.

He heard a movement off to his left, turned his head quickly, and nearly groaned with the slicing pain in his head. Blessed stood not six feet from him. He looked taller than Ethan remembered when he'd been propped against the wall in his guest bedroom, a bullet wound in his shoulder, his mad eyes blindfolded to protect anyone who looked at him. Ethan froze, quickly looked down.

"You're awake, are you? No, I won't stymie you, but I could, real fast, you know that."

"Ethan!" Autumn ran to him and threw herself against his chest. "You're awake. Are you back again, Ethan?"

"Yes, sweetheart, I'm back."

"But maybe not for long, Sheriff," Blessed said.

Ethan said quickly, "Where are we?"

"You're in a lovely motel tied to a chair. The woman is tied to the chair behind you. She's still asleep. Don't worry about her; she'll come out of it when she's ready to. It's interesting that you woke up first. Usually women wake up faster. Grace always says—" Blessed broke off, swallowed once, then again. He rubbed his shoulder where Savich had shot him.

Ethan said, "You need to get that bandage changed, Blessed, or you might die of gangrene. It still hurts pretty bad, doesn't it? And how about your arm where Joanna shot you?"

"I'll be a lot better than you'll be when this is all over."

"I saw him take lots of aspirin," Autumn said.

Blessed walked to Joanna, slapped her face lightly. "Come on, you bitch, face me."

Autumn jumped back from Ethan and hurled herself at Blessed. "Don't you dare call my mama a bitch! My mama isn't a bitch. And don't you hit her again, you hear me? You're a monster, you're crazy. Leave Ethan alone. Leave my mama alone!"

"Now, now, Autumn, child, calm down." Blessed's voice had gone all low and soothing, but that sounded bizarre to Ethan, and evidently to Autumn too. Ethan could hear her hitting him, hear her panting, then Blessed must have grabbed her. "Calm down, Autumn, or I'll stymie the sheriff right now."

Silence.

He heard her fierce little voice: "Don't you stymie him again! Don't, or I'll run away from you, I'll hide, and you'll never find me."

"I can always find you."

"Then I'll go hide in another place and then another and another until you're dead. You're old, you'll die soon. Don't you dare stymie Ethan again!"

More silence, then Blessed said, "All I have to do is tie you up, little girl. Don't threaten me."

Ethan twisted about in the chair so he could see them. There was fear in Autumn's voice, and rage, and hysteria, building. She started to hyperventilate, and then she was crying, ugly, tearing sobs.

Blessed wasn't deaf; he heard it too. Ethan heard the desperation in his voice as Blessed said, "Stop breathing so hard, stop it. And stop crying."

Autumn cried harder.

"Oh, all right, all right. If the sheriff doesn't try to do anything stupid, I'll let him be, but only as long as you do what I tell you to do."

Autumn stopped crying. She started to hiccup.

"Do you promise?"

"Yes, I promise. But you better keep your word or I'll run and hide from you." Ethan knew a hysterical child was the last thing Blessed needed. Autumn hiccupped again, but it sounded—it sounded like a fake hiccup to him. Despite the blasting pain in his head, Ethan smiled. She was an incredible kid.

"Sheriff?"

It was Blessed, and he was standing just off to Ethan's right side. "Your head hurt?"

"Yeah."

"Get him some aspirin, Blessed."

"Let him suffer, I don't have—"

Autumn did it again, the too-fast breathing, a single pathetic hiccup, and Blessed sighed. "All right, Autumn. You just stay still, all right?"

"I won't move," she said to Blessed. She stroked Ethan's hand.

The kid was playing him. *Good.* She wound her skinny arms around Ethan's neck, and he whispered against her cheek, "You're on a roll, kiddo, but be careful, all right? Blessed isn't stupid."

He felt her nod. When Blessed came back, she straightened and said, "You've got to untie him so he can take the aspirin."

Ethan groaned. Unlike Autumn, he wasn't faking.

He felt the pull of Blessed's fingers as he worked the knots at his wrists. Soon they fell away, not that it mattered much since he couldn't feel his hands. Ethan slowly brought his arms in front of him and began rubbing his hands together, then shaking them. Slowly, they started to tingle and he began to feel them again. His fingers throbbed and ached, but it didn't bother him all that much because his head was about to explode.

"Don't even think about coming after me, Sheriff. I won't let you live next time. Here's your aspirin."

Come after him? As if he could, since his feet were tied. Ethan took the aspirin and dry-swallowed them. He looked at his watch. Eleven o'clock in the morning. But what morning?

"What day is it?"

"Thursday."

Okay, good. He'd slept a few hours at most. He closed his eyes and sat very still, waited for the aspirin to do something good.

Autumn said, "I want you to untie my mama too."

A beat of silence, then Blessed's voice, irritated now: "No, the bitch stays—"

Autumn screamed at him, "My mama's not a bitch! Don't you dare call her that, ever again!" She sounded wild and out of control. She flew at him, hitting him again and again. Ethan heard Blessed curse under his breath, heard him say, "All right all right, I'll untie her. Calm down, stop acting crazy, you hear me?"

Acting crazy?

Autumn sobbed again, whispering through her tears, "Untie my mama."

Ethan thought the kid should be in the movies.

Blessed tried to sound tough, but he fell short to Ethan's ears. "Maybe I will, but if she tries anything, she goes away again. I mean it."

"Just untie her."

He heard Joanna moan.

"Don't you stymie her, Blessed!"

Ethan said, his eyes still closed, "Get her some aspirin, Blessed; she'll need it bad."

A minute later, Autumn said, "Here, Mama, here's some aspirin. I got you some water so you don't have to choke them down like poor Ethan."

Joanna let her put the aspirin in her mouth and the glass to her lips.

"Untie her, Blessed."

Blessed, looking harassed, untied her hands.

"Mama, let me rub your hands for you. That's better, isn't it? Ethan? Are you feeling better yet?"

"Yes," he said, and surprisingly, he was. "Joanna?"

"I'm here, Ethan." Ethan felt the chair move, and knew Joanna had picked Autumn up and was rocking her.

He heard Blessed walking toward him. He didn't look up, which was stupid, really.

He looked down at Blessed's boots. He had small feet for a man. Ethan said, "Your boots are dirty, Blessed."

"Yeah? Well, you should see yourself, Sheriff, and the—woman."

Ethan knew Autumn was opening her mouth to blast him. Blessed had made a fast save. Ethan said, "What happens now, Blessed?"

55

"We'll be on our way when you and the woman can walk out of here."

"Where are we going?"

A pause, then, "We're going someplace else, Sheriff, a very special place where Autumn will be safe, and then we'll wait for Mama."

Wait for his mama? But Ethan wasn't sure she'd come—Savich had told him he was dealing with Shepherd Backman. He'd have given a great deal at the moment to know what Savich had done with the old lady.

Joanna asked, "And where would that be?"

"Shut your mouth, woman, it's none of your business. Autumn, you get off her lap now, it's time to leave."

"I have to go to the bathroom," Joanna said.

"I do too," Ethan said.

"All right, but make it fast. Anything funny and you're both gone again."

In ten minutes they were back on the road, Ethan driving. "We're on Highway Seventy-five," he said. "I think it turns into Highway Eighty-one past Chattanooga. Where are we—?"

"You just keep driving, boy, and keep your mouth shut. I'll tell you where to go."

He decided not to push it. The pain in his head was only a dull throb. He looked over at Joanna next to him in the front seat. He knew she was still in some pain because she was sitting very still, staring straight ahead, her hands clasped tightly together. He reached out, pulled a hand free, and squeezed. After a moment, she squeezed his hand back. He still held her hand when they crossed into Georgia.

Ethan steeled himself to look into the rearview mirror, afraid he'd meet Blessed's eyes, but he did look. They were damned creepy eyes. He met Ethan's gaze. Blessed smiled. Nothing happened. Maybe Blessed wouldn't stymie him now, because if he did, Ethan just might wreck the van. Something to think about. He said, "Autumn, are you all right?"

"Of course she's all right. She's asleep," Blessed said. "Shut up and drive or you and the bitch are no good to me at all."

Ethan said mildly, "You've got to be careful, Blessed, about what you call Joanna. Autumn could wake up at any time. I wonder what she'd do this time?"

"She'll do what I tell her to do. You'll see, she'll come to love and respect her family, as we will love her. There's so much waiting for her, a lovely surprise for her too. Now be quiet, Sheriff."

"I was just going to thank you for the Egg McMuffin and coffee back in Chattanooga."

Blessed grunted. "I didn't want my niece to be hungry. It took you long enough to eat it. Don't speak to me again."

Ethan knew the only reason he and Joanna were still alive was that Autumn wouldn't do what Blessed told her to. What was he talking about—a lovely surprise for Autumn? Ethan didn't think it would be a good idea to ask.

It was two hours before Blessed spoke again. "Turn here, Sheriff."

Ethan turned off the highway into the middle of nowhere. He continued driving some twenty more miles on an old two-lane country road. Traffic was light, just a couple of pickups and a Volkswagen, only a couple of houses every mile, mostly old split-level houses set way back from the road, separated by thickets of trees.

Blessed finally directed Ethan to turn again onto a narrow one-lane dirt road that looked more like a wide rutted path, and then told him to head toward a dense clump of pine, maple, and oak trees.

Ethan had believed he'd known where they were going, but he'd been wrong. He said, "So we're not going to the tobacco farm?"

Ethan saw the look of surprise on Blessed's face, but he recovered quickly. "What do you know about any of that?"

"I know quite a bit about the Children of Twilight. So does the FBI." Well, he didn't know that much, Savich hadn't had a chance to tell him more, but Blessed didn't know that. "I know the cult is housed on an old flue-cured tobacco farm." Ethan stopped, not wanting Blessed to know everything he knew, which wasn't much. "Well, Blessed, that isn't where we're going?"

"No, we're not going there, we're . . . Shut up, Sheriff, and keep driving."

"Hey, I was wondering, do many people contact you through your website? Is that how you get members? Are there Children of Twilight branches in Europe? How about Transylvania?"

He heard Blessed cursing under his breath, heard Savich's name, and smiled.

"You shut up now, Sheriff, or I'll stymie you, you hear me? Autumn's asleep, she won't know."

"While I'm driving? Won't I run us right off the road if you stymie me? Autumn might get hurt. Best not take the chance, Blessed."

Blessed said, "Stop your mouth, Sheriff. Slow down ahead, the road's pretty rough."

The road was soon filled with rocks and potholes, and patches of mud with tire tracks weaving in and out of them. Maples, pines, and oaks pressed in from both sides, a vivid green canopy so close the van scraped against the tree branches. The road wound upward, meandering from right to left and back again, always climbing.

He braked when they came to an old weathered black iron gate across the road, two large wooden poles holding it in place. Trees were thick on each side, so there was no going around the gate. Where were they?

"Get out, woman, and open the gate."

Joanna pulled her hand from Ethan's, climbed out of the van. She walked to the gate and opened it.

Blessed called out of the open window of the backseat, "Stay there until we're through, then close it again."

Ethan drove through and watched her close the gate in the rearview mirror.

Why have a gate if it wasn't even locked? If it wasn't meant to keep anyone out, why then—there had to be a camera in the trees, or an alarm. Each time the gate opened, whoever was at the other end of this road knew someone was coming.

The road continued to snake upward, then simply stopped in front of a thick stand of pines. They were in low foothills, covered with trees.

"Get out of the car, Sheriff."

Ethan stepped out of the van into air that was still and calm, the bright light of day starting to fade. It was still hot. Had to be near six o'clock.

Joanna turned to see Blessed wake Autumn.

The little girl looked dazed. Joanna whirled on him. "Did you drug her, you monster?"

"Only some sleeping pills I got from the Quik Mart while the sheriff pumped gas. She's fine. Be quiet. If either of you try to tell her how we got here, I'll drop you where you stand. Now shut up. The two of you walk on ahead. I'm keeping Autumn with me."

Autumn said, "No, I want to go with my mother."

"No, you will stay with me. Do you understand?"

Autumn thought about this, then slowly nodded.

"Sheriff, walk straight ahead and don't do anything stupid."

Blessed took Autumn's hand.

They made their way along a winding narrow path through the trees, and suddenly stepped into a large flat expanse, not natural but cleared.

"Here," Blessed said, his voice satisfied. "We're finally here, Autumn. This place is more special than you can imagine. This is where you belong."

Ethan and Joanna stared at a large, ancient three-story barn, the gray paint peeling, rotted boards hanging by nails. It looked as if it had been abandoned for at least a half century.

Ethan said, "I'd say the tobacco farm is a cover, right, Blessed? Maybe your cult was there once but not now. This lovely old barn must be cult central."

56

"Yes, this is Twilight," Blessed said, a kind of possessive reverence in his voice. "Enjoy your blasphemy, Sheriff. Hey, what are you doing? Why are you looking back toward the woods? Maybe you're hoping someone followed us?"

Ethan said, "I just thought I heard something, that's all. An animal, maybe. I can't imagine anyone could know where we are."

Blessed listened a moment before he shook his head. "No, no one knows. Now, you think you're going to escape, but you're not. Fact is, if either of you ends up going anywhere, you won't even know it." He laughed, sounding pleased with himself. "Remember when you stopped for gas, Sheriff? I left you pumping? Just after we left the McDonald's, I knew I'd seen a car that stayed with us too long. I'll tell you, Sheriff, I couldn't believe it, but there was the same car sitting off to the side in the station, next to the tire gauge and water hose, with three yahoos in suits inside, trying to act all nonchalant. I simply walked back to their car, had a guy roll down the window, and I stymied him. The other guys went for their guns, but it didn't matter. I stymied them too. Didn't matter they were wearing real dark sunglasses." He laughed. "I guess they were told to try to follow us, right? Well, they didn't. I do wonder what happened to the Three Stooges. Maybe the gas-station cashier got suspicious when they never moved out and called the cops? You wanna tell me how these guys found us?"

"I have no clue."

Blessed turned to Joanna. "Well, do you know?"

Joanna said, her voice steady, "No, but evidently the FBI knows about this cult, Blessed, knows where it's located. So if I were you, I'd be worried. They'll be coming, Blessed, they'll be coming."

She was holding it together, Ethan thought. Her hair straggled around her face, freckles marched across her nose, her jeans were dirty, her shirt ripped and wrinkled, but she hadn't given up. Ethan imagined he looked as bad as she did. Actually, now that he thought about it, he thought she looked terrific.

Blessed looked down at Autumn and smiled. His voice was gentle, admiring. "I know you did that, Autumn, you somehow called that agent at the motel when you were in the bathroom. But he's not coming, he doesn't have a clue where we are, and that's why I made sure you had a nice long nap. If you call him now, it won't matter because you don't know where you are."

Autumn stared up at him. She said, "You need to shave. All your whiskers are white. You're old."

Ethan decided in that instant that he'd do whatever he had to to keep that little kid in his life. He wanted to watch her grow up, with Joanna—

Blessed stared at Autumn for a moment, then threw back his head and laughed.

"You haven't seen old yet, Autumn. You just wait. Now, if you two want to stay conscious, you walk over to the barn."

Joanna didn't move. "I want Autumn with me."

"I want to be with my mama," Autumn said.

Blessed stared at her, then released her hand. Autumn ran to her mother. Joanna clutched her child to her, dropped a kiss on her hair, another on her forehead.

When they reached the barn, Blessed walked ahead of them to the huge set of double doors, so rotted Ethan didn't know how they were still standing. Blessed pulled the door out enough to slip inside. He stuck his head out. "Come this way."

When their eyes adjusted to the shadowed interior, they saw rotted hay bales stacked haphazardly, rusted tractor parts strewn over the rotted wooden floor planks, the parent of the parts, an ancient John Deere tractor, sitting off in a dim corner, missing two tires. The air smelled fetid and stale. At least it wasn't as hot in here as it was outside. Ethan's foot crushed down on an animal carcass.

He realized then that all the display of

rot, the rusted machine parts—it was all staged. This was what someone thought an abandoned barn should look like, down to the John Deere tractor.

They watched Blessed push aside a couple of hay bales and two old car seats, the material covering them long rotted, and kick away straw from the floor, clearing about a four-foot space. He leaned down and pulled on a rusted old handle that was nearly flat against the wood, and a hole appeared in the floor. Blessed stepped back and smiled, waved his hand toward it. Joanna and Ethan looked down onto blackness.

Blessed reached down into the darkness and pressed some buttons. There came three short beeps, and then light suddenly filled the dark hole, but there was still nothing to see except wooden stairs that led downward. Blessed nodded to them. "The two of you will climb carefully down the stairs. When you get to the bottom, wait for Autumn and me. Don't forget, I've got Autumn, so don't try anything."

Joanna and Ethan climbed down the wooden stairs. They were solid pine, thirty of them; Ethan counted them.

The stairs ended in a small square room with whitewashed walls and a clean wooden floor. There was a single table with a telephone sitting on it, and nothing else.

They heard the trap door close above them, the low hum of air-conditioning. The air was cool. It had to take a good-sized generator, Ethan thought, to run this place.

Blessed walked past them to the phone, picked it up, and said, "The Keeper is here."

Joanna arched an eyebrow at Ethan.

At the end of the small room they watched a panel in the opposite wall slide silently open. Blessed nodded for them to go inside.

Joanna went first, Ethan close behind her. *More than a rotted old barn for the Children of Twilight,* Ethan thought. They stopped and stared at the vast, empty white space, almost dizzying it was so white, no other color to break it. The room was maybe forty feet by forty feet, the wooden floor painted as white as the walls and ceiling. *Another stage setting,* Ethan thought, this one doubtless meant to represent purity and innocence, maybe a bit of heaven? Or more likely, this was another stage setting to prove to cult members this was a holy place.

A young black man came through a white door set into one of the walls. He was wearing a white linen shirt and loose white pants, a thin rope tied around his waist. His feet were bare.

"Hello, Kjell," Blessed said. "I've got her."

57

WINNETT, NORTH CAROLINA

It was late afternoon when the black FBI Bell helicopter landed at the small airstrip two miles west of Winnett. The mountains were thick around them, and yet it was so hot and humid when Savich stepped out of the helicopter, he wished he could strip down and find a hose. He helped Sherlock out, and both of them stood there a moment, even the hot gush of air from the helicopter blades better than the still, dead air.

Holding hands, they ducked down and ran toward a small tin building thirty feet away. They turned to see the helicopter lift off. The pilot, Curly Hames, waved to them. They veered off into the shade of the buildings to where a dark green Subaru sat next to a banged-up truck and a rotted-out SUV.

The keys were in the ignition. Savich gave the interior a tolerant look and turned the key.

Sherlock sniffed. "The car smells new; that's big of the field office. Okay, we're going to meet Cully at the Chevron gas station on Market Street, only about half a mile from Victor Nesser's apartment on Pulitzer Prize Road. Then we'll go to Victor's apartment, meet up with Bernie Benton, and wait until Lissy and Victor show." She grinned. "Weird name. Turns out that Winnett native Marvin Hemlick won a Pulitzer some forty years ago for writing about a nasty Ku Klux Klan chapter here. Anyway, when last I spoke to Cully, he said he and Bernie had Victor's place covered, but nothing was happening, and time was moving slow as molasses in this heat and both he and Bernie were getting antsy."

She pulled out her cell and dialed Cully's number. There was no answer, only voice mail. Sherlock frowned, dialed again, got voice mail again. "Why doesn't he pick up? I told him I'd call the minute we were here. Cully's known for being so type A, his shoes nearly walk by themselves. What could he be doing?"

"Do you have Bernie's cell phone number?" Savich asked as he negotiated a left turn onto Market Street.

She shook her head. "Let's get to the Chevron station, see if Cully's there. Maybe his phone's dead." Like either of them believed that, Sherlock thought, and tightened her seat belt. Even the seat belt smelled new.

"We'll be there in a minute; hang on, sweetheart."

She noticed the countryside was quite pretty as they drove by—tree-covered hills rising slowly to higher hills, and finally they saw the mountains behind them. Pine and oak trees crammed the slopes, enough for a thousand houses, Sherlock thought, without making a dent.

Savich slowed through Winnett's small downtown. The three-block center was set squarely on flat land; the townspeople must have long ago taken a bulldozer to smooth it out. Red brick and wooden buildings crowded together along Market Street, and wherever there weren't buildings, there were trees crowding in. It was quite lovely, really, but it was so hot even in the late afternoon, Savich imagined you could fry spit on the sidewalk.

The downtown was quiet, dead, only a couple of teenagers milling around outside. *Dinnertime,* he thought, and escape from the oppressive heat, maybe some hoses going to cool off in the backyards.

The Chevron sign appeared ahead on a right-hand corner. An old man stood in the doorway of the Quik Mart, arms folded over his chest, watching a young guy pump gas into a white Mustang convertible. There were a couple of cars waiting to be serviced, but there was no sign of Agent Cully Gwyn.

Savich didn't pause. "Let's go over to Pulitzer Prize Road, take a look at Victor's apartment building. Maybe they're there, watching, forgot the time, whatever."

Sherlock didn't say anything, but she didn't like it. She was tense, on edge. She punched her cell phone's GPS on, and a dulcet female voice told them to turn right in point-five miles. A minute later, they pulled onto Victor's street in a neighborhood of the small ranch-style houses set back from the road on big yards with pine and oak trees cozied up to the houses. They were lucky it rained here a lot, or the town would never have survived forest fires for so long.

Pulitzer Prize Road was unexpectedly long. Finally the houses began to peter out, and at the very end of the street, on the very edge of Winnett, stood Victor's apartment building. It wasn't much, a two-story brick building with maybe six apartments. But the yard was big and green, like all the other yards, and there was a red brick walkway that led up to the door. There was only one house beyond the apartment building, the grass overgrown, its windows boarded up, obviously vacant. Beyond that decrepit house stretched a narrow two-lane road that disappeared into the thick oak and pine trees. Everything looked limp.

"If the locals don't take care," Sherlock said, looking around, "the forest is going to consume the town. Nothing but oaks and pines everywhere. It looks like they swallow up the road."

"I wouldn't mind sitting under an oak tree about now," Savich said, looking up at the afternoon sun, hot and high in the cloudless sky, "what with the temperature hovering around a hundred, and the humidity at two thousand. Do you know what the problem is—the sun's too big down here."

"We could join that golden retriever over there snoozing away under that pine tree. Everybody must be huddled around their air conditioners."

"If Cully and Bernie are watching the apartment building from close by, they could be inside that empty house," Savich said. "Do you see anyone? A car? Anything?"

They looked around carefully, saw nothing but the sun beating down. The trees were utterly still, not a breath of moving air.

Savich turned the car around and headed back toward town. He parked a couple of blocks from the apartment building, between a Toyota SUV and an F-150 truck. They walked back toward the building, their SIGs pressed against their sides to avoid any panic from passersby. They needn't have bothered. Not a single soul appeared, not Cully or Bernie either. They could be well hidden, Savich thought, but surely they'd have recognized them, at least recognized Sherlock's bright hair. This wasn't good, Savich knew it.

Savich would swear the air pulsed with heat. He saw the humidity was making Sherlock's hair curlier. She turned to him. "Why don't Cully and Bernie let us know where they are?"

Savich said nothing; what was there to say? He opened the apartment-building front door and stepped into a tiny lobby that held one palm tree and six mailboxes, painted white. The temperature dropped at least thirty degrees.

"It's like I've died and gone to an ice locker," she said. She flapped her arms, enjoying it.

They looked at the mailboxes even though they knew Victor lived in apartment 403, but why was there a number like that in a two-story apartment building?

"Let's take the stairs," he said. "Stay alert."

They didn't meet anyone on the stairs. Savich imagined a lot of people were inside, eating dinner. They heard children arguing over whether to watch an old *Star Trek* episode or *Batman*, but no adult voices.

The hallway was wide and dark, all the apartment doors painted different colors. Victor Nesser's apartment was at the very end of the second-floor hall. His front door was painted bright green, with big brass numbers—403.

Sherlock stepped forward, knocked on the door, and waited a moment, her SIG ready. "Mr. Nesser? It's Clorie Smith, from the *Winnett Herald Weekly*. I'm here to offer you a full month's free subscription, four free issues."

No answer.

She knocked again. "Mr. Nesser?"

No sound, nothing from inside the apartment.

Savich pressed his ear to the door.

He didn't hear anything at first, pressed his ear closer. He heard a muffled sound— *a person's voice?* He didn't wait, motioned for Sherlock to step back, and he kicked the door in. It flew open, banging against the wall. They went in, fanning their SIGs, and found themselves in a small entry hall, a living room to the right connected to a small dining area and kitchen.

Empty.

A muffled voice yelled, "In here!"

The voice was coming from the bedroom. Savich stepped toward it when the man shouted again, "No! Don't come in! There's a bomb and a trip wire!"

58

Savich froze, Sherlock behind him. He called out, "Okay, we're not moving. Cully, is that you? What bomb?"

"Just a second, got to get this duct tape off my mouth. Damn, it's hard to talk without any lips. Okay, listen, the young guy— Victor Nesser—I saw him string a wire across the bedroom doorway, floor level. I guess he didn't mind I saw him, figured I would see you coming and not be able to do a thing about it. Thank God I finally managed to get the tape off my mouth or we'd all be dead."

Savich knelt down and saw the wire,

maybe a quarter inch off the floor, stretched taut. He called out, "We're stepping over it. Are you all right?"

"Yeah, yeah, I'm okay, just humiliated. I'm here, on the other side of the bed. Like I said, I finally got the tape off my mouth, but I'm still tied up. Victor's got me connected to a wire, too."

"Okay, don't move," Savich said and walked slowly over to the bed.

Cully said, "I can see the bomb from here. It's by the dresser."

"Got it," Sherlock said. "You just don't move, Cully. Dillon and I are going to check it out."

Cully said, "The girl—Lissy Smiley—she was laughing, really enjoying it, crowing that the instant some stupid fed tripped the wire the whole building would go boom—a hundred feet up, burn up the air, maybe all the way to heaven, she said. Then she hooted, doing a Madonna bump and grind, and said something about sending you, Savich, to heaven." Cully sucked in a breath. "I usually don't remember exactly what people say, but she was over the top."

Sherlock said, "Hey, we're really glad you

got the duct tape off your mouth. No heaven for any of us yet."

Cully Gwyn, amazingly, laughed. "I knew you guys would come here when you didn't see me at the Chevron station and I didn't answer my cell. Please tell me you've spoken to Bernie."

"No, we haven't," Savich said. "We don't have his cell number. Okay, Cully, I won't try to get you free until we see what's going on with this bomb."

Sherlock dropped to her knees beside an ancient pine dresser, vintage Goodwill. "Okay, just eyeballing it first. What we've got is a large black metal box about the size and shape of a small suitcase. There's a wire running from inside it across the floor over to the bedroom door and another to you, Cully, so don't move a whisker."

Cully said, "There's no bomb squad in Winnett, no surprise there. Please tell me you guys know about bombs."

Savich said, "Stop hyperventilating, Cully, it'll be all right. Sherlock took a course at Quantico. She knows enough not to set the sucker off. How did Victor and Lissy get you?"

"Bernie and I were close to the empty

house just down the street, the one that's been deserted for only a few months, we were told, but the grass looks ready to take up residence it grows so fast here. We were hunkered down in trees a bit beyond the house, close enough to keep an eye on Victor's end apartment, but not too close to spook them if they showed up." He sighed. "Bernie had to use the john, so he went into the house, through the back. I never looked away from the apartment building. I swear to you, I never heard a thing, not even a whisper of movement. One minute I was wondering why Bernie was taking so long and the next I felt a gun stuck in my ear, and a girl giggled, told me I was the easiest fed she'd ever got. I couldn't believe it, Savich. I have no clue how she snuck up on me. I didn't hear a thing."

Dillon said, "She and Victor were probably behind you, watching, for a good long time, waiting for their chance. When Bernie went into the house, you had no one covering your back." *Easy,* Savich thought, *so easy.*

Cully sighed again. "I tried for her, twisted around, sent my elbow at her face, but she jumped back, waved the gun at me, and told me if I tried anything again, she'd shoot me. Then Victor comes up and tells me we're going to his apartment, he's hungry, and he wants to see if the bologna in his fridge is still good.

"First though, Lissy went into the house where Bernie was. I didn't hear anything, not a yell from Bernie, nothing. When she comes out, she's popping bubble gum. I asked her what she did with Bernie, but she just gives me a sneer and hits my ribs real hard with the butt of her gun. 'That's for trying to hit me in the face,' she says.

"There was no one around, and believe me, I looked hard. They marched me over here to the apartment building, then Victor ties me up here in the bedroom while she's got the gun on me. I watched Victor hook up the bomb. I asked him where Bernie was, and Lissy just laughs again, tells me to shut up."

"You're very lucky she didn't just shoot you when you tried to take her down," Sherlock said. "That's what she does, Cully."

"Yeah, I know. Fortunately for me, I think she wanted a show; she was hoping you guys would come. She laughed and laughed, and wondered if they'd ever figure out what body part went with what fed."

"I recommend you forget that thought, Cully," Savich said. "Okay, I can't get you free until Sherlock disarms the bomb. Don't move."

Savich went down on his knees next to Sherlock. She'd gotten the lid of the black box open. "Okay, it's definitely homemade, not sophisticated—thank you, God—nice and straightforward. Victor probably got this off the Internet, or out of a book, which is very good for us. Dillon, give me your Swiss Army Knife."

He handed it to her without a word.

Sherlock looked down at a pair of wires, red and green twisted together, leading to a—timer. *Why a timer?* The bomb was supposed to explode if someone hit the trip wire across the bedroom doorway, or if Cully pulled out his wire. *Why a timer?* Had they tried to rig the front door too?

Sherlock cupped her hand around the small screen and read out 00:34 seconds. She sucked in her breath, forced herself to calm.

"We're on a timer here, guys, not much time left before the sucker explodes."

Savich looked at the timer over her shoulder.

Thirty seconds, twenty-nine. He saw his son's face clear as glass in his mind, bouncing a basketball, and then saw Sherlock leaning over him, tucking a sheet around his chest.

Eighteen seconds, seventeen.

He watched Sherlock untwist the wires, follow each one to its lead.

Thirteen seconds, twelve.

Time compressed itself into a moment, yet Savich felt each ticking second as a separate unit, each second a universe of time, yet each second somehow disappeared into the next. He couldn't guess how many people were right now in the building, how many could die because of Victor and Lissy. He thought of the children they'd heard arguing. He heard Cully talking softly—maybe he was praying, but he wasn't moving, and that was good since the wire connected to the duct tape around his ankles.

Seven seconds, six.

No more time.

He wanted to tell Sherlock he loved her, and he opened his mouth—

"Here we go," Sherlock said, and he watched her slice cleanly through a yellow wire.

His heart thudded, and his breath eased out of his mouth.

He reached out and wiped away the line of sweat streaking down her cheek. "You did it, sweetheart, you did it."

Cully gave a shout. "Good going, Sherlock. Hey, I can get this duct tape off—"

There was a loud pop.

Sherlock said, "Hold that thought, Cully. What's going on now?"

59

PEAS RIDGE, GEORGIA

Kjell was tall, well over six feet, angular, and good-looking. His shaved head glistened in the stark white light. He wore glasses.

He bowed from the waist to Blessed, and said in a clipped British accent, "Keeper, we did not know if you would come. I see you have the little girl. Excellent. But the man and woman?"

"The sheriff and the child's mother."

"Keeper, we have never before brought outsiders here. It is a danger. Are you certain you were not followed here?"

"I am very certain."

"But why did you bring them here? Why did you not rid us of them?"

Blessed said, "I could not stymie them because of the child. I needed them to get her here.

"Do not look away from the sheriff, Kjell. He is dangerous. As I said, no one followed us, I made very certain of that. Twilight will remain a secret. Kjell, I must see the Father immediately. There is news I must give him."

"Where is Grace?"

"I must see the Father," Blessed said again. "Take them to see the Master. Be careful with the sheriff."

Kjell gave him a small bow, drew a revolver from his loose pants. "The child, Keeper, she will come to embrace us, you will see."

Blessed gave Ethan and Joanna one last look, then smiled down at Autumn. "All will be well," he told her, and walked through the same door as Kjell. The door closed soundlessly behind him.

Autumn stood perfectly still and looked up at Kjell.

He said, "Sheriff, you and the woman

back up against that wall." He came down on his knees in front of Autumn. He lifted his hand and touched her face. Autumn didn't move, merely stared at him in his eyes.

"What can you do?" she asked.

Kjell smiled. "I am a student."

"Of what?"

"All who are here are students. We study with the Father and with the Master. We study miracles of the mind that reach back many hundreds of years. We watch and we learn. This is an amazing place, Autumn. I also protect Twilight from anyone who would try to harm us."

He rose again and turned to Ethan and Joanna.

Ethan said, "Blessed is the Keeper. What is your title, Kjell?"

"I? I am the Master's right hand."

"I can't say I care much for all the white."

Kjell said, "White is the essence of light, it is peace and tranquility, it is life to the devout. That is enough, Sheriff. I believe you are both small-minded, incapable of understanding something so sublime as what we are."

Ethan said, "We're the small-minded people who are going to bring you down, Kjell."

Kjell laughed. "Dream your little dreams, Sheriff. All of you will follow me. We will see what the Master wishes to do with you."

Joanna asked, "Where are all the cult members? You call them the devout?"

"The devout are here, but you will not see them. We do not wish them to be disrupted by outside corruption. You need know nothing more. Let us go. You will meet the Master."

60

They stepped into a wide corridor, its walls white, the ceiling lower here than in the large room, the low hum of air-conditioning the only sound other than that of their footsteps. Every several feet there were framed photographs, all of them of the sky, each an evocative moment of time. Ethan thought there was real talent here: a magnificent sunset, a slash of lightning with a dying sun behind it, moments he'd tried to capture himself.

Kjell walked soundlessly behind them, Joanna in front, Autumn pressed against her side, her hand held tightly in her mother's. Ethan knew he had a gun pointed at the back of his head.

They passed doors with glass windows and brass door handles, most of them with their blinds pulled tight. He saw a flash as one of the blinds fell, and caught a glimpse of a beautiful young woman's face through the window before she disappeared. One of the devout? Or someone else? Had they been warned to remain in their rooms to avoid being corrupted by the outsiders? Or did the leaders not want them to know what was happening?

Corridors veered off to the right and left as they walked. It seemed to be a huge place. They walked another twenty feet before Kjell said, "Knock on this door, Sheriff."

Ethan knocked.

"Enter."

"Open the door, Sheriff."

There was no window in this imposing door. Ethan opened it and stepped into a library that held books floor to ceiling on all four of its walls. It was twenty feet deep, and against the back wall there was a large mahogany desk, and behind it stood a man wearing a white robe belted at the waist with a gold-link chain. He was a fine-looking man, in his fifties, tall, slim, his eyes a deep, shocking blue, eyes that pinned you. He held a small pistol in his hand.

Joanna wanted to tell him he looked ridiculous, but the truth was he didn't. He looked like a biblical prophet. She saw a strange pendant hanging from the belt. She wasn't close enough to see what it was.

Ethan said, "Caldicot Whistler, I presume?"

"Yes." Whistler held the gun in an elegant hand, an artist's hand, long-fingered and graceful. If Ethan wasn't mistaken, it was a Colt-style 1911 .45 semiautomatic aimed at him, not Joanna or Autumn, and for that he was grateful.

"Blessed told me you were bringing them to me, Kjell. Please stay close. You will be needed again."

Kjell gave Whistler a slight bow and left the room, closing the door behind him.

Whistler stepped from behind his desk, but he didn't come close enough for Ethan to make a try for him. Smart man. He said, staring down at Autumn for a long moment, "So this is the child."

Autumn pressed harder against Joanna's side.

"Her name is Autumn Backman," Joanna said.

Whistler ignored her. "I did not know if Blessed would manage it. He is immensely powerful, but there were obviously problems for him this time, and so the two of you are here with her."

Ethan said, "Did Blessed tell you that Grace is dead?"

Whistler paled. "Yes," he whispered. "Blessed gave me that tragic news. And it is you who brings it up, Sheriff? You kill a great man, and you think to mock me with it?"

"If I indeed killed him, I have no memory of it, since Blessed had stymied both me and Joanna."

Whistler closed his eyes an instant, then stared again at Ethan. "Blessed was so upset he ran to see the Father with the news. I knew Blessed was shot in the shoulder by that FBI agent, but this—it is too terrible."

Joanna said, "What's terrible is murdering an innocent man and kidnapping a child."

"Shut up, woman, you don't know what

you're talking about. Ah, this is unbearable. Grace was incredibly powerful. He was unique; nothing like his talent has ever before been recorded." He waved a graceful white hand at the shelves of books.

"How could you possibly get close enough to shoot Grace?"

"As I told you, I have no memory of anything."

Whistler's face went hard. "It doesn't matter." He raised his gun hand.

Joanna said, "The child is watching you, Caldicot. What will happen if you shoot Ethan? What will this Father person think of you then?"

Whistler slowly lowered the gun. "You are alive, Sheriff, only as long as it suits the Father. You need to remember that." He fell silent, shook his head back and forth. "It is hard to believe Grace is dead. What a huge loss for all of us. The devout will miss him. And the Father will be desolate."

Ethan said, "Even the powerful die, you know that."

Whistler looked at each of them, his eyes coming to rest on Autumn. "Blessed knew I would want to see you, speak to you. I fear you cannot take your uncle's place; no one can. It is a pity, child, that you will never know your uncle's devotion, his loyalty to his family, his infinite patience with our people. He held such high hopes for you, but now he will never see what you become. He hoped that in the fullness of time you would achieve powers that will astound everyone, as he knew his did. He died for you."

Ethan said, "No, he died because he tried to kidnap her and murder us. Whatever else he was, he was a criminal."

"It would give me infinite pleasure to shoot you, Sheriff."

Ethan decided he just might, despite Autumn's being there. He gave Whistler a big smile. "Your room is quite professorial. Is that your role here? To teach all the people who sign on here?"

"Like all the devout, I am also a student. I learn as they learn, pray for powers as they pray. In addition, I am the financial officer of Twilight."

"It must have cost very big bucks to build this underground bunker."

"Indeed, but then, money is very easy to come by for us, Sheriff. Even with Grace's passing, it will not be a problem. Blessed can simply walk into a bank and walk out with whatever amount is available. If one is accepted among us, poor or rich, money isn't necessary."

Joanna said slowly, "You mean people contact you through your blog and you interview them? You decide if they're worthy to be buried in this white tomb? They actually come?"

Whistler looked enraged at what she'd said, Ethan thought, but he held himself in check. Whistler looked down at Autumn, saw she was staring up at him, and said, "Naturally they are screened. We are serious about our secrecy here. Those who witness Blessed and Grace's gifts are enthralled. They eagerly accept our rules. They come to learn about all those who came before us, hoping they might come to understand those gifts from God. When they see unlimited wealth and the promise of psychic powers, the problem is to select among them, to keep the unworthy out."

Ethan said, "Do you enthrall them as well, Caldicot? Do you have a gift?"

"I will be given what is rightfully mine—"

"—in the fullness of time?" Joanna finished.

He swung the gun at her. Ethan was an instant away from jumping at him when Whistler took a quick step back. "Stop, Sheriff. I will kill you. Believe me."

Ethan said, "I do indeed believe you, Caldicot. Do you know, I think you could be a model for Jesus except for the gun in your hand, and the blue eyes."

"Ah, Jesus. I believe he was a good man, but I prefer the prophet Corinth. He is the Alpha and the Omega; he is the one we worship."

Ethan's eyebrow went up. "Corinth?"

"His was a magnificent power, not in the same way as Grace, but remarkable nonetheless. Perhaps Corinth did not have the goodness of Jesus and Grace, but he was a chaste man, a man of infinite wisdom, a man who could control those around him with a click of his fingers." He snapped his fingers in their faces.

"I've never heard of a prophet named Corinth," Joanna said.

He scarcely gave her a glance. "You are a woman. Why would you have heard of anything important?"

"I haven't heard of him either," Ethan

said. "So this Corinth had a psychic ability that astounded people?"

"Corinth could read the secrets in men's minds, knew what they truly wanted and how to manipulate them to gain whatever he wished. He was powerful and he was feared; no one dared touch him. All of us are here to try to understand the source of his powers, and of those who are gifted here among us. I wish Corinth were here, but he is not. Like poor Grace, Corinth is no longer of this earth."

"Where did he do all these things to manipulate his fellow man?" Joanna asked.

"Corinth was an intimate of the Medici—first Cosimo, then Piero, and finally Lorenzo. He was their confidant, their adviser. It is written he left Italy after Lorenzo's death in 1492. His death marked the end of the Golden Age of Florence. After came strife and war."

Ethan said, "And you believe everything fell apart because Corinth was no longer there as the power behind the throne?"

"Yes, of course. It is said he died, that his time was at an end."

"Where is all this written?" Joanna asked.

"You will ask no more stupid questions, woman."

Joanna said, her face expressionless, "All right. Are we to assume that you seek to make yourself into this Corinth? Peas Ridge, Georgia—not exactly Florence, is it? Where's your Lorenzo?"

Whistler looked as if he would explode.

"I never heard of him either," Autumn said.

Whistler calmed at her voice. He smiled down at her. "You will, child, you will. It is believed by many, the Father included, that Corinth did not die. Father believes Corinth went to Spain after he left Florence, that he joined a cult of psychics that eventually ran afoul of Torquemada. They were called Los Niños en el Atardecer—Children of Twilight. Torquemada murdered them. He wrote of it, in great detail. He called them *Adoradores del Diablo*—devil worshippers.

"It is a concern that Torquemada did not write of Corinth's capture along with the cult members in Spain, since the lunatic wrote about everything.

"The Father believes his incredible

family descends from Corinth." Whistler shrugged. "Who can say? It is appealing."

Ethan said, "I thought you said Corinth was chaste."

"He was. It was written that he had no family, but who knows?"

"So you see yourself as re-creating this group in fifteenth-century Spain? Who is this Father you keep mentioning?"

Whistler nodded. "You will find that out if he wishes it, Sheriff." He looked again at Autumn, and his voice softened. "We have made great strides here at Twilight. This is a place of peace and seeking. It is a place where you will be happy, child."

Autumn didn't answer him. She didn't look happy yet.

Ethan said quickly, "How many people are here now, Caldicot?"

"We have only twelve here at present. One is from Spain. Of course all who are admitted to Twilight vow secrecy, just as the Children of Twilight did so long ago. But it did not save them. Torquemada heard of them, hunted them down, and destroyed them. That will not happen to us. We have always known we must be careful, we must guard our secrecy well. Very few people know of this place, and it will remain that way."

"How can you be certain they don't tell others of this place once they leave?"

Whistler shrugged. "Some doubtless do. But it hardly profits them. They all agree to arrive blindfolded and leave the same way. And always at night. They do not know our location. And if they did know and were unwise enough to try to lead someone back here, they know our reaction would be—extreme."

Joanna asked, "What do they all do here?"

"All those who come witness incredible powers. They seek to understand and to learn if perhaps they can develop these powers in themselves."

"Have you found another Blessed?" Ethan asked.

"No, not as yet, but it is early. Today Autumn will join our ranks; she will become one of us. It will take time to find other gifted ones, the ones who will stand beside Blessed and the Father. Eventually we will become more powerful than your common minds can imagine. Perhaps the boy from Spain is right. Perhaps Corinth will appear again."

Ethan hadn't noticed the phone on Caldicot's desk until it rang. Whistler picked it up, listened. When he hung it up, he said, "It is time for you to return to the meeting hall with Kjell. Autumn, you will remain here with me."

Autumn went nuts. She screamed, "No, I won't leave my mother, I won't leave Ethan! I won't!"

Whistler looked ready to blow. Then he pressed a button on the side of his desk.

They'd come to a decision, Ethan thought, and he knew what it was. He had to be ready.

A moment later, Kjell appeared. He motioned them all back into the corridor. "I will see you soon, child," Caldicot called to Autumn.

Autumn turned around and said, "I don't think you look like Jesus at all. Jesus wasn't crazy."

61

WINNETT, NORTH CAROLINA

Another popping sound came from the black metal box and sounded like a gunshot in the small room. None of them breathed.

Sherlock bent down and examined the disarmed bomb and casing. She looked up. "One of the leads, it sparked. I'm going to remove it entirely away from the pack of dynamite." She lifted the wire, touched her fingers to the tip, felt the heat, held it until it was cool, and laid it on the floor. "I think that's what that noise was. I'm sure there's nothing left in there to send us to heaven." She held up the two detached wires.

Once Savich got the duct tape off Cully, he jumped up and stomped his feet to get feeling back into them. When he could hold his own weight, Cully walked over to look at the now harmless bomb case. "Thanks, Sherlock. Do you know when the next bomb course is at Quantico?"

Sherlock laughed, then she looked down at the remains of the bomb at her feet. "Homemade, professional—they're all scary. My heart's still pumping out of my chest."

Cully said, "I knew if I couldn't get that duct tape off my mouth, it was all over. I heard you guys kick the front door open and I'll tell you, I never chewed and worked my jaws so hard in my life. I found out duct tape doesn't taste anything like chicken. Damn, we've got to find Bernie."

Bernie was probably dead, Savich thought, murdered silently by Lissy and stuffed into a closet. They were out of Victor Nesser's apartment building in under a minute, running toward the deserted house.

Bernie wasn't anywhere in the house, dead or alive, and they didn't see any blood. It was one of those good news/bad news deals, Savich thought. If Bernie wasn't dead, it meant he was a hostage, and they all knew it.

"We've gotta think positive here," Cully said. "As long as he's a hostage, he's got a chance. Damn, that sounds lame. Why couldn't he have peed against the oak tree right behind us? No, he had to go be civilized and use the toilet in the house." Cully slammed his fist into the hallway wall and crumpled the thin wallboard. "Okay, they coldcocked Bernie, tied him up, stuck him in a closet. After they left me to explode, they came back here, collected Bernie, and took him somewhere. Where?"

Savich said matter-of-factly, "They took him to a spot where they could see the explosion. There's no way they'd want to miss that—all three of us history. As for the other apartment tenants, they didn't care about them. Okay, Cully, you've got to think back and concentrate. Did Lissy and Victor give any indication about what they were going to do when they left you? Anything about where they were headed, where they'd been hiding before they came up behind you?"

Cully leaned against the peeling wallpaper in the small living room and closed his eyes. He said finally, "They were talking while Victor duct-taped me, like I wasn't even there, they were that sure I was going to be blown up, you guys along with me—if they were lucky. Lissy starting chanting, 'I'm going to be lucky,' over and over again until Victor told her to shut up."

Sherlock said, "Let me interrupt a minute, Cully. I'm wondering how they knew Dillon and I would be coming to Winnett."

Cully looked blank, then he shook his head, sighed. "If they were watching me and Bernie—and they were—they must have been close enough to listen to me talking to you guys on my cell, just figured you'd be coming here."

Sherlock nodded. "Okay, go on. What else do you remember?"

Cully said, "Before they left me, she leaned down and kissed me—not just a peck, she Frenched me. I nearly fainted. She laughed. Then they waltzed out. As far as I could tell, Victor left all his stuff in the apartment, didn't take a thing. Maybe he'd already taken what he wanted.

"On their way out I heard Victor's voice, but I couldn't make out what he said, but then Lissy said real loud like they were arguing, 'I'm going to kill that bastard who murdered her, or my mama will never forgive me.' And you know what? She burst into tears, sobbed her heart out. It was weird. I heard Victor consoling her, soothing words. Then they left, and Lissy yelled out right before they closed the apartment door, 'Bada-boom!' Then she was laughing her head off, right after she was crying her eyes out. She's crazier than a loon, guys. You know what? I think Victor knows it."

Cully paused, looked like he was trying to make sense of things. "You know, I'm not really sure, but one minute Victor's bossing her around, and the next it's like he's afraid she'll turn on him. But when she Frenched me, I knew he was mad, really mad."

Savich said, "But he didn't do anything. Say anything?"

"No, he turned away, like he wasn't interested. And then Lissy ran after him, laughing. Who was she talking about killing? It wasn't you; I mean, she wanted to blow you up in Victor's apartment."

Savich said, "She was talking about Buzz Riley, the security guard at the bank in Georgetown they tried to rob. He's the one who saved my life, killed Lissy's mother, Jennifer Smiley. Buzz is safe; he took a long-overdue vacation in the Caribbean. Lissy was probably nagging Victor about trying to get down there."

Sherlock nodded. "Even if they thought of it, no way could they manage it. Victor knows that. They've got to plan on waiting until Buzz comes home."

"For sure killing Buzz is on Lissy's to-do list. Sherlock's right, they'll simply wait for him to come home." Savich fell silent. He stared at his hands, thinking.

Sherlock, who knew her husband as well as she knew herself, was content to wait. She lightly laid her hand on Cully's forearm when he would have spoken.

Savich looked up. "I'm thinking Victor and Lissy stayed close enough to see the apartment building blow. They probably watched to see Sherlock and me go in, then they saw all of us running over here a few minutes later to look for Bernie."

Sherlock said slowly, "But they didn't try to shoot us when we ran out of the building. We were all in the open, running, sure, but we were open targets."

Savich said, "We must have come out faster than they expected. Remember, we were running flat out. Maybe they were still dealing with Bernie.

"Bottom line, we've got to assume Victor and Lissy are still out there waiting for us to waltz out this front door, then they'll try to kill us all."

"Now there's a happy thought," Sherlock said. She walked to the front living room window and scanned the surrounding trees. "We're at the very edge of town, all trees and hills out there. They could be anywhere. You really think they're watching us, Dillon?"

"Oh, yeah, I would be," he said, "watching and waiting."

Cully said, "There's only two of them. You think they'd split up—one watching the back and one watching the front?"

"Sounds reasonable," Savich said.

Sherlock said, "Agreed. Now, what are we going to do?"

Savich pulled out his cell. "I'm going to call in the cavalry."

62

PEAS RIDGE, GEORGIA

They were walked back to the meeting hall, Kjell's gun shoved against Ethan's back.

The door slid silently open.

"Go in, Sheriff, Mrs. Backman."

At the last instant, Kjell tried to grab Autumn, but she jumped out of the way. She ran behind Ethan.

Kjell stood there, obviously uncertain what to do. Then he called over his shoulder, "Keeper, I need your assistance."

Blessed came into the room behind him. He looked haggard, his eyes red from weeping.

"Stymie them, Keeper."

"No!" Autumn jerked away and faced Blessed, her arms out, trying to cover both her mother and Ethan. "No, no, Blessed, don't you dare stymie them!"

Blessed grabbed her and lifted her into his arms. "Be quiet, Autumn. You will be quiet."

Autumn sank her teeth into Blessed's arm.

Kjell said when Blessed moaned, "Give her to her mother before she chews your arm off."

Blessed lowered a flailing Autumn to the floor. She ran to her mother, wrapped her arms around Joanna's waist, and pressed her face into her stomach. She was crying huge, deep sobs that sounded—fake.

Kjell crossed his arms over his chest and merely looked at each of them in turn, but his focus, his real interest, was Autumn. Blessed pressed his fingers to his arm where she'd bitten him. There was blood on his fingers. He looked at them, his eyes angry. He was panting. "No more of this. It's time."

Autumn screamed, "No!" She ran at Blessed, hitting his stomach with her fists.

Blessed grabbed her wrists and stared down at her, and then something very strange happened.

Blessed didn't talk, didn't seem to be able to move.

Suddenly, his eyes rolled back in his head and he collapsed to the floor.

Kjell was at Blessed's side in an instant. He dropped to his knees and shook him. "Keeper! Wake up!" He reached out to grab Autumn. "What did you do to him? What?"

Kjell realized the danger too late. He leaped to his feet, brought up his gun, but Ethan was on him. He kicked the gun from his hand.

Ethan had wondered if Kjell was trained to fight, and he was. But Ethan had learned karate and some of the dirtiest street fighting on the planet—in the Philippines. He'd gotten himself stomped before he learned being vicious could be the only way to stay alive. He went after Kjell with everything he knew, with all the rage he felt. Joanna pulled Autumn to her, her hand over her eyes so she couldn't see the violence, but she knew Autumn heard the slamming of fists against flesh, the grunts, the brief silences, which were worse, and knew the instant Ethan broke Kjell's nose and his glasses. Blood flew out to streak down the white wall behind him.

She watched Kjell, blood pouring down his face, land a kick in Ethan's kidney, watched him stumble back and fall, then roll back onto his feet. He went at Kjell furiously, his fist to his jaw, a kick to his belly, his other fist hard into his broken nose. Kjell, utterly silent to this point, fell back and moaned.

Joanna's heart nearly stopped when Kjell jumped at Ethan, dragged him down to the white floor. They rolled over and over, grunting, hitting each other in the head, each trying to gain leverage.

And then it was over. Ethan, on top, reared back and sent the heel of his hand into Kjell's broken nose, sending droplets of his blood flying. Kjell didn't make a sound. His eyes rolled back and he went limp. Ethan shook his hand, rubbed his bloody knuckles.

Joanna's mouth was so dry she couldn't find the spit to speak. Finally she whispered, "Is he dead?"

"Yes." Ethan got slowly to his feet and stared down at the young man. What had

Caldicot Whistler promised him if Kjell obeyed him? Great wealth? Power? Had Kjell killed the people Autumn had seen the Backmans burying? Now nothing mattered to him. He was dead. Ethan picked up Kjell's gun and put it in his belt.

Blessed moaned and sat up. He clapped his hands to his head and began to weave back and forth. He looked at Ethan, then at Joanna, looked hard, but he didn't look at Autumn. He clutched his forehead in his hands and whispered, "This cannot be, it cannot," and he fell onto his side again and began crying.

Ethan said, "Autumn, what did you do to Blessed?"

Autumn was deathly pale. Ethan went down on his knees and pulled her against him. "I'm sorry, sweetheart. I know it's bad, but I need you to pay attention to me right now, okay? This is super-important. Tell me what you did to Blessed."

"I didn't do anything, Ethan, I only—"

The door in the wall suddenly closed again.

Ethan knew they didn't have much time. He said, "We're going to get out of here. We'll go back the way we came."

"Ethan."

He turned to see Joanna staring down low on the wall. He heard gas snaking out from a small white vent not six inches above the floor. He cursed under his breath. "We've got to get out of here."

He scooped Autumn up in his arms and ran to where they'd first entered the white room, Joanna right behind him. Even though he could see the outline of the sliding door, he couldn't see how to open it.

"There has to be something," Joanna said. "There has to be." Ethan went on his knees in front of Autumn. "We're going to run our palms over this wall, look for a button, anything. Breathe real light; try not to let the gas get to you."

They couldn't find a way out. Ethan slammed his shoulder against the door, but it was solid. He could smell the gas, feel it against his skin. He ripped off his shirt, ran back to the low vent in the wall, and dropped to his knees. He stuffed his shirt as best as he could between the narrow slats. But to do any good at all, he had to hold the shirt in place.

Joanna fell to her knees beside him, shoved up her shirt, and unclipped her bra. "Move your shirt." As she stuffed her bra between the slats, Ethan yelled, "Autumn, go over by the far wall and pull your T-shirt up over your nose and mouth!"

Joanna pulled off her sneakers and stripped off her socks. He did the same. They stuffed the socks in, trying to hold their breath as they worked.

Objectively, Ethan knew there would be no stopping the gas, and there wasn't. "Sorry, Joanna, this isn't going to cut it. We've got to find the way out of this place. There's got to be some mechanism."

"Yes, there has to be something," Joanna said. "There has to be."

But there wasn't. Ethan felt the world spin, felt as if he were rising off the floor. He passed out.

63

WINNETT, NORTH CAROLINA

Eight minutes passed before Savich's cell phone rang.

"Savich." After a moment, he nodded. "Good." And he punched off his phone.

He said to Cully and Sherlock, "The cavalry's here. The chief of police and every single deputy Winnett has on the payroll are in position. They can't cover the woods, but they've got Pulitzer Prize Road blocked on both ends. They're forming a big perimeter, hunkering down where there are breaks in the trees, but trying to stay out of sight.

"The chief said he posted a couple of

marksmen on top of Victor's apartment building, came in through the back and up the stairs to the roof. The chief assures me everyone did their best to keep Victor and Lissy from knowing they're there. We didn't hear any cars from here, so maybe they didn't either. They're looking for Victor and Lissy's car or, rather, for a car that's hidden, since we don't know what car Victor and Lissy are driving right now."

Cully said, "They've probably got it stashed in some trees off the road."

"Can't be too far from here. Maybe the chief will find it. Then we've got them."

"So in the best of all possible worlds, Lissy and Victor have no clue they're surrounded," Sherlock said.

Cully slammed his fist into the wall. "I hate this, I really do. What if Bernie is dead?" He looked into Savich's eyes. "I guess you don't know. Bernie's wife, Jessie—she's my sister. They've got two kids, my nephews."

Sherlock touched her fingers to his forearm. "He's their hostage until they nail us and drive out of Winnett, Cully. He's alive, at least for now."

He nodded, but she knew he wasn't holding out much hope.

She said again, "Dillon, it's time to see if they split up, see if one of them is waiting out back for us to step out the kitchen door. It's about thirty feet from the back of the house to the edge of the woods, and the neighboring house is a good fifty feet away. It's all forest on our other side. Now, since it wouldn't be bright to go out the back door, I'm thinking to go out the bedroom window, there's a whole mess of oaks out there. Great cover." Sherlock saw his face and added real fast, "I'm the smallest, I can slip through the window, they won't see me. You know I can dodge and duck with the best of them. I'll slip into those trees and work my way back—"

Savich said, "No way. You just had your spleen removed, Sherlock."

"Come on, Dillon, it's been months since the surgery. I'm fine. You know I'm fine. Stop playing Mr. Protector."

"Forget it, you're still not up to running all out in the woods. I want you and Cully to stay put, keep a sharp eye out. Look at it this way, we've got backup in place. I'll probably be redundant. Don't worry. I'll be back soon. Good plan, by the way." And before Sherlock could jump on him or yell at him, Savich moved away from the front windows back down the hall to the bedroom.

He heard Sherlock say behind him, "Who needs a spleen anyway?"

64

Victor Nesser threw his binoculars to the ground. *"Where are they?"*

Lissy jumped a bit, picked up the binoculars, and looked through them. "There's still no movement in the house, not even a face looking out the front windows. Even though they couldn't find our federal cop buddy here—I'll bet you they called for their crime scene team, Victor, and that's why they're still inside the house."

Victor said, "But why isn't the crime scene team here yet? Why aren't they *doing* something?"

"I remember, it's *forensic* team, that's

what they call them on TV," Lissy said. "You're right, it's been way too long." She handed him back the binoculars.

"Yeah, but, you know, this is a hick town. Where would anybody get a forensic team? Maybe at Bud's Bowling Bonanza or down at O'Malley's Dairy Queen? What's taking them so long to get it together? *Why aren't they coming out of the house?*"

Lissy patted Victor's cheek. "They will, baby, they will. They're stupid. They don't know anything. They'll come trotting out of the front door any minute now and we'll blow them into a gazillion pieces." She frowned suddenly, punched his arm. "Some bomb you made, Victor. First you couldn't manage to stall out that security guard's car in Washington, and now you couldn't get the bomb to go off. Some computer expert you are."

"It should have gone off," Victor said, rubbing his arm. "I followed the instructions carefully; you watched me do it. Don't hit me again, Lissy, I don't like it."

"Still," she said, then looked over at Bernie. "We've got Mr. Fed here, and that's something."

Victor leaned over and punched Bernie

hard in the arm. "Hey, wake up, pigface. You know why your buddies aren't out here looking for you?"

Bernie was awake, had been for some time now, trying to control his roaring headache from the blow on the back of his head. Actually, he'd been whispering hallelujahs. Victor's bomb hadn't exploded, thank the good Lord, which meant Savich and Sherlock had disarmed it. Cully was still alive, and that was all Bernie wanted to think about. He'd hoped they'd say something useful if he kept playing possum, but then Victor hit him.

"Come on, pigface, open your baby blues!"

"His eyes aren't blue, Victor, they're brown."

"Yeah? How do you know that, Lissy?"

"He's all big and dark; no blue eyes for him."

Bernie opened his brown eyes and stared up at Victor. He didn't have to fake looking dazed. "What?"

"Hey, were you trying to fake it? Or are you still knocked stupid?" Lissy punched him in the belly with her fist. He barely responded. "See? He's still stupid. I hit him

so hard his cop brains are still scrambled."
She leaned down and whispered in his
ear as her palm flattened out on his stomach. "Hey, Mr. Agent, I like the feel of your
gut. No fat, good muscle tone. Let me see."
Lissy jerked his shirt out of his pants, ripped
the buttons off, and spread it open. "Wow,
Victor, look at our buff cop here." She
stroked her hand over his stomach, and,
to his horror, Bernie felt her fingers slide
down into his shorts.

He tried to jerk away, then coughed,
wheezed.

Victor jerked when he saw her hand.
"What are you doing, Lissy? Stop that,
you hear me? You don't even know him.
Stop it!"

Lissy laughed, pulled her hand out of
his pants. "That's the way to wake up a
cop, Victor. All you gotta do is touch their
brains." And she laughed again. "Hey,
that's true of any guy, isn't it? From what I
could tell, our cop here's got a pretty good
brain."

Victor looked at her like he hated her,
then kicked a rock on the ground beside
him. "Why's it taking them so long to come
out of the house? Forget the forensic crap.

There's no way they know we're here; they've got to figure we're gone. So where are they?" But Victor didn't really care at that moment what the federal agents were doing because his heart was still pounding at what Lissy had done—she'd actually touched another man, she'd actually *felt* the damned cop, and right in front of him. His hands shook. He wanted to hurt her; he wanted to kill the damned agent. He said again, "They should have come out. Why haven't they?"

Bernie heard the shrillness in Victor Nesser's voice, knew he was furious, near violence, at what Lissy had done. He had to calm things down. He said matter-of-factly, "Since I'm not in the house, they're checking everywhere for clues. They're thorough, so it takes time." *And they know you two didn't leave. They figured it out, they're holding tight, waiting for the local cops to show up.* But Bernie hadn't heard any sirens, hadn't heard a blessed thing. Were they coming in silent?

"Our pretty boy here is right," Lissy said. "There's been time for a whole battalion of cops to get here, but no one's come to save their butts. I think they're still looking around, still looking for *clues*. Don't worry about it, Victor, those clowns don't know we're out here. They're stupid." She thought about the constant ache in her stomach and rubbed her fingers along the row of ugly metal staples still dug into her flesh. She saw Savich clear in her mind, on his back on the bank's marble floor. He'd kicked up so fast, kicked her so hard, she hadn't even seen his leg, just felt the horrible pain that knocked her backward, knocked all her breath out of her. She remembered lying there, a fire in her belly, and she couldn't breathe.

"We'll get them." Victor saw she was in pain and smacked his fist against his leg once, twice. "We just didn't have time."

Lissy said, "I could have killed all three of them when they came running out, exploded their heads right off. But you were saying wait, wait, wait." She frowned. "Too bad that redheaded woman is going to eat one of my bullets. Her hair is cool; I want to know how she makes it look like that. She must be Savich's partner. Do you think they're sleeping together? Hey, pretty boy? Savich and that redheaded woman, they doing the dirty?"

"I don't know," Bernie said, and hoped it sounded believable.

Victor said, "Look, Lissy, you need to focus. Listen, I stopped you from shooting at them because it was too big a risk. Why take chances? If you missed even one of them we'd be in a deep crap pit now. No, this is better. We'll wait. When they come out of that front door, not expecting a thing, we'll take them down, take them all down, because we'll be ready. It'll be like shooting those Coke cans off tree stumps in your backyard, remember? Don't forget, we've got their buddy here, and they'll figure it out eventually. He's a big, important FBI agent. He gives us an edge, if we need it."

Lissy said suddenly, "Wait, what if they're worried we could be out here waiting for them? What if they go out the back door?"

Victor said patiently, "There's no reason for them to go out the back door. There's nothing back there but miles of woods. Why would they do that? They haven't figured out a thing. Stop your worrying and keep your eyes on the front of the house."

Bernie was praying Lissy would listen to him.

Lissy got to her feet. "I'm going to jump out of my skin if I have to wait here another minute. I'm going to check it out. I can circle around through the woods, get right up to the back door." She kicked Bernie with her toe. "You think they're still looking for clues? Dusting for fingerprints on the kitchen floor? Maybe using one of those fancy machines that shines blue and shows up bloodstains? It takes that long? They're up to something, Victor. Hey, if I come in through the back maybe I'll catch them all by surprise, shoot 'em before they even know I'm there. Maybe I can talk to that redhead about her hair. I'm thinking she must use some special hair products."

Down the rabbit hole, Bernie thought, and kept his eyes closed.

"Open your eyes, lover boy, say good-bye."

Bernie opened his eyes and said to the beautiful fresh-faced teenager who was anything but, "Good-bye."

She laughed and blew Victor a kiss, looked again at Bernie's belly, and said, "Keep him close, Victor, you never know when you'll need yourself a shield." She smacked her lips and laughed. "If he's still alive tonight, I might have myself some fun with him. You know, give him an IQ test."

Victor didn't say anything to that until Lissy disappeared into the trees. Then he bent down to the man lying bound at his feet, and stuck his gun against Bernie's mouth and shoved his lips apart. "You're never going to touch Lissy," he said. Bernie nearly gagged at the barrel close to the back of his throat. There was nothing he could do. He thought of Jessie and his boys.

Victor got himself back under control. He pulled the barrel slowly out of Bernie's mouth, shrugged, and eased down, his back pressed against an oak tree.

Bernie thanked God it wasn't Lissy who was enraged, because she'd have shot him without a thought. He tested his wrists again. He wasn't going to get himself free, his hands and feet were tied too tight. Victor held a gun on his lap, which meant Bernie was a half a second away from being dead. There was nothing he could do, nothing except pray, and that's what he did.

He prayed Savich and Sherlock and Cully had realized what was happening, prayed this insane Lolita wouldn't come in through the back door, laughing like a maniac, and empty a clip into them.

Victor said in a meditative voice, never looking away from the front of the house, "Do you know I've never killed anyone myself? That's why I drove the van for my aunt. I told her I didn't want to do that. A couple of days ago I shot a highway patrol officer woman in the chest. Lissy was yelling at me to shoot her between the eyes so she couldn't rat us out, but she was looking up at me, you know? And I shot the ground next to her head. I really didn't think she'd live; there was blood all over her chest." Victor leaned his head back and closed his eyes. "I guess Lissy was right, that woman cop did live, and she did rat us out, she told them exactly who we were. It was all over the car radio news, this big news bulletin about us."

Victor turned to look at Bernie. "But you, buddy, you're coming on to Lissy, and that makes me mad. Maybe I could kill you and not feel bad about it."

65

PEAS RIDGE, GEORGIA

When Ethan managed to open his eyes, he was lying on his back on a soft, pale blue rug, staring up at a white ceiling. He managed to sit up. He was in a nice-sized room, with a large bed with a pale blue coverlet, a desk that looked like an antique, and shelves built in behind it filled with books and what looked like journals. There was a gooseneck lamp on top of the desk, next to a computer. He saw a door that probably led to a bathroom.

The room looked like a superior hotel accommodation. There were raised blinds over the glass window in the door.

He walked to the door. It was locked, but he looked out the window. He could see only a window down the hall a ways from him.

He was in one of the members' rooms. *No mortification of the flesh in this place,* he thought, and touched the frame of a photograph on the wall, this one of a sky filled with stars.

He felt dizzy and slightly nauseated from the gas. Where were Joanna and Autumn? *Probably in a room of their own,* he thought. He stretched out on the comfortable bed and looked up at the white ceiling.

Who had brought him here? Whistler? There had to be others who worked for him. He had to be ready when they came.

He lay silent and still for a while longer, until the vagueness and nausea slowly receded a few minutes later. Ethan realized he was hungry. He pulled an old wrapped mint out of his pants pocket, peeled off the wrapper, and sucked on it. He closed his eyes.

He had nothing to do but wait.

He heard a key turn in the lock, and the door opened. Whistler stood there, his hand out, holding a gun. "I see you're awake already, Sheriff, as you should be," he said. "We've never had to use the gas before. I see now it was a prudent measure, after all. We couldn't have you leaving through the outer door."

"Were you watching the whole time?"

"Another precaution. I saw how you overcame my poor Kjell. I was fond of him." Whistler continued in a meditative voice, "Truth be told, I believed Kjell was invincible. I saw him fight at his dojo in Seoul; he never lost. Evidently I thought too highly of his skills, since you killed him.

"You have cost us dearly, Sheriff, and I hope to see you pay for it."

"Where are Joanna and Autumn?"

"They are in a comfortable room. Now it's time, Sheriff. You wanted to meet the Father. You will now."

66

WINNETT, NORTH CAROLINA

Savich eased open the bedroom window and climbed out. He ran bent over into the thick oak and pine trees before making his way around to the back of the house. Once in position, he dropped to his knees and looked across the large overgrown backyard. He didn't see anything, and no face through the window. Good, Sherlock and Cully were still in the dilapidated living room in the front. He moved deeper into the trees, stopping every few steps to listen. He was surprised when the land sloped downward. He realized there was no way Victor and Lissy had hunkered down back here; they wouldn't be able to see much of anything from this position. Climbing a tree would probably give them a view of the front of Victor's apartment building, but they'd be too exposed. No, they were on higher ground, with a full view of the front of the house. Still, he could never be certain of anything Lissy Smiley might do. One of them could be here in the woods behind the house figuring it was a perfect way to surprise them.

Savich studied the patterning of the trees, the play of light and shadows, the shapes of the branches, watching for any sort of movement, anything at all.

He stopped cold when he heard a soft popping noise. Did an animal make that sound? Then he heard a man moan, nothing more, just a low moan of pain. Another moan, this one deeper. Whoever it was, he was in trouble. If it was Bernie, that meant Lissy and Victor were close by.

Savich waited another moment, listened. He moved as quickly and quietly as he could through the trees, keeping low, in the direction of the man's moan.

It was oddly silent, not even the sound

of a bird or an animal. Every creature was listening, as he was.

The ferocious humid heat had slackened some in the early evening, but still sweat poured off him. He paused again, listened, but he heard nothing. Had he misjudged the direction of the moans?

Through the trees in front of him, Savich saw a small clearing, and in the middle of it a man in a deputy's uniform lay on his side, his face turned away from Savich. Savich couldn't tell if he was alive. Lissy or Victor did this, which meant they were close by, maybe waiting for him, or anyone, to step clear of the trees. He'd be hopelessly exposed. Savich didn't want to go into that clearing, but he also knew he didn't have a choice. If the deputy was alive, he couldn't leave him lying there helpless. He ran crouched over, dropped to his knees beside the deputy. The man was unconscious. He was young, not more than twenty-two, fresh out of the police academy. He had a bullet wound to his shoulder. Savich hadn't heard a gunshot, just the quiet popping sound. It was a silencer he'd heard, and the shooter had to be near.

If it was Lissy, he wondered why she hadn't shot him between the eyes. He pressed his fingers to the deputy's throat. A pulse, fairly steady. Savich pressed his palms down hard on the wound to slow the bleeding. What could he use for a pressure dressing? He ripped off one of his shirt sleeves and tied it tight around the deputy's shoulder. Then he pressed his palms down over the wound again.

In that moment, Savich knew someone was close, but there was nothing he could do about it, not with this young man's blood all over his hands. He heard the popping sound again at the same moment he felt a shock of frigid cold in his leg. And he heard Lissy's voice, all high and excited. "Hey, Agent Savich. Lookee here, lookee here!"

Savich nearly fell over but shifted his weight to his other leg, and kept the pressure on the deputy's shoulder. He didn't even look around at her. He called out over his shoulder, "Hey, Lissy, what took you so long? Where'd you get the silencer for your gun?"

"Oh, I haven't been far away. I've been watching you take care of the little boy cop here. My silencer—it's the coolest thing. I got it from a really cute redneck gun dealer in Tumis Springs yesterday; gave him two big ones for it. It was marked three hundred dollars, but he gave me a deal."

"I guess he didn't ask for any ID."

"Oh, no. He was smart."

The redneck gun dealer had known she was crazy and didn't want to die. Slowly, without reducing the pressure, he turned to see Lissy Smiley standing not six feet away from him in the shadow of a skinny pine tree. She was smiling hugely at him. He said, "I admit I'm surprised here, Lissy. Why didn't you kill the deputy right off?"

"Fact is, I didn't clock him because I hoped one of his partners would hear him moaning and thrashing around and come help him. He just folded right down, just managed a couple of wimpy moans. No one came. Isn't that just the sweetest thing? Here I was getting ready to give him a little tap to the forehead, get back to Victor, but then you came, Agent Savich, the big hero cop, running to save the little punk's life. Like, who cares if he was around or not?"

"Wouldn't anybody care if you died?"

He saw momentary panic in her pretty eyes. Was she seeing herself lying on the ground instead of this deputy, bleeding her life away?

"My mama would have cared if I'd died, but she's dead, so it doesn't matter."

"This guy has a mother too."

She was shaking, waving the gun at him, hysteria hot in her voice. "Shut up, you hear me? You're responsible for my mother dying, you bastard, so shut up, you hear me?"

He thought she was going to kill him then, but instead she relaxed a bit and actually sneered at him. He realized she wanted to gloat, she wanted to rub his face in her victory, and it gave him precious time. She said, "Hey, I sure hope your leg's hurting bad, like I can see it bleeding from here. I didn't kill you because I got some things to say first. You wanna know why I shot you in the leg? Because that's the leg you kicked me with. No way you can kick me now.

"No, don't you move, don't you even twitch. I will kill you if you try for your gun. You stay right there. I see your gun right beside the deputy. You throw it over here or I'll shoot your head off. *Now!*"

He didn't want to let up the pressure on the deputy's shoulder. He saw blood was seeping from the wound on the outside of his leg, but it wasn't bad. He said, "Lissy, I don't want this man to die. I can't let up the pressure."

She laughed, then yelled, "You throw your gun over here or I'll shoot you in the face, then I'll put another bullet in that idiot deputy, get him out of his misery."

Savich picked up his SIG and tossed it toward her. It landed only about three feet from the bottom of the deputy's left boot, too far away for her to get it, but Lissy didn't seem to notice. He kept pressing both hands on the deputy's shoulder, fully aware he had to get some pressure on his own leg soon.

She sang out, her voice high and manic, "I got you, I got you. Now it's you and me. You want to talk about dying, Agent Savich? Why not? I can't wait to watch you die slow."

"Yes, you sure do have me," Savich said, voice low, controlled. He held himself perfectly still. "You know, Lissy, this deputy wasn't just lost. There are deputies all around us. There could be one coming up on you right now. Fact is, you and Victor will end your spree right here, tonight. I'm thinking maybe there's a way out for you, but then again, maybe not."

"What way? Come on, spit it out, you bastard." She twisted her head around, then back to him again.

"I know you've got Bernie Benton for a hostage already, right?"

"Yeah, we got him."

"Fact is, he's a very little fish, of little importance in the FBI. He's just not enough. I've got juice, Lissy, everyone knows that. I'd say about the smartest thing you could do is take me as a hostage. You need me, Lissy, otherwise it'll be all over for you and Victor."

She laughed, clasped both hands around the gun, and aimed it right at his chest, but he saw that her eyes were more focused, more sane. "Well, now, maybe you've got a point there, maybe you don't. Tell you what, you and I will take a nice hike back to Victor, see if he thinks we can use you." She looked at the unconscious deputy. "You even tore off your shirtsleeve for this loser. I'll tell you, I couldn't believe it when I saw him trying to be cool, sniffing around, poking his gun into every damned bush, looking around every tree. I shot him

fast, he didn't even have time to crap himself. Then look what I bagged—the big
honcho himself." She studied him a moment as he continued to press down on
the young guy's shoulder. He heard the
bewilderment in her young voice when she
said slowly, "You'd have come running if I
only shot an animal, wouldn't you? I don't
understand that. They kill each other all
the time."

"Actually, Lissy," he said, "an animal only
kills for food, not for the fun of it. And people don't leave other people lying on the
ground bleeding. Except maybe Jeff, I think
his name was. Your mother wanted him to
help you, but he ran, didn't he?"

Lissy shouted, "That puking creep! He
couldn't get out of there fast enough. I'm
glad he's dead, glad!" Just as suddenly the
mad light left her eyes and she shrugged.
She tossed her head. "See, Jeff's dead,
and no one cares." She looked at him like
she was ready to put a bullet in his head.

He said, "Let me ask you, Lissy, would
you come running if someone shot Victor?
Or would you run away to save your own
skin, like Jeff did to you?"

"Sure, I'd come running for Victor, but

that's different. He's not some stranger out to bring me down like you and these jerk-face cops. Victor loves me. He'd do anything for me. I know him. He's like the other half of me. He thinks things through, real careful, you know?" She paused a moment, and for a second she looked oddly vulnerable. "Mama said you got to take care of number one first, or number one might just die and then what did it matter about number two or number three, or anyone else? Mama always said Victor was too sweet. Sometimes he is sweet, but not always." She shook her head, as if focusing herself again, and scuffed the toe of her sneaker into a mess of leaves at her feet. Her eyes flicked to the deputy. "I wondered what this little twerp was doing here in the woods. You knew we were close and you called the cops, didn't you?"

Pain flashed hot in his leg and he almost moaned with it. He'd never been shot in the leg before. It was like a searing knife was stuck in his flesh, deep and twisting now, that blessed numbing cold long gone, and there was nothing he could do about it.

Savich said, "You got me, Lissy. Are you

ready to see what Victor thinks of me as your hostage? You know, that other agent isn't really worth much at all, you could even let him go, no loss. He's with Victor, right?"

"Oh, sure, he's with Victor. Me, I decided to do some reconnaissance. I was looking real hard at the back door of that dumpy house, praying for one of you to come strolling out, but no one did."

She was angry again and frowned at him, her gun steady on his chest. "You think you're going to get out of this, big boy? Maybe you didn't fire the shot that killed my mama, but you threw the gun to that damned security guard, and he shot her. He shot her in the neck! I saw it, saw all her blood spurt out. I saw her die!" Her hand was shaking again, and Savich waited, ready. "I'm going to kill him too. I wonder if my pretty boy Bernie has anyone who'll care when he dies?"

"Yes, he does, a wife and two small kids."

"Well, boo-hoo, the kids aren't going to get a bedtime story from Daddy tonight. He's one of you, out to bring me down. He's the enemy. His wife won't be sad for long. Mama told me after Daddy was out of the picture she had herself lots of fun."

She rubbed her palm across her chest. "You know, I can't dance right now because of you. I don't have stitches, they put in those staples. I don't know how to get them out. Victor doesn't like to look at them." She studied him, then shrugged. "All right, Mr. Big Shot, you've earned yourself ten minutes. We'll see what Victor has to say about you being our hostage. Get your hands off that deputy's shoulder and stand up."

Savich slowly lifted his hand from the deputy's chest. He'd had enough time and the bleeding had stopped.

He had a chance.

67

Savich looked at his SIG from the corner of his eye, then looked at her closely, weighed his chances of diving for his gun, raising it, and shooting her. He figured his odds and realized it was a no-go. He couldn't trust his leg.

He said, "Let me get some pressure on my leg, okay? You don't want me to bleed to death, do you? How could I walk you and Victor to safety?"

She chewed on her lower lip. "All right, use your belt, that'll do it."

Savich pulled off his belt and pulled it tight around his leg. He knew he'd been lucky, the bullet was in and out, torn flesh and muscle, not all that deep. He'd be in big trouble if the bullet had lodged in him. He tried to put weight on the leg and it held up. The pain was bad, throbbing hard. It didn't matter, he had to move his leg, work it.

"Now let's get back to Victor. We gotta talk about you. Then I'll say good-bye to poor Bernie with the two little kids. Then we gotta get our money. I'm thinking Victor and I should head out west, maybe Montana. What do you think?"

"You and Victor don't have the money with you?"

"Mama hid most of the money in our house in Fort Pessel. When Victor and I went there, cops were all over the house so we couldn't get to it." He saw her hand shake from the memory. "Doesn't matter. After I take care of you, we'll go back and get it. It won't be a problem—all those ya-hoos will be swarming down here looking for us. Then we'll be set. Do you know how long it takes to drive to Montana?"

"Three, four days."

She nodded. "That's what I was thinking. I don't want to go fast, just sort of see all the tourist sights. Now, step back."

He did, and his leg held. He put his weight on it, moved it, tensed the muscles.

"Back up six feet."

He backed up. The movement was good.

He watched Lissy pick up his SIG, shove it into her wide belt with its big turquoise buckle. She waved her gun at him. He walked slowly, carefully, Lissy six feet behind him, not taking any chance he could reach her.

He prayed they wouldn't run into anyone. He didn't want to see anyone else die.

He knew Sherlock had to be planning something. He'd been gone too long.

"You're walking too slow. Move!" He limped faster between the thick trees.

"You know, Bernie's got a real good body, and he's old, at least thirty. I'm thinking you're even better. I was watching you pushing down on the deputy's shoulder, and I really like your muscles. You look meaner than Bernie does too, like a guy who's bashed some heads together. I like mean and hot. When I was thirteen, there was this biker dude, he was twenty and he was meaner than a gator, real bad, and so hot all the girls wanted him." She stopped, frowned at the memory, shook her head. "I had sex with him once, but then he left. Victor was eighteen and I got him instead, took his virginity while I was thinking about my biker dude.

"When I get you all settled down and tied up, I'll see. Hey, you married? You got a wife who'll miss you for maybe five minutes? You got little kiddies?"

"No, I'm not married."

"That redheaded girl, she your partner? You screwing her?"

"Why?"

"I want to talk to her before I blow her head off. I really like what she's done to her hair. I'm thinking I want to go red, get me some curls like she has." She fluffed her hair. "Think she'll tell me how to get what she's got?"

"Probably not if she realizes you're going to kill her. I mean, why should she?" Lissy Smiley was crazy and she was sixteen. He limped badly, even managed a big grimace of pain, which wasn't all that much of a stretch.

"I'll bet you're lying to me. You are screwing her, aren't you?"

"Nah. I don't even like her much."

"Well," Lissy said and laughed, "she a lesbian?"

Savich didn't say anything; he was listening. He heard something, a footfall. Was it Sherlock? Another deputy? He said quickly, to distract her, "About her hair, I'm thinking maybe she dyes it. But her eyebrows are a sort of dark red-brown, so maybe not."

Lissy laughed again, high and manic. "I'll be sure to ask her. Okay, lover boy, move it. We've got to get back to Victor. Hey, she any good with a gun?"

"Good enough." His leg hurt bad, but he had it under control. Could he manage enough of his weight on the left leg and kick out with his right? He didn't know. He knew if he tried and missed, he'd be dead.

He made his limp impressive.

"Wait, lover boy. Hold up a minute. I think I heard something. Maybe it's that little redheaded partner of yours. That would be good."

68

PEAS RIDGE, GEORGIA

When the door closed behind him, Ethan whirled around, but Caldicot hadn't come in.

Ethan turned to see an old man sitting on an immense, beautifully carved golden chair that would have suited Queen Victoria. He had to be at least eighty. He looked frail and insubstantial, with wispy clumps of white hair on his head and a seamed face. All in all, he would have looked like a pleasant old geezer if not for his pinched mouth, small and mean. Despite the gentle voice, what Ethan saw was decade upon decade of pettiness and ill will toward others. The old man's eyes were dark with intelligence, and with power, as he looked at Ethan. His body might be old, but his mind was fit. He wore a long white robe pulled together at his meager waist with a gold belt, like Whistler's.

"Good evening, Sheriff Merriweather. You will be fine in just another moment. The gas is a special compound that acts very quickly and dissipates just as quickly. Caldicot told me about the clothes both you and Joanna used to try to keep out the gas. Very creative. Caldicot was amused, except for the fact that you killed poor Kjell. And of course Blessed is injured. He is on the floor of my study, weeping. He is inconsolable. What did Autumn do to him, Sheriff?"

"I don't know."

"Surely you must have an idea. You have been with the child and her mother for nearly a week now. I must know, Sheriff."

"Where are Joanna and Autumn?"

"They are both fine at the moment. What did the child do to Blessed?"

"Who are you, Whistler's father?" Ethan had the mad desire to laugh.

The old man didn't say anything, continued to look at him, as if he was trying to figure something out.

Ethan said, "Who are you?"

"I, Sheriff Merriweather? Why, I am the Father, but I am not, however, related to Whistler. This is my home, and all those who reside here, for however long a time, are my children. They obey my wishes and in return are enlightened about powers beyond themselves."

"So Caldicot doesn't run things around here?"

"I'll tell you what, Sheriff. It seems we need each other, and so I will answer your questions and then you will have no reason not to answer mine. Caldicot does not run things here. Caldicot is my fine first lieutenant. He fancied the name Master, and so I gave it to him. Sometimes, when he doesn't realize I'm looking, he struts like he is the important one here, but he is not. I allow him his little conceits since he is something of a financial wizard, a blessing, since I find such things boring. He gathers our people from all over the world, and if he deems them worthy, he brings them here."

He raised a gnarled hand, pointed a thin

finger at Ethan. His fingernails were long and curved inward. His old voice quaked with anger. "I have answered your questions, Sheriff. Now you will tell me what Autumn did to Blessed. I must know."

"I have told you, I don't know what she did. As far as I know, she only looked at him, that was it."

"I don't believe you. All of this—the death of Kjell, my poor Grace shot by your hand, my wife calling me, desperate because they were taking her to jail, and it's all your fault, Sheriff. But Blessed, we cannot do without Blessed!"

Ethan said slowly, "Well, if this doesn't beat all—you must be Theodore Backman."

The old man gave him a regal nod. "Of course. Autumn is my granddaughter. I have lost two of my three sons, Sheriff. I will not lose my granddaughter as well. She appears to have more power than Blessed, even at her young age. She belongs to me, to my family, to Twilight. Her gift will draw the devout from all over the world. She will be revered. Under my tutelage who knows what she will become, the power she will have."

Ethan said, "Your wife said you died in a mugging in Reno some time ago. So, it didn't happen. It was all a fiction so you would be free to set up this cult. It occurs to me you could have done this without dying."

"I had no choice. I had to die. The gangsters who ran the casinos decided they didn't want to lose any more money to me, that I was stealing from them, though I played by their rules. The mugger was an assassin they sent to kill me, but I killed him instead. I was forced to cut all ties to Bricker's Bowl because of those vermin."

The old man sighed.

Ethan said, "So that's when you decided to open this place? *Children of Twilight?* I'm wondering, Mr. Backman, why all the white? And the robes—you wish to be seen as a prophet? Or perhaps as something more than that?"

"You speak so very simply, Sheriff, so unequivocally. You don't know anything about it. All of this, it was a huge undertaking. I was not a young man, even then."

"And Caldicot? What does he get from this?"

Theodore shrugged. "Shepherd and I

found Caldicot one day in a strip mall in Huntersville, an out-of-the-way place we chose because we had to be careful. Caldicot was selling cars, can you believe that? He tried to con us. I admired his abilities, and we talked.

"Two months later we bought the old tobacco farm some twenty miles down the road, using his mother's name. It served for a while, but I feared the assassins would find me. We decided to build my beautiful temple. As you know, money is never an issue in any decision I make.

"You know that my family is extraordinary. You've seen what Grace and Blessed can do." Theodore's face spasmed and his breathing hitched. He began to breathe too fast. He nearly rose out of his chair as he shouted at Ethan, "My poor Grace, my poor Shepherd! What have you done to my family?" Theodore's thin chest heaved. For a moment, Ethan thought he was ill.

After a moment, the old man settled himself back onto his throne. "Caldicot already believed he could read some people's minds on occasion. When he saw Blessed and Grace he was, of course, astounded. He is an ambitious man, and I convinced him he could achieve whatever he wanted if he joined with me.

"And so he did. Whistler is a Harvard man. He brings us fervent, eager people, thrilled that I will teach them."

"Caldicot said you haven't found another gifted person as yet."

"No, not as yet, but tomorrow Caldicot is leaving for Denver to see a gentleman who professes to foresee the future. We will see."

Ethan said, "So tell me again why people come to this big white concrete vault?"

Theodore waved a veiny old hand. "Enough! Look around you, Sheriff. My sanctuary is magnificent. My holdings are large here, and my children can explore the woods with me as much as they wish. Why would they not wish to stay?"

Ethan looked around the large, completely white room, the beautiful Impressionist paintings on the wall. Was that a Monet? There was a beautiful antique Persian carpet under the old man's sandaled feet.

It was a gem, this room, save for a ridiculous dais with its golden throne at the center. "You build underground to hide from the Mafia?"

Theodore said, "In part. I feared I would not be so lucky twice. There were other reasons. When you are nearly beaten to death for being who you are, Sheriff, you think about what that means. I left the business of gathering earthly wealth to my sons, and I was free to read and to contemplate, to think about the gifts we Backmans have been given, and the history of others like us. I came to believe my nearly being beaten to death had a purpose— indeed, that I have a purpose, a mission, to find others like us and to build our own community away from our murderers, a community of the elect."

"'A community of the elect'?" Ethan raised a brow. "I don't see that Caldicot has any extraordinary powers. And all these people here, are they being taught something, or are they being used? You have gathered so much money and power by putting your sons to use that you can convince these people to do just about anything, at least for a while. How long do people stay here, Mr. Backman? How long before they realize there is nothing here for them?"

"Are you quite done, Sheriff? I don't care for your sarcasm. This is where I choose to be. I'm safe here, and I come and go as I please. That old barn is set a good half-mile from the county road, a road that few drive."

"If everyone here is free to leave, then why did Autumn see your family burying people in the family cemetery?"

The old man's eyes held a momentary look of regret, and then he let it go. "Two of our visitors—not worthy of us, a rare mistake by Caldicot—threatened to expose us unless we paid them. It was a grave decision, not arrived at easily, but they were not as important as Twilight. I had to protect our secrecy, no matter what. Kjell had to remove them, unfortunately. It has been a difficult time for me, Sheriff."

"And just how did Grace and Blessed find Autumn?"

"Ah, that was a simple matter for Caldicot. He is a clever man. He knew Joanna lived in Boston. All he had to do was look up my poor Martin's obituary, and there was her maiden name. With that and what she and Autumn had told us, it required only a few well-placed phone calls to search out her family and friends, and her connection to Titusville, Virginia.

"Now, Sheriff, I have answered your questions. I have an offer for you. You will leave here alive and the woman with you if she wishes, if you convince Autumn to remain with her family. She will not suffer; she will come to be happy here, I promise you. She will be with her family, and I always protect what is mine."

69

Suddenly Theodore lowered his face in his hands a moment and whispered through his fingers, "But I couldn't protect poor Blessed." He raised his head. "My firstborn is not possessed of an agile mind. It was foolhardy of him to follow you into the Titus Hitch Wilderness. He should have waited for a better time. But he could not conceive of failing—he and Grace had never failed before, at anything we asked them to do.

"And now Grace is dead. The two of them were always so very close, in their minds, in their hearts." Theodore raised his head.

"You took part of my family, Sheriff; you owe me Autumn to pay for what you've done to me."

Ethan smiled at the profane old man. "You're worried Blessed will never be able to stymie anyone again, isn't that right, Theo?"

Theodore slammed his fist onto his throne arm. "You will call me Father or Mr. Backman!"

He sighed, then straightened, trying, Ethan thought, to look like a monarch rather than a pathetic old man. His hands fisted, making the veins ride high under his parchment skin.

He said, pride bursting in his voice, "Whatever happens, it is my granddaughter who did it to him. With no direction from anyone, with no training, with no understanding at all, this little seven-year-old girl simply pulled it out of herself. Did she destroy his power? Wipe it out of him forever? I hope not. But this child is amazing. Blessed was helpless against her. She is her father's daughter, my own granddaughter. Ah, Martin, another tragedy. I wonder what he would have achieved if he'd only remained with me in Bricker's Bowl."

"Why did he leave, Mr. Backman?"

"He was a boy, and he did not understand that with our gifts the Backmans behave as we choose, we are not bound by ordinary rules. We fought, always fought. One evening he said I was crazy, that I was using him, and I lost my temper and beat him. It never occurred to me that he would leave, but he did, and that was his choice. That left Grace and Blessed with us, and now only Blessed. I believe Autumn can help him. What she took she can give back. She must stay, Sheriff. Do you wish to live? Do you wish Autumn's mother to live? If so, you must convince the child to stay here, with her grandfather, with her uncle."

Ethan said, "Listen to me, sir, you must. You believe her mother and I can convince Autumn to stay. But Autumn doesn't want to be here, and when she meets you, I doubt she'll be leaping into your lap. She loves her mother, and if you harm me or her mother, she will never trust you, and she will find a way to leave, or to do you in. You must let her go."

Theodore's old voice was shrill. "You will listen to me, Sheriff. I have lost too much to let her go. No, Sheriff. The child will not leave Twilight."

Ethan laughed. "Twilight? I don't see any sky. Being in this place is like being buried alive."

Theodore slammed his fist onto the arm of his throne. "You will be quiet! You are common, Sheriff, and you understand nothing. I am having Autumn brought in, and you will convince her. You will tell her if she does not stay with me, you will die. Do you understand? I am her grandfather. She will come to accept that. If you value your life, you will help us come to terms."

The old man slowly pulled a gun from the sleeve of his robe, then pressed a button on the arm of his chair.

Ethan heard the door open behind him. He turned to see Caldicot come into the room, his hand around Autumn's arm, shoving Joanna in front of him. Autumn pulled and pushed at him, trying to get to her mother, but he wouldn't allow it.

Whistler tightened his hold on the little girl's arm. Why was she still fighting him? Didn't she realize how important she was to all their future plans? Didn't she realize how lucky she was, what incredible power she had, a power they would teach her to use? If only he could do what she'd done to Blessed—he'd prayed for such a talent. "Stop fighting me," he yelled down at her, and shook her arm.

"You leave her alone, you bastard!" Joanna dove at him, but her hands were tied behind her and she could only butt her head against him.

Whistler wanted to backhand the woman, but he merely shoved her hard, sending her to the floor. He shouted down at the child, "Look, that's your grandfather over there! Your grandfather! Your daddy's father! Get control of yourself!"

Autumn's eyes went blank, her pupils fixed. She became still, no expression at all on her small face.

Whistler grabbed both her arms, shook her again. "What are you doing? Damn you, what are you doing? What are you see-ing?"

Joanna jumped up at him.

Ethan yelled, "Let her go!"

Whistler sent his fist into the woman's jaw, knocking her backward. He saw the sheriff coming at him and grabbed the little girl around her chest and hauled her back against him. He raised his right hand, and Ethan saw a snub-nosed .38. "Stay back, Sheriff, or I'll shoot you! Or her, I don't care."

"Caldicot, don't harm Autumn!" Theodore yelled. "Bring her to me. Then you can take the mother and the sheriff out. Look at her eyes—her eyes are like Blessed's, the intensity burns within her."

She was looking off, away from all of them, seeing something he couldn't see. "What are you doing, child? What are you doing?"

70

WINNETT, NORTH CAROLINA

Victor heard something, like the rustling of leaves beneath someone's foot, someone who was trying to walk really quietly. Lissy? He raised his gun and turned toward the sound.

Bernie watched Victor unwind and slowly get to his feet, his gun swinging around him. Bernie hadn't heard anything.

Was it a cop? Lissy coming back? He couldn't do anything except wait and work at the damned duct tape on his hands.

From the trees he heard Lissy's excited voice: "Hey, Victor. Look at what I've got me!"

She wasn't alone. Bernie didn't want to believe it. Dillon Savich, his leg wounded, his belt wrapped around it, limped in front of Lissy.

She did a little dance. "The macho man told me all the cops in this pitiful town are on the other side of the woods, waiting for us to waltz out. All of them but one. Yep, a young deputy nearly walked right into me before I nailed him. Then Special Agent Savich here comes running to save him. See what I did, Victor? I shot him in the leg."

Victor stared at Savich, a complete stranger to him, except for his picture in the papers. Lissy was still dancing in place, she was so excited.

Victor said, "It makes sense he'd bring all the local cops in. I'm thinking they probably found our car. It's going to be tough for us to get out of here."

Lissy waved her gun around. "Big deal, a bunch of hick clucks, probably as brainless as the one I shot." She giggled. "Do you know, if I raise my face to the sky and breathe in, I can actually smell cops?" She shoved her gun into Savich's back. "This is my prize cop. Just look at his leg, he's not going to kick me anymore. Sit down, pretty boy, next to Bernie with the two little kiddies." Lissy started lightly rubbing her chest. When she saw Savich looking at her, she dropped her hand.

They were maybe a hundred yards inside the police line, Savich thought, in the thick trees that ringed the area, on high ground. He and Lissy had trekked slowly through the unending maze of oak trees, at least a quarter mile of woods, to this small hollow that sat on a sharp rise. Through the trees, he could see Victor's apartment building and the front of the ramshackle house where he'd left Sherlock and Cully.

He said to Bernie, "You okay?"

"Yeah. Yeah, I'm okay, I just feel really stupid."

"Shut up," Victor said. "I don't want you two talking, you got that? Sit down next to him and don't try anything." Victor pointed his gun right at Savich as he slowly eased down against an oak trunk, stretching out his wounded leg in front of him. He eased his belt loose, studied the wound. It had stopped bleeding. He pulled the belt off.

"Why'd you bring him here, Lissy? Why

didn't you just put a bullet through his head where you found him?"

"Big boy here tells me he's got lots more juice than poor Bernie with the two little kids, says we need a hostage cops will listen to and he's the only one who can get us out of here. What do you think?"

Victor looked from Savich to Bernie, then back to Lissy. "I don't like it, but I gotta admit, he does have more juice. Maybe he could get us out."

She cocked her head to one side and stroked her long, graceful fingers over her jaw. "When he does get us away, well, then, maybe you should be the one to put a bullet between his eyes, Victor. I'm thinking you need the practice. Remember you didn't have the balls to kill that highway patrol cop, even after I told you to punch her between the eyes?"

Victor's fist shot out so fast Lissy didn't have a chance. His fist smashed into her jaw. She reeled back, falling. Savich was halfway to his feet, his leg on fire, when Lissy screamed, "You sit back down or I'll put a bullet in Bernie! You got that, Mr. Special Agent? He'll be dead and it'll be all your fault!"

She was lying on her side, her gun aimed right at Bernie.

Savich eased back down, closer to Bernie this time, maybe close enough to get the duct tape off his wrists.

There were tears streaking down Lissy's cheeks. Victor leaned over her, his voice all soft and concerned, his fingers lightly touching her hair. "You shouldn't have said that, Lissy; you shouldn't have made me feel less a man. Look at what you made me do."

She worked her jaw with her fingers, her eyes never leaving Savich's face.

"You hurt me, Victor. You're lucky my jaw isn't broken."

"Yeah, well, you'll be okay, you won't have to go to the hospital again. No matter what you say, no matter how bad you insult me, I don't want you to have to go back to the hospital."

"I'm gonna have a big bruise."

"Not bad, I don't think," Victor said. He looked over at Savich. "You really brought this FBI agent back here as a hostage? Then you expect me to kill him? I could kill him, I could, if I wanted to. He doesn't look so tough all laid out there. We'll see, after he gets us out of here." He gave her a hand up.

Lissy continued to work her fingers over her jaw. "You could pop him right between the eyes? I could take care of Bernie. Then we'd be free and away from this hick town. We'll find us a car. I want to go to Montana."

"Montana might be good. I wonder how long it takes to drive there."

"We'll take five days, take it easy." Lissy looked up to see Bernie speaking low to Savich. "Shut up, or I'll shoot your heads off! Victor, before Super Cop takes us out of here, I've got an idea. Hand me his cell phone. I want to look at his speed dial."

Victor pressed the muzzle of his gun against Savich's throat as he pulled his cell phone out of his shirt pocket. Victor jumped to his feet and took two steps back and handed Lissy the cell. She flicked it to his stored numbers. "Isn't this a kick! The very first name, it's Sherlock."

"What kind of name is that? I wonder who he is."

"Probably a stupid nickname," Lissy said. "Let me place a call, see who this Sherlock is."

Bernie sent Savich a look, saw his face was perfectly still, expressionless.

The cell rang once, then a woman answered. "Yes?"

"Hey, is this Sherlock?"

"Yeah, I'm Sherlock. Who wants to know?"

"Smart mouth, aren't you? This is Lissy Smiley. I got me two big federal agents right here. Special Agent Savich, and Special Agent Bernie with two little kids. You're Savich's partner, right? You're the one with all that red hair?"

"That's me."

"You're really not sleeping with him? He said he didn't even like you much. Still, why wouldn't you want to get in his pants?"

"Why are you calling me, Lissy?"

"I want to know what hair color to buy to get your shade. And is that a perm?"

"Sorry, what you see is what you get."

"Well, that's too bad, now, isn't it? I called to warn you to stay inside that dumpy house or you'll get blood all over that pretty hair. I want you to tell the cops if they try anything I'll shoot these guys' heads off. Oh, yeah, the big guy is now our hostage. He's going to accompany us out of here."

And Lissy flipped off Savich's cell, threw it back at him. He caught it, stuck it in his shirt pocket. His right hand was only inches from Bernie's wrists, and neither Victor nor Lissy seemed to notice.

In that instant Autumn yelled for him.

71

Savich heard her yelling, louder than ever before. Her face was white, her eyes wild. She was panting.

What's wrong, Autumn? What's going on?

It's my grandfather, Dillon, he's alive and he's here, and I think he's going to hurt Ethan and Mama!

Whoa, wait a minute. Where are you?

In this building, it's underground, all white rooms and bad, real bad.

Autumn, listen to me. I've got a huge problem of my own right now—

Show me.

He looked over at Bernie, bound, propped up against a tree trunk, then at Victor and Lissy, their guns pointed at him. Could Autumn see what he was seeing, as he had seen that motel sign? Could she possibly see through his eyes?

"What are you doing?" Lissy yelled at him and took a step forward. "Whatever you're doing, you stop it or I'll have Victor drill you right now!"

Savich didn't think he'd moved. What had he done to spook them? He said, calm and easy, "I don't know what you're talking about, Lissy."

"Your eyes went all funny, then you stared at Victor and me and you looked like some weirdo freak, like you were looking through us. *What did you do*?"

Savich smiled. "Well, the thing is, and this is the absolute truth, there's this little girl who was looking at you guys through my eyes."

Victor whirled around, shouting, "What little girl? Where is she? There isn't a little girl! *What are you talking about*?"

Whatever the two of them had seen on

his face, he'd shaken them up. He said, "Her name is Autumn, and she's in Georgia, I think."

Lissy screamed at him, "You lying piece of—"

Victor grabbed her arm, shook it. "Lissy, no, he's doing this on purpose, trying to rattle us, get us to make a mistake. Look, he's not moving, it's all right. Whatever he does, whatever he says, it doesn't mean anything. He's just trying to creep us out. We've got to decide what to do, use him as a hostage or shoot his head off. Thing is, they can't shoot us if we've got him in front of us as a shield."

She screamed, "No! He'll do something; he'll kill us. He won't let us use him, he won't! I want him dead, Victor, now! You said you could do it if you wanted to. Well, it's time to step up." She traded guns with him. "Use mine. The silencer's on it, so no one will hear the shots. Shoot both of them, Victor. Prove to me you can do it."

Victor held the gun straight out in front of him, aimed it at Savich. His face was pale, his whole body rigid. He looked deathly afraid. Of killing them?

"Come on, Victor, drill both of them, right between the eyes!"

Savich heard Autumn scream *No!* and Victor staggered and went flying to the rocky ground, twisting and turning as if someone were physically pummeling him. Just as suddenly he stopped, and he sat up, terrified, and looked at Savich. He yelled, "Run, Lissy," and he took off into the trees.

Autumn, you did this?

"Hold it, Lissy!"

Lissy's eyes went wide with shock. Savich knew she thought Autumn was here now, but it wasn't Autumn. It was Sherlock, her SIG pointed directly at Lissy's back. Cully came running out from behind her and fired five fast rounds after Victor. They heard the cry of pain when one of the bullets struck him. Then Cully took off after Victor.

Sherlock said, "Turn around, Lissy. Very slowly, I don't want to kill you. Toss your gun to the ground right this minute."

Lissy looked over her shoulder, stared at the woman with the wild red hair. "Nice hair," she said. And she ran, firing wildly in Sherlock's direction.

Sherlock stumbled back and fell, got back up on her knees, and returned fire. She got her, heard the cry of pain, but she didn't know how badly the girl was hurt.

More shots came toward them.

"Stay down, Sherlock," Savich yelled. He stumbled over to her, half fell to his knees, and pulled her up against him. "You'd better be okay, you hear me?"

"Yeah, I'm good. Dillon, your leg!"

"It's not so bad. I can use it. Get Bernie free, then the two of you go after Victor. You'll probably have to split up to find him. Sherlock, Lissy took my gun."

Without a word, Sherlock handed him hers. He willed his leg to move, and it did, awkwardly but well enough, and he took off at a trot after her. Sherlock whispered after him, "You'd better be careful."

Savich soon saw Lissy weaving through the trees ahead of him. Sherlock's bullet was slowing her down. She jerked around, saw him, and fired. The bullet ripped past his head as he dove behind a tree. His leg screamed at him, and he waited a beat.

He heard gunfire, prayed they'd finally brought Victor down. He saw a flash of Lissy's white blouse and fired. She yelled.

He turned and ran toward her, his left leg dragging now. He yelled, "Lissy! It's over, stop now, you hear me?"

He heard her laugh, her manic laugh, loaded with pain. He knew she was on the move again, despite having two bullets in her. Lissy yelled, "You'll never catch me, you bastard. I'm going to kill you, and then I'm going to kill every single cop you brought here with you!"

He stumbled after her. Another bullet struck a tree a foot from his left shoulder. **Come on, you damned leg, keep going. Move!**

His leg must have heard him because he sprinted, moving quickly through the trees. She had to be bleeding; she had to slow down soon.

He saw her leaning against an oak tree, panting, hunched over. Blood covered her white shirt and flowed down her side over her jeans. She held his SIG in one hand and pressed her other hand to her chest. He saw blood seeping out between her fingers.

"Lissy, it's over. Drop the gun. You're hurt, we've got to get you help."

She looked toward where he was hidden

and fired. The shot went wide, sliced a small branch off an oak tree to his left. She fired again and again even when he knew she couldn't see him.

He remained quiet, solidly behind a tree, out of her line of fire.

She cursed him, and through her rage he heard the pain. A bullet took the bark off right by his face, sliced his cheek. Another damned scar. How many more rounds could she have in his SIG?

Savich knew she wouldn't stop.

It was enough, he thought; it was too much. He came out from behind the tree.

"Drop the gun, Lissy!"

She didn't. She yelled at him, "I hate you! I'm going to kill you!" She ran straight at him, screaming curses, her blood dripping from her arm, and she aimed her gun at his chest.

Savich pulled the trigger. The bullet struck her between the eyes. The force of it lifted her off her feet and flung her backward. Lissy was dead before she hit the ground.

He limped to her and stared down at the pretty eyes that no longer looked mad, at the pretty eyes that no longer saw him, no longer saw anything. Her fingers were still curled around his SIG. He pulled it free, shoved it into his waistband.

He had to get back to Sherlock. He turned on his heel and stumbled back as fast as he could.

72

Sherlock stood over Victor Nesser, panting, very aware of the tugging ache where her spleen had once resided, the heel of her boot against his chest. She'd shot at him with the Lady Colt she carried in her ankle holster a good four or five times, missed because her Colt was good only at short range. Then she shot at his feet and hit him in the ankle. He'd stumbled, kept hurtling forward, and she'd tackled him from four feet back, her adrenaline pumping hard. Now he lay on his back, breathing heavy but not moving. His ankle had to hurt. She said, trying to catch her breath, "All over now, Victor. Don't you think of twitching. Hey, we got you on both ends, head and toe."

Victor didn't move, just lay there and moaned. Sherlock yelled over her shoulder, "Cully, Bernie, I've got him. We're good here. Victor isn't going anywhere."

Victor closed his eyes tight. He heard the woman's voice, felt the weight of her foot against his chest and the god-awful pain in his shattered ankle, shooting up to his belly. He felt a sharp pain on the side of his head, licked his lips, and tasted blood. He was afraid to touch his ankle, afraid of what he'd feel. He'd rather walk around with half his head blown away than never be able to walk again. And there was nothing he could do about it. What was worse, he knew he couldn't help Lissy.

Where was Lissy? Had she killed Savich? He didn't think so; he didn't think the guy could be killed. And this redheaded agent who'd shot him was his partner.

Who was Autumn? What had she done to him? He remembered rolling around on the ground, helpless, his body twitching and heaving. Autumn was a little girl? No, that wasn't possible, there'd been no one there. It was all a lie, it was something Savich did, but what did he do, and how? He felt himself growing cold, felt fear nibble at the edges of his brain.

If only he'd shot Savich right away when he was stretched out and helpless beside Bernie, shot both of them, it would have been done, over with. And Lissy would know she could always count on him. Of course Lissy could have killed them herself, but she'd wanted to toy with them, toy with him too. It was a huge mistake, the biggest mistake they'd ever made. Their last mistake.

Victor remembered how it was before all of this, his years with his parents, his father knocking the crap out of his mother whenever the mood struck him, and then she'd gone back to Jordan with him to be knocked around some more. Was she even still alive? And Aunt Jennifer, the years that insane woman told him when to eat, when to brush his teeth, who he could speak to, and how she was going to kill him if he ever touched her precious thirteen-year-old daughter, the only human being he'd ever loved, spawned by that insane woman. He could still feel the edge of the butcher knife she'd held against his neck while she was screaming at him. Aunt Jennifer thought he was molesting Lissy. What a joke that was, but he hadn't defended himself, hadn't told her how it was Lissy with her newly budding breasts who came to his tiny bedroom under the eaves. Lissy had stopped her mother, grabbed away the knife, but still, not an hour later, Aunt Jennifer had struck him with a hammer even though she'd known it was Lissy—oh, yes, she'd known. He thought he was going to die then, but he didn't.

Victor knew there was no future for him. He guessed he'd known that from the moment Lissy got in his bed. And now Lissy could be dead. There was no way she was going to walk away from the cops this time. It was over, all of it.

Tears streamed down through the rivulets of blood on his face, not from the horrible pain of his shattered ankle but because he'd never see Lissy again. He didn't think he wanted a future. He opened his eyes and looked up at the agent standing over him, holding a small gun in her hand, aimed right at his bloody face.

Cully came up behind her, slowly lowered

his weapon, and looked down at him. He said, his voice emotionless, "You remember me, Victor? I'm the guy you trussed up on your bedroom floor, the guy you wanted to blow to pieces? Do you even remember that mother and father you and Lissy shot down in their kitchen in Alexandria? You shot two people for a damned car. How many other people have you and Lissy shot for no good reason? You're both rabid, Victor. You're both crazy."

Victor said, "I'm not crazy."

"Yeah, right," Cully said. "You going to blame it all on that teenager you've been screwing since she was thirteen?"

Sherlock lightly laid her palm against Cully's shoulder, felt him shaking with rage.

"I never screwed Lissy! Do you hear me, it wasn't ever like that. She needed me, only me. She always said she knew me, from the moment I came, she said she knew me to my soul. You're trying to kill her! You want to see her dead!"

Cully kicked Victor in the side, but Victor didn't even appear to notice. He shouted down at him, "Time for you to listen, punk. You're lucky you didn't kill Bernie or I'd kill you myself."

Sherlock saw that Cully was still shaking with rage and she said calmly, "But since you didn't kill Bernie or kill Agent Savich, Cully and I are going to take you to a hospital. We'll even help you, since your ankle's shot to pieces. You want a handkerchief to wipe the blood off your face? Ah, here's Bernie. We've got him, Bernie, no problem."

Bernie opened his mouth, but Cully overrode him. "I just wish I'd been the one to find you first," Cully said, and kicked Victor again. "I bet Bernie wishes the same thing. Then you wouldn't have gotten off with this puny foot wound."

Victor looked at them through pain-dead eyes. "You should be dead. All of you would be dead if it wasn't for that girl Autumn. Who is Autumn? There wasn't any little girl up there."

"You're right, Autumn wasn't nearby," Sherlock said. "But it doesn't really concern you now, Victor."

Victor tried to rise, hissed in pain, and fell on his side. They heard him whisper, "Lissy wanted to go to Montana. I guess that's not going to happen now."

Cully and Bernie lifted him, each of them

with a shoulder under his arms. He was crying and moaning, and he left a trail of blood on the rocky ground. Sherlock didn't care what he said; she was too worried about Dillon. Lissy could still be out there, and it was Sherlock's fault. She could have taken her down, should have, but she couldn't bring herself to shoot that young girl in the back. She'd let her focus slip for that instant of time, and Lissy had been so fast, moved in a blur, all of it unexpected, and then Sherlock had fired at her, but only a wound, maybe not even a bad one. Dillon could be dead because—Sherlock shook her head. No excuses. She'd screwed up royally, put all of them in danger. She hadn't done her job.

If it hadn't been for Autumn, Victor would have killed Dillon. "Autumn," she whispered, vaguely aware that Victor was cursing and crying, both together, "thank you for our lives."

"Sherlock, you guys all right?"

Savich came limping through the trees. He was almost whole. Good enough. She gave him a huge smile.

Victor stopped cold. He yelled, "Where's Lissy? What did you do to Lissy?"

Savich looked at the young man's ravaged face, at the soul-eating fear in his eyes. He said, "She's gone, Victor."

Victor raised his face to the darkening sky. "Lissy! Oh, God, Lissy, you can't die, you can't!" He wept like a lost soul from hell.

73

PEAS RIDGE, GEORGIA

Whistler looked down at her, and Ethan took his chance. He threw himself at Whistler, hurled him against the wall. His gun went skidding across the floor.

"Autumn, untie me!"

Autumn fell to her knees beside her mother and began to work at the knots. Joanna had to watch Ethan and Whistler trade blows until finally she pulled free. Joanna staggered to her feet and pushed Autumn behind her. She wanted to help Ethan, but she'd seen him fight. He didn't need her.

Whistler was stronger than Ethan had thought, but he had no real chance. Ethan had rage on his side, rage so deep it resounded in the most primitive part of him. He wanted blood. He staggered Whistler with a kick to his chest and managed to grab his head between his hands. He pounded his head against the white wall. He didn't stop even when he saw smudges of red against the stark white, heard Whistler moaning.

"No!" Theodore Backman stumbled off the high dais, fell to his knees. "No!" he yelled again and pointed a long finger toward the two men. He turned to look at his granddaughter, that precious little girl he had waited for to be the future of his family. He felt a searing pain in his chest, slowly fell onto his side. He sucked in air, trying to breathe.

Ethan smashed Whistler's head a final time against the wall and released him. Whistler slid down the wall, leaving his blood to streak in bizarre patterns, as if painted on by smudged fingers.

Ethan stood over him, sucked in air, and tried to quiet his rage. He turned to see the old man lying on the beautiful rug, his legs drawn up. He was awake and staring at Ethan. "You killed Caldicot?"

"I doubt it." He did not say whether he'd tried. Ethan turned to Autumn and Joanna. "Are you all right?"

Autumn nodded as Joanna hugged her close, smoothed her hand over her daughter's hair. "It's okay, baby, it's okay now. We're all right, Ethan. You?"

Theodore Backman called out, sitting up on the floor now, his hands outstretched to Autumn. "Autumn! My precious grandchild, you will reach the stars with me, you will conquer the heavens. Come here, child, come to your grandfather." He turned his head slowly toward the door. They stared at it, watched it open slowly.

There stood Blessed, his dark eyes burning bright with anger.

Theodore yelled, "Blessed, my son. Quickly, the sheriff and Joanna!"

But Ethan didn't look at him. He kept his head down and bulled ahead at Blessed, throwing himself as hard as he could into his stomach, sending Blessed back through the open door and hard against the hall-way wall. Blessed moaned with pain as the dressing on his shoulder turned red with blood. But he slammed his elbow into the

back of Ethan's head, sending him stag-
gering to his knees.

Joanna flew at Blessed, knocked her
own head into his chest just as Ethan had
done. Blessed grabbed her neck and jerked
her upright, but Joanna wouldn't look at
him. "It doesn't matter." Blessed struck her
hard in the jaw. Joanna went down.

"No!"

Blessed came running back into the
room just as Autumn landed against him.
She screamed at him and pummeled her
fists into his stomach. Blessed grabbed
her, shook her.

Autumn looked up and stared at him.
He whimpered, deep in his throat, and fell
backward. He hit the wall behind him and
slowly slipped to the floor, unmoving.

"Mama!" Autumn ran into the hall, fell to
her knees, and shook her mother's shoulders, lightly tapped her face, crying, beg-
ging her to wake up.

Ethan was at their side in an instant.
He gathered Joanna up in his arms and
rocked her. They turned as one to see
Theodore Backman stagger toward them.
He yelled, and his voice echoed in the

small space, like Moses calling out from the mountaintop, "You have failed me, Autumn. You are not worthy to carry on my name. You are like your common mother, of no use at all. I disavow you as I disavowed your father!"

He raised his gun and fired.

The bullet struck Autumn in the chest.

74

PALMERTON COMMUNITY HOSPITAL
TWENTY MILES EAST OF PEAS RIDGE

It was a miracle she'd survived the transport, Joanna told Savich, but she had. She'd survived two hours of surgery and was still alive when Savich and Sherlock got to the hospital the next morning, Savich on crutches. He ignored the pull of the newly sewn stitches on his thigh, and he ignored the constant hurt too, now, in the face of Autumn's dying.

Ethan had told the hospital staff he and Joanna were married, he'd explained to Savich on his cell when their FBI helicopter landed at Ricketts Field, only five miles from the hospital, so there would be no question he and Joanna could remain with Autumn in the ICU.

Ethan had called in a huge favor and gotten a medevac helicopter to pick them up in the clearing by the barn. He'd told Sherlock, his voice too calm—numb, really—that Peas Ridge Chief of Police Annie Parkes and all six of her deputies had arrived to deal with Theodore and Blessed Backman, and with Caldicot Whistler, all of them still alive, just as the medevac helicopter arrived. He'd told her about Kjell, about the people who'd stayed hidden when the violence had erupted, and about those who couldn't get out of there fast enough. He told her to look for a fresh grave when it was light again.

Savich and Sherlock looked at Autumn through the open curtain of the ICU cubicle, her pale little face very still, both her impossibly small wrists tethered to IVs, an oxygen mask on her face. She looked terrifyingly fragile, and Savich hated it. He kept talking to her in his mind, telling her over and over that she would pull through this, that he'd introduce her to Sean and she could be his big sister and boss him around. He told her he wanted to see her smile, just for him, told her about Astro, how when she was well, she and Sean could throw a Frisbee for him, and how he'd lick her mouth if she wasn't careful.

He never heard a whisper of her voice, never felt even a shadow of her. He prayed somehow she would hear him. He felt he had to keep talking, since there was nothing else he could do. And he wondered again and again how a small being like that could survive a bullet to her chest.

It was a good sign, an ICU nurse told them, that she was breathing on her own and didn't need a respirator anymore.

Dr. Maddox, Autumn's thoracic surgeon, fresh from a few hours' precious sleep, followed Ethan and Joanna out of the cubicle. He said to them, "I won't lie to you, like I told you, it was close, but she came through surgery like a champ"—a lie, but Dr. Maddox wasn't about to tell her parents he'd nearly lost her. "She's a strong little girl."

A sheriff and two FBI agents, he thought. At least he could leave it to them to sort out how it was that a seven-year-old girl got herself shot in the chest. He hadn't paid much attention to all the wild talk he'd heard about it. There hadn't been time for that. He touched his hand to Joanna's arm, shook Ethan's hand. "The two of you can stay, but I'll have to ask the agents here to keep it short. We have an ICU to run. Try not to worry too much, either of you, it will do no one any good. She's in good hands. I'll be in the hospital if she needs me."

"She's so small," Sherlock whispered. "She looks smaller than Sean." She turned in to him. Savich stroked her back as she sucked in a light breath, holding back tears that stung his eyes. He swallowed. He remembered his father telling him everyone expected the man to be strong, no breaking down, and in his opinion that just sucked. The memory almost made him smile. He said to Joanna and Ethan, "I've called her more times than I can count. She's—not there."

Joanna's voice was a thread. "Or maybe she's just not feeling strong enough. That could be it—sure it could. One of the ICU nurses told me she's got a long way to go to get well again. . . ." Her voice fell away.

Joanna and Ethan went back into the cubicle, taking their place beside the narrow bed, Savich and Sherlock behind them, standing at the end of the bed. The same nurse, Elaine Amos, came in. They watched her take Autumn's blood pressure. She paused, straightened, and said to them, "Look, I've seen people die, and I've seen some miracles too along the way, and with Autumn, I feel it here"—she touched her fingertips to her heart—"I know she'll make it. All of us here want to bring her through this. What happened to your leg?"

Sherlock said matter-of-factly, "He got shot." She saw Elaine's eyes go wide, briefly, but she didn't care. If this hospital was true to form, gossip was already rife now that two FBI agents had come running in, one of them on crutches. *If they only knew.* She wanted to touch Autumn's face, to feel the warmth of that small child's flesh, but Joanna's head was close to her child's, and she was lightly stroking her fingertips over Autumn's cheek.

Elaine said, "Look, guys, give me a minute with her, all right?" A final kiss, a final touch, and the four of them left Autumn's cubicle, Joanna looking over her shoulder at her daughter, her face so pale it looked bloodless.

Ethan said, "You should know, Savich, Theodore Backman died soon after he reached the hospital, a massive heart attack." He slammed his fist against his palm. "It was too easy for that perverted old man. Blessed, last I heard, is unresponsive— catatonic, they called it. They've moved him to a secured psych ward, where we've got him isolated and under guard anyway. As for Mrs. Backman, she's six rooms down the hall, raving and chanting, mad as a hatter. And Caldicot, that psycho is still in Chief Parkes's jail at Peas Ridge." He paused a moment, turned back, looking through the open curtains at the nurse bending over Autumn, fiddling with one of her IV lines. He said, his eyes never leaving Autumn's face, "Chief Parkes found the fresh grave, fifty feet behind the barn. I'm glad they did. At least the two people they found can go home now."

Savich's cell phone played Eric Hummer's "Milwaukee Blues." What now, Sherlock wondered, and wished she could rip the phone out of Dillon's hand and throw it out the window. But of course she couldn't. *Damned duty,* she thought.

Savich flipped his cell closed after a couple of minutes. He motioned the three of them out of the ICU. "Ethan, Joanna, you know Sherlock and I flew here directly from North Carolina. We have to go back to Washington, D.C. Mr. Maitland says the media's going nuts, he admits he's got a truckload of questions for us himself, and Director Mueller, even though he understands the situation with Autumn, has asked us to come back until everything can be sorted out. I don't want to leave—"

Ethan pulled Joanna to his side and squeezed. "We'll be here. Thank you for everything you've done."

Sherlock touched her fingers to his shoulder, then to Joanna's. *Silent, praying,* Savich thought. He looked down at her face, at the pain in her eyes. He said, "Listen, all of you. Elaine told us she'll make it. She promised us a miracle."

Epilogue

Five days later

Savich stood in the doorway of Autumn's private room on the second floor. He and Sherlock had just arrived at Palmerton after five long days of worry. The sun poured through the bank of windows, setting the pale yellow walls of her room aglow. She was still hooked up to IVs, but there were no longer oxygen clips in her nose, and he saw a bit of color on her cheeks. She was so small in that narrow hospital bed, so very thin. But she'd lived; she would make it. Soon she would be whole again.

She was asleep, her breathing even and soft. He watched Joanna lean down and kiss her cheek, then Ethan kiss her forehead. They walked hand in hand out of the room, both looking pale and drawn, their eyes still shadowed from days of worry and lack of sleep, but both of them were smiling.

Ethan shook Savich's hand, hugged Sherlock. "Autumn should sleep for a while now. Both Joanna and I are running on low. How about some coffee—and tea for you, Savich—in the hospital cafeteria? It's not bad at all, kept us alive these past days. I like the cane. Is that an eagle's head on it?"

The walls of the Palmerton hospital cafeteria were sunshine-yellow, the chairs and tables alternately bright green and blue. You couldn't help but feel your spirits lift a little when you walked in.

Joanna said, "We're very glad you guys are back. Even though we've spoken every day, it's wonderful to see you, to have you here." She drew in a deep breath. "It's been—difficult." Then she smiled up at Ethan, squeezed his hand.

Ethan said, "She's been improving steadily. Every single day, she's better and better. Only a couple of minor setbacks, a fever that scared the spit out of us, but it passed quickly. Dr. Maddox came out of her room this morning and he was beaming and did a little skip." Without thought, Ethan leaned over and touched his forehead to Joanna's. "We are very, very lucky," he said, and kissed her cheek.

Joanna gave them a brilliant smile. "Five very long days, but they're in the past now. You should hear Nurse Elaine talk about her miracle."

Ethan said, "We've seen some of the hoopla on TV about Victor Nesser. What's happening?"

Sherlock said, "The media frenzy over Victor and Lissy is still playing itself out, mostly in the tabloids now, and a couple of the talking-head cable networks. More speculation than fact now, shrinks and legal analysts using it to get airtime. There's been nothing new in the past day and a half to rev them up again, thank God."

Joanna said, "We saw an interview with that bank security guard, Buzz Riley, on one of the major stations. He was something, a very funny man."

Savich nodded. "Buzz called us after the show aired. He was pumped up, said he'd always wanted to be on TV, wondered if he'd get some calls from Hollywood."

Joanna laughed. It sounded a bit rusty, but it was still a laugh, no shadows beneath it. "Do you know I wouldn't be at all surprised if he made it into the next *Die Hard* movie, maybe as Willis's newest sidekick?"

Ethan said, "He sure sang your praises, Savich, about what you did at the Georgetown bank."

Savich said, "Buzz is very glad to be back home. He says water and sun are okay with him, but since no one could ever tell if he had a tan or not, why bother?" Savich shook his head, smiling.

Ethan rose, held up his hand. "All right, guys, don't talk about the good stuff until I get back. I'm going to get us some drinks."

Sherlock saw Joanna watch Ethan make his way to the buffet line along the back wall of the cafeteria. He turned and smiled brightly at them, gave Joanna a little wave.

It was hard for Joanna, Savich saw, to turn away from Ethan, but she finally managed it. She said, "Dillon, tell me first how your leg's doing."

He did exactly what he always did when he was hurt—he simply shrugged, said he was fine.

Joanna said, "All right, then, I can see you're not the one to ask. So you tell me, Sherlock, how's his leg?"

Sherlock said matter-of-factly, "The stitches come out in a couple of days. There wasn't too much muscle damage, so Dillon limps less every day, needs fewer pain pills. The doctor said he could begin some gentle workouts the end of next week."

"How's Sean doing?"

"He saw his father moving around on crutches. Since Dillon made light of it, Sean wasn't worried or scared about it. He decided it was cool. When Dillon graduated to a cane, Sean got himself a long stick and tried to walk like his father. He got his first taste of reporters a couple of days ago. They ambushed the three of us at Danby Park where we play Frisbee. Picture this, Dillon's sitting under a tree watching me throw a Frisbee to Sean, then Sean throws the Frisbee to Astro, grinning at the reporters over his shoulder, and all those people with their microphones and cameras surround him, looking for a big dose of cute." She smiled. "I fear Sean's a ham. Like Buzz, he loved it. Like Buzz, he's a natural."

"I wanted to grab him up and limp away," Savich said, "but to be honest about it, the crews were great with him. You don't often see a rabid pack of newshounds charmed like that, but Sean did it. He made it on most every news station that evening, even on one of the major network stations."

"Most of the ICU saw him," Joanna said. "He was fantastic. I can't wait for him to get together with Autumn."

While Sherlock told them another Sean story, Savich thought about things. He realized that even his gut now accepted that Autumn would live. She would be herself again. But the other, her incredible gift— since she'd been shot, he'd picture her in his mind many times every day, but he couldn't reach her. Nor had she called to him. It would be nice, he kept thinking, to speak to Autumn, no matter where she was, just to know how she was doing, what she'd done that day.

Would Autumn tell Sean about her gift? Would she be able to speak to Sean? Who knew? Sean was his son, after all. But the question now was, and he hated even to consider it, would she still have her ability at all?

Savich said, "The evening Sean was on TV, it was next to impossible to get him to bed. He was so high, I had to pull him off the ceiling. His grandmother—my mom—didn't help. She was stuffing him with brownies she'd brought over, telling him he was the next Matt Damon." Savich grinned. "I'll bet he's missing all the attention, with only Gabriella for a slave until we get home. I understand, though, that his best friend, Marty, from right next door, isn't happy with him. She called him a show-off, said he should have talked about her on TV, since she's been his friend all these years, and he was boring."

Ethan returned with three coffees and a cup of tea, four fat bagels, and a dozen packets of cream cheese and butter. He grinned. "Ambrosia for the arteries."

Joanna was smiling as she spread a thick coat of cream cheese on her bagel. "Do you know, this is the first time in a week I've been hungry?" She took a huge bite. "Ah, that tastes nearly as good as you do, Ethan . . ." Her voice dropped off, her face turned red.

Ethan laughed at her. It sounded so sane, so normal.

Joanna cleared her throat. "I have always blushed. It is my curse, along with my freckles. Dillon, you were talking about Victor Nesser?"

"Well, not really."

"Who cares?" Sherlock said, and poked him in the side. "Tell Joanna what's going to happen to Victor."

Savich said after he'd sipped the lovely Lipton tea, "Marvin Cutler, Esquire, from L.A., has taken Victor's case pro bono. He announced to a dozen cameras and fifty reporters that he's putting together a team and—har, har—he is doing this for the public good, not for the publicity. He's claiming Victor was Lissy's puppet, a slave under her control, and he only did what she forced him to do. It was Lissy who did all the killing.

"He's also saying the FBI brutalized Victor, even shot him in the foot for the fun of it after they'd captured him, and the poor young man will limp badly for the rest of his life."

"Fact is," Savich continued, "I'm doubtful Victor will go to court when the DOJ prosecutors present all the evidence to Victor's dream team. I'm thinking Victor will agree to life without parole rather than risk being tried in Virginia where there's the death penalty. That's where Lissy shot both a father and mother to steal their car. The mother died."

Sherlock said as she broke off a piece of bagel, "We heard yesterday that Victor is refusing to eat, refusing to talk, refusing even to see his lawyer. I'm thinking he's grieving for Lissy. What was between the two of them, no matter how twisted and perverse, it was strong and deep. She was the center of his life. I don't think he knows what to do or think or how to act without her. Was Victor the center of Lissy's life? Maybe so. Dillon suggested they put him on a suicide watch."

Ethan said, "A DEA friend of mine told me Lissy Smiley was buried yesterday beside her mother in Fort Pessel, Virginia. He said the local media plastered a photo of Lissy all over the TV, from back when she was ten years old and looked adorable. The media never fails to astonish me. They go after a criminal tooth and nail until the criminal is captured. Then they do a one-eighty and scream it's not his fault, point to all the dreadful things that happened in his childhood, how society failed him, *blah, blah.*"

Savich was chewing on his bagel as he listened. He looked across the small table at Joanna and Ethan, the two of them sitting close together, their arms touching, their body language screaming intimacy. A blind man could see it, and it had all come about in only a couple of weeks. He was looking at two people who'd battled death together and beat the odds, their child with them. *Yes,* he thought, Autumn was their child now. He wondered when Joanna and Ethan had realized their future was together. All he knew was that when they left the hospital, Autumn between them, they'd be a family. Would they all go back to Titusville and move in with Big Louie, Lula, and Mackie? He asked Ethan, "Who's taking care of your critters?"

"Faydeen, my dispatcher, moved in right after, well, after Blessed took us away. She said Lula has taken over the roost. Even my black Lab, Big Louie, won't cross her.

Faydeen reported that Mackie, the little wuss, sleeps under her armpit to avoid Lula. She tells him to search out his machismo and stand up to Lula, but Mackie just burrows deeper."

Savich saw a wonderful picture in his mind. A bachelor party for Ethan at his Georgetown gym with a bunch of hell-raising DEA and FBI guys who would joyfully beat the crap out of each other before eating a dozen pizzas at Dizzy Dan's. He laughed. Three pairs of eyes fastened on him. Savich cleared his throat. "Just thinking," he said.

"About what?" Joanna said.

"Sorry, can't divulge that, national security."

Ethan laughed. "I'll make him tell me later, Jo."

Joanna said, "Do you know Uncle Tollie finally made it back from the Everglades? I spoke to him, and he's on his way here." She shook her head and gave Ethan a look. "If it weren't for Uncle Tollie living in Titusville, I never would have gone there, I wouldn't have ever met Ethan or you guys or—well, I'm glad he does."

Ethan said, "Do you know the last thing

Autumn remembers clearly is the cave we went to in the Titus Hitch Wilderness?" He paused a moment, played with his coffee spoon. "All of it was such a shock to her, it's as if she can't let herself remember yet. I asked her if she called you, Savich, and she said she tried but she couldn't reach you."

It was a blow. Savich said, "No memory at all of what she did to Victor and Blessed?"

Ethan shook his head.

"What she did, it was incredible. She saved both Sherlock's life and mine."

Joanna said, "It's hard enough to say it out loud, much less bring myself to believe it, to accept it. How could she have done such a thing?"

Ethan said, "We may never know, but I'll tell you, in that underground vault of Theodore Backman's, Joanna and I watched her change. She became so powerful it scared the bejesus out of us. Is her ability gone now? Did she burn out? Maybe so."

Sherlock said, "As you said, maybe she's not ready to remember all of it."

Joanna said, "Autumn will come into her own, whatever that may be. And what does it matter if there won't be any psychic gifts in her future? I have my child back."

Savich stood in the doorway, watching Ethan and Joanna stroke their fingers through Autumn's hair, lightly touching her cheek.

He saw Autumn open her eyes, beautiful blue eyes that were bright and clear, no shadows of pain anymore. He saw her smile up at her mother and at Ethan. Joanna said, "Dillon and Sherlock are here, sweetie."

"Dillon's here? Where is he?"

"He's standing in the doorway."

Autumn turned her head, looked at him, and gave him a huge smile. *Dillon,* she called to him.